"Briana, what's wrong? Is it Nealie?"

"Oh, Josh, she's sick. She might be—so sick."

He had the sensation of falling toward a devouring darkness. "How sick? Is she in the hospital?"

"I don't know how sick. It's in the early stages. She doesn't know yet. Nobody knows."

"What's wrong with her?" Damn, his hands were shaking. His hands never shook.

"It's a—an anemia," she stammered. "It's very rare. And—and serious."

"What can I do?" He sat on the edge of the bathtub, his head down. He felt as if he was going to pass out.

She seemed to pull herself together, but she still sounded shattered. "Can you come home? I mean come *here*?"

"I'll be there as soon as I can. I'll get on the first flight out. But what can *we* do for her?"

"Oh, Josh," she said, despair naked in her voice, "I've thought and thought. I think there's only one thing. One thing in the world."

"What? I'll do anything. You know that."

She was silent a long moment. He knew she was having trouble speaking. At last she whispered, "To save her, I think we have to have another baby."

Dear Reader,

"Individuals in every generation must decide what they will preserve for those who follow."

Those are the opening words of a fine book, *The Heirloom Gardener* by Carolyn Jabs. I bought two copies of this book, one for me and one for my dad.

My father taught me that to see a seed sprout, grow and change was a miracle. *The Baby Gift* is a story about miracles and how, in our time, miracles can get mixed up with science.

About the science, I tried to be accurate, but I have probably made errors, and for this I apologize. As for the art of growing things, I turned to the wonderful organization called Seed Savers. What I got right is due to them and the delightful Lyn Jabs. What I got wrong, I got wrong on my own, drat it.

Growing heirloom vegetables is a lovely and rewarding (and, okay, delicious) pastime. Anyone who would like more information about heirloom gardening can contact The Seed Savers Exchange, 3076 North Winn Road, Decorah, Iowa 52101. On the Internet, you can find information at www. seedsavers.org

Best wishes,

Bethany Campbell

The Baby Gift
Bethany Campbell

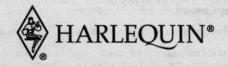

HARLEQUIN®

TORONTO • NEW YORK • LONDON
AMSTERDAM • PARIS • SYDNEY • HAMBURG
STOCKHOLM • ATHENS • TOKYO • MILAN • MADRID
PRAGUE • WARSAW • BUDAPEST • AUCKLAND

ISBN 0-373-71052-6

THE BABY GIFT

To Howard Martinson Bostwick, with love and gratitude.

Printed in U.S.A.

CHAPTER ONE

THE LITTLE GIRL dreamed of her daddy.

He was the handsomest daddy in the world and the funniest and the smartest—he knew things that nobody *else's* daddy knew.

He knew, for instance, how to escape from a giant octopus.

The little girl lived hundreds of miles from any ocean, she had never seen the ocean or an octopus, but still, she wondered about situations like this.

"The thing to do is not to panic," her daddy said. "If an octopus grabs you and wants to eat you, just stay calm."

"Calm?" she said dubiously.

"Between his eyes the octopus has a bump like a wart. Surprise him—bite his wart!"

"Yuck!" said the little girl.

"No," her father said, tapping her temple. "It's using your smarts. All the octopus's nerves are centered in that bump. When it hurts, he drops you and swims off fast as he can. He'll never want to see *you* again."

"Well," she said with a thoughtful frown, "what if a giant clam grabs my foot and won't let go?"

"Ah," said Daddy, "that's why you always carry a knife when you dive. If a giant clam snaps shut on you, cut his hinge. Snip-snip, you're free. And he's learned his lesson."

"Will it kill him?" she asked. She wanted only to escape the clam, not murder it.

Her father shook his head. "No. He'll have to lie low and grow his hinge back. Of course, some sand may drift in his shell, so maybe he'll make a giant pearl while he's waiting.''

"Hmm," said the little girl. "Well, what about crocodiles?''

"Easiest of all," said her daddy. "The crocodile has all sorts of muscles to snap his mouth *shut*. But he's got very weak muscles to open it up. Grab him by the snoot when his mouth is closed. Then he can't open it.''

"Then what?''

"Then move him someplace where he won't bite people and where the hunters won't get him.''

"Why would hunters want him?''

"To make wallets and suitcases and watch straps out of him. It's a sad fate, becoming a watch strap.''

"Mm," said the little girl. Then, as dreams do, hers drifted off. She was on an imaginary seashore, warm with caressing breezes. There, she and her faithful partner, Zorro the cat, stalked crocodiles. She was not afraid, because her daddy had taught her how to escape all dangers.

She strode across the sand, as fearless and strong as her father was. The sky was blue, the sun shone down with tropic brightness, and she moved, safe and invincible, through a world of eternal summer.

WHILE THE CHILD SLEPT, snow fell. It had fallen all morning.

It glistened, silver and white, on the greenhouse roofs. Like ragged lace, it covered the cold frames still empty of seedlings. It eddied around the corners of the barn, dancing with the wind as if alive and bewitched.

But the inside of the little farmhouse was warm. Briana had been up and working for almost an hour. The scents of coffee and bacon and biscuits hung in the kitchen air like country ambrosia.

It was a scene of almost perfect peace.

Then Briana smashed her finger with the hammer. A swear word flew to her mouth, but she sucked it back in pain. This almost made her swallow the spare tack she held between her teeth.

Through sheer willpower, she recovered and bit on the tack more firmly. She had a job to do, and with all her Missouri stubbornness, she meant to get it done.

She settled herself more steadily on the top rung of the ladder and gripped the hammer. She tapped the last crepe-paper streamer into place on the ceiling beam. Now kitchen, living room and dining room were festooned with spirals of red and white.

Briana cocked her head and examined the effect. It looked fine, it looked festive, it looked—happy.

Happy, she thought numbly. *Good. I want things to look happy.*

She climbed down the ladder and plucked the unused tack from her mouth, then thrust it into the pocket of her carpenter's apron. She stowed her hammer in its proper drawer and hung the apron on its peg inside the pantry.

She checked the food warming in the oven, then called her daughter to breakfast. She made sure her voice was firm, steady and, above all, cheerful.

"Nealie! Up and at 'em. Breakfast time."

From the bedroom came a groan that was impressively loud for such a small girl. "Agh!"

"No dramatics," Briana ordered. "They scare the cat."

With even greater drama, Nealie shouted, "I hate mornings!" This time her groan ended with a horrible gurgle. "Aargh-gack-gack."

The black cat, Zorro, streaked out of Nealie's room, down the stairs and to his sanctuary behind the washing machine. Zorro was of a nervous disposition.

Briana looked at all that remained visible of the cat, the twitching tip of his black tail. She crooked an eyebrow. "Good morning, Zorro. I'd hide, too, if I were you. Some mice were around earlier asking for you. Big mice. One of them had a baseball bat."

"Mom!" Nealie stood in the doorway looking sleepy and indignant. "You know Zorro's scared of mice."

"And he knows I'm kidding."

Nealie gave her mother a rueful smile. She was a small child with big glasses that made her look like an impish owl. Her new plaid bathrobe was too large, and the sleeves hung to her fingertips. From under its hem peeped large brown fuzzy slippers made to look like bear paws. The slippers were ridiculous, but Nealie loved them.

The girl dropped to her knees beside the washer. "Poor Zorro," she cooed, pulling him from his hiding place. Pieces of lint clung to his black whiskers and fur. She began to pick them off.

"Come on, Zorro," Nealie said comfortingly. "You can sit on my lap. I'll pet you."

She plunked down cross-legged on the floor and laid the cat on his back. She stroked his fat stomach, scratched his ears and babbled affectionate nonsense to him. He purred his almost noiseless Zorro purr.

Briana bit her lip and put the oatmeal into the microwave. All business, she opened a container of yogurt, then poured orange juice into a glass.

"I didn't want to wake up." Nealie yawned, stroking the cat. "I was wrestling a crocodile. I was winning, too."

"Of course, you were," Briana said loyally.

"I'm going to hunt crocodiles when I get big," said Nealie. "To help them, not to hurt them. Zorro and I'll build them a safe place so people can't make them into watch straps. Won't we, Zorro?"

Zorro's green eyes rolled unhappily, as if the thought of crocodiles made him queasy.

Briana stood by the counter, one hand on her hip, watching the timid cat and her fearless child.

Nealie was such a *little* girl. She was smart and imaginative, but much too small for her age, and delicate, as well. It was as if nature had not given her a body sturdy enough to contain so much spirit.

Nealie yawned again, then looked up, noticing the red and white streamers for the first time. Behind her big glasses, her eyes squinted.

"Hey! What's this? When'd you do all this?"

"This morning. I can't believe you didn't hear me," Briana said, setting out Nealie's vitamins.

"What's it for?" Then the child's face brightened like a sunrise. "Is it for Daddy? Is he coming home? Is he? Is it a surprise for him?"

Briana fought not to wince. "No. You know he won't be back for a while."

The sunshine in Nealie's expression clouded over. "Oh," she said. "Then what's all this *for?*"

"Your uncle Larry's birthday," Briana said. "We'll have fun. There'll be cake and ice cream and—"

"—and Rupert and Neville and Marsh," Nealie said in disgust. "Blech."

Rupert and Neville and Marsh were her cousins. They were all boys, all younger than Nealie, but bigger. Their idea of fun was running, shouting, scuffling and tormenting cats and girls.

"Why can't Aunt Glenda have the party?" Nealie asked. "Then the boys can break their *own* stuff."

"She wanted to have it," Briana said, defending her sister-in-law. "She's not feeling so good lately. So last night I said I'd do it."

"I know why she doesn't feel good." Nealie pouted. "She's going to have another baby. I hope it's not another boy—ugh."

Briana knew the baby would be a boy, so she made no reply. Instead she said, "Wash your hands and come eat."

"Zorro's not dirty," Nealie protested, kissing him on the nose. "He's sterile. I heard you telling Mrs. Feeney."

Caught by surprise, Briana laughed. "That's a different kind of sterile. It means he can't make kittens. But germs he can make—and does. Wash."

"I love Zorro's germs," Nealie said, straightening her

glasses. "They're wonderful, beautiful germs because they're his."

She kissed him again, then rose and washed her hands, then plunked herself down at the table. After the first few bites, she only picked at her food.

"Try a little more," Briana said as gently as she could.

"I'm not hungry," Nealie said. "My stomach feels kind of funny. You know."

A chill pierced Briana, but she allowed herself only an understanding smile, a mild nod. "Okay. Take your vitamins and go change. Your clothes are laid out on the dresser. Wear your new shoes. I'll drive you to school today."

"Aw, Mommy," Nealie grumbled, "you haven't let me ride the bus for *weeks*."

Briana's answer was ready. "All those Tandrup children have colds. Mrs. Feeney said so. They sneeze all over everybody."

Nealie didn't look convinced. Briana added, "Besides, I have to go to town anyway. I've got to mail the seed catalogs."

Briana gestured at the stacks of catalogs on the entryway table. The covers showed jewel-colored fruits and vegetables—tomatoes red as rubies, snow peas green as jade, pears the deep golden of amber.

Hanlon's Heritage Farm, proud letters announced. Your Source of Heirloom Seeds and Rare Fruits and Vegetables. Only the Best and Strongest. A Quarter Century of Quality.

"Why does Grandpa have to grow seeds?" Nealie asked. "Why can't he grow jellyfish or woolly worms or something interesting?"

"Seeds are what he knows," Briana said.

"He could learn something else," Nealie complained. "I think I'll tell him so tonight."

"Not tonight," Briana said firmly. "We're having a celebration. Remember?"

Nealie's eyes shot to the Heritage Farm calendar on the

kitchen wall, then widened in alarm. "But Mama. It's the first of the month. *Daddy* might call. What if he calls when everybody's here? We won't be able to talk. Rupert will hit and yell and pull the phone plug out. He's done it before."

"I won't let Rupert near the phone. Besides, Daddy's so far away he might not be able to get through tonight."

"He will if he can," Nealie objected. "You *know* he will." She paused, her expression saddening. "How much longer has he got to be in Khanty—Khanty…"

"Khanty-Mansiysk," Briana said. "He stays until he gets enough pictures. Then he'll be back to see you."

Josh Morris was in Siberia, just south of the Arctic Circle, shooting photographs for *Smithsonian* magazine. Before that he had been in Oaxaca, Mexico, taking pictures of Olmec ruins. Before that he'd been photographing moths in Belize and a live volcano in Java.

Briana had married Josh seven years ago, when he'd come to Missouri for a piece on farmers specializing in saving endangered fruits and vegetables. It should have been a tame assignment for him, mere routine, but when he and Briana met, routine flew away, and all tameness vanished.

Theirs was a heedless, passionate affair that swept them into a marriage barely three weeks after they'd met. Everyone who knew Briana had warned her. She'd ignored them.

Everybody who knew Josh had warned him, too, and he, too, had paid no attention. He was crazy in love, so was she, and nothing could stop them.

The marriage could not last, and everyone but them had seemed to know it. Josh was a man born with a hunger to roam. She was a woman tied strongly to one place. They stayed together only long enough to produce Nealie.

Josh had already been gone by the time Nealie was born—Albania, where he'd nearly gotten himself killed more than once. But he'd flown to Missouri as soon as he'd heard that the child was premature and fighting to survive.

Josh Morris loved his daughter. Nobody, not even Briana's disapproving brother, could deny that. Josh kept in touch with Nealie as much as possible, he sent funny cards and silly presents, he came to see her whenever he could. But he was always on the move, often far away, and his schedule was erratic.

"I wish he'd come home to stay," Nealie said with a wistfulness she seldom showed.

Briana stroked the child's brown hair. "He has to make a living."

Nealie wasn't consoled. "He could do something else."

Briana touch softened. "No. He's like Grandpa. This is what he does. He educates people. He helps tell important stories. A picture is worth a thousand words.

"It isn't worth one daddy."

For this Briana had no answer. She turned away and said, "I'm sorry."

"I wish you'd marry him again and he'd stay here, and we'd all be together," Nealie said in a burst of emotion. "Why won't he stay with us? Is there something wrong with us? With me?"

Coldness gripped Briana. She wheeled to face her daughter. "Don't talk like that. He loves you. He thinks you're the most wonderful daughter in the world."

"But why—" Nealie began.

"It's time for school. Go change your clothes."

Nealie tossed her head defiantly, but she turned and stalked to her room. Her big robe trailed behind her, and her bear paws made clumsy thumps on the floor.

Briana tried not to notice the limp in the child's determined step. She turned and began to clear the breakfast dishes.

I won't cry. I won't, she told herself fiercely. *Nobody's going to know how I feel. Nobody.*

But she knew this could not remain true. She could no longer keep things to herself.

The time had come. She must act.

FRANKLIN HINKS was the postmaster of Illyria, Missouri. His father had been postmaster before him, and Franklin could clearly remember Victory Mail, the three-cent letter stamp and the penny postcard.

He had vivid recollections of many things—including Briana Morris as a child, back when she'd been little Briana Hanlon. He'd seen her every day she'd gone to Illyria Elementary School, right across the street from the post office.

This morning he'd seen her stop her aging pickup truck in front of that same red brick schoolhouse. He'd seen her kiss her daughter goodbye and the child run up the snowy walk to the building.

He had watched Briana signal for a turn, then pull into his parking lot. She got out of the truck and came up the walk, her arms full of seed catalogs and her breath feathering behind her, a silver plume on the gray air.

She had been a pretty child, Briana had, and now she was a pretty woman—tall but not too tall, slim but not too slim. She had long dark hair with the hint of a wave and dark eyes that had something exotic in them.

She looked nothing at all like her father or brother, big Scottish-Irishmen with pale eyes and square faces. No, Briana looked like her mother, a quiet brunette with a slightly Mediterranean air.

Briana came in the door of the post office. She wore an old plaid jacket and a black knit hat and gloves. The wind had tossed her hair and burnished her cheeks to the color of fiery gold.

She smiled at him. She had a good smile, but lately—for the past two months or so—he'd discerned something troubled in it, deeply troubled. But he could tell she didn't want people to know. Franklin was discreet. He pretended he noticed nothing.

"Morning, Franklin," she said with a fine imitation of blitheness.

"Morning, Briana," he said and nodded at her stack of catalogs. "Folks must be dreaming of spring."

"They must be," she said. "We got thirty-two orders by the Internet this weekend."

Franklin made a tsking noise. "That Internet's going to put me out of business."

She set the catalogs on the counter. "Nope—look at all this. It's *bringing* you business. And next week, I'll start sending seeds out. I've got a huge pile of orders to fill."

"Hmm," Franklin said, stamping the catalogs. "Well, don't send every seed away. Save me some for those tomatoes I like. What are the kinds I like?"

"Brandywine and Mortgage Lifter," Briana said with a grin. "You'll have 'em. I'll even start them for you."

He knew she'd keep her word and that she wouldn't take any money from him, either. That was Briana.

"You'd save yourself some postage if you'd bulk mail," Franklin advised, "Keep a mailing list and send out two hundred or more at a time."

"Someday," she said. "I have to talk Poppa into it. Getting the farm into the computer age was tough enough."

Franklin nodded but said nothing. Leo Hanlon was a good man, a kindly man, but set in his ways. Didn't he realize the greatest asset he had on his farm was his pretty, brainy daughter, a woman who wasn't afraid of new ideas?

"Well, guess I'll check the mail and be out of here," Briana said. "It's Larry's birthday. Got lots to do to get ready."

"Oh, you got mail, all right," Franklin said. "One package too big to fit into the box. For Nealie. Maybe from the neighborhood of—oh, from the stamps, I'd say Russia."

Briana was always careful to guard her expression, but a light came into her eyes. He thought what he'd thought so many times in the last years—she still had strong feelings for Josh Morris, more than she'd ever admit.

"I'll get it for you," he said. "It's in the back."

The glow faded from her face, and the trouble crept into her dark gaze. "I'll check our box."

He moved toward the back room, knowing, of course,

what was in her post office box. It included a letter for Nealie, also from Russia.

Franklin had got a card from Josh in the morning's mail. Josh knew the older man saved stamps, and he always remembered to send him colorful ones from his travels. Such a man could not be bad, Franklin thought, no matter what some people liked to say.

When he returned to the counter, Briana was there, her mail tucked under her arm. She made no comment about Nealie's letter from Josh. She showed no emotion when Franklin set down the tattered package.

"It looks like it had a rough journey," she said.

"It's come a long way," he said. "Across half the world."

"Yes," she said in almost a whisper. "A long way."

She picked up the bulky package gingerly, as if it might have some magical power she didn't want brushing off on her. Then she flashed Franklin a smile and set off, her gait sprightly.

A man less observant than Franklin might have been fooled by that sprightliness. She had a problem, and from the kind of mail she'd been getting—support groups, medical foundations—he thought he could guess what.

He prayed to heaven he was wrong.

JUST AS BRIANA was stowing Nealie's package in her truck's cab, a sleek Cadillac swept in and parked beside her.

Briana suppressed a groan and forced herself to smile, even though the cold hurt her face. The car's driver, Wendell Semple, heaved himself out of the driver's seat.

"Briana," he said heartily. "Just the woman I want to see. Come over to the café. Have a cup of coffee with me. I need to talk to you."

Briana's smile felt as if it were freezing into place. "Sorry. My limit's two cups a day, and I've already had it. Thanks for the offer, though."

Wendell was vice president of the bank. He was heavy with what Briana thought of as a prosperous man's solid weight. He had a prosperous man's confidence, as well, the booming voice, the air that all his opinions were important and all his decisions were right.

"I said I need to talk to you, little lady."

She didn't like his tone and she feared what he wanted to talk about. "Sorry. I'm on a tight schedule."

Wendell's smile didn't fade, but it hardened. "Briana, this is about money. Tell me. Aren't you happy with the way I do business?"

Her heart plunged, and she felt caught out.

"I'd really like to know," he said. "Why'd you take all your own money out of my bank? Weren't you satisfied?"

Stay out of my affairs, she wanted to snap, but instead she made an airy gesture. "Nothing like that. It's no big deal."

He leaned closer. "It is to me. When I lose a customer, it's always a big deal. Your family's done business with my bank for what? Almost fifty years."

She said nothing.

He went on. "We've not only done business together, we've been neighbors all this time. But now you've taken away your personal business. I'd like an explanation. I think I deserve one."

"It's simple," she lied. "I wanted to try Internet banking—"

"But why?" he prodded. "Are you thinking of changing the farm account, too? That farm's an important business in this county. I *don't* want to lose it."

She turned her collar up against the cold wind. "You won't lose it. I did it as an experiment, that's all. To streamline things. I thought I could give more time to the family business if my own's handled automatically."

He raised one eyebrow. "Now that *sounds* good. But is it the truth?"

"Of course, it is," she said, lying with spirit. "I've got

to run, Wendell. We'll have coffee another time. Tell your wife hello. And that I'm starting her some begonia cuttings.''

She edged away from him, smiled again and got into her truck. Her heart banged in her chest.

Wendell stood in the snowy lot, looking like a man who didn't intend to be thwarted. She gunned the motor and escaped.

He was prying into her money matters, but money was his business. She didn't want him to know what she'd been doing. Not him or anyone else.

She'd changed her finances so all her bills were sent electronically to a St. Louis bank. No one in town saw them and no one in town knew what she was paying or to whom.

She had things to hide. She had fought hard to keep them hidden. But once again she had a frightening sense of urgency, that time was running out. *Now,* she thought. *I've got to do something now.*

HE HAD SPENT five weeks living in a flat, featureless wasteland of ice, taking pictures of nomads and reindeer and a way of life that was probably doomed.

He had slept in his clothes on pine boughs, bark and reindeer skins in a tent made of felt and hides. He'd kept from freezing at night with a portable stove that burned peat and pine branches. He stank of smoke and he hadn't bathed or shaved for over a month.

Now he was in Moscow, with what felt like a permanent chill in his bones. He stood in the lobby of one of the city's finest hotels, looking like a cross between the abominable snowman, an escaped prisoner and a bag of rags.

Other patrons looked at him as if he exquisitely pained their senses of sight and smell. From across the lobby, the pretty desk clerk shot him furtive glances of positive alarm. Josh Morris didn't care.

He'd picked the Hotel Kampinski because after five weeks in Siberia, he wanted every luxury in the world, and the Kampinski had them all. It lavished its guests with saunas and masseuses, a gourmet restaurant and fine rooms. It had phones and computers, fax machines and color television.

He wanted to get in his room, unlock the private bar and open a bottle of real American whiskey. Then he'd climb into the marble bathtub and stay there all night, soaking and sipping and feeling his blood start to circulate.

Tomorrow he'd put on the Turkish robe the hotel provided, send his clothes out with orders to burn them and have new ones brought from the American store on Arbat Street.

And then, as the grand finale, he would call his delightful daughter and talk to her for an hour, maybe more. To hell with the long-distance rates.

Josh wanted to phone her tonight—he hadn't even stopped over in the village of Kazym to clean up and rest. He'd promised Nealie he'd get through tonight if it was possible, but it was ten o'clock in Missouri now—past her bedtime.

After he talked to her tomorrow, he'd go shopping and stock up on Russian souvenirs for her. The nesting Matryoshka dolls, a set of Mishka bears, a small—but real—Fabergé pendant. Nothing but the best for his kid.

Briana wouldn't let Nealie wear the pendant yet—she'd say the girl was too young and make her put it away. But Nealie would have it and plenty else, besides.

He thought of buying Briana something—Baltic amber or Siberian cashmere—but she didn't like him to give her gifts. Still, she would look beautiful in white cashmere with her dark, dark hair and eyes....

A pang of bitter yearning struck him. He'd lost Briana. But he still had Nealie, and Nealie he would spoil to his heart's content.

He reached the registration desk, set down his camera bags and gave the clerk his name and affiliation. "Josh I. Morris. *Smithsonian* magazine, Washington, D.C., U.S.A."

"Ooh, Mr. Morris," said the desk clerk in her lovely accent. "Oh, yes. I'm sorry I didn't recognize you."

He probably wouldn't recognize himself, he thought.

"I made reservations for two nights," he said. He usually booked himself into the more downscale Mezhudunarod-naya, but he needed serious de-Siberiazation.

"Your magazine extend it to four nights," she told him. "They send message that you are to stay and rest a few days."

He shrugged. It was a bonus, like battle pay. Besides, they probably expected him to pick up some file shots of Moscow while he was here.

She frowned slightly. "You have many messages—many, many."

He frowned. From the *Smithsonian*? Did they have another assignment for him already? Was that why he was getting the royal treatment? Good Lord, he thought, were they plotting to send him somewhere even *worse*? What was worse in winter? The South Pole?

Visions of emperor penguins danced unpleasantly in his head. He didn't want another cold-weather assignment. He wanted to get back to the States and see Nealie.

He shoved the faxed messages unread into his camera case, took his key and headed for the bank of elevators. His room was on the fourth floor, overlooking the Raushskaya Embankment and the Moscow River. Beyond the river were the lights of the Kremlin.

He took the faxes from the case and laid them on the gilt and glass table next to the phone. The parka, his hat, gloves and boots he put into the laundry bag he found in the closet.

He stripped down to his skivvies and began running his bath. His underwear would soon join his other clothes in the trash. He unlatched the bar, opened a bottle of whiskey and filled a crystal tumbler.

Then he carried his messages and his glass into the bathroom. While he ran the bath, he yanked off his underwear and kicked it under the sink. At last he settled naked and belly deep in the hot water.

He read the first fax. It was from his agent.

"Morris, *Adventure* magazine says the Pitcairn Island assignment may be shaping up. Be prepared to move fast if it does. Remember you're contractually obligated. You've owed them an article since hell was a pup. Best, Carson."

Josh snorted, crumpled the fax paper and flung it into the gilt wastebasket beside the sink. *Adventure* had been trying to put that freakish assignment together for years. It was never going to happen. He wished he'd never signed the damned contract. *Adventure*'s editors were crazy, and their assignments bizarre.

He settled more luxuriantly into the water and read the next message. It was also from his agent.

"Morris, Know you're coming off a tough assignment, but would you consider shooting a piece on Greater Abaco for *Islands*? Would not take more than a few days. Writer is Stacy Leverett. Would start in two weeks—Feb. 15. Short notice, but Gullickson caught bad bug in Dominica. Best, Carson."

For Josh, this was a no-brainer. Abaco with Stacy Leverett? Go to a Caribbean island with a statuesque blonde who looked great in cargo shorts and had a taste for short-term relationships? Just what the doctor ordered for a poor frostbitten man.

The third fax was yet another from the agent. Carson curtly reminded Josh that he was still on call for another *Adventure* assignment, Burma. His permission from the Ministry of Tourism might come through within four weeks, and he needed to be ready. But, cautioned the message, remember that if the Pitcairn assignment jelled, it was the magazine's top priority.

Josh gritted his teeth. Burma would be a rough assignment and dangerous—typical for *Adventure*. At the moment, he would rather think of the Bahamas and getting Stacy Leverett out of her cargo shorts.

He'd go to Missouri for a week and see his daughter, then the Bahamas, then, if need be, Burma. At least Burma would cancel out Pitcairn.

He sipped his whiskey and looked at the next fax. It, too, was from his agent. Good Lord, didn't anyone else in the world write to him?

"Morris, Your ex-wife called from Missouri at ten o'clock this morning, New York time. She says please get in touch immediately. It's crucial. Best, Carson."

Briana? Briana wanted him to call? It was crucial?

She did not use words like *crucial* lightly. She hardly ever contacted him when he was in the field.

Unless something was wrong. Very wrong.

Visions of the Bahamas and statuesque blondes fled. Instead his mind was taken total hostage by a slim brunette woman—and a very small girl with very big glasses.

Troubled, haunted by images of his ex-wife and his daughter, he went on to the next fax. Again it was from Carson.

"Morris, Your wife called again at one. She says she needs to talk to you as soon as possible. Please phone her, no matter what the hour. She says it's an emergency. Yours, Carson."

The last fax was from Carson.

"Morris, Your wife phoned again at four, Eastern Time. She says please call as soon as possible. It's urgent. Yours, C."

Josh swore under his breath, not from anger but from a deep and instinctive terror. He rose out of the tub, knocking the glass of whiskey to the floor. It shattered, and he stepped on it, cutting his heel. He hardly felt it.

He wrapped a towel around his middle and grabbed the bathroom phone.

Getting connected to Missouri from Moscow was approximately as difficult as arranging a rocket launch to the moon. Josh's imagination ran to places that were haunted and dangerous.

He bled on the marble floor. While the transatlantic connections buzzed and hummed, he had time to pull the shards of glass from his heel and pack the wound with tissues.

Briana, Briana, Briana, he thought, his pulses skipping *What's wrong?*

From across the ocean, he heard her phone ringing. He pictured the little farmhouse—tight and cozy. He pictured Briana with her dark hair and mysterious dark eyes, her mouth that was at once stubborn and vulnerable. He imagined his daughter, who resembled Briana far more than him. His bright, funny, unique, fragile little daughter.

Then he heard Briana's voice, and his heart seemed to stumble upward and lodge in his throat.

"Briana?" he said.

"Josh?" she said in return. She didn't sound like herself. Her tone was strained, taut with control.

He heard voices in the background, those of adults, those of children.

"Are people there?" he asked.

"It's Larry's birthday," she said. "Just a minute. Let me take the phone into the bedroom so we can talk."

He heard the background noise growing dimmer. "There," she quavered. "I shut the door. They can't hear."

"Briana, what's wrong?" he said desperately, but he already knew. "Is it Nealie?"

"Oh, Josh, she's sick. She might be—so sick."

He had the sensation of falling toward a devouring darkness. "How sick? Is she in the hospital?"

"I don't know how sick. It's—it's in the early stages. She doesn't know yet. Nobody in the family knows. You're the first one I've told."

"Briana, what *is* it? What's wrong with her?" Damn, he thought, his hands were shaking. His hands never shook, no matter what.

"It's a—an anemia," she stammered. "It's very rare. And—and serious."

"How serious?" He sat on the edge of the bathtub, his head down. He felt as if he was going to pass out.

"She could—she could..."

Briana started to cry. Josh put his hand over his eyes. "Okay," he told her raggedly. "You don't have to say it. What can be done? What can I do?"

She seemed to pull herself together, but she still sounded shattered. "Can you come home? I mean come *here?*"

"Yes. Yes. I'll be there as soon as I can. I'll book a flight as soon as I can. But what can we *do* for her?"

"Oh, Josh," she said, despair naked in her voice, "I've thought and thought. I think there's only one thing. One thing in the world."

"What? I'd do anything. You know that."

She was silent a long moment. He knew she was having trouble speaking.

At last she whispered, "To save her, I think we have to have another baby."

CHAPTER TWO

Josh was stunned, stupefied.

"What?" he said.

"I—I said," she stammered, "I—I think we have to have another baby. To save her."

"Another baby." He repeated the words, but they made no sense. They fell like great, meaningless stones on his consciousness.

Briana began to talk, low and swiftly. She said Nealie had something called Yates's Anemia.

Josh had never so much as heard of such a disease. Now she was telling him his child—their child—might die of it.

"It'll lead to aplastic anemia," Briana said. "Her blood count's unstable. Her system can't fight infection. She gets tired too easily. She bruises too easily. When she's cut, she doesn't heal right. She could have complete bone marrow failure. Or other diseases. Even—stroke."

Stroke? How could so young a child have a stroke?

He shook his head to clear it. Briana sounded as if she were on automatic pilot now, as if she'd rehearsed saying this to him a hundred times. Her words tumbled out in a breathless rush.

"Wait," he begged her. "You're sure of all this?"

"Yes. Yes. I took her to a doctor in St. Louis. She had a complete blood count and a—a chromosome test. It had to be sent away to a special lab. She has what they call chromosome breakage. It's Yates's anemia and it's life-threatening. It's one of the hereditary anemias."

He put his hand on his bare stomach because he was starting to feel physically ill. "She inherited it?"

My God, he thought, *was it from me? Did I somehow give my own child a death sentence?*

Briana seemed to read his thoughts. "Yes. But, listen, Josh. She had to inherit it from both of us. We—we both carry a recessive gene."

"Briana—I don't get it. This runs in both our families? I never heard of it."

"Neither did I. It's recessive—and rare. Very rare. We couldn't have known."

We couldn't have known. He knew she meant to comfort him, but he felt no comfort, only a growing desperation.

Briana went on as if possessed. "Her bone marrow isn't at failure stage—yet. It might not fail for years. Or it might start tomorrow. There's no predicting it. But she hasn't been well, Josh. Not well at all…"

She talked about strange drugs he'd never heard of. She used terms that sounded as mysterious as witchcraft. But everything she said boiled down to one fact—for Nealie's illness there was no simple cure and no sure one.

The best chance was a transplant involving either marrow or umbilical cord blood. By far the best donor of either would be a healthy sibling.

Nealie had no sibling.

Briana paused, then plunged on again. "If she has a crisis, she'll need a donor immediately. But finding a match can take months, years. We need to find a donor before a crisis occurs."

"I understand that," he said. "But how much time are we talking here? It's inevitable this disease gets worse?"

"Yes. It's inevitable." In her voice resignation warred with determination to fight.

Josh swallowed. "So…how long could she live?"

He heard her take a deep breath. "Without a perfect donor? The average life expectancy is—she'd live to be fifteen. Maybe longer. Maybe not. She's—already outlived some children who've had it.''

A shifting blackness wavered before his eyes. He shut his eyes and began to think, *God, God, God.* He didn't know if he was cursing or praying.

He said, ''With a perfect donor?''

''She might get well.''

Might, he thought, pressing his eyes shut harder.

Briana said, ''So I've thought about it, Josh. I've thought about all of it. The best chance for her—is for us to have another baby.''

He fought to think. ''But we both carry this gene. We could have another child who's sick.''

''No. There are ways to make sure we have one who's healthy.''

He frowned, eyes still shut. ''What do you mean?''

''Josh, I've talked to the doctors about it. I mean, it *can* be done. It's complicated to explain. It'll be easier to talk about it face-to-face.''

''Just tell me.''

She was silent a moment. ''We don't even have to touch each other. We can have my eggs artificially inseminated.''

His eyes snapped open in shock. *''What?''*

''There are tests,'' she said. ''The doctors can tell if there's a healthy embryo that's a match for Nealie. If there is, they can implant it in me—''

This was crazy, Josh thought. This was mad-scientist stuff, fantasies out of a future world.

Was she *really* saying they'd have a child but they wouldn't touch? That under the cold lights of a lab, strangers would quicken the eggs into life without either of them being there? And that then tests—not nature—would decide which of these tiny entities would survive and which would not?

Something deep within him rebelled.

''You want us to play God, Briana?''

"Josh, it's for *Nealie*." Her voice broke, and with it so did his heart. There was no answering her argument.

Still, he tried. "Look, I love her, too. You know that. But have you thought about—"

"I've thought of nothing else."

"Briana, let's talk this over—"

"I can't talk much longer right now or people will get suspicious. Rupert's already banging on the door."

Josh could hear him. Larry's boys were little louts, and they were the plague of Nealie's life.

Oh, God. Nealie's life. Nealie's *life*.

"Aunt Briana, come out!" It was Rupert's voice. "Neville made the cat throw up!"

Josh furrowed his brow in concentration, as he tried to block out the kid. He said, "Briana, tell me one thing. Does Nealie know how sick she is? Does she suspect?"

"No. I told her all the testing was for allergies. I told everyone that. I've lied to the whole world. Only you know the truth. Oh, Josh, please come home. Together maybe we can save her."

"I'll be there as soon as I can."

Rupert was banging louder. Josh heard Briana shush him. "Nealie's asleep," she told the boy. "Be quiet. You'll wake her."

"Nealie's a wimp," Rupert shouted. "I didn't *mean* to give her a nosebleed. I said I was sorry."

Alarm and anger rose in Josh. "A nosebleed?"

"She gets them all the time," Briana said wearily. "I made her lie on the couch with a cold cloth on her face. She fell asleep. I put her to bed. She has no energy lately." To Rupert, she said, "Rupert, stop that. If you wake Nealie, you'll be in *real* trouble." To Josh she said, "I've got to go. And I've got to pull myself together before I face them. I've been dreading telling you this. I'm sorry, Josh. So sorry."

"Tell Nealie I love her and that I'm coming home. I'll let you know when as soon as I get a flight."

"Thank you. Josh. Goodbye."

She sounded almost humble—his proud, cheerful, independent Briana.

The line went dead. He sat for a moment, then hung up the phone on its gold-colored hook.

His head swam with sorrow and shock. He did something he had not done since he was eleven years old. He put his face into his hands and wept.

RUPERT WAS JOINED at the door by his brother Neville, who began to kick. "Aunt Bri, Aunt Bri," Neville called. "You've gotta come. The cat threw up. Mama tried to clean it up, but she started to get sick. And Marsh spilled root beer on Grandpa's pants."

Briana was torn between laughter and weeping in despair. It was all surreal—the downstairs decked with balloons and streamers, her rambunctious nephews, the tormented cat, the nauseated sister-in-law, her father with his pants full of root beer.

She fought the hysteria and dashed the tears from her eyes. She forced her mouth to stop quivering and by sheer willpower composed herself.

Josh was coming home. That's what was important. He would help her face the tumultuous emotions, the terrifying decisions about Nealie. As for her feelings about Josh, she could not worry about that now.

She swung open the door and looked at her two oldest nephews. "Rupert," she said calmly, "you are never to *batter* this door again. Or any door in this house. Or anything else."

Rupert looked hangdog. He often disobeyed his mother, but Briana had a steely moral force that could wither him when she got him eye to eye.

"I thought you'd want to know about the cat," he said sulkily.

"I got the message the first time you said it." She swung

to face the other boy. "The same goes for you, Neville. In my house, no kicking."

"Daddy sent me to get you," Neville said righteously. "He said he wasn't going to clean up after that old cat. And Grandpa needs—needs soda pop for his pants."

Briana deciphered this. "You mean club soda. Let's go downstairs."

"Can Nealie get up and play?" Neville asked.

"No. She needs her rest."

"Why's she always gotta rest?" Neville asked, hopping heavily down the stairs. "I don't have to rest. I'm not even tired. I could go all night."

"I wasn't trying to hit Nealie," Rupert whined. "Her nose got in front of my fist, that's all. I was showing her how to box."

"Well, don't," Briana ordered and herded both boys into the living room.

"There you are," her brother, Larry, said almost accusingly. "Help me with Dad's pants." He stood by the sink tearing off great swaths of paper towel and handing them to Leo Hanlon, who looked bewildered.

The scene was as chaotic as Briana had feared. Glenda, her sister-in-law, was three months pregnant and lying on the couch, her feet up on a cushion. Her face had a greenish cast.

She smiled weakly. "Hi, Briana. Have you got a cracker or something? To settle my stomach?"

Little Marsh toddled toward Briana with an empty plastic mug. "More root beer," he said. "More root beer."

"No more root beer," Larry said. "You ruined these pants. These are your good pants, aren't they, Dad? Your Sunday pants?

"I just had 'em cleaned," said Leo and did his best to glower at Marsh. Marsh glowered far more fearsomely.

Briana marched into the kitchen. She opened the refrigerator door and pulled out a bottle of club soda. She thrust it into her father's hands. "There. Go into the bathroom and scrub those pants."

"How do I get them dry?" Leo asked with a helpless air.

"Use the hair dryer," Briana said. "It's under the sink."

"I'll get scorched," Leo complained.

"Take off your pants and *then* dry them," Briana said.

"Oh. Well. I would have thought of that. Of course." He took the club soda and went into the bathroom.

Larry leaned against the closed door and looked at Briana. He waggled his brows. "I bet Harve Oldman would *love* it if you told him to take off *his* pants. He'd probably pass out with happiness."

Briana said nothing. Harve Oldman was a neighboring farmer, a bachelor and a would-be suitor. She had cut off all contact with him as soon as she knew Nealie was sick.

"Where is good old Harve, anyhow?" Larry asked. "He hasn't been around lately."

Briana still said nothing. She reached into the cupboard and pulled out the box of soda crackers. As she arranged half a dozen on a plate, Larry gave her a friendly leer. "I mean Harve's well off. And he's got the hots for you."

"Please," Briana said. "The cat is nauseated, your wife is nauseated. Don't make it three of us."

Larry shrugged. "Easy to love a rich man as a poor man."

She didn't answer. She carried the crackers to Glenda, who forced herself into a sitting position and began to nibble.

Briana put her hands on her hips and surveyed the living room. "Where's the cat?"

"Hiding from Neville," Rupert said. "Neville dragged Zorro out from behind the washer and held him upside down and shook him."

Glenda gave an apologetic smile over the cracker. "I told him not to."

"Boys will be boys." Larry shrugged. Then he squinted

at Briana. "Who you talking to for so long on the phone?" he asked. "The whole family's *here*."

"It was personal," said Briana, getting disinfectant and cleaning cloths from the pantry.

Larry shrugged again and said, "Poppa figured it was Josh. He said he knows that look you get on your face when the phone rings and it's Josh."

"I said it was personal." Briana set about cleaning up the mess the cat had made. The boys were chasing each other around the dining room table.

"You boys be quiet," Glenda said from the couch.

"Ah, let 'em alone," Larry told her.

The boys chased on.

"Don't those sons of guns got energy?" Larry said with a proud laugh.

I can last until they've all gone home, Briana told herself. It became her mantra for surviving the rest of the night. *Till they've all gone home.*

AT LAST, the little house was empty of its guests. Her father returned to the main farmhouse, where he had lived all his life. Her brother and his family went home to the neighboring house Larry had built when he'd married.

Briana lived in the house that years ago had belonged to Uncle Collin, her father's bachelor brother. It was far smaller than the others, only two bedrooms, but it was set nicely apart from the main house, and its simplicity suited her.

Now it was quiet, blessedly so. She washed the last of the dishes and put them away. Still restless, she got out the ladder and took down all the balloons and the crepe-paper streamers.

There. It was her normal, peaceful little house again. She made herself a cup of hot chocolate and sat down on the couch to savor the hush that had at last settled.

Zorro came padding soundlessly from behind the washer.

He leaped to the couch and settled heavily into her lap, thrumming with his almost silent purr.

"Poor Zorro," Briana whispered. "Neville got you, hmm? Poor kitty." She scratched him between his black ears.

Briana loved her family, but she was glad they were gone.

She could not tell them of Nealie's illness. She could not. She knew some of this was simple, cowardly denial. Every person who knew Nealie was sick made her sickness seem more real.

Nobody would treat Nealie the same, or Briana, either. The boys would not understand, and they might say wounding things to Nealie. Glenda would be too sympathetic, and Larry wouldn't want to talk about it at all. He wouldn't know how to deal with it.

And her father—her father's heart would break. He was a sentimental man, especially when it came to his family, and he worried incessantly over his loved ones. Larry was big and strong and a hard worker but, unlike Briana, he'd never done well in school. Neither was he skilled with people. He talked too loudly, made inappropriate jokes, and he could be chauvinistic.

Glenda, his wife, was sweet and docile. This was her fourth pregnancy in six years, and she was always exhausted. Leo Hanlon wanted his son to hire a woman to come in and help Glenda, but Larry said it was her job, she should do it.

And although Leo was proud of his big, sturdy, handsome grandsons, he fretted about their rowdiness. *He* could by God control them. So could Briana. Why wouldn't their parents? Leo fumed and grumbled at Larry, but nothing changed.

Leo's favorite grandchild was Nealie. Larry couldn't understand this. After all, Nealie wasn't big, strong or good-looking. Worse than that, she was only a *girl*.

But Leo had never been able to resist his granddaughter's

spirit or smile. He fondly nicknamed her Funnyface. He was proud of her intelligence and imagination—he adored her. To know how ill she was would destroy him.

No, Briana wouldn't tell them. How could she? She wouldn't say anything until another child was clearly on the way.

For two months her daughter's sickness had been her secret. Soon Josh would be here. She would no longer be alone with it.

She lifted Zorro from her lap and set him on the floor. She shut off the lights and went upstairs to bed, Zorro waddling silently behind her.

She opened the door to Nealie's room and peered inside. The child stirred and rose on her elbow. "Mama?"

"Hi, sweetie. I didn't mean to wake you."

"My clothes woke me up," Nealie said. "I want my jammies."

Briana switched on the bedside lamp.

"How come I still have my clothes on?" Nealie squinted at the sudden brightness. Her big glasses lay beside the lamp.

"You fell asleep on the couch," Briana said, going to the dresser. "I brought you up to bed. I didn't want to wake you up."

Nealie rose on both elbows, frowning. "I remember. Rupert gave me a nosebleed."

"Yes, well, he likes to roughhouse. I scolded him for it."

"Ha!" crowed Nealie. She knew how Rupert hated Briana's scolding.

Briana rummaged in the drawer for pajamas. "Do you want the ones with cows or the ones with flowers?"

"Cows," said Nealie with a yawn. Then she fell back against the pillow. "Why do I have so many nosebleeds?"

Briana's hand tightened convulsively around the flannel. "Your allergies, I guess," she lied.

"Rupert woke me up, too," Nealie said in a sulky voice. "I heard him kicking on a door and yelling."

"Those are rude things to do," Briana said. "I don't want you ever to do them. Here, sit up, let me get that shirt off you."

She got the child into her pajamas and then made her settle back against the pillow. Briana pulled the quilt to Nealie's chin and bent to kiss her.

Nealie blinked, as if truly awake for the first time. "Daddy—did he call tonight? He always tries to call on the first of the month. Did he?"

Briana hesitated. If she told Nealie the truth, it would take at least half an hour to get her back to sleep.

But she had told the child lie after lie, and this time the truth would make her happy. She kissed the soft cheek. "He called. He says he's coming home soon."

Nealie sat up with a start, hazel eyes widening. "Really? Honest?"

"Honest. He's finished his assignment in Khanty-Mansiysk. He's in Moscow, ready to start back."

"And he's coming *here?*" Nealie's body seemed so charged with energy she looked ready to bounce. "Here? To see us?"

"Yes. To see you."

Nealie bounced in a sitting position. "When? When?"

"As soon as he can catch a plane. He should be here by the end of the week."

"For how long?" Nealie asked, bouncing harder.

Briana's heart wrenched. "I don't know. We'll see. Don't bounce, sweetie. You'll make your nose bleed again."

"Maybe he'll stay," Nealie said. She stopped bouncing, but she wriggled. "Stay and never go away again."

"No. We've talked about that. Daddy can't stay in one place. But this time, maybe he can stay—a longer time."

"Till my birthday?"

Nealie's birthday was in April, more than two months

away. God willing when spring returned, the child's strength would return with it, and she would be better, not worse.

"Could he?" Nealie asked. "Still be here for my birthday?"

"I don't know. He'll tell us when he gets here. Now lay down and close your eyes and go to sleep. When you wake up, it'll be morning, and he'll be one day closer."

She slipped her arm around her daughter, leaned back with her against the pillow. Nealie's little body, warm and lithe, snuggled against hers.

"Why didn't you wake me up when he called?" Nealie demanded. She was tired. She tried to hide her yawn as she said it.

"Shh. It was late. It's a different time in Moscow. He would have called earlier if he could. You know that."

Nealie nestled closer. "*What* time is it in Moscow?"

"Moscow time," Briana said, and they both giggled. She smoothed the child's hair and kissed her cheek again. She stayed until Nealie was asleep.

Then, because Briana couldn't bear to let her go, she switched off the light and slipped under the quilt with her. But she could not sleep. She lay in the darkness, holding on to her child.

ON SATURDAY, Josh watched the airport loom beneath the plane as his flight descended into St. Louis. A light snow fell, dusting the runways, but after Russia, he saw such a snow as insignificant. It was like a season of buds and bluebirds, practically springtime in Paris.

His head, however, felt nothing like the merry month of May. It felt like hurricane season in hell.

For three days he'd lived in a nightmare of bad airline connections and endless delays. He'd spent too many hours crouched in cramped plane cabins, missed too much sleep, been able to stomach too little food.

Truth be told, he'd also nursed too many Scotches and

vodkas to dull the pain. The pain came not from his physical discomfort, but out of fear for his daughter.

Along his jerking, twisted journey, he'd kept in touch with Briana as best he could. He told her he'd rent a car in St. Louis and drive to Illyria, for her not to drag Nealie out into the cold.

But when he got to the gate, his heavy camera bags slung over his shoulder, he saw them both, his ex-wife and his child. It was as if the rest of the sea of waiting people parted and vanished.

They stood at the edge of the walkway. Briana looked beautiful but pale and tense. Nealie, his little, bespectacled elfin Nealie, looked radiant.

His daughter grinned at him. She had lost a tooth. For some reason, this nearly undid him. He ran toward her, and she ran to him, her arms out wide.

Then he had her in his embrace, and she seemed to be both clinging to him and climbing him like a little monkey. "Daddy, Daddy, Daddy," she cried, her arms tightening around his neck.

He kissed her all over her face, knocking her glasses askew. She laughed and kissed him back.

"Daddy," she said again with such deep contentment that the words tore his heart.

She tried to wrap her skinny legs around his waist, but she was too small, and his parka made him too big. He let his camera bags fall to the floor and held her as tightly as he could. She buried her face in the harsh fur of his new parka, giggling.

He stared over the top of her head into Briana's dark eyes. She was holding back tears, he could tell.

For a few seconds, everything that had ever gone wrong between them disappeared. For those few beats of his jittery pulse, once again he loved her, and she loved him.

But he knew it was an illusion and he knew that it couldn't and wouldn't last. There were some things in life so broken they could never be fixed. His marriage was one of them.

CHAPTER THREE

FOR A MOMENT Briana's gaze locked with Josh's. There was a wildness in his hazel eyes, a desperation she'd never before seen. In that look she read the depths of his love and fear for Nealie.

She understood his feelings, shared them. She had an impulse to join him and Nealie in their crazy embrace. But she did not. Instead she turned away and let them have their moment.

She bit her lower lip and wished her heart wouldn't beat so hard that its every stroke felt like a stab wound. The airport looked blurry through her unshed tears, and she gave all her will to blinking them back.

But then she felt Josh's touch and, helpless, she turned to him. Nealie clung to his neck, and he carried her in his left arm. His right hand gripped Briana's shoulder.

He said nothing, only stared. His looks had always been a paradox to her, his face both boyish and rough-hewn. The jaw was pugnacious. The nose had a thin scar across the bridge from having been cut in a street fight when he was twelve.

But the eyes under the dark brows were alert and sensitive, and she had never seen such vulnerability in them. Still, his mouth had a crooked, slapdash grin that she knew he put there for Nealie's sake.

His brown hair was long and not quite even. He had a close-trimmed beard, and the harsh winter had burnished his cheekbones and etched fine lines at the corners of his eyes.

He put his free arm around her. "Briana," he said. He bent and kissed her on the mouth. His beard tickled and scratched. He smelled of Scotch and airline peanuts. His lips were chapped.

None of it mattered. Something turned cartwheels inside her, and to steady herself, she put her hand on the thick gray fur of his parka.

He drew back too soon, or maybe not soon enough.

He shook his head in mock disapproval. "You weren't supposed to come for me."

"She insisted," Briana said, giving Nealie a shaky smile. "You think I could keep her away?"

Nealie's arms tightened around his neck. "You came all the way from Russia. We just came from Illyria."

He shifted her to hold her closer. "It doesn't matter where we started out, does it, shrimp? We ended up together."

She smiled and buried her face in his shoulder. He hugged the child and pressed his cheek against her hair. "I love you," he said. "I've missed you. Every day, every night, I've missed you."

NEALIE CHATTERED on the way home, bombarding Josh with volleys of questions. "The people really have reindeer that pull their sleds?"

"Indeed they do."

"Just like Santa Claus?"

"Pretty much. Except Santa lives in one place. And these people move around."

"Why?"

"Because they're nomads."

"What are nomads?"

"People who move around," Josh said. "They have to hunt. They have to have fresh grazing for the reindeer. They change places when the seasons change."

"Why do the seasons change?"

"Because the earth goes round the sun."

"Why?"

"Because of gravity."

"What's gravity?"

"It keeps things fastened down."

"Why doesn't it keep the nomads fastened down?"

Josh darted a helpless glance at Briana's profile. She had a strange, sad little smile, but she kept her eyes on the road.

"That's a good question," Josh hedged. "I'll have to think about that one. Ask me again tomorrow."

Nealie settled more comfortably into her booster seat. She was growing tired, he could tell. He held her hand, and her head lolled against his shoulder.

"Daddy?"

"What, Panda Girl?"

"Why do you always call me Panda Girl?"

She knew the answer to that. It was a game they played. "Because when you were born, you had an extra thumb on one hand. Pandas have extra thumbs."

"Why?"

"Because they're special. Everybody loves pandas."

"Then why'd the doctor cut off my panda thumb?"

"So you'd match on both sides."

She held out her left hand, staring at it. A small white scar marked the operation. "Why didn't the doctor put another one on my other hand?"

"He couldn't find one. Panda Girl thumbs are very rare."

"I wish I kept the one I had."

"Naw," he said and kissed her ear. "Then everybody would have been jealous."

"Rupert says I was born a freak. That I had too many thumbs and a hole in my heart."

He resisted to the urge to say what he thought of Rupert. "See," he said. "Rupert's clearly jealous. Too bad. Poor old Rupert."

"Too bad," she echoed. "Poor old Rupert."

She dozed off. For a time neither Josh nor Briana spoke.

The only sound was the soft stroking of the windshield wipers.

Josh shifted so the child leaned more comfortably against his arm. He took off her glasses and slipped them into the pocket of his travel vest. His parka lay in the back seat, flung atop his bags.

"Does your family know I'm coming?" he asked, trying to keep the sarcasm out of his voice.

"Of course," Briana said, eyes on the road. "I had to tell them as soon as Nealie knew. She couldn't keep it secret. Not possibly."

"Do they know why I've come?"

Briana shook her head. Her dark hair swung about the shoulders of her white sweater. "No. I told everybody your assignment was done and you wanted to come back to the States to see Nealie. That's all."

He cocked his head, examining her. Oh, she was still something, all right, with her golden skin and exotic eyes. When she was serious, like now, she was a pretty girl. But when she smiled, he remembered, she was dazzling. She had the best smile he'd ever seen. He wondered how long it had been since she'd really used it.

"So," he drawled, "how'd your family take the news I'd be here? Great wailing and gnashing of teeth?"

"Poppa was polite," Briana said. "He said you could stay in his guest room if you want."

"No, thanks," Josh said and looked out the window on the passenger's side. Leo Hanlon was a deceptively amiable man, but his true feelings for Josh were as cold as the ice that glittered in the trees.

Josh had almost succeeded at the unthinkable—he had almost taken Briana away from Leo. But the old man had won. He'd won with one of the oldest plays in the game— just when Briana had to choose between the two men, Leo had gotten sick.

"How's his health?" Josh asked. This time he couldn't keep the edge out of his tone.

She stared straight ahead. "He's doing well. He went to the cardiologist last week. His heart's good. He hasn't had any episodes lately."

Episodes, Josh thought sourly, *are what you have on soap operas.* "But," he said, "I suppose he can't work much."

"No," she said.

"So Larry oversees the farm."

"Larry's a physical guy. He likes it."

He turned to Briana. "And what about Larry? Did *he* offer to let me use his guest room?"

"No." She cast him a cool look. "He hasn't got one. All his rooms are full of kids."

"He still thinks of me as the guy who deserted his big sister?"

"He doesn't change his mind easily."

No. He's like a Rottweiler or a water buffalo that way. Once an idea worked its way into his thick skull, it seldom found its way out again.

Josh didn't really care about Larry's opinions. But he knew down the line he'd have to grapple with them. As well as the far more complex ones of Leo Hanlon.

"Just when do you plan to tell them?" Josh asked. "About her?" He nodded toward Nealie, who was sleeping with her head on his shoulder. "And about—us?"

Every visible muscle in Briana's body seemed to tighten. "I don't want to discuss it now."

"Have you thought about it? How you're going to tell them? When?"

Her chin was stubborn. It was a look he knew well. "I said not now. She might wake up."

As if to prove Briana right, Nealie stirred, rubbed her eyes, murmured something incomprehensible, then nestled against him.

She's so small, Josh thought, *so thin. She wasn't this thin last time I saw her.* She was light as a bird, like a creature with air in its bones.

"You and I," he told Briana, his voice hard, "have to talk soon. And for a long time. I didn't come all this way to be stonewalled."

She nodded without looking at him. "Tonight. When she's in bed."

He frowned. "This thing you want to do—another baby—it's going to cause all kinds of—"

"Shh. Tonight."

"Fine," he countered. "Tonight. And where am I supposed to stay? Am I invited to use *your* guest room?"

She shot him a look. "I don't have one, either."

"I'll sleep on the couch."

"No. People would talk."

He sighed in exasperation. She was worried what people thought? She wanted him to father another child for her— like *that* wasn't going to make people talk?

She said, "If you don't want to stay with Poppa, you can stay at the motel. I'll loan you my truck to get back and forth."

He groaned. He remembered Illyria's motel from the photo shoot when he'd met Briana. It was a far cry from the five-star Kempinski in Moscow. Instead of private bars in every suite and a view of the Kremlin, it had a soda machine at the end of the hall and a view of a cornfield.

But that wasn't what bothered him. What bothered him was that he and Briana had spent their wedding night there. They'd married in a kind of ecstatic haste, too hungry for each other to go anywhere else. They'd made love, then dozed, woke, made love again, and when the sun came up, they made love again.

If Briana remembered, she didn't show it.

He tried to steer the conversation to neutral ground, not sure they had any.

"The farm's a success?" he asked.

"Oh, yes," she said, businesslike. "These days people are careful about what they eat. The more particular they get, the more they like us."

"No preservatives," he quoted from memory. "No additives. No artificial fertilizers. Only natural pesticides. No hybrid or patented seeds. The heritage of pure, old-fashioned food."

"You've got it," she said with a hint of the smile that used to make him crazy with wanting her.

"As George Washington said, 'agriculture is the most healthful, most useful and most noble employment of man.'"

"Wow," Briana said. "You really *do* remember."

I remember much more. Too much.

"Yeah. I remember," he said.

"In growing season, we do well at the farmers' market," she said. "We always sell out. We have buyers from restaurants as far away as St. Louis."

He thought about this past growing season. During it he had traveled over half the earth. She'd stayed home and tended her garden. And their child.

She said, "Was it a problem, getting time to come here?"

He shook his head. "No. Gave up a couple of short assignments. Nothing major."

"Where do you go next?"

He tried to sound casual. "I'm not sure."

"Are you still tied up with that crazy *Adventure* magazine?" she asked, an edge in her voice.

"I've got one more assignment," he said. "That's all."

She tossed him a displeased glance. "Where?"

"Don't know. Maybe Burma. An outside chance of Pitcairn Island."

"Burma?" she asked with alarm. "Pitcairn Island? Josh, those are *dangerous* places. When would you have to go?"

He shrugged. "Burma? Probably not for a month, maybe more."

"Burma has terrorists," she said. "It has *land mines*."

"I'll be careful. Besides, a few weeks in Burma beats months on Pitcairn."

Briana had said he needed to be in Missouri for at least

three weeks. He'd told Carson he wasn't touching *anything* for three weeks, and Carson had been bitter because there was money at stake, a lot of it.

From the unhappy look on Briana's face, he decided the subject needed changing. "So how's the seed business?"

She seemed relieved to talk of something else. "It keeps me busy. We've got a Web site now. And I computerized as much of the business as I could."

One corner of his mouth pulled down. "Computerized? Didn't Poppa object to that?"

The ghost of her smile flickered again. "Until he saw the results. He liked the profits."

"So it's the same as just after his heart attack. Larry's the brawn, you're the brains. In fact, it's the same as *before* his heart attack."

Her mouth went grim. "That's not fair. He's never been the same since my mother died. I told you that when we met."

"Sorry," he said, but he felt little true sympathy.

Briana's mother had died two years before Josh came to Missouri. She had been the one with the business mind. She kept the books, made the payments, studied new directions to take the business.

Leo Hanlon had neither the patience nor the sort of mind to take over the job his wife had done. It fell to Briana to do, and she did it brilliantly.

Leo's bachelor brother, Collin, a true workhorse of a man, died shortly after Leo's wife did. He had done all the farm's heavy work.

Without his wife and brother, Leo was nearly helpless. His back bothered him, his joints ached, and he was lonely. He wore his depression like a badge that exempted him from responsibility. He hired out more and more of the physical work. He was a genial man, sweet-natured, but he seemed to Josh to have drifted into a sort of privileged laziness.

"So what exactly is your father doing these days?" he asked, trying to quash the sarcasm in his tone.

She detected it anyway. He could tell by the way her jaw tightened. "He's owner and president, same as always. This whole business started with his vision."

His vision, his brother's sweat and his wife's smarts, Josh thought. Leo Hanlon's shaping dream had been a simple but good one. Most important, it came at exactly the right time.

Twenty-five years ago, the time of the small farmer in America was nearly over. People were not merely migrating to the cities, they were swarming there. Big farms gobbled up the small ones, and corporations bought out the big farms.

But America had begun as a country of farmers and settlers. Many who had gone to the cities missed the cycles of planting, growing and harvesting. They missed the feel of dirt between their fingers and the taste of tomatoes fresh-picked and still warm from the sun.

Leo Hanlon might not have succeeded as a farmer, but he prospered as a nurseryman. He supplied seeds and seedlings and potting mixtures to those city-dwellers who still yearned to garden.

But Leo's true stroke of genius was not to sell just *any* seeds and plants. He specialized in the old-fashioned varieties with old-fashioned flavor. He was in short, one of the pioneers in heirloom gardening.

The big seed companies often didn't offer the older classic breeds. Instead, they came up with new, improved, scientifically developed strains. They grew fast, uniformly and well. They just didn't seem to taste as good.

Heirloom varieties were in vogue again, and across the country a few dozen places like Hanlon Heritage Farms kept gardeners in supply. Leo Hanlon's mission was good. It was even noble. Josh sincerely admired it.

But Leo himself was a different matter.

When they first met, Josh had thought Hanlon likable,

well-intentioned and slightly comic. But Josh had underestimated him.

Leo Hanlon had proved to be the strongest adversary he'd ever met.

The two of them waged a stubborn war, and Hanlon won, hands down. What he had won was Briana.

THE TRUCK PASSED between the gates of Hanlon's Heritage Farms. *We're home again,* Briana thought.

At least she and Nealie were home. She wondered how the farm looked to Josh's worldly eyes.

The main farmhouse, where Leon lived alone, stood on the hill, a stark shape against the gray sky. Set in the valley was the ranch house Larry had built for his family. There were the old greenhouses as well as two new ones, modern and utilitarian.

Her house was on the next rise, clearly visible through the winter-bare trees. Her brother would be in one of the sheds, tinkering with the tractors. It was that time of year.

Her father would be in the room that served as his office, pottering with his endless notes. Was he watching? Did he suspect anything?

She glanced at Josh, who peered at the landscape, frowning.

"It looks pretty boring to you, eh?" she said. "It's not exactly Moscow or Paris."

"That's not what I was thinking."

"Oh?"

"I was thinking of the fields. They'd make a nice shot. A black and white abstract."

Briana looked at the familiar fields. Snow filled the furrows but hadn't stuck to the black ridges of dirt that ran between. The effect was like a painting, a great, complex design of sensuously rolling stripes.

How wonderfully he sees things, she thought. *I think Nealie sees things that way, too.*

Nealie stirred. "Are we home yet?" She rubbed her eyes

with her fists. Josh took her glasses from his pocket and helped her settle them on her nose. "We're home, Panda."

The girl looked out the window, then settled against him with an air of contentment. "You're really here," she said to him. "I thought maybe I only dreamed it."

"No dream, kid." His voice was gruff. He kissed her tousled hair.

Briana's emotions made a hard, painful knot in her throat.

"How long can you stay?" It was the third time Nealie had asked him the same question.

"I don't know. As long as I can. A while, I guess." For the third time he gave her the same answer.

"Then you have to go back to work," Nealie said with unhappy resignation.

"But for now, I'm here," he said. "With you."

Briana pulled into her driveway, pushed the button to open the garage door and drove in. "I guess we can leave your things in the back," she said to Josh. "There's no sense unloading them. You'll be going to the motel."

He said nothing. He gave her a look that clearly said, *We'll see about that.*

THE MOMENT CAME that Briana had dreaded.

Josh came down the narrow stairs. "She's asleep."

Briana stood by the couch, nervously folding the afghan. Josh had been upstairs for almost an hour. He had promised to read Nealie to sleep.

He crossed the room and stopped, looking at Briana. She felt threatened in a dozen conflicting ways. She was glad they had the couch between them, like a barrier.

"It's time," he said. "Now we talk."

She paused, biting the inside of her cheek. At last she said, "Let me pour us some wine. I think I'm going to need a drink for this."

She moved toward the kitchen, and he moved with her. He said, "Now what's all this about artificial insemination and healthy embryos?"

Why do you have to start with the hardest question?

She tried to keep her hands from shaking as she took the wine from the cabinet and poured two glasses. But she knew what she had to say. She'd rehearsed it enough. The words came to her lips almost as if someone else were saying them, and she was only mouthing them, a ventriloquist's doll.

She explained about the Center for Reproductive Health in St. Louis. There specialists could fertilize a group of eggs in vitro, a test tube union. The fertilized eggs would grow and divide until they produced what was called a blastocyst or pre-embryo.

When the pre-embryos were three days old, geneticists would test to see whether they showed signs of Yates's anemia. If a fertilized egg was healthy, it could be placed in the mother's womb before the end of the week.

"So that's it," Briana finished. "It's pretty simple, really."

"It's anything but simple," Josh said.

She shrugged and moved to the living room, wineglass in hand. She sat in the easy chair so he would be forced to sit on the couch. She crossed her legs. "Should I explain it again? I—I have some brochures and magazine articles and things if you want—"

He cut her off with a sharp gesture of his free hand. "The science I understand. At least well enough. It's the ethics that bother me."

"What do you want? Your ethics or your daughter's life?"

The coldness of her voice surprised her. But he didn't flinch, and his eyes didn't waver from hers.

"What about the *baby?*" he demanded. "We bring a child into the world for one reason. To save another child who's sick. Not because we want him, but because we don't want to lose the one we've got."

She raised her chin. "I'd love him. You know I would. I love children. I always wanted a big family."

Josh shook his head. "And what am I supposed to feel for him? I mean, we're talking about a child who's mine, too, you know."

She wished he'd sit down, but he stood in front of her as if rooted in place. She was ready for his argument. She'd anticipated it.

"Your feelings are your own business. But I know you. You'd care for him. You know you would."

He studied her as if she were a being from another planet. "But suppose, Briana, it doesn't work."

She turned her face away so she wouldn't have to look at him, but he went on, his voice relentless. "Suppose we have this child, but the transplant doesn't work, and we still lose Nealie. What then? Is it the baby's fault? Would you still want him? Or every time you looked at him, would you wonder why he was there but Nealie was gone?"

"Don't talk about her being gone, dammit!"

"And how would he feel? Knowing that he was born not because we wanted a child but we wanted a donor? And, unfortunately, he just didn't work out."

She clenched her fist on the arm of the chair until she felt her nails cutting into her palm. "I said I would love this child. That love is without condition. I would love him no matter what happened."

"Would you love him if he had Yates's anemia?"

Her head jerked up, and she glared at him. "I'm trying to make sure *neither* of them has it. That's the point."

He turned from her with a sound that was part sadness, part disgust. He walked to the mantel and struck it with the flat of his hand. He swore. "What if none of these hypothetical embryos is healthy? What if they all carry the disease? What do you do then? Flush them away and start over?"

"You can freeze them," she said, setting her jaw.

"Freeze them," he mocked. "That's nice. Do you have any other children? Yes, but they're in the freezer. They would have been flawed, so we didn't let them get born."

"Someday there may be another way to cure this disease." She shot the words back. "A sure way. Then they could be born and grow up safe."

"There may not be another cure for years. Decades. What then? We just keep the little nippers on ice for eternity?"

"Someone else could bring them into the world," she argued. "Someone who couldn't conceive on their own. It happens all the time."

"You've got all the pie-in-the-sky answers, don't you?" he said. "I'm not asking for just myself, you know. Other people are going to be raising the same questions."

"I don't care about other people," she said with passion. "I care about my daughter."

"And your other child, too, of course. The one you want for spare parts."

She could have slapped his face. Instead she took a long drink of wine. It tasted bitter as gall.

"I'm sorry," he said. "That was a cheap shot."

"Yes. It was."

"But people will say worse things. About us. To us. And to our children."

"I said I don't *care* about other people. And what's more, they don't have to know. It's none of their business."

He blinked. He set his untasted wine on the mantel. He stared at her in disbelief. "They wouldn't have to *know?*"

Her chin shot up. "I mean it. Why would they have to know?"

"Sweetheart, if you're pregnant and you have a baby, somebody's going to notice, I'll guarantee you."

"They don't have to know how we did it. The center has a confidentiality agreement. Nobody else ever has to know."

"And how do you explain this baby? Say we had a wild fling? And then we decided it wouldn't work, but there's a baby on the way, so what the hell, you'll just go ahead and have it?"

"Why not?" she challenged. "People try to reconcile all the time, and it doesn't work out. One of us got careless, I got pregnant. I wanted another child, so I had it."

"Good Lord," he said from between his teeth. "You're something, you know that?"

"Isn't it better?" she asked. "It's a white lie, it's not meant for an evil purpose. It's just to protect us—all of us, the whole family."

He picked up his glass and took a deep drink. "You should have been a lawyer. Your powers of equivocation are wasted on tomatoes."

She ignored the gibe. "If the truth got out, it'd be a media circus. Other people have done this. They ended up being national news stories. Do you want that? Do you want it for Nealie? Or the baby?"

Suddenly he looked older, and more tired than she'd ever seen him. He rubbed his forehead. "The baby. You talk about this kid like he's real."

"He could be a she," she said.

"Don't change the subject." He turned his back to her. He put his elbow on the mantel and leaned his forehead on his hand. "Look," he said. "I don't know if I can go through with this."

Panic flooded her. "But you said—"

"I was in shock. I'm still in shock. None of this seems real."

"Oh, Josh," she said, her throat tight. "It's *too* real. You've seen her. How little she is. How frail."

He made no answer.

She said, "We have two choices. We can do nothing for her. Or we can do—this."

He swore.

Desperate, she said, "It's hard to accept, I know. It's taken me two months to come to terms with it."

She knew immediately she'd said the wrong thing. She saw the tension seize his body. For a moment he was as immobile as if turned to stone.

Then he dropped his hand from his eyes, straightened and turned to face her. "You've known about this for two months?"

"I—I guess I was—in denial."

"Oh, please," he said with contempt, "spare me the psychobabble."

"If that's the wrong word, I don't know the right one."

"My child's seriously ill and you waited *two months* to tell me?"

"I couldn't face it. I couldn't talk about it. I couldn't believe it. I had to think about what to do."

He glared at her. She knew she deserved it. Tears welled in her eyes.

"I'm sorry. Be as angry as you want. But take it out on me. Not her."

He put his hand to his forehead again. "Look, I'm still on Moscow time. I've got jet lag. Denial's a lousy word. But I understand what you mean. Maybe I can't forgive, yet. But I understand."

She knew what he felt—grief, fright, anger and a terrible sense of isolation. He was full of the same roiling welter of emotions that had overwhelmed her when she'd first learned. And he was clearly exhausted, as well.

"Oh, Josh," she said. "you need rest. Let me give you the keys to the truck."

He said nothing, just stood there with his eyes covered.

She rose from the chair, then stood behind it, clasping its back, unsure what to do. "I'd drive you, but I can't leave Nealie alone. I—I could call Poppa. It's still early. You could just walk over there."

He shook his head no. "I don't want the keys. I certainly don't want *Poppa*."

"Then…"

He dropped his hand and met her gaze. He moved to her with a quickness that belied his fatigue. His hands gripped her shoulders. "What I want," he said, "is you."

Then his arms were around her, and hers were around him.

They clung to each other so desperately it was as if they were trying to forge their two bodies into one. She wanted to be as close to him as possible.

"Briana," he said, "oh, Briana."

Then his mouth was on hers, as hungry and seeking as her own, and she was lost in her need for him.

CHAPTER FOUR

HE WANTED HER. He had always wanted her. But never this much and never this badly.

She was the only one who understood—who could begin to understand—what he felt for his child, the depth of it, the complexity, the pain, the fear. To hold Briana meant he was not alone, that there was one person who shared the unspeakable emotions that tore him.

Yet it was more. She was not just a person, she was Briana, and he loved her. Together they had created a child, and together, God willing, they might save her.

But it was all tangled together in his head, the looming terror of loss, the wild desire to fight for his daughter's life and his sheer, aching physical need for not any woman, but *this* woman.

She felt the same for him. He knew she did. He could sense the need and yearning coursing through her body.

He took her face between his hands. Her skin felt soft and flawless as the finest silk. He kissed her so deeply it dizzied him. Behind his closed eyes, lights danced and exploded, dying into darkness, then exploding again.

"Don't—" she whispered against his mouth.

"Yes," he said, and when she turned her face away, he kissed the smooth spot beneath her ear.

"No."

"Yes."

"Don't—please. *Please.*"

"I need you," he said, his lips against the throbbing vein in her throat. "I need to hold you. Hold me. Be with me."

She struggled to pull away. The movement seemed tinged with both reluctance and determination.

"Don't," she said for the third time, and to his despair, she seemed to mean it.

He gripped her shoulders. "We need each other. You know it. I know it. Let it happen."

He tried to kiss her again, but she drew back, shaking her head. "We can't. That's not why I asked you here."

His clasp tightened. "You said you'd tell people we had an affair. It doesn't have to be a lie. Let that part be true."

She refused to meet his eyes. He could feel her body turning more rigid. "It can't be true," she said. "We can't do anything. For lots of reasons. For one, you—you're supposed to—to refrain from ejaculation for now."

She'd done it to him again. He was stunned. He could only stare at her, uncomprehending. "I'm what?"

She raised her face to his, her face defensive but stubborn. "Refrain. At the lab they'll need to test your semen. They'll want a good sample. And I'll be taking fertility drugs. I have to. I have to—to give them multiple eggs."

"Multiple eggs? You make yourself sound like the Easter rabbit."

"Don't laugh," she warned. "I'm serious. We can't make love. It's what the lab ordered. We go Monday."

His groin ached, and his head was beginning to hurt. "What about afterward?"

"No. I told you. I'll be taking hormones. Something might go wrong. I won't chance an accidental pregnancy."

"I thought the point of me being here was that we have another child."

Her chin quivered. "The point is that we have a *healthy* child."

A slow resentment was rising in him. "You must have been damn sure I'd go along with doing it your way."

"No. I wasn't sure. I just prayed you would."

"And what if I said let's not do the bit with the lab and the mad scientists. Let's have a kid the old-fashioned way."

To his consternation, her eyes filled with tears. "I couldn't stand to take the chance. I couldn't stand to have another child at risk the way she is. I'd rather die. You can call me a coward, but I c-couldn't."

She began to cry, and she was a woman who cried so rarely that the sight half-killed him. He understood her torment and hated himself for fueling it. "You're not a coward," he said. "Not you. Never you."

He folded her into his arms, gently this time, making no erotic demand, only holding her and letting her weep. "We'll do it your way," he said. "You're right. The baby will be safe. Shh. Our baby will be strong and healthy and fine."

Our baby, he thought with a conflict of emotion that half-dazed him. *We won't make love. But we'll have a baby.*

At last her tears slowed, then stopped. She stepped back from him, shamefaced, wiping her eyes. "I'm sorry. I didn't mean to do that."

"Maybe you needed to do it."

"I'll try not to do it again."

He looked at her streaked face. "In all my life I've only seen two woman who could cry and still be beautiful. Ingrid Bergman—and you."

She gave him a weak smile that made his heart twist in his chest. His desire for her hadn't vanished. It intensified so keenly that it hurt.

"I should go." He said it abruptly, but she didn't look surprised.

She seemed to understand and nodded. "I'll get you the keys." She went to the kitchen counter, where her handbag lay.

To have something to say, he asked, "Did my package for Nealie come?"

She opened her bag, took out the keys. "Yes. I put it away for Valentine's Day, like you asked. She doesn't know it's here."

"Maybe I should give it to her tomorrow," he said. "I

didn't have time to buy her much in Moscow. I'll get her something else for Valentine's.''

She came to him, dropped the keys into his outstretched hand. "Whatever you want," she said.

He knew he needed to leave before the urge to take her in his arms again grew irresistible. He fingered the keys. "I'll leave. For now."

"Yes," she said. "There's more to talk about, of course."

"Of course. What we tell Nealie about this. About the baby."

"Yes. That's the hardest part. But it's late. And you've had a long trip."

"Yeah." At this point it seemed a thousand years long.

She walked him to the door. He wanted to kiss her good-bye. He confined himself to the lightest brushing of his lips against her cheek. She did not return the caress. She only gave him a small, pensive smile.

"So I guess it's good-night," he said.

"I guess it is."

She opened the door for him. He paused halfway through it and turned to her again. "Call me as soon as Nealie wakes up."

"I will," she said. "Get rested. Do you remember the way to the motel?"

"I think so," he said. He remembered. He had been back to it in his memory too many times to forget.

He closed the door and walked alone into the night.

BRIANA HEARD HIM drive off. Then she sat in the silence, rotating the stem of her wineglass and staring at the dancing flames in the fireplace.

She had not been surprised by the fervor of Josh's embrace or the hunger of his kiss. Her eager response didn't shock her. Perhaps it should have shamed her, but it did not.

In spite of everything, they still desired each other. And

they both loved Nealie. Those two things would never change. Perhaps loving Nealie made them want each other more—pain sometimes needed the narcotic of touch, fear needed the consolation of nearness.

Briana put her hand to her temple, for it ached. She considered herself a simple woman whose life had become too complex. Josh was a wonderful man and a devoted father. She loved him, and he loved her in return, but they could not live together.

She loved this place, this farm, this work, and she could not leave it. It was her home, and her father needed her. The business could not survive without her. Her *father* could not survive without her. He was an unhealthy, absentminded man who, left to his own devices, forgot to take his pills or eat right or do his exercises.

No, Briana belonged to this place as surely as if she were one of the plants rooted here.

But Josh belonged nowhere, or else he belonged everywhere. The far places on the map called him, the siren stories chanted out for him come and help tell their tales, and he always went.

For five months he'd tried to stay on the farm, pretending to be a steady man committed to a steady place. He worked to learn a business foreign in every way to his nature. What he learned was to hate compost and pruning and predatory insects.

Then his agent had phoned with the irresistible offer to cover the trouble in Albania, and Josh had wanted to go. He wanted Briana to go and wait for him in Italy. Briana thought it all sounded too unsafe, especially with a baby on the way.

With horror, she realized her husband liked danger, that it tempted him with a lure just as strong as that of distant lands and exotic sights. Then her father had his heart attack. She could not leave him.

After that, the marriage swiftly unraveled. But their love for their daughter never changed. And the old undercurrent of desire that had drawn them together, that, too, stayed strong as ever. Briana had found that although pride was a cold bedmate, it was a safe one.

She rose to empty the wineglass and tidy the kitchen before she went to bed. She was emotionally exhausted, and Nealie would be up early, wanting her daddy.

Halfway to the kitchen, she heard a knock at her door. She turned and went to answer it. Her father stood on the little cement porch, a knitted cap pulled over his ears, a matching muffler wound around his neck.

"Poppa," she said in surprise. "It's cold. Why are you out?"

"I came to see if you were all right," Leo said, stepping inside. He looked at her living room suspiciously, as if were somehow contaminated. Then he gazed studiously at the wineglass in her hand. "Does he have you drinking alone? I hope it's not come to that already."

Briana gave him a rueful smile. "I was about to throw it out. Do you want a glass for yourself? A cup of cocoa?"

He waved away the suggestion, then sat down heavily on the couch. He unbuttoned his jacket but didn't take it off. He watched her go into the kitchen, pour the wine down the drain, then rinse the glass.

She turned to face him. "Make yourself comfortable, Poppa. Can I take your hat and coat?"

He shook his head, but took off his cap and held it scrunched in his fist. "I won't stay. Like I say, I just came to see if you're all right."

"Of course, I am," she fibbed.

"He stayed a long time." Leo said, his tone unhappy.

"Not so long. He read Nealie to sleep. Then we talked a little."

"He made you cry," Leo said. "I can see the streaks on your face."

She felt shamefully caught. She put her hand up to her cheek. "It's nothing," she said.

"What did he do to make you cry?" Leo demanded.

"Nothing. He did nothing."

"Then what did he say?" Her father's face was grim.

Briana sat in the armchair, trying to look as composed as possible. "He didn't say *anything*. Really, Poppa, it's—private. It's not easy having a broken marriage. I'm sorry for Nealie, that's all."

Leo didn't look as if he believed her. "He wants you back, doesn't he?"

"No." She bit off the word. "He doesn't."

"It would never work," Leo warned her. "He's not a man who'll settle down. The roaming—it's in his blood."

"Poppa, you don't need to tell me that."

"He'll certainly never make a farmer. Not him. Not that one."

"He doesn't *want* to be a farmer," she retorted. "He's a photographer, a world-class one. He's got a gift, and it's his duty to use it."

Leo's face turned sad. "He's got a family. It's his duty to stand by them." He paused. "He doesn't want you to come with him, does he? That wouldn't be good for Nealie. All that moving around. She's a delicate child. And this is the only world she's ever known."

Briana clutched the arms of the chair so tightly her fingertips were numb. "He hasn't asked us to come with him."

"That's good," Leo said, nodding. "This is the only family Nealie has. Josh has none to speak of."

"No. He doesn't."

Josh had no one. He had grown up in a series of foster homes in Detroit. His mother had abandoned him when he was four, saying she was too sick to keep him. She died a year later of hepatitis. He did not know who his father was.

A difficult child, he was moved from home to home. He didn't begin to find his way until he was fourteen, when he'd traded a stolen fifth of rum for a used camera.

No, Briana thought bitterly, Josh had no family, and why shouldn't such a rootless boy grow up into a rootless man?

The camera was his real soul mate, the great love of his life.

"I don't know what I'd do if you and Nealie left us," Leo said. "I guess I'd have to curl up my toes and die."

An infinite weariness sank into Briana's bones. "We're not leaving. And he's not staying. Let's not talk about it anymore. Please."

"Well, it bothers me," Leo said, crushing his cap into a ball. "Every time he shows up here—every time he even phones, you moon around as if your heart's half broke."

"I do not."

"And Nealie." Leo rolled his eyes. "He goes away, and you'd think the sun had fallen out of the sky forever. It takes her days to get over it. The longer he stays, the worse she gets. So how long is he staying *this* time?"

"I don't know." That, at least, was the truth.

"Sometimes I think it'd be better if he never came at all."

"That's wrong. He loves her. And she loves him."

"Indeed he does, and indeed she does. But it's a painful thing to watch, that's all I'm telling you," Leo said.

"Poppa," she said, "I understand how you feel. I really do. Just be civil to him, that's all I ask."

"Have I ever been less than civil?" he asked, his tone pained. "Have I ever so much as raised my voice to him? No. I even asked him to stop and stay with me. Well, he'd have none of it, and maybe it's better."

"Maybe it is," she said.

He rose unsteadily to his feet. His arthritis must be bad tonight, she thought. "I'll go," he said, buttoning his jacket. "You'll think me an interfering old man. It was only that I was worried. He stayed so late."

"Not so late," she said, coming to her father and adjusting his muffler.

He pulled on his cap. She walked him to the door. He put his hand on the knob, then leaned and kissed her brusquely on the cheek.

"Maybe this time you'll get him out of your system," he said. "Find a different man, a real family man. Have more children. You were never meant to have only one child, you know. That's been my prayer many a time. To see you with another baby in your arms."

He kissed her again and left. For a moment, she leaned against the closed door, hearing his last words echo in her head.

She put her hands over her eyes, not knowing whether to laugh or cry.

THE BEDSIDE PHONE rang, and Josh picked it up immediately.

"Hi, Daddy," said Nealie. "I just got up. Can you come for breakfast?"

He'd been awake since dawn, waiting for this call. He was showered, shaved, dressed, had been ready for an hour to go to her. "I'll be there as soon as I can, Panda."

"Maybe you could take me to church."

He set his jaw. He had never been the churchgoing sort. But he had expected this. "Sure, Panda. I'll take you."

"Hurry. Mama's making something special."

"I'll be there in two shakes."

"Bye, Daddy. I love you."

"I love you, too, baby."

He hung up the phone, stood and went to the bathroom mirror. He'd tried this morning to shave off the rest of his beard. The job hadn't been a complete success.

The upper part of his face was burned and blasted brown by the Siberian snow glare and wind. The lower part seemed city pale in contrast, and he had nicked his chin in two places and his throat in one.

He tried to adjust the collar of his white shirt to cover the scrape on his throat. He wore a black tie, as well. How long since he had worn a tie? Months. Maybe a year. Maybe more.

He put on his parka and picked up his camera case and left the spartan little room.

BRIANA'S BROTHER, Larry, was sitting in his van in the motel lot, parked next to Briana's empty truck.

Josh swore under his breath. He knew Larry was not there by accident or coincidence. He was waiting to talk, and from his face the conversation would be grim.

Larry got out of the van slowly and deliberately. He was a big man, four inches taller than Josh's five eleven, at least sixty pounds heavier. He wore a down jacket that made his shoulders look as wide as an ox yoke.

"Hello, Larry," Josh said. He did not bother pretending to smile.

Neither did Larry. He wore no hat, and his curling hair was like a dull gold flame under the gray sky. "I want to have a few words with you."

"Fine," said Josh.

"First," Larry said, narrowing his eyes to a squint, "I want to know what you're doing back in Illyria."

"I came to see my daughter."

"If you'd stayed here, you could see her all the time," Larry said.

That's none of your business, you moron. But Josh tried to quench the flare of his anger. Larry was Briana's brother, and although she knew his shortcomings, she was protective of him and loved him. He was family.

"I wish things had worked out differently," Josh said, and this he meant.

"We all do." Larry's words came out in a plume like a dragon's breath.

Josh said, "I hear your family's growing. There's going to be another addition. Congratulations."

"Yeah. And my kids know one thing for sure. I'll always be there for them. I won't never go gallivanting off and leave them."

You've got your job, bullyboy. I've got mine. Step aside

before I want to break your self-satisfied face. Josh kept his expression impassive. "I'm due to meet Nealie. She's expecting me. Have you had your say?"

Larry stepped more squarely in front of him. "I hear you made my sister cry last night."

Oh, hell, Josh thought in exasperation. "She didn't tell you that."

"No." Larry crossed his big arms. "My pop went over there last night to make sure she was all right. He said she'd been crying. You've got no right to make her do that."

The blood banged in Josh's temples. What could he say to this man that wouldn't widen the breach between them, make everything harder than it already was? Once again, he tried to push anger aside. "I would never willingly hurt your sister. I would cut off my right arm before I'd knowingly cause her pain."

"You wouldn't have to cut it off," Larry said. "Because I'd tear it off. I mean that. You ever hurt that girl again and you'll answer to *me.*"

He put out his ungloved hand and pushed Josh's chest. It was a slight touch, but full of warning. He brought his face closer. "Understand?"

When Josh was growing up in Detroit, if anybody had been foolish enough to push him, the guy would have gotten a mouthful of shattered teeth. Josh was smaller than Larry, but he knew he could flatten him.

What he did was harder. He held up his hands as in a sign of peace. "I understand," he said. "And I don't want trouble with you. You're Briana's brother and Nealie's uncle."

"You remember that," Larry said. But he stepped aside.

LARRY'S VAN was faster than Briana's old truck. He beat Josh to the farm by five minutes. When he walked in the door of his house, his wife gave him a disapproving look.

"Well," she said. "Did you find him?"

"Yeah," Larry said. "I found him, all right."

Larry had gone hunting for Josh Morris with a sense of righteousness. He had convinced himself the man was a threat to his sister's happiness, his father's health and his family honor.

His father had phoned last night, upset that Briana had been crying. Leo had fretted and dithered and worked himself into a state.

Larry loved his father, but he knew Leo was not a confrontational man. He would never be able to face down somebody like Josh Morris. Larry considered himself the real man of the family, and it was his duty to protect his father and his sister. If he didn't, it was a blot on his manhood and a blow to his tender self-esteem.

This morning he had risen early. He had watched Briana's house, waiting for the lights to go on. When Nealie was awake, she would want her father to come, so as soon as Larry saw her bedroom light flicker into life, he'd gone to meet Morris one-on-one.

Glenda crossed her arms over her softly swelling stomach. She was a lovely blond woman, but lately she looked worn. He supposed it was just her pregnancy, some woman thing like that.

"Well?" She said it with a peculiar edge of aggression in her voice.

"Well what?" Larry asked, hanging his jacket on its hall peg.

"What did you say to him?"

Larry turned to face her, feeling smug, the top dog. "I told him never to make my sister cry again. That if he hurt her again, I'd rip his arm off."

She looked pained. "You didn't *really* say that."

"Yes, I did," said Larry. "Where are the boys? I'm ready for breakfast."

"I let them sleep late. I wanted to talk to you."

He looked at her suspiciously. "So? Talk."

"I told you last night what I thought. You didn't pay any

attention. I laid awake a long time thinking about it. You should stay out of your sister's business. It's got nothing to do with you.''

Larry bristled. "It's got everything to do with me. It's family, dammit. He made her cry."

"You don't know why she cried," Glenda argued.

"Because he hurts her feelings," Larry said. "He gets her all upset."

"You weren't there. You don't know what happened."

"Yeah? Well, that's what Pop thinks. And you know Briana. She's not the crybaby type. She fell out of a tree once when we were kids and broke her arm. She didn't even sniffle."

Glenda thrust out her delicate little jaw. "Maybe she's crying because she still loves him. She still cares for him, you know. You can see it—if you'd look."

"She shouldn't care. He's no good. He went off and left her once."

"He's not a bad man, Larry. He loves his child, and I think he still loves Briana."

"He's not one of us," Larry returned.

"That means he's different. It doesn't mean he's bad."

"She's *my* sister. I'll decide what I think is good or bad for her."

Glenda crossed her arms more tightly. "Let them make their own decisions. In short, Larry, you should butt out."

He blinked. This was unlike Glenda, who was usually so adoring, so compliant. "Hey," he said. "Whose side are you on, anyhow?"

"I don't know," she said. "But I'm starting to think it isn't yours."

She turned her back and walked away.

"Hey!" he said again. "What is this? And where's breakfast? Haven't you even got coffee made?"

"Make it yourself," she said and walked out of the room.

He stared at her, his mouth open in stupefaction.

NEALIE FINISHED her breakfast because her daddy told her to. Briana sat at the table across from Josh, her chin resting in her hand. He was good with the child, so good.

He looked weary but, to her, still handsome. He had shaved off his beard, and it made him look younger, but his sideburns were tipped with silver that hadn't been there when he'd visited last.

"And now," Josh said, "if you'll promise to eat a breakfast like that every day, I'll give you a present."

Nealie's expression was excited, yet tinged with conflict. "But, Daddy, sometimes my tummy feels funny. And I'm not hungry."

"I know," he said. "But you could try. You could remember your promise and try, couldn't you?"

Nealie's brow puckered. "Yes. But if I *couldn't* eat everything…"

"The important thing is you try, okay?"

"Okay," she said solemnly.

Josh turned to Briana. "You know where that present is, don't you?"

She smiled and nodded, rose and went to the pantry. From the top shelf she took the tattered package with its Russian stamps. She carried it to the table and set it beside Nealie's empty plate. "Daddy sent this. It came a few days ago."

"Wow," Nealie said, staring at the exotic stamps. "What is it?"

"Open it and see," Josh said.

Nealie's small fingers struggled with the taped box, and finally Briana helped her. She had no idea what the package held.

At last Nealie lifted the flaps of the box. She stared inside at something beautifully white and furry. "What *is* it?" she repeated.

Josh gave her a cryptic smile. Nealie opened the box. Inside was a pair of boots like none Briana had ever seen. They were white as cream, with dark leather soles and ornamental insets of brown fur at their tops.

"They're from the Khanty-Mansiysk district in Russia," Josh told Nealie. "They're made of reindeer hide, sewn with deer sinew. A white hide like that is special. It's for someone specially loved."

Nealie held the boots and looked at them with pleasure and awe. But then a shadow crossed her face. "This was a reindeer?"

"That's how the Khanty people live," Josh said. "They herd reindeer. For over five thousand years they've taken care of the deer, and the deer take care of them. The deer are grateful so they give them food and clothing and hides to make shelter. A woman named Vika made these for you. She said they'd keep you warm all winter long. That the spirit of the forest would protect you from the cold."

"They're beautiful," Nealie said, stroking the thick white hair. She kicked off her slippers and pulled on the boots. "Can I wear them to church?" she asked Briana. "Please? Can I?"

"Yes," Briana said, smiling at how the girl wriggled her feet and stared at them in admiration. "But run and change your clothes. Wear your brown pantsuit. They'll look good with that."

"Wow," Nealie said, sliding out of her chair. "Nobody I know has boots clear from *Russia*. Thank you, Daddy."

She gave Josh a smacking kiss on the cheek then clomped happily up the stairs, enjoying the sound of each boot step.

Together they watched as she disappeared into her room. Josh gave a sigh of mock relief. "For a minute, I thought I'd goofed. I'd become a purveyor of murdered reindeer."

"She has leather shoes," Briana said. "So do I. I thought you explained it nicely."

"Spend a few months in Siberia, you forget about political correctness."

She rested her chin on her hand again and studied him. "You never were a great one for political correctness, as I recall."

"I don't want to make her unhappy."

The only way you make her unhappy is when you go away, Briana thought, but she said nothing. Instead she rose and said, "I'd better clear this off and get ready for church."

She reached for his empty plate, but he clasped her wrist gently and held it. "Briana?"

She looked into his eyes, which were serious. "Yes?"

"Larry came to see me this morning. He doesn't want me to make you unhappy, either."

She made a sound of exasperation. "Oh, *why* does he have to put in his two cents? This is none of his business. Not at all."

"No. It's ours."

"That's right," she said, feeling a surge of defiance. "And it's *only* ours."

"Other people won't feel that way," he said, stroking her wrist with his thumb. "Not when they find out there's a baby on the way."

"I don't care what people think." She believed this. She had convinced herself of it.

"You'll stand against them all if you have to?"

"Yes." She spoke without hesitation.

"And you'll do it alone?"

"I can handle it. I know I can," she said. She prayed that this was the truth and that she had the strength.

He stood, sliding his hand down to lock with hers. He took a step nearer. "You don't have to," he said. "I've thought about it."

Her flesh tingled at his nearness, but she did not move away. She felt she must stand her ground. "I've thought about it, too. I can do it."

"You don't have to face it alone," he said, his voice quiet. "Briana—marry me. Marry me again."

CHAPTER FIVE

HIS WORDS struck her like numbing blows, and his nearness overwhelmed her.

"No," she said, her throat constricted. "I'd never ask you here for that. Never."

"I know that," he said. "But think about it. It's best for everyone."

She shook her head to clear it. "No. We didn't get it right before. We—we just can't live together."

He bent so close she felt the warmth of his breath on her lips. "We don't have to. Who says it has to be a conventional marriage?"

She stared at him, bewildered. "You mean it wouldn't be *real?*"

Something flashed deep within his eyes—something he immediately shuttered. "Sham? If that's how you want it."

"I can't—" she began.

But Nealie came stamping importantly down the stairs in her new boots. "I *love* these," she declared. "I feel like I've got big furry rabbit feet. Like Bugs Bunny."

Briana wrenched her hand from Josh, and he took a step backward.

But Nealie had seen. She stopped halfway down the stairs. Behind her big glasses, her eyes widened, and her face looked both hopeful and perplexed. "You were holding hands. Do you like each other again?"

"I'll always like your mother," Josh said. "I hold her hand once in a while. Like she was—my sister."

"Oh, Nealie," Briana said, desperate to change the subject, "you're sweater's buttoned all crooked. Let me fix it."

Nealie's small hand tightened on the banister. She came down the stairs, no longer stepping proudly. Briana went to her to rebutton the cardigan. The child, in her excitement, had gotten it comically askew.

But her face was solemn and puzzled. Briana knew the girl was confused by what she had seen. "Daddy and I are friends, that's all." She fastened the sweater. "Look at you. You've got one sleeve up and one sleeve down. There. Now you're perfect. And your boots are beautiful."

Nealie looked at them, and slowly her smile came back.

Briana straightened and took Nealie's hand in hers, her fingers still tingling from Josh's grasp. She went to the coat closet, painfully conscious of him but avoiding his eyes.

As they stepped out the door, he leaned near and whispered, "Think about what I said. We'll talk later."

She made no answer. Her ear burned as if he had breathed a live spark into it.

SHE WALKED into church with him, each of them holding one of Nealie's hands. Everyone stared except her brother, who nodded mechanically, then fixed his eyes on the church program.

Beside Larry, Glenda smiled uneasily and mouthed hello. The little boys gaped and whispered and poked each other with excitement.

Beside Larry, Briana's father sat. He, too, tried to smile, but there was nervous pain in his face. He gave Josh a weak wave of greeting. Josh nodded in return.

The sermon seemed the longest Briana had ever sat through. The subject was the importance of the traditional family.

AFTER THE SERVICE, in front of the church, Josh suffered through a reunion with Briana's family.

He could feel the force of Larry's disapproval. It came at him like a great, invisible wave pulsing through the wintry air. Glenda, still pretty but looking wan, tried hard to offset her husband's unfriendliness.

She didn't so much ask Josh questions as chirp them nervously, one after another. How was his trip? How long had he been in Russia? Were the people nice? What had he photographed? Oh, my, wasn't that *interesting?*

As she chattered, her sons watched Josh with a hostile suspicion they seemed to have absorbed from their father. Glenda ran out of questions. An awkward silence weighted the air.

Then Rupert stared at Nealie's boots, his nostrils flaring. "What are those?"

"They're boots," Nealie said. "They're clear from Siberia, Russia. My daddy gave them to me. He had them made special."

"Why'd he do such a dumb thing?"

"It's not dumb," Nealie retorted. "He did it because he loves me."

"If he loved you, he'd stay home with you." Rupert sneered and stepped on Nealie's toe, smudging her boot.

With a fiery look, Nealie shoved him so hard he fell into the snow on his bottom. Josh wanted to kiss her and raise her to sit on his shoulders like the champion she was. Rupert began to cry.

"You kids stop that," Briana's father commanded with surprising sternness. "You're right in the front yard of the church, for Pete's sake. Rupert, stop yowling."

Rupert stopped crying. He thrust out his lip and sulked instead.

Leo turned to Josh. "The boy's high-strung," he said gruffly.

Josh bit back a sarcastic reply and forced a smile that he hoped would pass for understanding. From the corner of his eye he watched Nealie bend and polish her boot tip clean.

On the surface, Briana's father acted friendly enough. But

he eyed Josh strangely, as if taking measure of a dangerous competitor. Glenda invited everyone to Sunday dinner, but Josh declined. He made his excuses as gallantly as he could, but he did not want to spend the afternoon with this family. He wanted only his own child—and Briana.

He said he and Briana and Nealie had to drive over to Springfield so he could rent a car of his own. That, at least, was true enough.

The trip was short, and Nealie rode home with him. At the house, Briana put on an apron and made spaghetti because Nealie remembered it was Josh's favorite. He sat at the counter, playing word games with Nealie, but he could not keep his eyes from Briana.

She moved like a dancer, he thought with a pang, every movement marked by grace and efficiency. She bantered with them as she worked, and he marveled at her ability to act as if nothing had passed between them, either last night or this morning.

But he knew she was as aware of what had happened as he was. The memory of it tingled around them like an electrically charged field. He had always been good at hiding his feelings. He'd never before realized Briana was every bit as good as he was and maybe better.

He loved Nealie dearly but was glad when after dinner she began to yawn and at last fell asleep on the couch. He carried her up the stairs, put her on her bed and covered her with an afghan.

When he went downstairs, he saw her empty boots standing by the couch. The sight touched him for a reason he could not name. He picked them up, stroked them, then set them down.

"She loves them," Briana said, drying the last of the dishes. "She really does. You made a great choice."

He leaned against the counter nearest her. "You should have let me help you with those."

"No," she said, hanging up the dish towel. "You're company."

"I'm not company," he said, looking her up and down. "I'm the father of your child. And your child-to-be."

"It's only biology," she said. "Technically, you're a guest." She said it coolly and briskly, as if she were warding him off.

"Am I?" He arched an eyebrow.

He moved behind her and undid the bow of her apron strings. When she took off the apron and set it aside, he let his hands settle on her waist, his thumbs just above the swell of her hips.

She went stiff and still. "Don't."

"We're about to make a baby. We've still got lots to talk about."

He felt her muscles go even more rigid. She pulled away from him and moved to the other side of the counter. *She's keeping it between us like a damn chastity belt,* he thought.

"Then talk," she said. "But no touching. That's not part of the bargain."

"Bargain?" he said. "Is that what you call it?"

She shrugged. She had changed from her church clothes into jeans and a long-sleeved white T-shirt. When she shrugged, her breasts did things that made his mouth water.

He tried to keep his voice cool, businesslike. "There's plenty about this bargain that's not resolved."

She shrugged again, and the movement of her breasts forced him to look away so she wouldn't see the hunger in his eyes.

"We can't talk about it in front of Nealie," she said. "It's—difficult."

"Difficult. Yes."

"It's strange," she said with sadness. "We tell children truth is important but in front of them we lie. We turn into the hypocrites we warn them not to be."

He said, "Seems to me you've got a lot more hypocrisy ahead of you."

Her dark eyes snapped. "What do you mean?"

"You'll have another child. But you'll lie about it to your

family. And to Nealie. And someday to the child, too. That's a lot of lying for a woman who used to be honest to a fault.''

"That's different."

"Is it?"

"Yes. I was talking about things—things like this morning, about Nealie seeing us touching. What to say to her about other things, that's all."

He crossed his arms, a gesture of resolve not to try to touch her again. "This morning. That's a loaded subject. But let's talk about it."

Her face went wary. "I—I'm sorry my brother came to see you like that. It's always been part of the problem, I know. Somehow my family keeps pushing itself into the foreground."

"Yes," he said, crossing his arms more tightly still. "They do."

"And you *don't* get along with them," she said.

"You could phrase that the other way, too. They don't get along with *me*. Your brother doesn't try, and your father doesn't want to. They were scared to death I'd take you away from them. Then where would they be?"

She pushed her hand through her long, dark hair. "Oh, please," she pleaded. "I could see it after church. Nobody said anything, but it was there. It's hopeless between you and them. The way it's always been."

"And the way it'll always be?" he said, a bite in his voice.

"I suppose," she said and stared past him.

She would never leave them. He knew that. They had laid the perfect trap for her. They *needed* her. She was the strongest of them, the smartest, the most giving. She was the one who held everything together for them, including their finances.

He took a deep breath and set his jaw. "Now you want to tell them we had a fling, I got you pregnant, then went on my merry way again."

Her head jerked so that she met his eyes square on. "I'd never say that."

"It doesn't matter what you say. It's how they'll see it. They'll hate my guts even more than they do now."

"They don't hate you," she hedged. "They just—"

He cut her off. "Don't dodge it. It's a real issue. It'll affect my relationship with Nealie. And with—the new one."

For once she didn't have a fast answer for him. She jammed her hands into her pockets and looked stubborn. All she said was, "I won't let that happen. I promise."

"You *can't* promise," he argued. "You can't promise how other people are going to feel. Nealie, for instance. What's she going to think? What will other people say to her? That I came back here, knocked you up—"

"Don't be crude." Her eyes flashed again.

"I can be a lot cruder than that," he warned. "They'll say I knocked you up, then left you. What kind of man will she think I am?"

She tossed her head. "She *knows* what kind of man you are. She adores you. She'd never turn against you."

"Oh, Briana. What an idealist you are. What a scheming, lying, hypocritical little idealist."

Her hands flew out of her pockets, clenched into fists. "Schemer? Liar? All I'm trying to do is save my child's life. If you want to call me names, go ahead. I'll do what I damn well have to."

Beneath his crossed arms he felt the brutal hammering of his heart. But he kept his calm facade. "And exactly how are you going to explain all this to her? What lies have you cooked up especially for her?"

Briana's eyes narrowed, and she set her fists on the countertop, like someone getting ready to fight. "I'll tell her the truth—mostly. That I got pregnant and that though you and I both love her and love the baby, we knew getting married again would never work. But we wanted the baby—both of us did—and we decided this way was best."

"In short, a very complicated lie. Hard for a child to understand. Even one as bright as Nealie."

Briana leaned toward him, her fists on the counter, her stance militant. "You apparently didn't hear me. I will do this. My child is in danger. If I have to bend the truth, or if everyone gossips about me, I don't care."

"I wasn't talking about you, Joan of Arc. I was talking about my daughter."

"I will make her understand and accept it," Briana said emphatically.

"Yeah, yeah," he sighed cynically. "And next you'll be out in the radish patch shaking your fist at the sky and crying, 'With God as my witness.' From Joan of Arc to Scarlett O'Hara in ten seconds. Speedy."

"Ooh," she said from between clenched teeth. "You are the most impossible man—"

"Put on earth, obviously, to deal with you, the most impossible woman. Briana, you don't have to put the truth through all these contortions. You don't have to run this gauntlet. There's a simpler way. This morning I made you a proposition—"

"A proposition." She hissed the word. "You have an interesting way of putting things yourself."

"All I'm saying is marry me. We don't have to live together. We can live the way we live now. You stay here with your precious family—"

"It's no sin to love your family," she interjected.

He ignored her. "—and I make my living the only way I know how. I'll come to see Nealie and the baby as often as I can. It won't be a conventional marriage, but at least your family can't object to a baby if we're married. Nobody can say things to Nealie that are mean—or at least too mean. And you—you're saved from living in a jungle of lies."

She straightened and put her hands on her hips. "Except for the marriage, of course. *That's* a complete lie."

"Better a simple lie than a complicated one." He smiled.

"Didn't you hear a word of that sermon this morning?" she challenged. "About the importance of marriage? About husbands and wives committing to each other? About the sanctity of the union?"

He laughed. He shook his head. "Briana, you're hopeless. You're both the most conventional woman I've ever known—and the least. You'd tell a thousand improbable lies that will only hurt you and everyone else. But you reject the plausible one that's best for us all."

"I don't want a sham marriage," she said, squaring her shoulders. "Or for you to marry me out of pity or because it's the right thing."

"Either way you play it, your life will be a sham, won't it?" he said, raising one eyebrow. "Why not a respectable marriage that's a lie instead of a misguided affair that's a lie? I don't ask that you be faithful. If you want someone else, fine. I couldn't care less."

She looked more stricken than angry. He played his trump card. "And one more thing, Briana."

She looked at him, her eyes full of uneasy questions.

"This is the only way our baby won't be a bastard. You're not the only one who'd have to live with that. So would he. So would Nealie and your family."

He let the words sink in, and he could tell he'd made a point she couldn't counter. At last she said, "I don't want you to be noble. It's so unlike you."

"I'm not being noble. I'm being stone-cold practical. I don't want to marry anybody else. So I might as well marry you again. If I find somebody else someday—or you do—we'll deal with it then. One problem at a time. Okay?"

She raked her hand through her hair again, a gesture of weary frustration. All she said was, "You make my head spin."

"Likewise," he said.

They were silent for a long moment. He thought of going to her, of taking her in his arms, of saying he wanted to be married to her again because he loved her and would do so until he was in his grave.

But Nealie's voice cried out from upstairs, startling them both. She sounded confused and alarmed. "Mommy! Come help me! My nose is bleeding—bad!"

NEALIE SAT QUIETLY in Josh's arms, her head resting against his shoulder. He held his finger against her nostril, applying pressure to stop the bleeding.

Briana came upstairs with a cold compress—ice cubes wrapped in a washcloth. Josh took it from her and put it over the bridge of Nealie's nose.

Nealie looked pale but no longer frightened, and she seemed to feel safe in her father's embrace. Briana knelt and began to clean Nealie's hands with a second washcloth. She gave Josh a troubled glance.

After church he had taken off his sweater and tie. His white shirt was spotted with blood. "Your shirt—" she said.

"It's not big deal," Josh said and smoothed Nealie's hair.

"I messed up everything," Nealie said unhappily. "The pillowcase, my good sweater—"

"Shh," Briana said, "I can get them clean again."

"Even Daddy's shirt?"

"Sure she can," Josh said. "She's Supermom. You know that. Now be quiet. I think the bleeding's stopped."

Nealie sighed and settled even closer to him. "The nosebleed woke me up," she complained, then yawned. "I was dreaming about white mice. They could talk."

"Close your eyes," Josh said. "Maybe they'll come back. Here, we'll just lean against the backboard and be quiet."

"Can I take off my sweater?"

"If you're careful," he said.

"I'll help," said Briana. She unbuttoned the brown cardigan, then helped ease Nealie out of it and her undershirt.

She dressed her in a pajama top and let her sink back against Josh.

"Shhh," he said. "Be still."

"Will you tell me a mouse story?" Nealie asked in a croaky little voice.

"Yes," said Josh, "but first close your eyes."

"I'll get a clean pillow," Briana said. She and Josh exchanged looks that spoke the silent language of parents.

He was saying, *I'll stay with her and try to get her back to sleep.*

She was saying, *I'm scared, Josh.*

So am I. But we can't let it show. And we're going to take good care of her. I promise you this.

He turned to Nealie. In a meditative voice, he said, "Once upon a time there was a white mouse named Wilberforce. He lived with his mother and father and seventeen brothers and sisters in a cheese factory...."

Briana kept her face immobile, picked up the stained pillow and sweater and took them downstairs to the laundry nook. She went back upstairs and got a fresh pillow and pillowcase from the linen closet.

She took them into Nealie's room. Nealie, eyes closed, rested against her father's chest. In a low droning voice, he said, "The mother mouse said, 'What kind of cheese do you want for supper tonight, dear? American, Swiss, Cheddar, Monterey Jack, Gouda, Edam, Roquefort, Stilton, Parmesan, mozzarella, provolone or Liederkranz?'

"And the father mouse said, 'Excuse me, my dear, I was reading the paper. Did you say something?'

"And the mother mouse sighed and said, 'I asked what sort of cheese you wanted for supper. American, Swiss, Cheddar, Monterey Jack, Gouda, Edam, Roquefort, Stilton, Parmesan, mozzarella, provolone or Liederkranz?'

"'Let me see if I have this straight,' said the father. 'The choices are American, Swiss, Cheddar...'"

Briana laid the clean pillow on the bed and smiled at him

in spite of herself. He was clearly trying to lull the child to sleep. She turned and left him reciting his hypnotic lists.

He was a good father, a wonderful father. But to marry him again? A marriage in name only was repellent. To try a real marriage would never work, she told herself, never. She couldn't face the thought of losing him a second time. It would kill her.

HE CAME DOWNSTAIRS when she was soaking Nealie's cardigan in the kitchen sink. Since the nosebleeds had begun, she kept a special bottle of soap for removing the stains. She was determined to save the sweater, which was one of Nealie's favorites.

He moved beside her, and his nearness, as always, made her skin prickle and her blood flow too fast. He said, "She's asleep. I think she'll be out for a while." She felt the warmth of his breath on the side of her neck.

Briana cast him a quick sideways look. "I never heard of cheese used as a lullaby."

"I nearly put myself asleep," he admitted. He nodded at the sweater, which she was still scrubbing. "Can you get it clean?"

"I think so. I've had enough practice. Too much practice."

He shook his head. "It's one thing to hear about her nose bleeding. It's another to see it. I felt my heart stall. It just quit beating for a minute."

"I know the feeling," she said, keeping her gaze on the sweater.

"We'll get her through this, Briana. We will if it's humanly possible." He put his hand on her shoulder, not erotically, not possessively, but as a friend would. Yet his touch still set a tremor through her.

She said, "Your shirt—I'll try to clean it."

"I don't have another one here."

"I'll find something for you," she said. "Please take it

off. It'll upset Nealie to see you in it. And she'll want to know she didn't ruin it.''

"She probably did. It doesn't matter. I've got other shirts. I'll tell her it all came out. She won't be able to tell the difference.''

She took a deep breath. "Weren't you just criticizing *me* for lying?''

"Touché,'' he said.

It becomes a habit, she wanted to say. *It becomes easy. Pretend this. Lie about that. Leave out this bit of truth. Twist that one. It becomes second nature.*

Instead she dried her hands and said, "I'll find you a shirt.''

She went upstairs. quietly so as not to wake Nealie. She looked in the least used drawer of the least used bureau in her room. She knew she had a few old sweatshirts and T-shirts stored there, work clothes.

Rummaging, she found, near the bottom, something she had not expected. One of his old sweatshirts—Josh's. A pang of memory shot through her. She lifted the shirt from the drawer.

It was a souvenir of one of his travels, long past. It was faded blue, from Canada, and had a picture of a white wolf on it. Almost reluctantly she ran her fingers over the fabric, remembering its feel.

When he had first gone away, sometimes she'd missed him so much she'd gotten out of bed and changed her night-gown for this shirt, just to be touching something that had touched his body. She had been hurt and angry at his going, but she'd still believed he'd come back to her to stay.

"Oh, my God,'' she whispered, remembering. How long had the shirt been lying there forgotten? Six years at least, six long years.

But she squared her shoulders, carried it downstairs and thrust it at him. "Here,'' she said brusquely.

He looked at it in disbelief. "You saved this? All these

years? Remember? I loaned it to you one chilly night and you liked it so much, I told you to keep it.''

She remembered. But she said, ''Obviously I should clean out my drawers more often. I forgot it was there.''

He gave her a sardonic look. ''For a moment I was flattered. I should have known better.''

He unbuttoned the shirt. ''You're sure you want to mess with this?''

''You're the one who told her I'd get it clean.''

''Quite the little washerwoman, aren't you? And pretty, to boot.''

He peeled off the shirt, and she sucked in her breath in shock.

He was still lean and muscular and she knew his body all too well. But there was something different—a scar. A crooked, purplish welt zigzagged across his left bicep and continued across his chest, stopping just under the left nipple.

''Good heavens,'' she said. ''What happened?''

''New Guinea,'' he said without emotion.

''How?''

''A guy with a spear. We'd been staying in this village several days. He'd been fine. Then one morning he came out of his hut in a rage, holding this spear and threatening us.''

''But why?'' she asked, unable to take her eyes from the scar.

Josh shrugged. ''I don't know. None of us knew. Maybe he'd had a bad dream. Maybe he just snapped.''

''He tried to kill you?'' she said in disbelief.

''He tried to kill Lieberman, the writer. I was trying to talk to him, get between them. Ellison got behind him, grabbed him. He was already throwing the spear, but Ellison knocked his aim off. They finally wrestled him to the ground.''

She could not stop herself. She lifted her forefinger and ran it in dread over the scar. She had not felt the bare flesh of his body for years. The sight and feel of it were achingly familiar.

Yet the scar was not familiar. It was unlike any she'd ever seen. "You could have died," she breathed, touching the part of it nearest his heart.

"It was mostly a flesh wound," he said. "He nicked a few ribs."

"B-but," she stammered, laying her hand over the scar, "you could have got an infection or—"

He put his hand over hers, pressed it against his chest so she could feel the strong beating of his heart. "No," he said gently. "Ellison patched me up, radioed for a plane, I got taken to a hospital at Moresby Port. I was back on the job in a week."

She stared at him as if he were a creature she could never fathom. She tried to draw her hand away. He kept it where it was, on the scar over his heart.

Her voice went ragged. "When did this happen?"

"A year and a half ago. Maybe a little more."

She raised her dark eyebrows in hurt resentment. "You never told me. You never said a word."

"I didn't want to worry you. Or Nealie."

"You shouldn't hide the truth from us, either."

"Ah," he said. "Back to the issue of truth again, are we? Would you really feel so bad if I got killed?"

She wrenched away from him and snatched the bloody white shirt. "Get your clothes on," she said, twisting the faucets to fill the sink. "Yes, I'd feel bad. I'd feel bad for Nealie. She worships you. She couldn't stand it if you got yourself killed for some damn—*picture*."

"You know," he said, picking up the sweatshirt, "I think you're a little jealous of the pictures."

She shot him a look over her shoulder. "Of course, I am. They took you away from us. And half the time when you go, I wonder—I wonder if you're ever coming back."

He pulled the sweatshirt on. She was glad his torso was covered again. But it haunted her memory, and now she wanted to smooth his brown hair, which was mussed by pulling on the shirt.

"You've got it backward," he said, leaning against the cupboard door. "I go to make a living, not to get killed. I'm careful."

She concentrated on rubbing the shirt. "I'm afraid you'll fall off a mountain or be eaten by sharks or trampled by a rhinoceros."

He gave her a smile that was almost a smirk. "Beats dying of boredom on a tomato farm."

How did we every get married? she asked herself miserably. *Why? How did it last as long as it did?*

His smile died, and he recognized he had made a mistake. He eased a bit closer to her. "I'm sorry," he said, and he seemed to mean it. "I shouldn't have said that. It was a stupid thing to say."

"No," she said, staring unseeing into the suds. "You're right. This is my home, and you'd always be bored here. You'd always be going away, and I'd always resent it and be afraid. We both do what we have to do."

She rubbed at the shirt until it seemed clean, then rinsed it repeatedly and wrung it out. He stood in silence, watching her. She straightened the shirt, smoothed it and put it in the dryer. She wiped her hands on a towel, and Josh suddenly seized one in both of his.

"You're going to ruin your hands." He stroked the rough skin on her knuckle.

"What difference does it make?" she asked. "I'm a farmer's daughter. I get in the dirt and I plant and I weed. I don't need to hold anybody's hand. I shouldn't hold yours. So let me go. Please."

He raised one hand and set it on the back of her neck. "I don't want to let you go. I want to keep you."

"I don't want to be kept," she said, raising her chin. "And that's what it would be, wouldn't it? You keeping me? No. I'm never going to depend on anyone again except myself.''

"Well, Miss Independence,'' he said, bringing his mouth closer to hers, "then how do you expect to have this baby?''

CHAPTER SIX

HER PRETTY MOUTH twitched in agitation. But she didn't have to give him an answer, because someone tapped at the front door, a gentle, almost timid sound. Rap, rap, rap.

"That's Glenda's knock," she said. "And I told you to stop touching me. I meant it."

"Glenda? What's *she* want?" Josh demanded. But reluctantly he let his hands fall away.

"She's my sister-in-law and my neighbor. She doesn't need an invitation. She can come over any time she wants," Briana said. She moved quickly to the door, and Josh stood looking after her, flexing and clenching his hands in frustration.

She composed herself—what a good little actress she was—and flung open the door. "Hello, Glenda. What a nice surprise. Come in."

Glenda stood at the threshold, her thin face red with cold. She stepped inside and stamped her snowy boots on the welcome mat.

"The phones are out," she said in her breathless way. "I think ice may have brought down a line. I didn't know if you knew."

"I didn't," Briana said. She patted Glenda's snowy sleeve, urging her inside. "Come in. I'll make you a cup of hot chocolate."

Glenda shook her head. "No. I can't stay. I came to say that Leo isn't feeling well. Right after dinner, he started feeling queasy and weak. I've got him lying down in Rupert's room. He says he wants to see you."

Briana's face blanched, and her hand tightened on Glenda's arm. "He's sick? Is it his heart?"

"I don't think so," Glenda said. "I'm hoping he just overate. And lately he's been kind of—you know, on edge."

She cast an apologetic look at Josh, who knew that he, of course, was the reason Leo was on edge.

"And he wants to see me?" Briana said, worried that her father was sicker than he would admit.

"Yes," Glenda said. She fidgeted with her left glove, pulling and picking at it. "I don't know what about. You know how he gets when he doesn't feel well. Antsy. He worries about little things."

Briana pressed her lips together and nodded.

"He wanted somebody to go to the old greenhouse, too," Glenda said. "Just to make sure the latest seedlings don't need thinning. You know—"

"Yes, yes," Briana said. "He gets a bee in his bonnet. Does he want me to do that, too?"

"No," Glenda said, still nervously plucking her glove. "I'm going down there now. Larry can't do it. He's too ham-handed." She gave Josh another of her strained smiles. "But if you want to go with Briana, I'll stay here with Nealie."

Josh watched Briana, who was pulling her coat out of the hall closet. "Thanks," he said. "I'll stay here. Nealie's taking a nap."

"Oh," Glenda said and shrugged. "Well, if she wakes and you get cabin fever or something, the two of you can come down. The old greenhouse. The big one, you know?"

"I remember," he said. And he remembered how vulnerable Briana was when it came to her father. Leo was an expert at sensing when he had a rival for her loyalty and attention.

Is the old boy really sick? Josh knew the question was too cynical to be voiced, but he had to ask himself. The old man wanted no outsider luring away his daughter.

Briana sat on the couch, pulling on her snowboots. Her face was pale, but a hectic flush colored her cheeks. "I'll check on him. If I think he needs to go to the emergency room, I'll drive him." She darted Josh a worried look. "If I have to take him, you'll stay with Nealie, won't you?"

"You know I will," he said.

She stood and wrapped a crocheted muffler around her neck, donned a cap and mittens. "I don't know when I'll be back," she told him.

"I understand," he said.

When she went out the door, Josh felt he was watching her being pulled away from him and toward Leo as if on an unbreakable string.

LARRY OPENED the door. He was in his stocking feet and had the Sunday funny papers in one hand. A basketball game was on television, the sound turned low. Rupert lay on the rug in front of the set with a bag of potato chips and his toy guillotine. He was trying to decapitate his GI Joe doll.

"Be quiet," Larry told Briana. "The two little ones are asleep. Don't wake 'em up."

She was already unsettled, and his tone set her teeth on edge. Larry could be boorish, there was no denying it.

Yet paradoxically, this was one of the reasons she felt protective of him. He had no social skills, nary a one. He had always been athletic and handsome, but from childhood, he had an awkward way about him. People did not take to him.

He had many good qualities. He worked hard, he was a good provider, he was faithful to his wife, and when he made a promise he kept it. But he did not have an iota of charm. He wanted to be liked, but outside the family circle, he was not. Briana felt sorry for him.

So she nodded and said hello to Rupert.

"Shh," Rupert admonished her. "The kids are sleeping. Wow! Three-point shot! Cool!"

Briana gave the boy a look that told him to keep a civil tongue in his head. Rupert looked guilty and stuffed a handful of chips into his mouth.

"Pop's laying down in Rupert's room," Larry said, scratching his stomach.

"How is he?" Briana asked.

"Aw, he's okay. He just pigged out," Larry said. "He had three helpings of chicken."

"He's supposed to watch his cholesterol," Briana said.

"Yeah? Well, tell him, not me."

She sighed and started to take off her boots so she could leave them on the mat in the entryway. Larry went to the couch and flopped down on it, opening the comics pages.

Briana hung her coat in the closet and went down the hall to the back bedroom. She knocked softly on the door, but there was no answer. She eased it open and peeped inside.

Rupert's walls were covered with posters of Arnold Schwartzenegger as The Terminator, his idol. Over his bed was a large picture of Godzilla stepping on a bus.

On the bed lay Leo, his cheeks rosy, sleeping as peacefully as a cherub. His snoring was light and even.

Oh, Poppa, she thought in frustration. *I thought you wanted to talk.*

But she knew better than to wake him. Leo was cranky when wakened from a nap. And deep down she did not want to go to her own house. Josh made her fear her emotions too much.

She sat in the chair beside the bed. She would wait here, alone with her dozing father, trying desperately to sort out her thoughts.

NEALIE WAS wide-awake.

She was also surging with restless energy, so Josh dressed her for outdoors and walked her down to the greenhouse.

Glenda looked up when they walked in, and her face

brightened at the sight of Nealie. She might feel uneasy with Josh, but he saw that her affection for the little girl was deep and real.

"Nealie," she said with pleasure. "Just the person I need to see. You can help me thin these tomato seedlings."

"All right!" Nealie said. "What kind?"

"Nebraska Wedding," Glenda answered. "And they need thinning. This batch looks a bit leggy. I guess your grandpa can just sense these things."

Nealie stripped off hat, gloves and jacket. She dragged a little step stool to Glenda's side and stood on it. She began to work, and Josh marveled at her. Although her hands were small, they were quick and sure.

Josh hung his parka on the peg beside Nealie's and Glenda's. The heat of the greenhouse seemed tropical after trudging through the February snow, and the aroma of growing things and soil filled his nostrils.

"Now that you're here," Glenda said to Nealie, "would you mind if I took a little break?" To Josh, her voice sounded falsely bright.

"No," Nealie answered. "I like this."

Glenda left the worktable and sat in a folding chair in the corner. She moved slowly, almost painfully.

Nealie had started singing to herself, a song from *Beauty and the Beast.* "Bonjour," she caroled, "bonjour!"

Josh went to Glenda's side. "You're tired," he said. "You should quit for the day."

She looked at him with a self-conscious smile. "I'm fine. Really."

He said, "It's a long walk from here to your house. I'll go and get the car and drive you home."

Her smile fled. "No. Please. I like being here. It's so peaceful."

Not like your house, he thought. He said, "Briana says you're going to have another boy."

"I'd hoped—" She shrugged. "Well, it doesn't matter.

I'm used to little boys." She nodded toward Nealie. "Look at her. She's a natural gardener. She's got it in her blood."

Josh fought not to flinch at the mention of Nealie's blood. He said, "I guess Leo casts a long shadow."

She stared at him, and he realized he had used the wrong words. He said, "I mean, he's got a gift for this. He passed it on to Larry and Briana and Nealie, too."

She nodded. But she said, "You were right the first time, too, though. He does cast a long shadow. We all stand in it." In a rush, she added, "I don't mean he's a bad man. He's not. But somehow he has such influence. Larry wants his approval so much. And Briana feels so protective about him. I try to be the perfect daughter-in-law, but I know my kids don't behave, and Larry won't help. I don't know why, maybe it's some sort of rebellion. You know, passive-aggressive. At first I didn't have the nerve to fight it. Now I don't have the energy."

Her candor surprised Josh. He looked at her with interest.

"I guess I'm feeling sorry for myself," she said. "It's just that I always have this sense that I don't live up to Leo's expectations."

"I know that feeling exactly," Josh said. "He isn't exactly crazy about me. And that's an understatement."

"You're a threat," she said with the same frankness. "He was afraid you'd take Briana away. Now he's afraid you'll take them both."

Her gaze moved to Nealie. She was still thinning the seedlings, singing another song, this one from *Pocahantas*.

Glenda said, "Leo loves Nealie and Briana. But he *needs* Briana. So does Larry. We all do. It isn't fair."

Josh had the feeling of a man who is deep in enemy territory and comes across an unsuspected ally. "Fair?" he echoed.

"All this," she said, making a gesture that took in the greenhouse and everything within it. "It's on her shoulders to run it. Leo's never done it by himself. I doubt he could. Larry couldn't. I couldn't. So we all depend on Briana."

He raised one eyebrow. "Why are you saying this to me?"

She looked into her lap at her soil-stained hands. "To tell you that if you want her, you're going to have to fight for her. Hard."

He kept his face impassive, but his heart seemed to stumble and keep stumbling. "And if I fight hard—will I win?"

She raised her eyes to his. She looked half hopeful, half fearful.

"I don't know," she said.

LEO'S EYES fluttered open. He yawned lavishly. Then he saw Briana at his bedside and blinked in surprise.

"Hello, Poppa," she said. "How do you feel?"

His expression, bland and sleepy, changed to worried. He put his hand over his heart. "I felt queasy, a bit weak. I guess I needed rest."

He glanced at the opposite wall. Multiple Arnold Schwartzeneggers scowled at him, and Leo scowled back.

"Besides, those kids get on my nerves. Neville threw a handful of mashed potatoes at Rupert, and Rupert spit a pea in his eye. I want to go home. I want the peace and quiet of my own house. Walk me back."

Briana put her hand on his shoulder. "I'll borrow Larry's van and drive you."

"Nonsense." He snorted. "I walked here. I'll walk back. The doctor told me to exercise. And I feel restless. I've got a lot on my mind."

Apprehension rippled through her. "What's on your mind?" She hoped it wasn't Josh.

"I'll tell you on the way," Leo said. "Let's get out of here." He rose with more spryness than she'd thought possible.

Briana worried that the frigid air would be a shock to Leo's lungs, but once outside, he seemed invigorated. He inhaled as if savoring the briskness of the cold. His cheeks turned even rosier.

Their boots crunched on the snow, and she put her arm through his. "Now," she said, "what's bothering you?"

"Those kids don't help matters," he answered. "Why doesn't Glenda make them mind? It's her job to teach them manners."

"She can't do it alone. Larry has to back her up. And he never does."

"Larry," he said with an edge of exasperation. "Larry's just a big kid himself. But he told me he wants more responsibility. More of a hand in running the place. Him? Ha!"

Briana lifted a questioning eyebrow. "What kind of responsibility?"

"He wants to expand the mail order business. Sell equipment. Tools. Fancy sprinklers. Water timers. Drip irrigation kits. Machines."

Briana had often thought of expanding the business, but never in that direction. "Actually, Poppa, it's not a bad idea. Larry understands machines. He's very good with water systems. He knows his stuff."

"This is a farm, not a toolshed," Leo answered.

She said, "And maybe Larry should have more responsibility."

"He doesn't know squat about running a business."

"He never will if he doesn't get any experience."

They had reached the crest of a gentle rise. "Let's stop for a minute," Leo said, putting his hand on his chest again. "I want to catch my breath."

She tightened her hold on his arm. "Are you all right?"

He ignored the question. Instead he surveyed the view. Briana's gaze followed his. From this vantage point she could see all four greenhouses nestled in the valley, the machine shed, the rows of cold frames, the empty fields.

"Look at it," Leo said with reverence. "Twenty-five years ago, it was nothing but cornfields and pastures. This is what your uncle and your mother and I started creating way back then."

"I know, Poppa. It's a great accomplishment."

A quaver entered his voice. "It's a dream come true. But I could never trust it to Larry. He's not—capable."

Briana said nothing. She could see her little house in the grove of winter-bare trees. She wondered if Nealie was still asleep. She thought of Josh, and her heart tightened.

Leo harumphed. "I'm not saying Larry's a bad boy, you know. It's just that he never did well in school, the way you did. And he's not good with people. Not like you."

Briana turned to gaze at Larry's house, looking cozy and well kept in the snowy landscape. "It's not fair to compare us, Poppa. We're different people. Larry can do a lot of things I can't."

"And you can do a lot he can't," Leo countered. He was silent a moment, then said, "When I'm gone, he'd never last alone, you know. Without you to supervise things. He just couldn't handle it."

His words made responsibility and guilt weigh on her like a bag of stones strapped to her back. She thought of what Josh had said about her family and tried to push the memory away. It only made her emotions more complex.

She patted his arm. "Don't talk about being gone."

"I thank the Lord for you and Nealie," Leo said, putting his hand over hers. "The two of you make everything worthwhile. And when I'm gone, I know the farm and Larry will be safe—with you here."

"Poppa," she said, "is this what you wanted to talk about? Larry and the farm?"

"No, no. It's only an old man's rambling. I'm rested. Let's move on. I want to show you something at the house."

Briana's spirits sank. She could guess what he wanted to show her. And it was the last thing she wanted to see.

"I SHOULD GO HOME," Glenda said, standing. "The boys will be waking up."

"We'll go, too," Josh said. "I don't want Nealie to wear

herself out. We'll walk you as far as Briana's, and I'll drive you back from there."

Glenda didn't object. She nodded with a small smile of gratitude.

"Come on, Panda Babe," he called to Nealie. "We're going back."

"Just two more minutes?" pleaded Nealie. "I'm almost done. Honest."

He looked at her, so delicate yet so efficient. She had potting soil on her fingers and a smudge across her chin. Her glasses had slipped down her nose. His heart ached with love for her. "Two more minutes," he said.

She began singing again, although not with the same energy. The song fell into an almost tuneless humming.

"She's not strong, is she?" Glenda asked softly. "I worry about her."

In spite of the hugging warmth of the greenhouse, Josh felt a chill trickle through him. "Yeah, well, allergies."

"I didn't know allergies could make you tired all the time. She's seemed—well, almost frail lately."

"Allergies are complicated," he said. "It takes a while to straighten them out." He saw how easy it was to fall into Briana's pattern of hiding the truth. He clamped his mouth shut and said no more. Glenda seemed to realize he didn't want to talk about it.

Nealie finished her thinning, jumped down from her step stool and washed her hands. Josh helped her and Glenda into their jackets. He knelt and zipped Nealie's, wound her scarf around her throat and straightened her cap when she jammed it on crookedly.

"Thank you, Nealie," Glenda said. "You did as much work as I did. I got a good rest."

"I know why you need rest," Nealie said brightly. "It's because you're going to have another baby."

"Yes."

"I wish *my* mommy and daddy would have another baby."

Josh had the sudden sensation of being hit in the head by a rock. Glenda blushed. He put on his parka and said, "That's not an appropriate subject, Nealie."

"Why?"

"For complicated reasons."

"What reasons?"

"We'll discuss it another time."

"When?"

"Later."

"How much later?"

He sighed and said, "Let's go."

They left the greenhouse, and Nealie was distracted by the sight of two cardinals sitting in a pine tree. "Why don't cardinals fly south in the winter?" she asked.

"We'll look it up in the encyclopedia when we get back."

"My goodness," said Glenda, looking at him. "You don't even have your coat fastened or your hood up. Aren't you cold?"

He smiled. "After Siberia, this seems balmy."

"My daddy is very strong," Nealie said proudly.

"Yes," Glenda agreed. "He is."

"That's why you thin the seedlings," Nealie told Josh. "To make sure the plants are really strong."

"Is that so?" he said, although he knew it well.

"You get rid of the weak ones," she said. Then she frowned unhappily. "Rupert said somebody should thin me out. Because I'm one of the wimpy ones."

A wave of shock and anger swept over him. But he could not say what he wanted to in front of Glenda.

Glenda looked profoundly embarrassed. "He shouldn't have said such a thing. And it's not true. I apologize for him saying it."

"It's okay," Nealie said. "I called him an imbecile. It made him really mad because he didn't know what it meant. But it kind of scared me."

She hit a deep patch of snow and staggered, almost fell.

Josh scooped her up in his arms. He would carry her the rest of the way home. He held her tight. "Don't be scared," he said. "Your mother and I will take care of you."

She put her arms around his neck, her mouth set in a determined line. Behind the big glasses, her eyes were thoughtful, almost solemn. "I don't want to be thinned out," she said.

"You won't be," he said and held her tighter still.

CHAPTER SEVEN

LEO'S HOUSE WAS LARGE, and although it had many windows, he kept it dark. When Briana's mother was alive, it was a bright place, always tidy and clean and cozy.

Sometimes when a man's wife dies, he keeps the house exactly as she had it, perhaps out of habit, perhaps out of sentiment or perhaps out of something deeper than either.

In contrast, Leo had changed everything—or he had started to. At different times he had begun to move the furniture, but halfway through he would give up, claiming he had hurt his back or changed his mind or he should throw it all out and buy new.

Both Briana and Larry had offered to help him finish rearranging, but Leo would fall into a pensive mood and refuse. The furniture stayed at odd angles in odd places.

Pictures hung off-kilter or were taken from their nails and leaned facing the wall. Magazines and newspapers were stacked haphazardly on almost every surface. This disorder bothered Briana, but not just for its own sake. She thought it symbolized some deep unhappiness in her father.

The heat in the house was turned to high, today. The smothering air and the disarray made her feel claustrophobic after walking through the sparkling snow and sharp, clean air. "Poppa," she said, trying not to sound like a nag, "you should really clean this place up."

"Phooey. Why?" Leo asked. "I live alone. What difference does it make?"

All this clutter—it's not a healthy atmosphere."

"Move in and change it," he teased. "It's too big for me. And you live in a cracker box."

He always made this joke, and she feared it was half serious. She said, "You should hire someone to come in and help you keep organized."

"I don't want a stranger in the house," Leo said. "I know where things are. That's what's important."

Briana knew he was set in his ways, so she changed the subject. "What did you want to show me, Poppa?"

"Ah," he said. "Come into my office."

NEALIE WAS TIRED from her walk in the snow. She took off her beloved boots, stretched out on the couch and watched her favorite video, *Beauty and the Beast*.

Josh sat beside her, and she lay her head on his thigh. "I love this story," Nealie said. "I think she looks like Mommy, don't you?"

She meant the brown-eyed heroine, singing with passion about how she wanted to live somewhere other than her provincial town.

"A little," Josh said.

The girl on the screen did resemble Briana, but she sang an altogether different song. Briana was happy in her small corner of the universe, and she wasn't about to be budged from it.

"I'd like to see all the places you get to see," Nealie said, nestling closer. He put his hand on her shoulder, which felt impossibly small to him.

"Someday you will," he said.

"Mama would, too," she said.

"I don't think so." His hand moved up to wind a lock of her hair around his forefinger. It felt finer than strands of silk.

Nealie said, "She likes to look at your pictures. She always does."

He was surprised. He thought she'd resented his work too much to want to see it. "Does she?"

"She keeps them all," Nealie said, turning to look at him.

"You mean she keeps them for you. I always send you a copy."

"No," Nealie insisted. "She gets other copies, too. She says it's so I can look at mine all I want but still have a good set. But she looks at them lots."

He said nothing, only put his hand on her shoulder again. She apparently took his silence for disbelief, because she propped herself up and adjusted her glasses, looking at him righteously.

"I'll *show* you," she said. She put the video on pause and hopped from the couch.

"Nealie," he began, not sure what she was up to.

She was already on her way, padding upstairs toward Briana's tiny second-floor office. She turned and looked at him over her shoulder. "Come *on*," she said.

Reluctant, but curious, he rose and followed her. At the top of the stairs, she waited for him at the closed door of the office. She reached behind an aspidistra plant in a glazed green pot and drew out a key. She thrust it into the lock and turned it.

"Nealie, don't. If it's locked, she wants it kept private."

"She knows I know where the key is," Nealie said with perfect confidence. "The lock is to keep out people like Rupert, not me. I can go in whenever I want and play computer games."

She swung open the door and switched on the lights. Feelings still mixed, Josh stepped in after her. She lifted a ceramic paperweight shaped like a large tomato. Beneath it was another, smaller key. She plucked it up as if she'd done it a hundred times.

She turned to Briana's four-drawer file cabinet, stood on her tiptoes and clicked open the single lock at the top. "Nealie, don't," he warned again, but already she was squatting, pulling open the bottom drawer.

"But these magazines are for me," Nealie countered.

"Mommy always said so. It's where she keeps her other pictures you took, too."

Josh inwardly swore, but he was unable to look away. There, in clear plastic covers, were the magazines that held his work of the last six years—*Adventure, Smithsonian, Islands, The Far Territory, Stepping Westward.*

That's it, he thought. *That's the last six years of my life. That's what I've done all the years that Nealie's been alive.*

It filled less than half a long file drawer. It suddenly didn't seem like very damn much. Next to the magazines were books he recognized as photograph albums.

My God, how many pictures did I take of Briana, of us together, of all the places she loved? And then Nealie? A thousand? More?

Briana had been wonderful to photograph, perfect to his discerning eye. Her beauty was not flashy, but deep and real, and the longer he'd looked at her, the lovelier she'd seemed.

What might seem like flaws on another woman made her only more interesting—the smattering of freckles across the nose, the mole under her jaw, the slightly asymmetrical widow's peak. And her smile, of course. Her smile.

Nealie said, "I'm not supposed to take out the magazines because I've got my own. I've come in here and seen her looking at them, though."

"Um," he said. "Well, that's how I met her, taking pictures. So I guess that's how you got here."

"I can look at the albums, though," she said, putting her hand on one. "Do you want to see them, the pictures you took back then?"

"I don't think so," he said. "I think you'd better lock up again. Your mother might not want me in here."

"Why?"

"Because this is her private place."

"But I can come into it," she said, looking puzzled.

He knelt and slid the drawer shut. "It's a private place

for you and her, then. You shouldn't bring anybody else into it without asking. As a courtesy to her.''

''Oh,'' Nealie said, clearly disappointed. But she stood and locked the filing cabinet.

She put the small key under the ceramic tomato. But he wasn't watching her. He was reading the labels on the file cabinet drawers. The first two were business. The third was marked Family, Financial, Medical.

Nealie's records would be in there. The records, the insurance, the bills. And he thought, *The bills. How does Briana think she's going to pay all these medical bills?*

She had never told him, never given so much as a hint, not even mentioned it. If there was an answer, he suspected this drawer held it.

He held Nealie's hand and led her downstairs. She turned on her video. But she was yawning, getting sleepy.

Josh kept his eyes on the screen, but he wasn't thinking of *Beauty and the Beast*. He was thinking that upstairs there were two keys that might unlock the secrets Briana was keeping from him.

LEO LED BRIANA through the neglected living room to a door he always kept locked. He took the old-fashioned brass key from his pocket and placed it in the keyhole.

He swung open the door and switched on the light. Leo's study wasn't nearly as disheveled as his living room. He kept the curtain half open so he could look out as he worked at his desk.

From his window he could see Larry's house and Briana's, as well as the greenhouses. Briana and her father paused and stared outside. Josh's rented car was parked in the drive. The only color he could get was flaming red, and it looked as brash and bright as a male cardinal against the backdrop of the snow.

Leo frowned at it. ''Hmph. Where's he going next?''

Briana's heart contracted. ''He doesn't know. He has an

assignment he has to take if they call. It'll probably be Burma. There's an outside chance it'll be Pitcairn Island.''

"Pitcairn Island?" Leo said with a sniff. "Isn't that the godforsaken place where all those pirates went?"

"Mutineers," she said. "From the *Bounty*."

"Burma. Pitcairn Island. I never saw a man with such wanderlust. When's he going?"

"I told you. He doesn't know."

Leo sighed, as if Josh's lack of plans was a great personal burden. He turned from the window. "Sit," he said, gesturing at the easy chair before the crowded bookshelves. The chair was full of gardening magazines, seed catalogs, pamphlets and a hot water bottle wrapped in a towel.

Briana moved it all aside. The water in the bottle was cold. "Poppa, is your arthritis bothering you again?"

"It always bothers me." Gingerly he lowered himself into his desk chair. "But I didn't bring you here to discuss my aches and pains. Sit, sit."

She sat, her fingers linked in her lap.

He gave her a long, significant look. His blue eyes twinkled. "I've done it. I've finally started my project. Where'd I put it? It was right here."

Briana's muscles were tense. For the last three years Leo had been talking about writing a newsletter to be mailed out with the catalog. At first she'd been delighted he had found a subject that interested him so passionately.

She was no longer delighted, for Leo's obsession fueled her secrecy about Nealie's disease. It was another reason she could never tell him what she and Josh must do and how they must do it.

"Ah," said Leo, "here it is." He picked up a pile of papers of different sizes, unevenly stacked. He handed it to her, pride aglow on his face. "Look—my first issue. Done except for a little touching up."

Briana gazed at the top page, which was blue. It said, Nature's Worst Nightmare—Genetic Engineering or a Bargain with the Devil, by Leo Lawrence Hanlon.

"I couldn't decide which title to use." Leo's smile was almost boyish. "So I used them both. Sometimes writers do that."

Briana could only nod, swallow and stare at the disorderly stack.

"There's a few little typos and things," Leo said with a dismissive wave. "But you can fix that. You got that computer, and you can check my spelling and sentences and stuff."

Briana's spirits withered as she thumbed through the pages. She knew all too well what the subject was. Her father hated genetic engineering. It frightened and infuriated him. He had begun by hating everything science could do to engineer plants.

Briana understood his concerns, and some of them she shared. But lately Leo's dislike had extended to all genetic engineering, especially when it concerned humans.

He said, "First they cloned mice, then sheep, now pigs. Next it'll be people. Some crazy jerk of a scientist wants to go back and clone Dracula. I read about it. Think of it—Dracula."

"I think that story was mostly for the sake of sensation," she offered.

"Still, it's possible," Leo said darkly. But then he smiled at the manuscript in her hands. "I mention it there. I touch a bit on everything."

Briana chose her words with care. "For starters maybe you'd better stick to plants, Poppa. That's our business. All by themselves, biotech plants are a controversial issue."

Leo crossed his arms, a stubborn gesture. "Not for my customers. They believe what I believe. The right way is nature's way. And that's that."

"Doctors are learning more about genetics all the time. What they learn can help people."

"Help, shmelp. Parents will start picking out what sex child they're going to have," Leo said. "Then they'll want to make sure it's good-looking. That it's smart. They'll try to create superchildren but they'll end up making Frankenstein monsters. Why, I wouldn't have such a child in my family. It'd be a freak. And its parents would be a worse freaks—not an ethical bone in their bodies.''

Oh, Poppa, if you had even an idea of what I'm about to do— It's best you never know. It's best nobody ever knows.

"Let's change the subject," Leo said. "I have other things to discuss."

Relief welled in her. She said, "Gladly. Anything."

He fixed her with a piercing stare. "Why have you taken all your money out of Wendell Semple's bank? And why aren't you seeing Harve Oldman anymore? *He's* the man you ought to marry."

NEALIE FELL ASLEEP during the closing credits of *Beauty and the Beast*. It seemed like a light sleep, almost a doze.

Josh stared at her, a frown line between his brows. It wasn't normal for a child to nap this much. It was one more sign of her illness.

He swore to himself. He wished Briana was back. There were a thousand things they needed to talk about. And he had to convince her to marry him again. Her idea of going it alone was gallant but foolhardy.

He wondered if the phones were working yet. He eased off the couch and padded on stocking feet to the counter. He lifted the receiver and listened. There was a dial tone. The line was in service. He hung up.

He stood for a moment, thinking of Briana's closed office, her locked file cabinet. He had no right to look in her private papers, he told himself. He would be worse than a busybody, he would be a sneaking rat.

With a sigh he moved toward the television to switch it off, then decided to let the closing song play until its end. He went to the front window and stared out for a long time.

He could see his and Nealie's footprints from when they'd walked together to the greenhouse. There were those when they returned, he carrying her and Glenda at their side.

Briana's tracks, leading in another direction, were the oldest set. They were slowly disappearing beneath the falling snow. So were his and Glenda's, which were larger. So were Nealie's, which were the smallest.

All of them disappearing beneath the snow. So transient. So fleeting.

Suddenly, under his breath, he said, "To hell with it." He had every right to look at Briana's papers about Nealie. The girl was his daughter, too.

I have conquered my goddam scruples, he thought as he went up the stairs two at a time.

For years Briana had indulged her father, coddled him, protected, defended and nurtured him. But his two questions appalled her. She felt the sudden swelling of an unfamiliar emotion, anger toward him.

"What?" she demanded.

Leo had taken on an air of injured authority. "After church, after you left with Nealie and *him*—"

"His name is Josh," Briana said, her voice brittle.

"After you left with him, Wendell Semple came up to me. He said you'd moved all your money out of your account. You wouldn't give him any reason except you wanted to try banking on that Internet thing."

"I don't *have* to give him any reason," she retorted. "It's my money, and I can move it where I want."

"He's been our banker for fifty years, through thick and thin. He deserves some loyalty."

"He'd deserve more if he'd respect my privacy. He has no right—"

"I hope you're not thinking of taking all our business from his bank. I might want another mortgage. I've been thinking of building a new greenhouse. We can't afford to get on his bad side because you've got some newfangled idea."

She put her hand to her forehead, which was starting to throb. They did not need another greenhouse. They had their hands full with four. This argument was starting to gallop off in too many directions.

She took a deep breath and let her hand drop to her lap. It rested on the manuscript. "Mortgage or no mortgage, he's got no call to discuss my private decisions with you. I'm an adult."

"I'm concerned about you," Leo countered. "You've been acting strange lately. Now this bank thing. What's it about?"

Briana found herself lying again, just as Josh had predicted she would. She told him the story she had told Wendell.

Leo did not look convinced. "No sooner did Wendell walk away than Harve Oldman came up. He said you'd been avoiding him lately. Harve saw you with *him*—"

"His name is Josh," she repeated through clenched teeth.

"—and wondered if that's why you didn't want to see him anymore. That you were getting back together with— Josh."

He said *Josh* with kindliness so false it was frightening. Briana felt as if her face had frozen.

"How I feel about Josh is nobody's business but mine," she said. "Harve has no right to ask, and I hope you told him so."

Leo gave a shrug of innocence. "I told him I was mystified. I said I didn't know why you'd broken off with him. That I had no idea that Josh was coming back. Or why he'd come now."

"Josh doesn't have to explain himself to anybody. He's welcome anytime. He's the father of my child."

"I told Harve not to worry. Josh wouldn't stick around. He'd be on his way again. He always is. You know that, don't you?"

She raised her chin. "Yes. Perfectly well."

"What you need is a man who's steady. Harve is steady."

If Harve were any steadier, Briana thought bitterly, he could walk around with a carpenter's level on his head. He had many virtues, and he managed to make all of them boring. Next to Josh, he seemed as sexually attractive to her as a cement block.

She heard the anger in her voice. "Poppa, I don't need you to pick me a husband. If I want one, I'll pick my own."

Leo looked both benign and wounded. "All I'm saying is Harve is your own kind. He's a farmer. He's a good businessman, a good manager. He's one of us. He could help you run this place, and he'd take good care of you and Nealie."

Briana could bear no more. She stood. "I can take care of myself *and* my daughter. I think I'll go home to her—now."

"I only told you the truth," Leo said, looking wounded. "Wendell wondered about you. Harve did, too. You come waltzing out in public with that man—Josh—and people talk."

"I'll waltz out in public with whoever I please—including the clone of Dracula."

She had not spoken this sharply to her father since her whirlwind courtship with Josh.

Tears rose in his blue eyes. "I'm sorry if I offended you," he said. "I'm only concerned about you and Nealie. And my conscience commands me to speak out."

"Mine commands me to end this conversation," she said. "It's upsetting both of us."

He sank back in his chair as if exhausted and defeated. "I only said what I said out of love. I love you. Forgive me." He leaned his elbow on his desk and put his face in his hand so she could not see his emotion.

"I love you, too, Poppa," she said. "But I have to go now."

She turned and left him. She still clutched the manuscript in which he denounced all genetic engineering.

She set it on the hall table while she jammed her arms into the sleeves of her coat and knotted her scarf around her neck. She pulled on her boots, stood and took the manuscript.

Then, from the office, she heard her father's voice. "Briana? Briana? Are you still there? I'm not well—I'm sick. I think I need a doctor."

She ran. He sat in his chair, slumped, clutching at his upper chest. His face had gone pale, and sweat misted his brow.

Good Lord, she thought in panic. *I've given him a heart attack.*

CHAPTER EIGHT

THIS WAS a hell of a turn, Josh thought with bitterness.

He had a thousand things to talk to Briana about in private. Instead he was stuck in a hospital waiting room with her whole family while they awaited word of Leo.

At last Leo's young doctor, Imat DeQueljo, entered.

"He's going to be fine," the doctor said with a smile. "Just a very minor attack of angina. We'd like to keep him under observation overnight. He can go home tomorrow at noon. When he does, he wants a family member staying with him, or to stay at one of your homes for a while. He's a little, you know, nervous about being alone at first. Insecure."

Expressions of distress sprang to the faces of both Larry and Glenda. They looked at each other and then they looked at Briana. They clearly expected her to do it.

No, no, no, Josh thought. *She can't move in with him. He can't move in with her. No, no, no.*

"I can't stay with him," Larry said defensively. "I'm no good with sick people. Besides, I got work."

Glenda fidgeted and wiped a rivulet of drool from Marsh's chin. She darted Briana a guilty look. "I don't think he'd be comfortable with us. The boys make him nervous."

No, thought Josh. *No, no, no. Don't do it, Briana.*

Briana met Josh's gaze and held it. "I'll take care of it," she said.

No, no, no, no, Josh thought. *A thousand times no.*

How could he ever talk to her with Leo always hovering

in the background? In his mind's eye, he saw Leo in drag, a male duenna with a shawl, a comb in his hair, a Spanish fan and gimlet eyes.

Briana faced Larry and Glenda. "I'll have to hire somebody. Nealie has doctor appointments. I have to take her to St. Louis. More than once."

"Change your appointments," Larry said.

"No," said Briana. "It took too long to set them up."

"Then," Larry challenged, "who're you going to get to stay with Poppa?"

"I'll find someone. I said I'd handle it and I will." She turned to Dr. DeQueljo. "Can we see him?"

"He's asleep. If you'd care to wait—"

"We got to get these kids home," Larry said. "He might sleep all night. Tell him I'll come see him tomorrow. Let's go, Glenda."

"Will Grandpa die?" Rupert asked, obviously interested by the prospect.

"No—and shush," scolded Glenda. "Put on your jacket."

Rupert looked disappointed. "I never been to a funeral."

He turned to Nealie. She sat on Josh's lap, her arm around his neck. Rupert said to her, "You still got on those stupid boots."

"They're not as stupid as you, Rupert Von Poopert," said Nealie.

"Hush, Nealie," Briana said. "Shame on you. Mind your manners."

Nealie bit her lip and kept silent until Larry had herded his family from the room and out of earshot. Then she sighed and tightened her arm around her father's neck. She looked at him. "There's something I don't understand."

He said, "What, Panda Girl?"

Her face had grown troubled. "What's angina?"

"It's a temporary chest pain," he said.

"Is it a heart attack?"

"No, babe. It just means for a little while not enough

blood got to his heart. It's a spasm. Like when you get a cramp in your foot.''

She did not seem reassured. "Can they fix him?"

"The doctor thinks they can fix him just fine."

"And now we're waiting for him to wake up? So we can talk to him?"

Briana reached over and smoothed the girl's hair. "I'll wait. You and Daddy go back to the house. It'll be your bedtime soon, too."

"But I'm not sleepy. I had *two* naps today." Nealie held up two fingers for emphasis.

"We'll wait with you for a while," Josh said. "If we go, you've got no way home. Somebody'll have to drive back for you."

Briana had called nine-one-one when Leo felt ill, and an ambulance had come screaming up the lane for Leo. Larry and his family followed in their van, and Josh took Briana and Nealie. Briana had been too upset to drive.

With a sigh, she rose from her chair. "Then let's go stretch our legs. I'm tired of this room. I could use some fresh air."

"Me, too," Nealie said, unwinding her arm from Josh's neck. "I don't like hospitals."

She stood, and Josh helped her into her jacket. He knew if everything went well, within a year Nealie, whether or not she liked it, would be in the hospital getting the blood cord transplant that might cure her.

If things did not go well, she could end up in the hospital anyway—and there would be no cure.

He buttoned her coat to the chin and tried to say the right words. "A hospital can be a good place. It can make sick people well. It's where we go to try to save lives. And it's where we get babies. When you were a baby, you came from this very hospital."

"Mm," Nealie said noncommittally and examined her new boots. "I'll be glad when Grandpa's home again, that's all."

"Me, too," Briana said and adjusted the girl's cap. "Now let's go outside. We won't stay there long. Especially if it's cold."

"I can't get cold," Nealie said, her chin high. "I have boots from Siberia. I'm safe forever and ever."

"Sure, kid," Josh said, tucking her muffler more tightly into her collar. "Sure, you are."

ODDLY, the night was not cold. The ever-fickle Missouri weather had changed again. No snow fell. No wind blew. No cloud marred the sky. No cars crunched by on the snowy streets, and no one besides the three of them seemed to be out on this perfect winter night.

Overhead, the vault of the sky was a luminous blue strewn with stars. A nearly full moon made the snow look like sweeps of white velvet. Across the street from the hospital was a small park, and Nealie wanted go to its playground.

Once there, she headed for her favorite toy, a blue plastic horse mounted on a big spring. She dusted the snow off his head, mane, saddle and tail. She climbed onto his back and began to bounce gently.

"Not too fast," called Briana. "Don't get too wild."

"I won't," Nealie answered. "I don't want to get another nosebleed."

Briana and Josh stood at the edge of a grove of evergreen trees, watching her. The branches were so mantled with white, they looked as if they were decorated for Christmas.

The snow on the ground was marked by no tracks except theirs. Briana knew she should step away when Josh slid his arm around her and drew her close, but she did not. It had been a grueling day, and she was glad to lean on someone else's strength for a change.

He fingered her scarf where it was knotted at her throat. "I'm sorry about your father," he said. He spoke quietly so Nealie wouldn't hear over the creaking and bouncing of her horse.

Briana shook her head. "I'm sorry, too. Sometimes it seems like there's so much to take care of—too much."

He turned toward her, putting a hand on each of her shoulders. She looked into his shadowed face, at once so tough and so kind. His shoulders seemed impossibly wide in the parka, wide enough to bear half the world's weight if he had to.

"You don't have to take care of everything alone," he told her. "I've tried to talk about it, but you always cut me off. This time don't. Please. Let me help you, Briana."

Almost reluctantly, she slid her hands up to grip the open sides of his parka. He was still so hardened by the Russian cold that he didn't bother to fasten his coat against the mild night.

She was tempted to lay her throbbing forehead between the furry halves of the parka, to rest it against the firmness of his chest. She remembered the hard muscularity of him when he was naked and they were in bed together. She had felt awed and proud that she could make such a powerful body respond to hers. Such love they had at the beginning and such desire, such wildness and tenderness—layer upon layer of emotion.

She only stood with him for a long moment, neither of them, perhaps, daring to inch closer to the other.

When he finally spoke his voice was gruff. "Which do you think brought on this attack of your father's—the three helpings of chicken or me?"

"A little bit of both, I suppose." She managed a melancholy smile. "But mostly me. I upset him when we talked."

His hands moved down to cup her elbows. "Same old stuff? That he worries about the farm? And Larry? And his own health?"

She nodded. Josh knew Leo's issues all too well. What he couldn't understand was that her father's concerns were real and that Leo had spells of fretfulness that weren't good for him.

"I have to find someone to stay with him," she said tiredly. "It's more than his health. It's how he lives. The house is a mess. It's dark and depressing. He doesn't like cooking for himself. Glenda and I take turns doing it for him. I keep telling him to get help. But he says no, he doesn't want a stranger in the house—"

Josh's hands moved to her shoulders, gripping her more tightly. "He's going to have to put up with it, Briana. You're running most of the business and your own house. Most important, you've got Nealie to take care of. And you're also going to be pregnant—if we're lucky."

She squared her jaw. "I know."

"You and I have to go to a lab tomorrow and do some very unromantic mumbo jumbo," he said. "Don't we?"

She gave him a sheepish look. "Yes."

"Let me see if I understand this," he said, stepping a bit closer to her. "You take drugs that make you—"

"Ovulate like crazy," she said.

His face looked pained. "Then they take these, er, ova—"

"Ova," she said, suddenly feeling more like her old self, "that's cute. That at a time like this, you'd want your plurals correct."

"Does it hurt you? When they take them?" he asked.

"No. Hardly at all. They sedate me a little, it's over fast."

"I, in the meantime, am to donate sperm into a paper cup or a beaker or test tube or some damn thing."

"I'm afraid that's right. Sorry."

"And then?" he said, still looking uncomfortable.

"The scientists do what you call their mumbo jumbo. If there's a healthy embryo, it's transferred to me. And from there, with luck, nature takes its course."

He clenched her shoulders. "What if nature doesn't take its course?"

In spite of the cold, still air, she felt her cheeks burn. She stared at the snow. "Then we try again. You don't have to do any more. They'll freeze your extra sperm. You wouldn't have to come back."

"Briana," he said, "I'd want to come back. But you've got to do one thing for me."

She looked at him, half in fear, half in desire, knowing what he was going to say.

He said, "Marry me. For God's sake. Say yes."

She felt giddily posed between laughter and tears. "I can't make that decision at a time like this. Poppa's sick. Nealie's sick. The whole world's turned upside down—"

Twenty feet away, Nealie bounced on her little blue horse, like an elf queen riding by moonlight. Josh drew Briana into the shelter of the trees. The snow-laden branches creaked, and sparkles of snow floated down. He pulled her close. His arms wrapped her, pressing her against him. "Marry me," he said and kissed her, then kissed her again.

The world, all blue and silver, reeled about her, and she felt she was falling upward, into him and into something larger and more intense and more complete than she could ever have without him.

HER MOUTH WAS WARM and deliciously familiar beneath his. He hated the thick coat she wore. He wanted to relearn by touch each curve of her body. He thrust his fingers into her hair, just to feel the heft and satiny thickness of it, once so familiar to his touch.

"Briana," he mumbled against her mouth. For a moment she clung to him as tightly as he did to her. But then she pushed away and stumbled to a nearby bench. Her mittened hands shaking, she dusted the snow from its surface and sat down almost as if collapsing. She put her face in her hands.

He could not let her go so abruptly. He swept aside snow and sat next to her. He put his arm around her, trying this time not to seem possessive and passionate, but only kindly. "Did I make you cry?"

"No." She raised her face. It was streaked with snow from her mittens, already starting to melt.

He said, "Briana, I just don't want you to be unhappy."

"Then don't push me all the time," she said, her voice strangled. "My father just had some—some kind of coronary incident. He's scared and he's sick, and this is *not* exactly the time to rush into marriage."

"Especially to a man he doesn't approve of?" Josh said.

"I didn't say that," she retorted, "you did."

"I might point out," he said, "that your having my illegitimate child might not be the best thing for his health, either."

"See?" she said, moving to face him. "You're pushing me again. I have things to work out."

"Like someone staying with your father?"

"That, too," she said. "And you and I have to go for our physicals tomorrow. Nealie has a checkup, too. So I need to find someone—fast."

"What about the woman who helps you at the office?"

"Penny? I'm practically working her to death now. She's got to cover everything when I'm gone—and I have to go into St. Louis a lot in the next couple weeks. Blood tests, ultrasounds, all sorts of monitoring."

"Then ask DeQueljo. He knows nurses, caregivers, people like that."

She nodded. He didn't like the way the moonlight shone on her face. The streaks of melted snow made it look as if she'd been crying. He had to turn his gaze away.

He stared instead at his daughter, *their* daughter. It was time to take her back to bright light and real warmth, out of the snow. "Come on, Nealie," he called. "Let's go inside. It's getting late. Your mother wants to talk to the doctor."

Nealie climbed obediently off her horse. She took Josh by one hand, Briana by the other. Linked together, they walked toward the hospital.

"In truth," Doctor DeQueljo said, "I'm shorthanded myself. A small hospital like this, it doesn't attract nurses, I'm sorry to say."

Nealie was yawning and looking restless. Josh held her, and she laid her head sleepily against his shoulder. "There must be somebody," Josh insisted. "Briana's got her hands full. Isn't there somebody retired, maybe not even a nurse, but a good, dependable woman—"

DeQueljo raised his eyebrows thoughtfully. "There's a woman just moved near here, a widow. She's trying to decide what to do next, but in the meantime, she's staying with her nephew. She came to me to get a prescription renewed. Had been a schoolteacher. Seemed basically sensible. Doesn't need to work, yet still might like to have some activity—just a chance to stay busy, feel useful."

"You know anything else about her?" Josh asked.

DeQueljo nodded. "She grew up here, left when she married—oh, thirty years ago. Went to New York but always wanted to come back to Illyria. Husband didn't."

"She grew up here?" Briana asked. This was beginning to sound hopeful to her, almost too good to be true. "And she still has family here?"

"Oh, yes," said Dr. DeQueljo. "Your neighbor, in fact. Harve Oldman. This is his aunt—Inga Swenson."

Briana felt the blood drain from her face. Mechanically she said, "Harve's aunt? I met her once. She seemed like a—a nice lady."

But still, she thought, *Harve's aunt? It could be awkward.*

"Give her a call," DeQueljo said, and put an encouraging hand on her shoulder. He threw Josh a shrewd glance. "I think Briana should go home now. She looks more worn out by all of this than Leo does, frankly. And he's still sleeping like a baby. He'll probably sleep through the night. The little girl's tired, too. She needs her rest."

DeQueljo gave Nealie a long look.

Briana thought, *He knows something's wrong with her.*

Does he know how wrong? He suspects. And Josh knows he does. I can see it in his face.

But Josh said nothing. He smiled and carried Nealie out of the room and into the hallway. After a moment, Briana followed, wordless. Nealie was asleep by the time Josh got her to the parking lot. He strapped her into her seat and helped Briana inside.

He got in and started the car. "This doctor," he said, "DeQueljo. How much have you told him about Nealie?"

"Nothing," she said. "He came here only two years ago. I've always taken Nealie to specialists. He's Poppa's doctor, not mine."

As Josh pulled out of the parking place, he gave her a sidelong look. "Shouldn't you tell him? What if there's an emergency? And you don't have time to get her to St. Louis?"

Briana felt defensive. "I've been going to tell him. I kept putting it off. Until after you and I talked."

She supposed it had been a foolish decision, postponing telling DeQueljo. It was just one more face of that hydra-headed monster, her denial. But DeQueljo might want her to confide the truth to Leo, and this was something she would resist with her last drop of strength. Leo would be shattered by Nealie's illness, but he would never approve of what she and Josh were going to do. Never.

She sat in silence as the car left the city limits and headed into the countryside. The moonlight gleamed on the thick snowfall, but she hardly saw the landscape. She could only wonder if Josh condemned her for not talking to DeQueljo or if he could understand her conflict.

When at last he spoke, his question took her by surprise. "Isn't Harve Oldman the guy you went out with?"

"Yes," she said, shifting nervously.

"How'd you meet his aunt?"

"She came to church with him a few weeks ago. He introduced us afterward, that's all. Poppa decided to sleep in that morning. He knows she's back, but he hasn't seen her yet. She only came to church that once.''

Silence fell between them, like a sharp, divisive blade, and Briana stared at the highway.

Josh said, ''I get the impression he—this Harve—is serious about you.''

She shrugged.

''I also got the impression you'd been seeing him for some time. A couple of years.''

''You get a lot of impressions,'' she said. ''Where exactly do you get them?''

''Here and there,'' he countered. ''When I've talked to Nealie. Your brother dropped hints. Glenda mentioned it, then acted like she wished she hadn't. She clammed up when I asked her more.''

Good for Glenda, thought Briana, but said nothing. She was reluctant to speak about Harve. She had hurt him, and he didn't deserve hurting.

But Josh wasn't going to let go of the subject. ''So how long have you and Harve been an item?''

''We're not an item,'' she returned. ''I stopped seeing him as soon as I learned the truth about Nealie. I hadn't been seeing him all that long. Sixteen months at the most.''

''Sixteen months is a long time. It's longer than we lived together.''

''Right. I learned from that not to rush a relationship. You taught me well.''

''Did I? How well? If this thing with Nealie hadn't happened, would you have stayed with him? Would you have married him?''

She shrugged again. ''He's a good man. Steady. But he won't want me after I do what I have to do.''

Then he's a fool, thought Josh. *But you didn't answer the question.*

''Do you love him?'' he asked. ''Is that it? Is that why you never give me a straight answer?''

"I love my child," she said wearily and pressed her forehead against the cold glass of the passenger window.

INGA OLDMAN SWENSON sat at the breakfast table with her only nephew, Harve.

He looked glum. He hadn't touched his bowl of cereal, and the cornflakes were growing limp and soggy in the milk. He sipped half-heartedly at his coffee, although she had made it strong and served it black, the way he liked it.

Over the top of his cup he gave her a searching look. "Are you going to do it? Help take care of Leo Hanlon?"

Poor baby, she thought. *You look like a lovelorn bean-pole.*

This was not an unkind comparison on her part, only honest, for Harve was uncommonly tall and slender. Although he was thirty-five, he had boyish features and the large, clumsy hands and feet of an adolescent who hadn't quite finished growing.

Inga loved him, and his sad eyes and innocent face only made her love him more. She was the sort of woman who liked taking care of people and managing them, and Harve seemed at a point in his life when he needed expert care and management.

An only child, he had been born late in his parents' life. Two years ago his mother and father had died within months of each other. He had never married, never even kept steady company with a woman—until Briana.

Briana had rejected him, and he seemed wounded and lost. Inga knew he did not want her to go to Briana's aid, that he felt betrayed by even the thought of it.

He had beautiful dark blue eyes, and they silently repeated his plea. *You're not really going to do it, are you? It will hurt all the time knowing you're so close to her, and I can't be.*

She reached across the table and patted his hand. "Yes," she told him. "I'm going to accept. These people need help."

So do I, said Harve's eyes. *Don't you see how lonely I am?*

She clamped her small, smooth hand over his big one. "Harve, sweetheart, don't feel like I'm going over to the enemy's side. You're too naive for your own good. If I go to Leo's house, I'll not only help him, I can help you."

He blinked in surprise. "Help me?"

"Yes," she said with a nod. "You love this woman?"

A blush mottled his face. "I—I don't like to use terms like that."

She smiled. "Terms like what? Like love?"

"Ummph," he muttered, clearly uncomfortable.

"Sweetheart, love isn't a term. It's a beautiful feeling, a beautiful thought, a beautiful word. Most women want to hear it. Did you ever tell her you loved her?"

"Ummph," Harve said again, and she knew that in this case, *ummph* meant *no.*

She gave him an affectionate look and shook her head. "Dear boy, you need a lecture from your aunt Inga."

"Why should I have to say all that mushy kind of stuff?" Harve asked, almost petulantly. "Actions should speak louder than words."

Inga lifted an eyebrow. She feared that in Harve's case, *inaction* had spoken louder than word or deed. He was not an aggressive man. *Poor guy,* she thought, *you need all the help you can get. Thank goodness I'm here for you.*

She squeezed his hand. "You really think that she broke off with you because she wants her ex-husband back?"

He managed to look even more crestfallen. "He's got something I'll never have. I don't know what you'd call it. He's been all over the world. I've hardly ever left this farm."

"Ah," said Inga, "but this can be like the fable of the tortoise and the hare. Slow and steady wins the race."

He frowned. "Are you calling me a tortoise?"

"No. I'm calling you a man who's good and dependable.

From what you've said, this ex-husband of hers is neither.
I've heard the same from other sources.''

He frowned harder. ''What other sources?''

''Well,'' she said wryly, ''at the beauty parlor, for instance.''

Twila Hansen, the beautician who owned the business,
was a motherly woman of forty. She hadn't approved of
Josh Morris the first time around and yesterday had told
Inga that the thought of Briana going back to such a man
appalled her.

Harve seemed shocked. ''Then it's true what they say
about beauty parlors? That women go there to gossip?''

Inga waved her hand as if shooing off such a sexist idea.
''A few do. Most don't. I listened because it was about the
woman *you* want. Knowledge is power. *Information* is
power.''

Harve looked dubious. ''That's the schoolteacher in you,
thinking things like that.''

''Maybe you could learn a thing or two from this old
schoolteacher. The heart of the matter is that he won't stay,
and she won't leave. *You're* the one she needs.''

''Well, he's the one she wants. I saw the way they looked
at each other in church. He'd slip her a glance on the sly,
like. She'd do the same to him. Her father isn't happy about
it at all. Neither's her brother.''

''See?'' Inga said, throwing her hands out for emphasis.
''How can such a relationship work? Her family doesn't
like him. He doesn't like them. But they like you fine. Don't
they?''

''Is that what people say at the beauty parlor?''

''Yes. And you've said much the same yourself. Be honest. They like you. Don't they?''

''Well, yeah,'' Harve admitted with becoming modesty.
''They seem to.''

''So you're not out of the picture, dear boy. You're very
much in it.''

''Not if she won't let me near her, I'm not.''

"Oh, you'll be near her, sweetheart. For starters, you'll drive me there and back every day. And I'll make sure you're thrown together."

"But why would I drive you? You got your own car. You drive fine."

"I have to take my car to the mechanic," Inga said, "something's wrong with its computer thingy."

This was only a small lie, one not only necessary in the service of love, but perhaps even noble. There was nothing terribly wrong with the car's computer system, and her mechanic in New York had told her it wasn't worth the time and money it would take to fix it. But Inga would put the car in the garage and keep it there as long as necessary.

She said, "I'll put in a good word for you whenever I can—without being obvious, of course. And as for that ex-husband of hers, well, I'll keep my eye on him. If I can do it, I'll show him up for what he really is."

Harve looked troubled. "I don't know." He shook his head. "It doesn't seem right. It doesn't seem fair."

Inga clasped his hand again. "My dear, all's fair in love and war."

She believed this with her whole heart. What she was about to do was slightly dishonest, but it was for everyone's best interests. She was acting out of love. And how could that ever be wrong?

LEO WAS SULKING. Briana had told him that she could not stay with him once he was home.

"I have too many appointments for Nealie," she said. "And I've got a bunch for myself."

"What's wrong with *you?*" he demanded. "And why can't you see Dr. DeQueljo?"

"It's just a little female complaint," she said. "Nothing serious. But I need to tend to it. And I'm more comfortable with a woman doctor."

Leo turned away from her. He hated any discussion of feminine health problems. They embarrassed him. He didn't want to meet her eyes. "I suppose that's why you've been acting funny lately."

"Partly," she said. "But I'll be fine."

"Well, that's a relief. Indeed it is. But who's going take care of me when *I* get home?" he asked. "I'm not going to Larry's. With all those boys it's a madhouse. I need peace and quiet."

Briana's expression was implacable. "I've hired someone."

Leo was appalled. "I told you before, I don't want a stranger in my house. I won't have it."

Briana looked stubborn. "She's not a stranger—exactly. She said she had known you years ago, in school. Her name then was Inga Oldman. She's Harve's aunt."

"Inga Oldman?" Leo practically howled. "Never! I didn't like her then, and I won't like her now."

"What's wrong with her?" Briana asked. "I met her at church, and she seemed perfectly nice. Dr. DeQueljo recommended her."

Leo made a sour face. He remembered Inga, all right. She had been such a perfect little lady he'd loathed her. She always got the outstanding student award and the best citizen medal.

"She was a priss and a do-gooder," he said. "And ugly. She didn't have any meat on her bones. Her hair was the color of a barn rat, and she had braces on her teeth. When she smiled, she looked like the bumper of a Chrysler."

Briana looked unconvinced. "I thought she was attractive."

"You're not a man. You can't see her through a man's eyes."

"I'm not saying marry her," Briana reasoned. "Just have her help you a few days a week."

"Phooey," said Leo.

"She wants to come in and visit you later this morning. Just give her a chance, for heaven's sake."

Leo rolled his eyes as if Briana had laid upon him an

affliction too awful to bear. "You wanted to talk to me alone. Well, we've talked. Bring in Nealie now."

Nealie was in the visitors' lounge with that worthless father of hers. But Briana didn't move. "You'll see Inga Swenson?"

"Inga whoever. I suppose I can stand her for one day. But after that, *you* can take care of me."

"I may have more appointments. In fact, I'm sure I will."

Leo's voice was cold as. "I want to see Nealie," he said. "This conversation's wearing me out. It's going to give me another attack."

AN HOUR LATER, after a refreshing nap, Leo lay in bed watching television. It was a rerun of *The Andy Griffith Show,* a good, wholesome show made back when children respected their parents.

He still felt that Briana had failed him, shut him out. He brooded on this, knowing it was Josh Morris's fault. The man had always had a peculiar hold on her—peculiar and, to Leo's mind, sinister.

A knock at his door startled him out of his dark reverie. Yes?" he almost snarled. The door was half closed, and he couldn't see his visitor.

"Leo Hanlon?" said a woman's voice. "It's Inga. Inga Oldman Swenson. May I come in?"

Leo thought, *Let's see this hag that Briana's forced on me, this insufferable crone.* "Come in," he said in his grumpiest tone.

The door opened, and in she walked. "You probably don't remember me," she said.

He remembered her, but he wouldn't have recognized her. She was one of those women who, like a fine wine, improved greatly with age.

Her brown hair had turned the color of pewter. She had once worn it in unbecoming pigtails. Now it was short, marvelously thick and wavy.

She had put on weight, and on her it looked good. Once she had been skinny as a stick, but now she looked downright cuddly. Why had he never noticed how beautifully blue her eyes were or how flawless her skin?

She was lovely, just as lovely as she could be.

She also had a pleasant air, a paradoxical mix of shyness and confidence. She stood straight but kept her head ducked and tilted to the side. Her smile was demure, but since she was looking at him from that angle, her eyes seemed almost flirtatious.

"I remember you," he managed to say, his voice no longer gruff.

She said, "You probably wouldn't have known me, I've gotten so plump. But I'd have known you. You've hardly changed at all."

Over the course of thirty years, Leo had added much weight and lost much hair. But he suddenly felt a decade younger because she had not only complimented him, but sounded as if she meant it.

"Time has been kind to you," he said gallantly.

She ducked her head more, but she looked pleased. "Your son's coming to pick you up at noon. And I guess I'm going to help you convalesce—if you'll have me."

Oh, thought Leo. Oh, I think I could learn to like this.

CHAPTER NINE

JOSH FELT GRIM.

He didn't like doctor's offices, hospitals or clinics, and lately it seemed he spent all his waking hours at such places. He and Briana had dropped Nealie off at the house of Briana's college friend, Cheryl. Cheryl had a six-month-old girl, and Nealie loved the baby.

This morning, Nealie's blood check showed she was no better, but neither was she worse. "She's holding her own," the doctor told Josh and Briana in his office. "I wish the medicines were doing more for her, but at least the disease isn't gaining ground."

Briana looked as if she was going to cry. But she didn't. She hated for people to see her cry. Josh saw her bite her lip, straighten her spine and grip the arms of her chair more tightly.

Now they were on their way to the fertility and genetic center. Josh hated the idea of such an intimate physical exam, but Briana didn't seem to think about it at all. She still seemed depressed at Nealie's lack of progress.

At a stoplight, he reached out and put his hand on the nape of her neck. "Cheer up. If she can stay stable until the baby comes, that's all we need."

"I just worry about her," Briana said. "I was terrified she'd be worse. I wanted so much for her to be better."

"I know," he said, his hand stroking her nape. "Believe me, I know."

He would have leaned over and kissed her, but the light changed. He put his hand on the wheel.

He said, "I've got to ask you something."

Her expression went wary, suspicious. "What?"

"This fertilization thing—using a lab for a stork. It's got to be expensive. You've got to let me pay for it."

She shook her head, her dark hair swinging with the motion. "No," she said, "I've got some things figured out. I'll manage."

"That's your answer to everything," he said. "If I said, 'Look out—a giant meteor's going to destroy the earth,' you'd say, 'I'll manage.'"

Her expression grew stubborn. "You can pay for your physical and the other work they have to do with you. I'll pay for the rest. It's my body."

"And it'll be my child in your body. What's more, there are all these expenses for Nealie. I want to pay for them from now on."

"All I ask is that you donate sperm. I never asked for money."

"Well, dammit, you should. What do you have? Some kind of martyr complex? Why do you always think you have to carry the whole world on your shoulders alone?"

"I don't want to be indebted to you," she said.

He pulled off the street so quickly that the tires screeched. He veered into the parking lot of a convenience store and stopped. He'd seen her records. He knew she was plunging into debt up to her neck.

"What are you doing?" she demanded.

"Getting ready to turn around and go back to Illyria. You want my tadpoles? You'll take my money. You've got one minute to change your mind. It's my way or the highway."

Her dark eyes flashed. "That's blackmail. You'd never do it. You have to help Nealie."

"Yes. And I want to help her in every way possible. I have that right. She's my child, too." He glanced at his watch. "Fifty seconds."

"You're pushing again," she accused. "What makes you think you can shove your way into this and take charge?"

"I'm her father. I've been paying child support. Right now, she's a special child, she needs special support. You're close to coming unraveled, Briana. You think you're Wonder Woman, but you'd better admit you're human. How will you take care of Nealie and a baby when every day you're worried sick about money? Forty seconds."

"I've been taking care of her all the time you've been gone," Briana countered. "Which has been most of her life."

"Ah," he said. "So now all my travels are guilt trips. It so happens I make my living moving around. You make yours staying put. And you know I make more than you do. So let me put it where it's needed. Use it for our little girl—and our baby. Thirty seconds, sweetheart."

"Look," she said, despair creeping into her voice, "we shouldn't be arguing. In twenty minutes we have to walk into that clinic and convince a counselor we're *fit* to be the parents of a new baby. If he saw us the way we are now, he'd kick us out the door."

Josh shook his head. He'd tried to make an honorable offer, but instead of comforting her, he'd only upset her. He needed to regain lost ground.

He spoke more gently. "You're right. We need to present a united front. Now when the doctor asks how we intend to support both these children, you can't sit there jutting out your chin and saying, 'I'll manage.' It'll be much better to say we'll work together. And that I, as the father, will pay child support for two and for all medical bills involving them."

He paused. Lightly, tentatively, he put his hand on her shoulder. "They won't think we're able to cooperate in bringing up two kids if we can't agree on anything. Trust me. Fifteen seconds, baby. Fifteen."

For the space of a heartbeat, she said nothing. Then she raised her shoulder so her cheek pressed against his hand. At last she whispered, "You're right. We have to pull together."

"Then let's kiss and make up," he said. "Okay?"

"Okay," she said, her voice unsteady. She lifted her face to his.

He would have unsnapped his seat belt and thrown it off, seized her and kissed her until they were both oblivious. But this was not the place and it was absolutely not the time.

He forced himself to be controlled. He leaned toward her and gave her the gentlest, most encouraging kiss he could. But her mouth against his made his soul spin.

THE CONSULTING DOCTOR was a small, wiry man with eyes as black as jet. Everything about him said that he wanted straight answers, and he wanted them without hesitation.

For one of the few times in her life, Briana felt intimidated. The man sat behind the desk and stared at them like a stern judge. His fingers were steepled, and his gaze never wavered.

She and Josh sat across from him, and she felt it was as if they had fallen into the clutches of the Grand Inquisitor. Her mouth was dry, and her muscles clenched into knots as hard as stone.

Beside her, Josh gave off an aura of seriousness and calm. He stretched out his hand and took hers, settling them on the arm of her chair. It might have been a theatrical gesture, simply for the doctor's sake, but it seemed sincere, and she was grateful he'd done it.

The doctor's name was Vargas. He said, "In vitro fertilization means the egg is fertilized outside the mother's body, then reimplanted. The process, as you know, is controversial."

Briana could find no words. Josh said, "We understand."

Vargas said, "But if IVF is controversial, the genetic testing of the fertilized eggs is a hundred times more controversial. Many people think it's playing God. That it's used to create some sort of designer child."

"We don't want a designer child," Josh answered,

squeezing Briana's hand. "We want a healthy child. We wouldn't want it to suffer the way Nealie has. And we don't want to bring another fatally sick child into the world."

"But," said Vargas, "there will be people who condemn you for doing this. They will look on you as meddling with the very process of creation. How do you intend to handle that?"

Briana's heart beat harder. Her mouth went dry. Josh said, "We'll handle it by keeping it as private as possible. Your clinic has a confidentiality policy. We'll keep this to ourselves. It's a family matter."

"But you're not a family, are you?" Vargas said with frost in his voice. "You're no longer married. Which makes this irregular."

"This is the only family I have," said Josh. "I care deeply for Briana and for our daughter. I'd like very much to have another child. Of all the women in the world, Briana is the one I'd want to be that child's mother."

Vargas's black eyes flicked to Briana. "And you? How do you feel?"

Briana struggled to find her voice and make it confident. "I feel exactly the same. I'd love another child. And I don't know any man I'd want to father it except Josh. We—we're still fond of each other. And it's nobody's business but ours how we choose to have a child. We want the baby to be healthy—and to be able to help Nealie. That's what medicine is for, isn't it? To promote health and save lives?"

Vargas looked at her skeptically. She felt exhausted by even such a short speech. She clung to Josh's hand more tightly.

Vargas said, "About the support of this new child—about the medical bills—you've made arrangements?"

"We've made arrangements," Josh assured him. "I'll support both children, including medical expenses. We've settled that."

Vargas had kept his gaze on Briana. "True? You have an agreement?"

"Yes," she said, her throat constricted. "We have." She did not dare say they had reached it only within the last hour, after arguing in the parking lot of a convenience store.

"I'm willing to sign a legal document to guarantee it," Josh said.

Vargas gave him a cool look. "That would be a good idea." He glanced at the forms they'd filled out. "Yet you say that you have, at present, no intention of remarrying. This is odd, when you protest how much you care for each other. It's also going to put a stigma on this second child, whom you both claim to want so much."

Briana was shocked and angered that he would bring up such a matter. *What business is it of his?* Then she realized, *It's exactly the kind of question that he's paid to ask.*

"Actually we've discussed this," Josh said. "But it's a difficult time for Briana to make a decision. Nealie's not the only member of her family who's sick. Her father has a history of heart trouble. In fact, he just had another spell and gets out of the hospital today. The situation is complicated for her."

Briana thought he'd given an adequate answer, but Vargas studied Josh intently. "Is it also complicated for you? Are you also unable to reach a decision?"

Josh turned to Briana and looked at her, not the doctor. "If she'd say yes, I'd marry her in a minute."

Briana's stomach fluttered. Suddenly she was able to meet the doctor's eyes without fear. "Our daughter wishes with all her heart that we'd marry again. But it didn't work the first time. She'd be devastated if it didn't work out a second time. I can't rush into a marriage *hoping* it'll work. I have to *know* it would work. I can't chance putting everyone through that pain again."

Vargas said, "And you really believe you can hide what we'd be doing here—whether you marry or not?"

"Yes," she said with conviction. "It's best that we keep it to ourselves. Nobody else has to know."

Vargas gave her a tight smile. "But people may find out.

It's quite possible. And if so, you will face intense criticism from some quarters.''

''I'll manage—'' She remembered what Josh had said and changed what she had started to say. She looked at Josh, her hand still linked with his. ''We'll manage. Together we'll work it out.''

Vargas looked unmoved. ''I hope for your sake you can.''

He reached for a form, wrote out their names, then signed his own at the bottom. ''Take these to the lab. You can start your tests.''

A disbelieving joy jolted through her. ''You mean we're approved?''

''The paper says I've counseled you and brought up some of the difficulties you face. You're in a dilemma, but you seem to have given it genuine thought. Yes, I have reservations about your case—it's unusual. You face a number of difficult problems. You seem to have the courage to face them. I wish you luck.''

He rose, shook each of their hands, and walked them to the doorway. Briana felt giddy and weak in the knees. They had won the first round. Josh slipped his arm around her shoulders, and she thought, *Thank you, thank you. I couldn't have made it through that interview without you.*

''I could hardly talk in there,'' she admitted. ''You had to give most of the answers.''

''Once you found your pace, you were fine. You did great.''

They went to the desk that scheduled preliminary interviews and tests. They filled out more forms. They sat and waited to be called.

Briana saw a copy of *Adventure* magazine. She paged through it idly until she came to a photo feature on Haiti. She recognized Josh's work immediately, although he hadn't sent her a copy of this article. She turned to face him. ''Haiti? When were you in Haiti?''

He shrugged nonchalantly. ''Early last year.''

She stared at the pictures in horror. "My God, this is the middle of a riot. Why didn't you tell me?"

"I didn't want you or Nealie to worry. I wasn't there that long."

A tide of resentment swept her. "One of these days you're going to walk into the wrong place and get yourself killed."

"I'm always careful."

"So you went there when there was fighting in the streets, and nothing happened to you? Nothing threatened you in the least?"

He wanted to lie to her. He knew any more lying would be wrong, so he tried to play down the truth. "Some guys fired at us. They didn't hit any of us. They were lousy shots."

He didn't tell her about the hand grenade that had nearly put out the eye of Wentz, the writer, and grazed Josh's calf with shrapnel. He could see she was upset enough.

"Oh, Josh," she said. "It destroys me when you do these things. That's one reason I can't think about remarrying. I'd live in dread that you'd be killed somewhere. I'd never stop thinking about it."

He had no chance to give her an answer. A nurse called their names. They rose, and the nurse guided them down a hall, then sent them two separate and opposite ways.

BRIANA WAS GLAD to let Josh drive when they went to get Nealie. She was a skillful driver, but he was even more so. Yet for all his ease weaving between lanes and negotiating complex routes, he looked unhappy.

"What's wrong?" she asked. "I thought your nurse said you were a strapping, healthy guy, strong as a horse." With an air of mischief she added, "And that your sperm is very lively."

"He did say it," grumbled Josh. "Good grief, why did they have to give me a male nurse?"

"He's not just a nurse," she said. "He's a clinical nurse

specialist. They can do all the basic things a doctor can. Give physicals, make diagnoses, even write prescriptions.''

Josh was not appeased. "Then what in hell do we need doctors for?''

"The doctor can spend more time with patients with special needs. He can put the more elementary things into the hands of the nurse.''

"Please don't remind me about the hands of the nurse.'' Josh gave a mock shudder. "They were cold as an arctic herring.''

She looked at him in amused disbelief. "You just came from Siberia, and now you're complaining about a man's chilly hands?''

"Nobody in Siberia put his chilly hands where this guy did. He poked me where I don't want to be poked. He squeezed me where I'd rather not be squeezed—at least by a guy. Then he shut me up in a bathroom with a girly magazine and two paper cups. Into one cup I was supposed to whiz. In the other I was to expel my own personal reproductive juice. Neither of which was easy with Mr. Herring Hands standing out there smirking.''

Briana smiled for the first time that day. "If the door was closed, how did you know he was smirking?''

"I could feel it. His smirk sent vibrations through the door.''

She put her hand on his shoulder in sympathy. "A physical's no fun for women, either. Trust me.'' She thought of the trial transfer she'd undergone. It was relatively painless but had filled her with anxiety.

"Yeah, but *you* got a female doctor.''

"I'm a woman, I got a woman doctor. You're a man, you got a male nurse. What's the difference?''

"It's different, that's all,'' he said.

She gave his arm a soft, playful swat. "I've learned two things about you today. Doctors' offices make you nervous, and you've got a phobia about male nurses. I used to think you were completely fearless.''

"Well, I'm not. Sorry."

"But you've climbed in the Himalayas. You went to Albania when it was a war zone. Haiti, too. You've been shot at, you've had a polar bear charge you, you were bitten by a moray eel in Tahiti."

"I'm used to that sort of stuff."

"Well, then what bothers you about having a male nurse?" she teased.

He was silent for a moment. At last he said, "I was in too many foster homes. Sometimes there were guys who tried to get touchy-feely. I could usually make them back off."

Shocked, she stared at him as if seeing him for the first time. "You're saying some of these men tried to *molest* you?"

"Yeah," he said, keeping his eyes on the road. "One guy told me to cooperate or he'd sneak in my room when I was sleeping and gag me with duct tape. I told him if he tried it, I'd kill him. But he was a lot bigger than me, and I had to sleep sometime. He did it."

Sickness filled her. "Oh, Josh, you never told me that."

"It's not the kind of thing you want people to know," he said. "When I fell for you, I fell so hard, I didn't want you to find out. I was afraid you'd think—less of me."

Her heart wrenched. "I think more of you—for surviving. But what did you *do?* How did you get away from this man?"

"I sneaked out my bedroom window the next morning, before he got up. I walked four miles to the police station. I told them what the SOB had done. I had to go to a doctor, have a damn physical. At that point it was the last thing I wanted to do."

"How old were you?" She was riven by sympathy for what he must have suffered.

"Eleven," he said between clenched teeth. "I'd just turned eleven."

"And the man?" she asked, still numb with horror. "What happened to him?"

The corner of his mouth twitched in bitterness. "Oh, they got him. They found out he'd had his way with my two older foster sisters, too. And others before us. He got twenty-five years in the state pen. He died there ten years later. A nice, peaceful death, lying on his cot, watching TV."

She laid her hand on his upper arm. "I wish you'd told me before. You were brave, Josh, to go to the police like that."

"No. I was scared out of my mind. I used to have nightmares that he'd break out of prison and come looking for me."

"You can be scared and brave at the same time," she told him.

He turned to her with a smile that didn't reach his eyes. "You've taught me that, Briana. You're the perfect example."

"I never went through anything like that. It must have been the most frightening thing that ever happened to you."

He shook his head. "No. Nealie's being sick is the most frightening thing. It's a thousand times worse."

She knew this had to be true. But she still burned to ask him more about his childhood. When they were falling so headlong into love, he'd fended off questions about growing up. *I spent a lot of time in foster homes,* he'd say. *I don't like to talk about.*

They were on Cheryl's block, only a few houses away. There was no time to ask anything.

"Guess we'd better put on our happy faces," Josh said.

He pulled into Cheryl's driveway. Wearing expressions that were falsely cheerful, they made their way to the porch to get their child.

"WELCOME HOME, Poppa," Briana said, kissing her father on the cheek. He sat in his recliner watching television. "Is Mrs. Swenson here?"

"She's in the kitchen, doing the supper dishes," Leo said rather pettishly. "She said *she* wouldn't leave until you came back. You took your time up in St. Louis. Have fun?"

Resentment rippled through her. "We didn't go for fun. Nealie and I both had appointments. We spent most of the day in doctor's offices."

"Well, I hope you can stay home for a while now. Where you belong."

Briana took a deep breath. The Center for Reproductive Health had never before dealt with a case related to Yates's anemia. They wanted to monitor her almost every day.

She said, "I have to go back and forth for more tests and things. For the next two or three weeks."

Leo reared back in his chair. "Two or three weeks? Is this something serious? You look plenty healthy."

Briana steeled herself to talk fast. She knew her father had a Victorian horror of discussing what he called women's problems. So she said, "It has to do with my, er, time of the month. It's a common problem, but they have a new treatment with high-dose vitamin B-12 shots."

Leo winced. "You can't get a vitamin shot here?"

"No—it's a very new thing. It takes a specialist. And I'm more comfortable with a woman doctor. These matters are so—personal."

Leo was embarrassed and displeased. "But how can you keep chasing off? You've got a business to run."

"Penny's coming in," Briana said.

Penny was her part-time assistant. She was thirty-two and lived in town with her older sister, Tammy, a music teacher. Penny had been a violinist in Branson, Missouri, but she'd broken her wrist in a bicycle accident and could no longer play with her former skill and precision.

She was taking correspondence courses in business and management. Her fingers were nimble enough to work a

computer keyboard. She was a quick learner and grateful
for the chance to earn money and learn at the same time.

"Penny hasn't got the experience you've got," Leo complained.

"The more she works here, the more experience she'll
have," Briana reasoned. "Besides, she helps at the greenhouses, too."

"Phooey," said Leo.

Briana changed the subject. She forced a hopeful smile.
"So how do you like Inga Swenson?"

Leo's expression grew strange. "She'll do, I guess. She
came back with me when Larry drove me home. But now
I'll have to have her here almost full-time—what with *you*
gallivanting all over."

Briana sensed that her father was pretending to be far
more displeased than he actually was. At that moment the
kitchen door swung open and Inga came into the living
room.

She radiated confidence and cheer. "Hello, Briana," she
said. "How's your little Nealie? Doing well, I hope."

"She's doing all right, thank you."

"That's good," said Inga. "That's good." She set about
straightening a disorganized pile of magazines. She seemed
a bustling sort of woman, born to set things in order.

"I would have come to say hello sooner, "Inga said,
"but I thought you and your father would want some time
alone. I'll be out of here soon. I've already phoned Harve
to come get me."

Briana blinked in displeased surprise. "Harve?"

Inga looked up with an innocent smile. "I'm having a
little problem with my car. But Harve said he'd take me
and bring me. He's such a sweet man. So generous."

Briana nodded and forced another smile. She said,
"Poppa's going to need you all week, and maybe then
some. I hope that's all right."

"Oh, yes," Inga said, moving to inspect a magazine rack
jammed with past copies of *TV Guide*. "Why, some of

these are three years old, Leo. Do you want me to throw them out?''

''I haven't done the crossword puzzles in them yet.''

''Whatever makes you happy, Leo. Do you want me to pick up anything special for your lunch tomorrow?''

''I'd like some more of that vegetable soup you brought with you today,'' Leo said. ''That stuff's good enough to eat seven days a week.''

Briana stiffened, still more surprised. Leo loved raising vegetables but often tired of eating them. He had long scorned vegetable soup.

''I'm trying to coax Leo into eating a more healthy diet,'' Inga said in a stage whisper. She ducked her head as if in shyness, then threw him a little glance.

Leo tried to look nonchalant. ''I suppose I should.''

The doorbell rang. Briana started. She had been so fascinated by the dynamics in the room she hadn't heard anyone pull into the drive.

Harve, she thought in dread. *It's Harve, and I have to be polite to him.*

Inga said, ''That must be my dear boy. Briana, if you'll answer the door, I'll get my coat. I'll be out of your way in no time at all.''

Reluctantly, Briana went to the front door and opened it. Harve stood on the welcome mat, his expression shy and full of yearning. He swallowed.

''Hi, B-Briana,'' he said. Sometimes, under duress, he stammered.

''Hi,'' she returned. ''Come on in.''

He entered, giving Leo a nod of greeting. Inga was slipping into her coat, which was stylish. ''You're such a kind fellow,'' Inga said to Harve, ''taking care of your old aunt like this.''

''It's a pleasure,'' said Harve and swallowed again.

Inga began to button her coat. She was leisurely about it. ''Harve,'' she said, ''when I looked out the window at

's happening?'' He led her to the far corner, where
e couldn't see. Josh kept hold of Briana's hands.
w,'' he said. ''What's up?''
oppa,'' she said. ''He's afraid to be alone. He's afraid
have another spell.''

oppa, Josh thought, *is afraid you'll slip out of his grasp.*
said, ''He doesn't need Nealie. She's missed a day
hool and she needs to get back into routine. She's
r than he is. Let her stay here.''

e nodded, but didn't look at him. ''Yes. You're right.
urse.''

studied her expression but could not read it. ''Some-
else happened up there,'' he said. ''I can tell. What's
g?

nga Swenson.'' She raised her eyes to his. ''The
an I hired. I think I made a mistake.''

Vhy? Doesn't your father like her?''

r mouth took on a rueful quirk. ''Maybe he likes her
vell. I think he's rather smitten with her.''

nd he doesn't see that she's really a wicked hellcat?''
lana shook her head. ''She's not that, at all. I have the
g she's basically goodhearted. But...''

ut what?''

he's manipulative, dammit. And she's having Harve
her there and pick her up. She's practically pushing
n my face. She told him to come here tomorrow and
y drainpipe.''

h's muscles tensed. ''*What?*''

nce Harve got there to pick her up, they wouldn't let
et a word in edgewise. It was like they circled and
l in on me.''

arve's coming *here?*'' Josh demanded.

said you could fix it. You know how, don't you?''

took a deep breath. He felt his masculinity being chal-
d, and he resented it. But he'd tell the truth. ''Actually,
d have to improvise. I like your drainpipe crooked.

Briana's house, I saw she's got a drainpipe coming loose.
Do you suppose you could fix it for her?''

No! Briana wanted to scream. Instead she said, very
softly, ''No. You don't have to—''

''Harve's such a wonderful fix-it man,'' Inga said, with
that fetching tilt of her head. ''He's got his own place in
such perfect shape, there's nothing left for him to do. He's
been itching for a project.''

''I *like* fixing drainpipes,'' said Harve.

''You're a good fellow, Harve,'' said Leo.

''Always glad to help a neighbor,'' Harve said, giving
Briana a shy look. *Help!* Briana thought. *They're ganging
up on me!*

''No,'' she repeated, ''really. You don't need to—''

Inga cut her off. ''Tut, tut, dear. It's a man's job. Your
father can't do it. And Larry works so hard, plus he's got
his own home to keep up. Harve will be glad to help. Won't
you, sweetheart?''

''I like to work, all right,'' said Harve. ''Keep things
fixed up.''

Briana struggled to take control of the conversation.
''You don't need to, Harve. My husband—my ex-
husband—Nealie's father can do it.''

''Harve can help him,'' said Inga, chipper as could be.
''Many hands make light work.''

''I don't think Josh does that kind of work,'' Leo said
with a disapproving slant to his mouth. ''He's more the
artistic type.''

''Oh, yes,'' said Inga, winding her scarf around her
throat. ''You said he's a photographer. And goes everywhere. How wonderful to travel all over the world, to see
exotic sights. Does he just love his work?''

''He certainly seems to,'' Leo said dryly.

''He's wonderful at his job,'' Briana countered. ''Not
many men have the courage to do what he does. Nealie's
very proud of him—and so am I.''

''Oh, to be free as a bird,'' Inga said dreamily. ''But of

all the world, I came back to Illyria. I may decide to settle down here. I guess that roots are what I may most want.''

"Me, too," said Leo.

"Me, too," said Harve.

"We're all of a kind," Inga said. "As alike as peas in a pod. But here I am chattering, and I should be on my way."

She walked to Harve's side and took his arm. "I'm going to hold on to you, dear. I wouldn't want to slip on that packed snow out there. But you'll take care of your old aunt, won't you?''

"I'll take good care of you," Harve vowed. He opened the door.

Inga laughed and looked over her shoulder at Leo and Briana. "He means what he says. He's a man of his word. Leo, I'll see you bright and early in the morning."

The door closed behind them. *Thank heaven they're gone,* thought Briana, her knees going weak with relief.

"Ah," Leo said with satisfaction. "They're *good* people. The best."

CHAPTER TEN

BRIANA LOOKED distressed. Her cheeks were
cold, her long hair tousled by the wind.

"Hi, Mommy," Nealie called from the c
curled under the afghan, watching *All Dogs G*

"Hi," Briana said, her voice tense. "You
go to Grandpa's for the night. We need to sta

"Aw, Mommy! I don't want to. Can't I s
Daddy?''

Josh went to Briana, gazing at her in conce
this? Yes, I'll stay with her. She'll sleep bette
bed. She's had a long day.''

Briana shrugged with an air of helplessnes
odds with her usual independence. "I—I
Poppa wants us both there.''

Irritation rose in Josh in a swelling tide. '
always get what Poppa wants?''

"No, of—of course not," she stammered.

The correct answer, Josh thought, *was yes
he didn't want to argue with her. With Nealie
Briana were both feeling their emotions sp
control. The result was that they bickered, ar
to make peace with her, a peace that lasted.

Nealie said, "Mommy, I don't want to go
It's always dark there, and he keeps it too h
makes me cough.''

"Daddy and I are talking it over," Briana

Josh took her hands and drew her towar
"Come on," he said as gently as he coul

It's got an interesting angle. I thought of taking some pictures of it. Black and white. Kind of an abstract.''

"Ooh!" she said, as if in despair.

"I'll try, I'll try," he consoled her.

"I don't want him coming here," she said with passion.

"Then I'll send him packing. I promise you."

"This woman seems sweet, but she's also sort of…relentless."

He gave her a crooked smile. "So am I, babe."

"I—I really wanted to talk to you tonight," she said.

He leaned closer until their foreheads touched. "Yeah. Me, too."

"I could phone you," she said. "When Poppa's asleep."

"I'd rather talk to you face-to-face," he said. "I could come up to your father's house when he's out for the night."

"No. Nealie shouldn't be left alone."

"You could come down here," he said.

"I'm not sure that would be a good idea."

He studied her. She looked so pretty—and so exhausted.

"Whatever you want," he said.

"About today," she said. "I don't know how to thank you for going through it."

"Give me a kiss," he said, and bent to take it.

Her lips were warm and pliant. He wished her jacket was off so he could feel the delicious curve of her breasts against his chest. He let himself slip his hands under her coat and grasp her waist, pulling her nearer.

She surprised him by putting her arms around his neck and pressing closer still. He felt his groin harden. He kissed her more deeply, and she strained upward, opening her lips.

He tasted her tongue, and it was an aphrodisiac to him. He slid his hands higher, inching them toward her breasts.

Nealie's voice interrupted his enchantment. She had a small, feminine voice, but it startled him as much as an air raid siren.

"Wow!" said Nealie, delighted. "Are you guys getting back together? Are you going to get married again?"

He and Briana sprang apart.

"Your daddy and I will always like each other," Briana said, straightening her jacket.

"That looked like more than just *liking* each other," Nealie observed. "Can I have a glass of apple juice?"

"Sure, sure," said Josh. "I'll pour it for you." He left Briana and moved to the refrigerator.

"I should be going back to Poppa's," Briana said.

"Do I have to go, too?" asked Nealie.

Josh paused, his hand hovering beside the bottle. His back was to Briana, and it went taut with tension while he waited for her answer, hoping she hadn't changed her mind.

"No," he heard her say. "Stay with Daddy. You'll rest better here."

Then she said "Good night, sweetheart," and he heard the sound of her kissing Nealie.

He took his time pouring the juice. He heard the front door open, then close. Nealie came to his side. "Why were you kissing like that? That's how people in the movies kiss."

He shrugged. "Once in a while she lets me. And I like it."

"She seemed to like it, too," said Nealie, with a challenging look.

He thrust the glass at her. "Drink your juice," he said.

AT EIGHT-THIRTY the next morning, Inga Swenson was already at Leo's house, making his breakfast. Briana was driving to the center in St. Louis for a blood test and ultrasound, and Josh was taking Nealie to school.

Harve saw his opening and he took it. Inga had convinced him he must assert himself and display his superior householder skills.

He drove his truck to Briana's from Leo's, where he had just repaired a faulty faucet. He parked and took his toolbox from the pickup's bed. He plodded to the drainpipe and began to wrestle it into its right position.

One of the metal clamps that held it in place had come loose and needed fastening. He began to hammer.

He was so engrossed that he didn't notice the woman come out of the house. He'd seen her car there, of course, but had hardly thought of her. Her voice startled him. Truth be told, it *scared* him.

"Hey, you!" she'd said with surprising vigor, "Harve Oldman! You're not to touch that."

Harve leaped away from the pipe and glowered at her. "Says who?" he demanded, trying to keep a manly edge in his voice.

"Briana did. So did Mr. Morris. He said he'd fix it, and if you came to send you away."

Harve looked her up and down. He'd seen her a few times here and there since she'd come back to Illyria— Penny Pfiefer. A feisty little redhead, her face peppered with freckles. The longer he looked at her, the more he realized she was kind of...cute. But he couldn't let a woman push him around.

She wore a green parka, unzipped, but no gloves or hat, and her fiery hair was tossed by the wind. She must have thrown on her coat and run out as soon as she heard him hammering.

"I mean it," she said, crossing her arms tightly. "He said not to let you do it."

"It's not his house," Harve said defensively.

"Well, it's hers, and she said the same thing. So please go. If you don't, you'll get me in trouble."

Harve's brow furrowed. This was a dilemma. To impress one woman, he would have to defy another who was only trying to do her job.

"I'm almost finished," he said. "A few more nails, and it's done."

"You've done a nice job," she admitted. "But please. No more. I have my orders."

"Well, drat," said Harve in disgust. "I do most of the work, and he'll take the credit."

"I don't think he's that kind of man."

"Umph," muttered Harve. He didn't believe her.

"Look," she said, "just help me out. I'm not trying to be a witch. It's cold out here. Why don't you come in? I'll give you a cup of coffee as a peace offering."

Harve studied her. She'd started to shiver. He felt sorry for her but was wary of going inside. "What if he comes back while I'm here? He won't like it."

"He said he had errands to run after he dropped Nealie off at school. That he wouldn't be back for over an hour. He left only fifteen minutes ago. Come on. I just made a fresh pot of coffee."

Against his better judgment, Harve followed her inside. He shucked off his gloves, cap and jacket and threw them on an empty kitchen chair. He sat down at the counter while she poured the coffee.

"I've seen you a couple times since you came back," he said. "You were a violinist up in Silver Dollar City?"

"Nope," she said, setting a cup in front of him. "Branson. And I'm not really a violinist. I'm a fiddler. I specialized in bluegrass music."

Harve brightened. A fiddle player seemed much less intimidating than a violinist. "But you had an accident," he said.

"I was riding my bike. The traffic's terrible in Branson. I got clipped and landed on my wrist, shattered it. I'll never play professionally again."

She seemed to have not an ounce of self-pity. She said everything matter-of-factly, as if it had happened to somebody else. Yet Harve felt sympathy welling up for her.

"Gee, that must have been tough."

She gave a philosophical shrug. "I was depressed for a while. Maybe six months. Finally I decided feeling sorry for myself wasn't going to do any good. Then our dad got

PLAY

Lucky 7

and you can get

FREE BOOKS AND A FREE GIFT!

PLAY LUCKY 7 and get FREE Gifts!

HOW TO PLAY:

1. With a coin, carefully scratch off the gold area at the right. Then check the claim chart to see what we have for you — **2 FREE BOOKS** and a **FREE GIFT** — **ALL YOURS FREE!**

2. Send back the card and you'll receive two brand-new Harlequin Superromance® novels. These books have a cover price of $4.99 each in the U.S. and $5.99 each in Canada, but they are yours to keep absolutely free.

3. There's no catch. You're under no obligation to buy anything. We charge nothing — **ZERO** — for your first shipment. And you don't have to make any minimum number of purchases — not even one!

4. The fact is, thousands of readers enjoy receiving books by mail from the Harlequin Reader Service®. They enjoy the convenience of home delivery...they like getting the best new novels at discount prices, BEFORE they're available in stores...and they love their *Heart to Heart* subscriber newsletter featuring author news, horoscopes, recipes, book reviews and much more!

5. We hope that after receiving your free books you'll want to remain a subscriber. But the choice is yours — to continue or cancel, any time at all! So why not take us up on our invitation, with no risk of any kind. You'll be glad you did!

We can't tell you what it is...but we're sure you'll like it! A surprise **FREE GIFT** just for playing LUCKY 7!

NO COST! NO OBLIGATION TO BUY!

NO PURCHASE NECESSARY!

**Scratch off the gold area with a coin.
Then check below to
see the gifts you get!**

YES! I have scratched off the gold area. Please send me
the 2 Free books and gift for which I qualify. I understand I am
under no obligation to purchase any books as explained on the
back and on the opposite page.

336 HDL DNKC   135 HDL DNJZ

FIRST NAME   LAST NAME

ADDRESS

APT.#   CITY

STATE/PROV.   ZIP/POSTAL CODE   (H-SR-04/02)

Worth **2 FREE BOOKS** plus a **FREE GIFT!**

Worth **2 FREE BOOKS!**

Worth **1 FREE BOOK!**

Try Again!

The Harlequin Reader Service® — Here's how it works:

Accepting your 2 free books and gift places you under no obligation to buy anything. You may keep the books and gift and return the shipping statement marked "cancel." If you do not cancel, about a month later we'll send you 6 additional books and bill you just $4.05 each in the U.S., or $4.46 each in Canada, plus 25¢ shipping & handling per book and applicable taxes if any.* That's the complete price and — compared to cover prices of $4.99 each in the U.S. and $5.99 each in Canada — it's quite a bargain! You may cancel at any time, but if you choose to continue, every month we'll send you 6 more books, which you may either purchase at the discount price or return to us and cancel your subscription.

*Terms and prices subject to change without notice. Sales tax applicable in N.Y. Canadian residents will be charged applicable provincial taxes and GST.

If offer card is missing write to: Harlequin Reader Service, 3010 Walden Ave., P.O. Box 1867, Buffalo NY 14240-1867

BUSINESS REPLY MAIL

FIRST-CLASS MAIL   PERMIT NO. 717-003   BUFFALO, NY

POSTAGE WILL BE PAID BY ADDRESSEE

HARLEQUIN READER SERVICE
3010 WALDEN AVE
PO BOX 1867
BUFFALO NY 14240-9952

NO POSTAGE
NECESSARY
IF MAILED
IN THE
UNITED STATES

sick, so I came back to Illyria to help out my sister and figure out what I was going to do.''

Harve didn't know what to say. To him, to have a talent and lose it was tragic, the kind of story they put on a television show.

She looked at him quizzically. ''Why do you look so sad?''

''Well, it *is* sad,'' he said. ''What happened to you, I mean.''

She laughed. ''It's not the end of the world. Besides, that level of show business wasn't very glamorous. I played with Cary Cameron's Cowgirl Band. It was only a novelty act, really. We'd stay in Branson for about eight months, then tour. Touring's not much fun. It gets old fast.''

Still, Harve thought, discreetly eyeing her as he sipped his coffee, she had been on stage, she had traveled, seen the world.

She poured cream in her coffee and toyed with the teaspoon, stirring first one way, then the other.

''What did you wear?'' he asked, astounding himself.

She looked up, blinking in surprise. ''What?''

''I mean did you have a—a costume? When you were a cowgirl?''

She gave him a dubious smile. ''Cameron wanted us to look like 1940 showbiz cowgirls. White hats. White high-heeled boots. Little blue skirts with stars on them, red and white striped blouses. A red sequined vest. And me, because I had long hair and wasn't pretty, he made me wear my hair in braids so I'd look cute.'' She wrinkled her nose in distaste.

To Harve she seemed very cute indeed. He thought she must have looked irresistible on stage. She'd cut her hair short and it was attractively curly, even windblown as it was now.

''You live with your sister?'' he asked.

''Yes.''

''I don't remember much of you when we were kids.''

"I was probably three grades behind you. Nothing to notice. I remember you, though. You live on the next farm, right?"

He nodded.

She said, "You had a white horse. One summer day, you rode it into town. I thought you looked like a cowboy hero. Young Clint Eastwood or something. Do you still have a horse?"

He shook his head numbly. He was stunned that anyone would compare him to Clint Eastwood.

"I like horses," she said. "But we lived in town."

Harve's thoughts spun. He drained his coffee cup. "I guess I should go," he said. "I hope I didn't get you in trouble. Working on that drainpipe.

He rose and fumbled into his jacket and hat. He put his gloves on his powerful hands. "I—I could pull a few nails out. So he'd have more to do when he gets back."

Her face brightened. "That would be a great idea. Thanks."

"Thanks for the coffee," he said.

"Thanks for the cooperation," she said.

He walked out of the house with the sense that he was being unfaithful to Briana. But he could not get out of his mind the image of Penny Pfiefer in her cowgirl outfit, spangles and all.

INGA SAT across from Leo, sipping her tea. He said, "I like bacon and eggs for breakfast."

Inga shook her head. "Leo, it would be poison to your system. Please just try the yogurt. I sliced bananas into it."

"That's not enough to keep a bird alive," Leo grumbled.

"I've just made you a sort of Danish pastry out of toast," she cajoled. She opened the oven door. "Ah, just right." She took it out with a flourish.

Leo looked at it with suspicion. "What's that white stuff on top?"

"Low-cal cottage cheese with sweetener and cinnamon."

"Phooey," said Leo, making a face.

She set the plate before him and gave him such a melting look, he decided to humor her. Besides the stuff, awful as it sounded, smelled delicious.

A few bites convinced him that it *was* delicious. Warily, he sampled the yogurt, which was also low-fat. Low-fat foods generally had no taste, but this glop was different, smooth and tasty. The sliced fruit made it even better.

"Mm," he said, dabbing a spot of yogurt from his chin. "Not bad."

Inga stood staring out the kitchen window. "That's odd," she said. "Harve was fixing the drainpipe, and this redheaded woman came out of the house. He went inside with her."

Leo gave a snort of disinterest. "That's Penny Pfieffer. She helps Briana out from time to time. Can I have more of both?"

She turned to him, her mouth a pink circle of disappointment, "Oh, Leo, I'd like you to diet for a little while. Can't you wait and have an orange for a snack in a few hours? It'd be so much better for you."

Leo frowned and tried flattery. "Well, it's your fault. If you didn't cook so well, I wouldn't want any more."

She laughed. "My late husband had heart problems. I had to learn to cook healthy meals for him. The doctors wouldn't guarantee he had six months. But I put him on a regimen and he lived another sixteen years."

Leo looked at her with fresh interest. *Sixteen* years? This woman was so capable she could extend life itself?

She bowed her head, swallowed, and her pretty face went sad. "His heart trouble didn't kill him, either. He stepped in front of a taxicab. I'm sure he had another ten good years in him."

Sixteen plus ten was twenty-six, Leo thought with growing enthusiasm. If he followed Inga's advice he might live to be eighty-six. Or even longer. After all, there were no taxicabs in Illyria.

"This regimen you mentioned," Leo said. "What is it?"

Inga stood beside the window, her hands clasped. The winter sunlight gave her hair a lovely gleam. She said, "First, I have a huge collection of tasty, healthful recipes. I've been collecting them for years. It's become my hobby, I suppose. But Harve's very picky, so I don't have much chance...."

Her voice trailed off, and she sighed. The she looked up and gave Leo a smile. "The other part is exercise. When the weather was nice, we'd take romantic walks and talk about whatever he wanted to talk about. I wanted to make it a pleasant time for him."

This sounded quite sensible to Leo, that if he exercised, it should be pleasant for him.

She tilted her head in that way she had. "If the weather was bad, we stayed inside and exercised together. We made a sort of game out of it. There are a series of exercises just for couples, you know."

Leo didn't know, but he began to imagine them. He began to imagine them rather vividly. "I might like to try that," he said.

"Good," she said. "Next week I'll bring my tapes and music and candles."

"Music and candles?" Leo asked. This was sounding even better.

"I always used music and candles. It created a nicer atmosphere. It made me feel that exercise wasn't just work, it was a special time-out for togetherness and fun."

Leo said, "Yeah, I'd like to try that."

Something caught her eye, and she turned toward the window. "Now this is strange. Harve's coming out of the house. She walked him to the door. My goodness, her hair is *very* red. I wish I'd had hair that color when I was young."

"Your hair was fine," said Leo. "Your hair was a lovely brown."

She said, "But what's this? It looks like Harve's pulling

out some nails. He's laying them on the windowsill. It doesn't look like he's finished the job.''

Leo was not interested in Harve. ''Tell me what we're having for lunch.''

Inga gave her attention fully to Leo. ''Oh,'' she said, ''I've brought that vegetable soup you wanted. And greens for a salad. I have a special dressing I think you'll like.''

''I know I'll love it,'' Leo said, basking in her attention.

''YOU FIXED the drainpipe,'' Briana said, pleased.

Josh watched her unzip her jacket and pull off her gloves. ''I just put the clip on. Harve was the one who wrenched it back in the place.''

She looked at him oddly. ''You and Harve worked together?''

He shook his head, his expression disgusted. ''No. He came while I was driving Nealie to school. It was a sneak attack. Penny stopped him.''

''Penny?'' Briana laughed. ''Good for her. How did the two of you get along?''

''I hardly saw her,'' Josh said. ''She stayed in your office most of the time. Came down for coffee once.''

''She's a hard worker,'' Briana nodded. She pushed up her sleeve and looked at her watch. ''It's a little early, but we could go pick up Nealie. You could say hello to Franklin Hinks at the post office.''

''My philatelist friend?'' he asked with a smile.

''He always asks about you,'' she said, watching him take his parka from the closet. ''And speaks well of you.''

''At least one person in town on my side?'' Josh asked ironically.

''There's Nealie and me,'' she said.

''Then I can conquer the world,'' he said.

JOSH HUGGED NEALIE and listened to her chatter about the schoolday. The class gerbil was pregnant and might have her babies tonight. The teacher had shown a video about coral reefs. They had drawn pictures of tropical fish.

"You've seen coral reefs, haven't you, Daddy?" she asked.

"Yes," he said. "In Florida. The Caribbean. The South Pacific."

"I'd like to see a coral reef. Some day will you take me to one?"

"Sure I will." *I'll take you to every coral reef in the world if you just get well.*

"Can Mommy come, too?"

"If she wants to." *I'd love for her to come. I'd show you both such wonderful things. I'd show you what an amazing world it is.*

"Did you ever take pictures of sharks and things, Daddy?"

"I've taken some."

"What's the scariest picture you ever took underwater?"

"A great white shark smiling at me."

"Why was he smiling?"

"He thought I was his breakfast."

"How did you escape?"

"I was in a special cage for photographers. Your mother would probably say photographers should always be kept in a cage."

Briana laughed. "No, I wouldn't."

Nealie said, "Did the shark bite the cage?"

"Yes. Until he got a toothache. Then he swam away."

"To the shark dentist?"

"Absolutely."

The conversation bounced along, a seemingly normal conversation in a seemingly normal family. Briana knew it was an illusion but was grateful for it. Josh kept his arm around Nealie and made her laugh all the way home.

BRIANA WASN'T FOOLED. "Something's bothering you," she said to Josh, frowning. "What?"

Nealie, still proud of her new boots, had gone upstairs to change out of her school clothes, clomping every step of the way. Josh and Briana had a few precious minutes alone together.

"You know what," he said. "I wish you wouldn't go up to your father's again tonight."

She sorted through the mail she had retrieved from the post office after picking up Nealie. She shook her head worriedly. "I know. There are so many things we have to talk about. I wish Poppa wasn't afraid to stay alone and you and I could have some time to ourselves."

She was a very efficient sorter. On the counter she laid in neat stacks the orders for farm products, bills, junk mail. He watched her with a mixture of admiration and desire.

"Let me take these up to the office," she said, picking up the business mail, "and tell Penny she can go home."

She ran lightly up the stairs.

Josh looked around the small living room as he took off his parka. It was cozy. He had lived here with her for six months and it had been home—in a way his first home. He thought of those days with nostalgia.

And he thought of the first days when Nealie came home from the hospital, and he'd flown back from Albania. The first time he'd given Nealie a bottle had been on that old sofa...and his heart had ached with love for the tiny creature in his arms.

Memories overwhelmed him. He had returned to Illyria for Nealie's heart surgery. He had come from Iceland that time. For the surgery on her hand, he'd come to her from Malaysia. And for all the other visits, too many to count. He came from one faraway place and left for another.

Yes. This little house might be as close as he would ever get to home. He had a condo in Los Angeles that he sublet most of the time. He liked California, but the place he always came back to was *here*.

Briana came down the stairs with Penny. Josh and Penny

nodded hello. He thought she was kind of cute in a freckled way. She seemed like a nice, bright woman.

Briana was taking off her jacket, and Penny was putting on hers, when the doorbell rang.

What now? thought Josh, gritting his teeth.

Briana rolled her eyes, stalked to the door and flung it open. Harve stood there. He wore a cap with earflaps. Josh thought uncharitably that it made him look like a goddamn beagle.

"Harve," Briana said, more dismay than welcome in her tone.

He took off his hat and held it in both hands in front of his chest. "We saw that you'd come home. I came to drive you to your father's."

Briana's dark eyes flashed. "I'm not ready. I just got here. I have things to do at my own house first."

Harve swallowed. His ears were turning red from the cold. "I could come in and fix something until you're ready. Your dad says you've got a slow drain in the bathroom sink. I've got my toolbox, and I could—"

"Harve, no!" Briana said emphatically. "I want a few minutes at home with my family. Please tell Poppa I'll be up in a little while. You can take your aunt home. Poppa will be fine by himself for a half hour or so."

Penny stepped forward, pulling a green wool cap over her red curls. "Harve, Briana's been on the run all day. If you're so primed to fix something, you can help me with my license plate. It's hanging on by one screw. If I back into a snowbank and lose it, I'll get a citation."

"But—" Harve said.

"No buts. Let's go," said Penny. She grabbed him by the elbow and steered him outside. The door shut behind them.

"She certainly took charge of *that*," Briana said with a crooked smile.

"Give her a raise," said Josh, putting his arm around her waist. "A big one."

CHAPTER ELEVEN

"LET GO," Harve ordered, shaking Penny's arm. "I've got to get my toolbox."

"Then get it," said Penny. She stepped away and crossed her arms. "Good grief, couldn't you give that poor woman a moment alone?"

Harve trudged to the truck bed and heaved out his toolbox. He stalked toward Penny's rusted green car and cast a look of rebuke toward the house. "I bet *he* can't fix a clogged U trap."

"Who? Josh Morris?" Penny asked, with a challenging tilt to her head.

"Yeah, him." Harve sneered. "I see he finished fixing that drainpipe. Those nails look whacked every which way. How long did it take him?"

Penny paused, suddenly not looking quite so superior. "About half an hour. Well, maybe more."

"Ha!" Harve said in triumph. "I could have done it in three minutes."

He knelt behind her car and opened his toolbox. Penny stepped closer, as if to supervise him. "Could you take a picture of a rhinoceros charging right at you?" she asked.

"No." Harve snorted. "I wouldn't want to. I'm not that big a fool."

"Could you if you had to?" she persisted.

He ignored her. "How long you been driving around like this? This license plate is so bent up it looks like a paper airplane."

"I don't know," she said. "A couple of weeks maybe."

"Well, why didn't you fix it sooner?" he grumped. He removed the license plate and bent it back into shape.

"Wow," she said with grudging admiration. "You did that with your bare hands."

"My hands aren't bare. I got on gloves."

"You know what I mean," she said.

Oddly, her words filled him with warm pride. "You could have fixed this yourself if you'd got to it soon enough. What's the matter? Don't you have a screwdriver?"

"No," she said matter-of-factly.

He stopped and stared at her. She leaned against a walnut tree, her green parka and cap in bright contrast to her flame-colored hair. He realized again that she was an attractive girl in her offbeat way.

"You don't have a screwdriver?" he said in disbelief.

"We lost it," she said without a note of embarrassment.

"You only got one?"

"There's another one somewhere, but we can't find that one, either," she said.

"Well, then," he said, head cocked, "how do you get anything *fixed?*"

"Mostly we don't. Our father used to do all those things. Since he died, we've been trying to cope. We're getting better. We do fine."

"I bet," Harve said and went back to screwing on her license plate. Her bumper looked crooked to him, too. Also, her tailpipe was rusted and bent.

"Umph," he said. "I bet your house needs a thousand things done to it."

"We get along just fine, thank you," she said. But she didn't sound quite so snippy.

He could hardly imagine two women silly enough to own only two screwdrivers and to lose both of them. Still, she was a feminine sort of little thing, and he supposed that accounted for it. Then he remembered he was supposed to be thinking of Briana.

"I'm going to come back tomorrow and fix that U trap," he said, standing. "It'll save her a plumber's bill."

"And what if she tells me not to let you do it?" Penny asked. The cold breeze blew a strand of hair across her eyes, and she swiped it away. Her eyes, he noticed, were almost as green as her cap and gloves.

"I'll come and see anyhow," he said stubbornly. "It's the neighborly thing to do."

"Suit yourself," she said with a toss of her head. "But if she gives me orders, I've got to carry them out."

"Fine," he said, standing tall. As if in afterthought, he said, "Maybe I'll straighten that bumper of yours, too. If you ever tried to tow anything, it'd pop right off."

"Why would I ever tow anything?" she asked. A smile played at the corner of her mouth.

"Because you never know what might happen," he told her.

She gave him a thoughtful look. "That's true. That's absolutely true."

An odd feeling stirred deep inside him.

"Thanks for the help," she said, moving toward her car. "See you tomorrow, I guess."

"Yeah," he said, his heart beating strangely hard. "Guess so." He picked up his toolbox and loaded it in the truck. He gazed after her as she drove down the frozen lane.

Was that a wobble in her right rear tire?

It ought to be fixed.

BRIANA HIKED up the snowy hill to Leo's house. She went reluctantly and only because she did not want to make a scene and upset her father.

But this could not go on, she told herself. She wanted to be with Nealie, and Nealie would rather stay with Josh. Briana didn't blame her. She yearned to talk to Josh herself. But right now Leo held the winning cards.

It was unpleasant to think in those terms. Josh had always

claimed that Leo played emotional games, that he manipulated her. She had always denied it.

She knew, of course, that her family had long deferred to Leo, that her mother had pampered him and trained Briana to do the same. He was her poppa. She had always thought him wonderful and adored him as her mother had.

He could be a man of enormous charm when he wanted to. Lately, he hadn't wanted to. He was by nature good-tempered—although again, not lately.

She felt guilty and disloyal thinking such things, but she couldn't help it. She opened the door and went inside. Leo sat in his recliner. He used his remote to turn down the volume of the television.

"You took your time," he said with a hurt look.

"I had things to do," she said. "I'm running behind these days. You're sick, Nealie has her allergies, and I have all these trips to the city."

"Feeling better?" he asked with his old air of kindness and concern.

"About the same," she said, but that was not quite true. She was taking fertility shots and could already feel them toying with her hormones.

"I wish you could do this closer to home," he said. "I worry about you being on the road so much."

"I wish it was possible, too, Poppa."

"Nealie didn't come again today," he said, clearly disappointed. "Doesn't she love her old grandpa any more?"

"Of course, she does. It's just that she gets to spend so little time with her father—"

"That's God's truth," said Leo, his tenderness vanishing.

"—and she hasn't been strong all this winter. She's missed a lot of school. It's best she sleeps in her own bed, sticks to her routine."

"She'll outgrow these allergies," Leo said with confidence. "She comes from strong stock. At least on *our* side. Besides, it's not like she's a boy."

Briana closed the coat closet and turned to him, her eyebrow lifted. "What do you mean by that?"

"She's not a boy," Leo said, laughing. "She's not going to have to grow up and use her back, like Larry does. She'll never have to take a wrench to a tractor and heave around hundred-pound bags of fertilizer. She'll use her brains." He tapped his forehead and winked his most beguiling wink. "Like you. And your mother. And Inga."

"Oh," said Briana. "So now it's Inga, not Mrs. Swenson?"

Leo looked at her with wide, innocent eyes. "For goodness' sake, I've known the woman from childhood."

Briana gave him a one-cornered smile. "Yes. When she had no meat on her bones and her hair was the color of a barn rat."

"Time changes all," Leo said, trying to sound philosophical.

"She was a priss and do-gooder, too, as I recall," teased Briana.

"I was young and inexperienced," Leo said. "I didn't appreciate her virtues. I was too busy being a red-blooded American boy."

"And her virtues are…?" Briana coaxed.

"She's a *very* organized woman," Leo said. "Remarkably organized. Also an excellent cook. I've never liked winter squash. Tried to. Couldn't. Yet she made a side dish—I can't describe it. I must give more time to promoting winter squash."

"Squash has long needed a champion," Briana said dryly. "So she takes good care of you, eh?"

"She does an adequate job," he admitted. Then, as if he felt he was revealing too much, he changed the subject. His look grew serious, even stern. "Why didn't you let Harve fix that bathroom sink?"

"Because I don't *want* him to."

"Why not? The sink's not working. He volunteered to take care of it. But you refused. That's not neighborly."

Briana sighed and prayed for patience. "I'm afraid his interest is more than neighborly. I don't want to give him false encouragement."

Leo raised one white eyebrow. "Sometimes there's a person who seems…very ordinary to you. Then one day—bam!—you look and everything's different. That could happen to you and Harve."

It could happen to you and Inga, she thought, not sure how she felt about the idea.

"Just be kind to the poor man," Leo said. "After all, he'll be here long after lover boy's gone."

Don't call him lover boy, Briana wanted to snap. Instead she said, "His name is Josh."

"Whatever," Leo said, turning his attention to the television screen. "Anyway, he'll be gone. And you know it. But Harve will be here for the rest of your life."

"Do I need to make you some supper?" she asked, her jaw clenched.

"I suppose," Leo said. "Inga made a diet meat loaf. It's in the refrigerator. All you have to do is warm it up. She said I should have a nice salad, too. She brought all the fixings."

Briana looked at him, nestling cherubically in his chair, so content to be served, so confident it would be done. *Don't blame him completely,* she scolded herself. *You helped make him this way.*

She set out for the kitchen. "I mean it," Leo called after her. "Harve'll be here for you forever. Think about it."

JOSH WAS ON THE COUCH nearly asleep when the phone rang. He raised himself with a start and glanced at his watch. It was past eleven.

He stood and made his way in stocking feet to grab the receiver.

"Josh?" The voice was Briana's, soft and low. Instantly he became alert.

"Babe?" he said.

"Is it too late?" she asked. "I looked down the hill. The living room lights were on. They were dim, but I thought you might still be up."

"I was watching the nature channel," he said. "Do you know that houseflies taste with their feet? Sounds unsanitary to me."

He was joking. The television set wasn't even on. He'd been trying to sleep on the couch because he didn't want to sleep in Briana's bed. He'd tried to last night. It had nearly driven him crazy.

The sheets smelled faintly of her sweetness. The whole room did. He remembered the warmth and pliancy of her body in that bed, of the hours they had spent there, the things they'd done, how she'd felt, how she'd tasted, how she'd sounded when she'd made little gasps of desire and fulfillment.

"I just wanted to talk to you," she said.

"I wanted to talk to you, too," he said. He imagined her in Leo's house and wondered if she was dressed for bed. Did she still wear funny nightgowns? He'd always had them off of her in record time.

"It took Poppa a long time to get drowsy," she said. "I think he'd been napping all day."

"So he could stay up all night guarding you with a shotgun?"

"Very funny."

"Very true."

"How's Nealie?"

"A superior child in every way. She went to bed with no trouble. But she misses you. She wants to know how long you'll keep spending nights up there."

He heard her sigh. He closed his eyes, remembering how she used to sigh against his neck, her bare body pressed to his, her naked legs twined with his.

He said, "Don't tell me. I know. He'll try to keep you there as long as I'm around."

She said, "I'm afraid you're right."

He was surprised. "Once you'd never have admitted that."

"I—I don't know what to think," she said. He could hear the unhappiness in her voice. "It's like Poppa's changed."

From a toad into what? Josh thought. Knowing this wasn't the most tactful of questions, he said, "Changed how?"

"He just seems a lot more calculating about Harve and me."

"And what time should I expect your rural Romeo next? About three a.m.? Is he bringing a concrete truck? Will he be pouring a new basement floor?"

She laughed, although he could tell she didn't want to. "Harve's not a *bad* man."

"To me he is. He's a rival. He fights dirty. He can fix things."

"Can't *you* fix a U trap?"

"I don't even know what a U trap is," he said in all honesty. "It sounds like something for catching U-boats."

"Well, I think Poppa and probably that Inga woman are encouraging him to be assertive."

"That Inga woman? Hmm. Sounds like you don't like her."

"Actually, she's done wonders for Poppa. The place already looks cleaner and brighter. She's gotten him to eat things he's never eaten before. She made him a meat loaf with tofu in it."

"Tofu? My God, next she'll have him doing yoga and standing on his head."

"She might. She's obviously got great persuasive powers. I'm just afraid she's trying to use them on Harve's behalf."

"So is he starting to look better to you? That cap with the earflaps bit, that was pretty sexy."

He liked joking with her like this, the old teasing way. Sometimes after sex, they'd lay in bed, cuddling and trying to make each other laugh.

But she didn't laugh. "I feel sorry for him. I have the feeling that his aunt truly feels she's doing the right thing. But she's not."

"No," he said. "She isn't."

"There's more," she said. "Poppa's much more openly hostile about you than he ever was before. I guess he feels threatened."

He should feel threatened. If I could, I'd carry you off and ravish you in ways he'd hate to imagine.

"I'm afraid he's a little jealous of how much Nealie cares for you."

Josh forced himself to be generous. "That's natural. Most of the time, he's the main man in her life."

"But not in her heart," Briana said, making his own heart crack a little. "Maybe Poppa's acting this way because he's getting older. He's facing his own mortality and worrying more than usual about the family and the farm."

And maybe he's getting careless and transparent, Josh thought. *And you're finally seeing through him.*

She said, "But all I'm doing is talking about me. I wanted to talk about you, Josh. Why didn't you ever tell me? About what happened when you were eleven?"

The old shame and sickness swelled in him, the old desire to keep his secret. "I don't like talking about it." But he knew he had to give her more than that. "I don't even like thinking about it. So most of the time I don't."

Denial, he thought. The same thing for which he'd criticized Briana. If you didn't think about it, never spoke of it, it was as if it never happened. But he'd been doing it for longer than she had. Years longer.

"I think I can understand," she said.

He thought this was true. If anyone one could, she could.

Softly she said, "I wish you'd told me about this years ago."

He stared at the afghan under which Nealie so often lay. One of her stuffed animals rested beside it. "What would it have changed?" he asked.

"I don't know," she replied. "You wouldn't have had to keep it locked up inside. You wouldn't have had to be alone with it."

He walked to the couch and picked up the toy, a small teddy bear, hardly larger than his hand. He said, "So now you know. After it was over and done with, I tried to forget it. You're the first person I ever told."

"Such a thing had to change you," she said.

He turned the small bear around to examine it. It was dressed like a farmer, wearing little overalls. "Yeah," he said in a rasping voice. "Maybe it did."

"Oh," she said, "Poppa's awake. He's calling that his throat's sore and he wants some cough syrup. I have to go."

He tossed the farmer bear up and caught it. It even had a tiny straw hat. "Will you call again?"

"If he goes back to sleep. He may want to stay up and watch television. If he does, I'll go to bed. Snow's predicted for tomorrow. They want to monitor me again at the clinic, and it's a slow drive when it's snowing."

"Good night, babe."

"Good night, Josh. Take care."

He hung up the phone. He looked at the toy bear and wanted, irrationally, to throw it against the wall. Instead he set it on the coffee table. It was, he supposed, the perfect toy for a child who lived on a farm, but he'd rather Nealie had a bear with cargo pants and a camera around its neck.

He lay down on the couch. He thought of going upstairs to Briana's room and sleeping alone in the bed they'd once shared. He couldn't do it.

THE DAYS went by slowly. Leo and Inga contrived dozens of ways to keep Briana and Josh from being alone. But Harve was not cooperative.

Every morning he brought Inga to Leo's. He stayed for an hour or so, repairing things that Larry hadn't had time to get to, but having been rebuffed by Briana once, he was reluctant to approach her again.

But Inga had been after him, and he knew he must try. At the kitchen table, Leo was happily eating his omelette. Inga was tidying a cupboard, and Harve watched Briana's house through the window. He had lingered there as he finished repairing a latch.

At Briana's, Penny Pfeiffer had arrived in her broken-down green car. The old wreck belched smoke, too. It obviously needed a new filter. Couldn't she *see* these things? Penny went into the house.

A moment later, Briana came out, laughing and blowing kisses over her shoulder to Nealie. Even from this distance, she looked so pretty and light on her feet that Harve's heart tightened. Her truck wasn't much newer than Penny's old compact, but at least she kept it in good shape. She got in it and drove off toward the mysteries of the city.

Harve wondered what was wrong with Briana that she needed to get so many shots from a fancy doctor. Inga hinted it was a delicate problem, soon to be cured. Harve could imagine no problem. Briana always seemed full of energy to him, could work hard as a little horse—the perfect farmer's wife.

Then Josh Morris came out of the house, holding Nealie by the hand. The kid was buttoned up, a muffler wound around her neck, big furry boots, a cap pulled down nearly to her eyes.

Josh strapped Nealie into her car seat in his rented car, got in, and they, too, disappeared down the lane. *Good riddance,* thought Harve. It was time for him to move.

He put his screwdriver into his tool belt. Without looking at his aunt, he said, "Think I'll go down to Briana's and start on that sink now."

"Better late than never," Inga said, but she sounded happy, not disapproving. "I've found some more things for you to do around here when you get back. I'm just determined to see this house put in order."

Harve put on his heavy jacket and zipped it to the throat. He put on his wool gloves and his cap with the earflaps.

He got in his pickup and drove the short distance to Briana's house.

He took a deep breath, and when he knocked at the door,
he tried to make the knock sound authoritative and mas-
culine. The door swung open almost immediately, and
Penny Pfeiffer stood there, all five feet two inches of her.

She pushed a red curl out of her eyes. "Well, look who's
here," she said. "I heard you drive up. I knew it was you."

"I came to fix the sink," Harve said, drawing himself to
his full height. He was well over a foot taller than she was.
It gave him an unfamiliar feeling of machismo.

"I'm sorry," she said. "My orders are *not* to let you fix
the sink. I'm sorry, but that's the way it is. If you want to
come in and have a cup of coffee, that's fine, but then you
have to go."

"But I even got a new U trap in case she needs one."

"Nope. And that's the final word from headquarters."

Penny's air was resolute, but he thought when he looked
into her green eyes that he saw something like fellow feeling.

"Oh, come in," she said, opening the door wider. "I've
got a fresh pot of coffee and I'm not good for anything
until I've had my second cup."

Harve wasn't sure. Having coffee was like settling for a
consolation prize. But she had such a natural, no-nonsense
air about her that he found himself inside the house and
once again sitting beside her at the counter.

She made coffee so strong a horseshoe would float in it.
"Good coffee," he said.

"Caffeine," she said, "nectar of the gods."

A silence settled between them. An uncomfortable silence.

At last she planted her elbow on the counter and leaned
her cheek against her fist. She regarded him with sympathy
that seemed half kindly, half amused. She said, "You've
got it bad, don't you?"

Her words startled him. His coffee cup stopped in midair. "What do you mean?"

With one forefinger she traced a heart on the countertop. "Briana. I've been watching you this past week or so. You really *do* have it bad for her, don't you?"

He tried to recapture his dignity. "I'm kind of partial to her," he said.

Penny laughed, but not in a mean way. "Kind of partial," she mocked. "Oh, Harve," she said. "Sometimes you're just too Jimmy Stewart."

"Whadya mean by that?" he sputtered.

"I mean, you're this big, tall, gentle guy who's so impossibly shy about his emotions. You come courting with a lug wrench."

"You mean I'm comical?" he asked. "Stupid?"

She shook her head, and the fiery curls bounced. "No. I'm sorry. It's kind of sweet, actually."

Embarrassment flooded through him. "But it shows? How I feel?"

"Is a bluebird blue?" she asked with a wry look.

"Of course, it's blue," he said. He set down the coffee cup. "Do people talk about me?" The thought was almost too horrible to bear.

She made a dismissive gesture. "A little tiny bit. This is a small town. Everybody gets talked about. Even me."

"You?" he asked, still more confounded. "What do they say about *you?*"

"Oh, that I went off to Branson and lived the wild life of a musician."

"Did you?"

"No. I was pretty square. I dated a drummer once. That was about it."

A drummer. That sounded fairly wild to Harve. Drummers were known to have long hair and smoke marijuana.

"So what do they say about *me?*" he asked.

"Nothing," she said, and her voice was kind. "Except that you've liked her a long time."

"But that she doesn't like me," he said, plunging into dejection.

"It's just she's got this thing she has to resolve with Josh," Penny said. "They saw each other and it was kismet—you know, fate."

"That's movie stuff. Life isn't like that," grumbled Harve. "What else do people say?"

She tapped the countertop thoughtfully. She gazed toward the kitchen window. "They say—well, they say if Briana doesn't, shall we say, return your affection? That it's her loss. There are plenty of other girls who wouldn't mind if you came calling."

He blushed so hard his ears burned. "W-what other girls?"

"There you go, being Jimmy Stewart again. Don't you ever notice anything?"

"I notice things. Your tailpipe is rusty. Your right rear wheel wobbles. I notice lots of things."

She laughed again. She rose and filled his coffee cup. He didn't object. The conversation was uncomfortable, but it was also interesting. Hardly anyone had ever sat down with Harve and talked to him about himself. Except Inga, and she talked to boss him.

He said, "You didn't answer. What girls?"

"Lots." She sat beside him again.

"Name one," he challenged.

Penny put her elbows on the counter, knitting her fingers together. "She'd kill me for saying this...."

"Yes?" Harve prodded.

"She'd never admit it in a million years...."

"Yes?" He leaned closer.

"She's never actually come out and said it, but..."

"Yes?" His curiosity was rising to flood tide.

"I just sort of suspect," she said slowly, "that my sister might kind of like you."

He recoiled. "Tammy? The schoolteacher?"

Tammy was short like Penny, and she wasn't bad looking, but she had no more personality than a fence post. Also, she sang soprano in the church choir, and when she hit high notes, she made Harve's ears hurt.

"You and Tammy are a lot alike," Penny offered. "You're both quiet, sweet-natured, dependable. That's an important quality, dependability."

Harve had gone from excitedly curious to depressed. "You think Briana doesn't want me, and you're trying to matchmake."

"No. I'm just saying there are other fish in the sea."

Harve was obdurate. "I don't want another fish. I want Briana."

"Okay, okay," Penny said, throwing her hands up in surrender. "It's just that I wanted to let you know other women have said you're attractive. You've got this kind of puppy-dog charm—"

"I'm tired of talking about fish and puppy dogs," he said, pushing away from the counter. "Look, is there something around here I could fix? Just so I don't feel like a complete fool for coming?"

She looked at him a long moment, as if having an argument with herself. "Maybe the doorknob on Briana's office," she said at last.

"What's wrong with it?" he asked, mollified only a bit.

"It's hard to turn. For her, it's nothing, but me, with this trick wrist? Sometimes I have a real problem with it. It tends to swing shut."

He sighed. "I can fix that with no problem. Will she get mad at me?"

She stood and motioned for him to follow her upstairs. "Don't worry. If she gets mad, I'll take the blame."

He followed her upstairs. She wore jeans and little black slippers. He imagined her in her little blue skirt with white stars swinging back and forth from her hips like a bell. He imagined her in white cowboy boots.

I've got a certain puppy-dog charm, he thought irrelevantly. *There are women who would welcome my attentions....*

WHEN JOSH CAME BACK to the house after taking Nealie to school, it seemed achingly empty without her and Briana. Penny was upstairs working, but she kept to herself, did her job. She said Harve had come to fix the sink, but she hadn't let him.

Josh was at loose ends. Bored. He decided to hike around the farm and take some art shots in black and white. He was checking his camera equipment when Glenda phoned.

Larry had a chest cold and was staying home. He could watch the kids while she went down to the greenhouses. The tomatoes were due for another transplanting, and she needed to get in all the work she could.

Would Josh like to come and keep her company? He said he would. He met her at the oldest greenhouse and tried to help. But his hands, so clever with a camera, were awkward with the seedlings. Glenda expertly transplanted six in the time it took him to do a bad job of one.

He knew, for the thousandth time, he wasn't meant to be a farmer.

"They're giving you a tough time, aren't they?" Glenda asked. "It's like they're trying to keep you and Briana apart."

"Trying," he said. "They're doing a damn good job, if you ask me." He accidentally snapped the stem off a plant and swore. He said, "I don't get this sudden ascendance of Inga. It's like she appears and is the puppet mistress, pulling everybody's strings."

"She's cast a spell on Leo, that's for sure," Glenda said. "But in a way it's good. She's getting the place cleaned up. She's getting him to eat right and even exercise a little more."

And she's keeping me away from my wife, he thought with acrimony.

He said, "She's pushing Harve at Briana for all she's worth."

Glenda tossed him a sad glance. "She's really fond of him. He's the only relative she has, you know. And she's convinced you won't stay around."

He broke another stem and spilled potting soil on the counter. "I don't quite fit in here, do I?"

"If you want Briana, keep fighting for her," Glenda advised. "They'll keep trying to come between you. You've known that from the start. It's just gotten more obvious. A lot more obvious."

They were silent for a moment. Then Josh said, "You wouldn't mind if she went away, would you? Briana, I mean."

Glenda looked at the tray of plants and picked up another seedling. When she spoke, it was with an air of reluctant confession.

"She's my sister-in-law, and I love her, but Larry will always be in her shadow. I'd like to see him come into his own. He never will with Briana always here. Leo never listens to *Larry's* ideas. It doesn't help Larry's disposition."

Uh-oh, thought Josh. He gave her a sidelong glance. "You and Larry. Are things okay between you?"

She nodded. "Mostly. But we—we've had words. I told him after this baby, no more children. He finally agreed. I think the babies were one of his ways of proving he's a man. I told him there are other ways."

"Yeah," Josh said.

"Harve's wrong for Briana," Glenda said. "I've always known that."

Josh stopped mutilating plants for a moment. "But am I right for her?"

She looked at him searchingly. "I wish I knew. Sometimes love just isn't enough. You know?"

Her cell phone rang. She wiped her hand on her apron and answered. "Yes, honey," she said. "Yes, honey. Well, make him stop. You're his father. Just *make* him. Yes. I'll be right there.''

She tucked the phone into its holder and untied her apron. "Larry. He can't hold the fort any longer. I've got to go back.''

He helped her into her coat, put on his own and walked her to her van. He watched her drive off. She was a brave woman in her own way.

He hiked uphill against the wind to Briana's house. Tonight he would somehow get her to himself and talk to her the whole night long, if necessary.

He vowed he would.

But it was not to happen.

Instead, it was the night Harve Oldman's farmhouse caught on fire.

CHAPTER TWELVE

AT EIGHT O'CLOCK, Harve heard his dog, Queenie, barking madly at something. Harve rose listlessly from the sofa and moved to the window. He blinked in shock.

Black smoke poured from his old machine shed, the outbuilding closest to the house. He blinked in surprise, and in the space of that blink, the first flames shot through the shed's windows.

"What is it?" Inga asked, stifling a yawn. She had been sitting beside him, watching television and darning his socks.

But Harve could not speak. He stood at the window as if rooted, watching the shed disappear in the growing fire and roiling smoke.

Grandpa's tractor, he thought, sick to the heart. The shed held only a few pieces of equipment, including the ancient tractor Harve kept for sentimental value.

The tractor had belonged to his grandfather, and Harve kept it in good working order and sometimes brought it to farm exhibits or let people drive it in parades. He was too shy to drive it in public himself.

Then the graveness of the situation hit him. Far more was at stake than the antique tractor. The night was cold but dry, the wind stiff and blowing straight toward the house. Already orange sparks flew through the night air like swift imps, intent on destruction.

"Fire!" cried Harve as he leaped for the phone. He called nine-one-one and babbled that his shed was on fire and his house in danger.

"Fire?" echoed Inga, jumping to her feet and dropping her darning. "Fire *here?*" She ran to the window. There was no more shed to be seen, only flames, and the flames were cloaked in great clouds of black smoke that rolled toward the house.

"Hurry," Harve ordered her. "Grab what you need, and let's get out of here!" She ran to her bedroom, and Harve looked wildly about his living room, at the furniture and framed pictures and vases and knickknacks he had known for years.

He snatched the family Bible, the photograph albums, the farm's account books and a metal file box of records. He ran to the garage, threw everything in the bed of the pickup and backed the truck out of the garage and upwind of the fire. He saw Inga running from the house carrying an armload of clothes, a suitcase banging against her knees, her laptop case slung over her shoulder.

He helped her stow her things in the truck and told her to stay where she was. He raced to the house. It still seemed safe, for the fire had not yet touched it. In the distance, he heard sirens. Wildly he ran inside and gathered things that had sentimental value.

He forgot to take any clothing but stripped from his bed a quilt his mother had made. He snatched a candlestick that had belonged to his grandmother, an old framed print of a dog howling over a lost lamb.

He threw everything into a dresser drawer and carried it outside. As he stumbled to his truck, the pump engine pulled up. The firemen, volunteers, were all neighbors, some he knew well.

The men spilled out of the truck and ran across the snow, dragging hoses. Something exploded in the shed, and they all staggered back. Pieces of the fiery shed sailed through the night sky. Some landed on the roof of the house, still burning. The wooden shingles caught fire almost immediately.

Harve had to be restrained from going into the house,

and the man who held him back was Briana's brother, Larry. He rasped, "Damn it, Harve, I'm sick as a dog, and I don't want to wrestle you. Settle down!"

Inga stood, weeping into her hands. Queenie, her tail between her legs, came whining to Harve and tried to lick his dangling, helpless hand. Harve wanted to be like Inga, to cover his eyes and not see what was happening. Something else in the shed exploded, and more fire rained on his house. The whole roof seemed ablaze.

Harve knew how hard it was to fight a fire in cold this intense. The water would freeze almost as fast as it came out of the hoses. He shook his head in dazed disbelief. "My house," he said. "Where will we go?"

Larry gripped him more tightly. "You'll come stay with us. That's what neighbors are for."

"WHAT DO YOU MEAN, they've come to *live* with you?" Josh demanded.

He'd been hoping to be with Briana tonight, but not this way.

Briana stood in the upstairs bathroom, the door open. She hadn't bothered taking off her jacket. She was filling an overnight bag with extra shampoo, toothpaste and other personal supplies.

She stopped and met Josh's disapproving eyes. "Josh, they've had a fire. Where else could they go? They're our neighbors."

Uncharitably Josh thought, *Don't they have any other neighbors? Does he have to move in practically on top of the woman I love?*

"Did the house burn all the way down?" he asked, leaning against the door frame, watching her.

"Not completely," she said, reaching for a bottle of lotion. "But they couldn't save much."

"Did the roof cave in?"

"Most of it," she said. "And I guess most of the upper story's gone."

"But does he still actually *have* a house?"

She gave him an impatient look. "Not really. Maybe there's enough to save. I don't know. Larry tried to explain, but he had a coughing fit. I got what I know from Glenda, and she didn't know details."

"But he's got possessions?" Josh asked, hoping against hope.

She put a fist on her hip. "I doubt it. Whatever's there has water and smoke damage. They really need help, Josh. Please don't begrudge it."

But Josh did begrudge it. There was Briana, all rosy-cheeked and agitated and full of kindly sympathy—for Harve. And his meddling aunt.

"How long will they stay?" Josh asked. To him it was as if Leo's farm was suddenly teeming with Oldmans, dozens of them, not simply two.

Her eyes flashed. "Good grief, don't tell me you're jealous. How petty—they may have lost everything."

"I'm not jealous," lied Josh, feeling the very incisors of the green-eyed monster sinking into his heart.

She moved past him to go to the linen closet in the hall. "I suppose I should take some extra towels," she said. "They're both covered with smoke. Oh, this is awful." She began to stack towels and washcloths on the sink. "Harve has hardly any clothes," she said almost to herself. "I guess he can wear some of Daddy's for now."

Great, seethed Josh. *Harve's going to be in Daddy's house, wearing Daddy's clothes and chasing Daddy's girl.*

"Can Harve eat by himself?" Josh asked sarcastically. "Or will you sit by his bedside and spoon peeled grapes into his mouth?"

She threw down the last towel and glared at him. "What is *wrong* with you?" she demanded. "Are you so devoid of human compassion that you'd deny a neighbor shelter for the night?"

"I'm sorry they had a fire," Josh said without emotion. "That's big of you."

"But when you phoned me, you said it was a little fire."

"I said it was a little fire that might spread. That's what Glenda told me when Larry got the call. And it did spread."

Josh sighed harshly. His first hint that something was wrong had been when he heard Larry squealing out of his drive as if all the devils in hell were chasing him. His second hint was the wail of sirens in the night.

Then Briana had phoned him from Leo's, breathless, saying the volunteer fire department had been called, that there was a fire at the Oldmans'. She'd said it was an outbuilding and hoped it wouldn't be more. Nealie had awakened, frightened by the keening fire trucks so nearby, and Josh had to go to her. He had told her there was only a small fire and the volunteers had gone to put it out.

He'd convinced himself it was the truth. He wished neither Harve nor his aunt harm. He didn't want them hurt, he didn't want the house to burn down, he did not wish so much as one scrap of their possessions to be scorched by a spark.

But he'd been flabbergasted when Larry's van had returned, followed by Harve's truck. Then Briana had phoned again, saying Harve and his aunt would be staying with Leo, and she didn't know for how long.

Now, Briana was in her own home like a delivering angel, but it wasn't Josh she had come to deliver. No, instead she was madly securing supplies to comfort his rival.

"Let me get this straight," Josh said from between his teeth. "You're staying with your father, and so are Inga and Harve. I am exiled down here, like I'm back in Siberia."

"No, you're not," she said. "Inga and I will stay with Poppa tonight. Harve's coming down to stay with you."

"*What?*" Josh practically howled.

She put both hands on her hips. "You're a logical man. Poppa is sick. He has three bedrooms and a lumpy old couch. Inga will stay in the guest room, and I'll stay in the room nobody ever uses. Harve can come down here to sleep on the couch. Mine is comfortable.''

''But *I* sleep on your couch.''

She gave him a long, quizzical stare. ''Why?''

He gestured toward the bedroom. ''Because I can't stand to sleep in our bed—your bed alone.''

''If you don't want it, then let Harve use it,'' she retorted.

''No. He might get to like it,'' Josh said.

She made a sound of displeasure. ''Sleep in it or let him. The poor man's exhausted.''

''Why can't you come home?'' he asked. ''Let him stay with your father? Your father's crazy about him. I'm not.''

She ran her fingers through her hair in frustration. ''You and I can't sleep under the same roof. How would that look?''

''You and I are going to have a baby together. How's that going to look? Am I never going to see you alone again except in a laboratory?''

Nealie's door swung open with a creak. She appeared in the hallway, struggling to get her glasses on straight. Her hair was mussed, and one pajama leg was hiked up to her knee.

She looked at them sleepily. ''What's going on?''

Josh watched as Briana's face changed. All trace of frustration and anger drained away. Her expression grew tender. She said, ''Honey, I'm sorry. Did we wake you?''

''No,'' said Nealie. ''I had to go potty. Then I heard you talking. Is something wrong?''

Briana licked her lips. ''There was a fire over at the Oldman farm.''

Nealie used her bare foot to push down her scrunched pajama leg. She yawned. ''That's what Daddy said. Is everything okay?''

''There was some damage,'' Briana said vaguely. ''They can't sleep in their house tonight. So Harve is coming here to stay with you and Daddy, and his aunt's coming to stay with Grandpa and me.''

Nealie seemed too sleepy to question the arrangement. But she showed concern. "Is Harve all right?"

Briana nodded. "Yes. A little shaken up, but not hurt. Not a bit."

"How's his aunt?"

"Exactly the same," said Briana. "Not hurt at all."

"Uncle Larry? He went with the firemen? He's okay?"

"He's fine, too."

"That's good," said Nealie and yawned again. She hobbled down the hall to the bathroom and went inside.

Briana threw Josh an accusing glance. "Did you see that? She's only six, but she asked how everyone *is*. She, at least, shows some concern."

Josh looked away, disgusted by the situation, disgusted by himself. He supposed he was a selfish bastard.

But he loved Briana. He wanted her. And it seemed not only her family, but the whole community was closing around her like a possessive fist he could never pry open.

"I'm sorry," he said.

She looked at the towels. "I'll set these aside for Harve. You know where more are."

"Yeah," he said. "I know where everything is. I remember."

They heard Nealie flush the toilet. The child opened the door and lurched to her bedroom, seeming already half-asleep again. "Night, everybody," she called.

"Good night," they said, almost together.

"I'll go kiss her," Briana said.

"She'll be asleep by the time her head hits the pillow," said Josh.

"I don't care, I want to kiss her anyway."

He watched as she went down the hall.

Tonight he would share the house with Harve. He hated the idea, but he would do it with no more complaint.

But by all that was holy, *he* was going to sleep in Briana's bed. Even if it killed him.

INGA SAT, DAZED, on the edge of the bed in the guest room. She wore one of Leo's old bathrobes.

Briana had made her take the guest room because the other bedroom was neglected, used mostly for storage. Inga had been through too much to sleep in the worst bed in the house, surrounded by boxes and cobwebs.

Briana gave her the clean towels and the night case. "I brought you a nightgown in case you need one," she said to the older woman.

Inga nodded and stared at the floor. "Harve's going to your place?"

"Yes," Briana said. She had already sent him on his way. He seemed in shock, not yet fully comprehending what had happened.

"Poor Harve," Inga said, shaking her head. Her hair was wet from the shower, she wore no makeup, and her shoulders slumped. Tonight she looked all of her years and no longer in control of her fate or anyone else's.

"That farm has memories for me," Inga murmured. "I grew up there. But I left when I was eighteen. I've had other homes. It's the only place Harve's ever known."

Briana searched for words of comfort. "Larry—my brother—says maybe there's less damage than it seems."

Inga was not consoled. "More than a building makes a home. There are possessions, too. Most of mine are safe. I put them in storage until I could decide where I'm going to settle down. But so many of Harve's things—his mother's furniture, the pictures she hung on the wall, her china—the things he's known from childhood."

"Maybe some will be all right," Briana offered. But she did not know, she could only hope.

"You probably think I'm a silly old woman," said Inga, twisting her fingers. "And that I'm feeling sorry for myself. I admit it, I am. It was frightening."

"It must have been," Briana said. "I'm sorry you had to go through it."

"Ah," Inga said with a sigh, "I'll bounce back. I always

do. It's just I feel so bad for Harve. If you could have seen the look on his face when your brother held him back from going in that house again—''

Briana was glad she hadn't.

A tear spilled down Inga's cheek, and she wiped it away as if angry at herself for shedding it. ''No. I'm not the one suffering tonight,'' she said. ''It's Harve. Home is everything to him. I never in my life met a man that loved home so much.''

Briana nodded stiffly. She said good-night and went to the spare room. It smelled of must and dust, but she put on her nightshirt and crawled between the sheets. She lay in the darkness and wished Josh, whom she loved, was a man who knew how to love a home.

THE NEXT MORNING, Briana threw on her clothes and made her way downstairs, anxious to get to her house and Nealie. She was not nearly as eager to see how Josh and Harve had gotten on as housemates.

Inga was already up, looking fatigued but much closer to her usual self. Her pewter hair was sculpted, her blue slacks and sweater clean, if a bit wrinkled, and she was polishing the oven as if her life depended on it.

''It's work that makes life tolerable,'' Inga said briskly. She yanked open a drawer that held a cluttered heap of pots and pans. ''My goodness, it looks like your poppa hasn't organized anything in here in years.''

''He hasn't let anybody touch it since my mother died,'' Briana said.

Inga whirled to face her, her cheeks flaring pink, apology in her eyes. ''Oh, my dear—I'm sorry. I'm practically a stranger to you, and here I am, pawing through your family things.''

Conflicting feelings surged through Briana, but she did not let them show. ''No,'' she said. ''If Poppa will let you do it, that's fine. It needs to be done.''

That was true. The job needed doing. The kitchen was

no longer the bright and orderly one her mother had run. It had fallen into such sad disarray it no longer seemed like the same room.

Inga brightened and turned to the drawer. "I'm letting your poppa sleep after all that turmoil last night."

"That's good, too," Briana said.

"I'm making salmon on toast for his breakfast. Won't you and Nealie and Mr. Morris join us? I'll call Harve, and he can bring them up."

"No, thanks," Briana said, "I want to spend at least a little time at home with Nealie. Things have been so hectic lately."

Inga sighed philosophically. "I suppose you want to see Mr. Morris, too. After all, he doesn't get here very often."

Briana went cold. She felt ambushed by the remark. "He gets here quite a bit, really," she said. "Tell Poppa I'll see him when I get back from St. Louis."

"Drive carefully, dear," Inga said, rearranging pans. But Briana was already out the kitchen door and at the hall closet, pulling out her jacket. Inga, she fumed, could seem as sweet as a fairy godmother, but she could also slip a poisonous comment into a conversation with neatness and ease.

She was still fuming when she reached her house, but Nealie met her at the door and flung herself at Briana, hugging her around the knees. "Mommy—you're home. I don't like it when you're gone all night."

"I don't like being gone, either, sugarplum," Briana said, kissing her. "Whoa! Look at you. You're still in your bathrobe. You need to get dressed for school. Better hurry. We're running late."

"Daddy's got my clothes all laid out. He helped me blow-dry my hair."

"Your hair looks lovely," Briana said, smoothing it. "Where is Daddy?"

"In the downstairs bathroom. I'll call him. Daddy! Mommy's home."

"Now scamper," Briana said. "Get dressed. I'll fix a quick breakfast."

Nealie ran up the stairs in her slippers shaped like bear's feet, then disappeared into her room. Briana was hanging up her jacket when the bathroom door swung open.

Josh strode into the living room wearing only a blue towel around his waist. He was barefoot, and his damp hair slanted across his forehead. He hadn't shaved.

He stopped and put his fists on his hips, looking her up and down with his head cocked at a derisive angle.

She blinked in surprise. It had been years since she had seen him so nearly naked. He was pale from the long Russian winter, but his skin had a natural gold tone that kept it from whiteness.

She'd forgotten the power of his legs, the leanness of his waist, the squareness and width of his shoulders. He had muscles he'd built in arduous work in jungle and tundra and mountains, not at any gym.

She saw the familiar scars that had always frightened her because they signified the dangers of his past. She saw new ones that frightened her more because they symbolized his present and his future.

"Ah," he said out of the corner of his mouth. "The lady of the house. You've decided to come home. Welcome."

"Where are your clothes?" she asked, unable to take her eyes from him.

"Mostly in the dryer," he said. "I had one clean set left. I loaned them to Harve."

For the first time, she noticed the familiar thump-thump of the clothes dryer running. "Don't you have a robe?" she asked.

"No. Do you want me to wear one of yours?"

"No." She tried not to stare at the ropy sinews of his arms, the hardness of his abs. With great willpower, she turned and moved toward the kitchen, but his image stayed burned into her mind. She said, "Where's Harve?"

He followed her. He smelled like minty soap, the way he

used to smell when he climbed into bed with her. "Harve? He's in the upstairs bathroom, using my shaving cream and shaving with my razor."

"Your generosity is astounding," she said, plucking the pancake mix out of the cupboard. "Can't you put on *something?* Nealie will see you."

"Nealie's seen me in less than this. We went swimming together last summer. This towel covers more than my trunks, for God's sake."

He leaned against the counter, standing too near her for comfort. She could see the mist of water droplets glistening in his chest hair.

"Harve will see you, then," she argued. With a clatter, she yanked a skillet from the oven drawer and smacked it on a stove burner.

He crossed his arms, which made his biceps swell. "So Harve sees me? So what?"

"It just isn't—seemly, you walking around like that," she retorted, swinging open the refrigerator door and snatching eggs, milk, the package of sausage. "It looks— too intimate."

"What am I supposed to do? Wear a blanket like *I'm* the disaster victim? He's the one whose house burned down."

"How are you going to take Nealie to school if you have no clothes?"

"My clothes will be dry by then. We've got half an hour."

He watched as she cracked the eggs, poured the milk, and began to stir furiously. "Ha," he said. "I know what it is. The sight of my manly body fills you with lust. You can barely contain yourself. You want to throw me on the counter and have your way with me among the place mats."

"I'd like to throw you out the door and into a snow-drift," she said between her teeth.

"Your loss," he said, almost idly.

Upstairs the bathroom door creaked. "Hark," Josh said, lifting an eyebrow. "Little Merry Sunshine approaches."

Briana looked up. Almost timidly Harve came out of the bathroom. He met no one's eyes. He stared downward as he descended the stairs.

He was clean-shaven but had a large nick on his chin. His wet hair was slicked to his head. He wore Josh's jeans, which were too short and came halfway up his shins. He had on Josh's sweater, which bulged over his midsection and left his wrists dangling nakedly from the sleeves.

He moved with funereal slowness, and Briana felt uncomfortable gazing on him in such a miserable state. She tried to turn her attention to fixing breakfast, but she kept stealing furtive looks.

"Hi, Harve," Josh said personably, still leaning against the counter, arms crossed over his bare chest. "Feeling better?"

Harve gave him a look that clearly said, *Do you always hang around half-naked like this?*

Harve's eyes were bloodshot, whether from smoke or sorrow, Briana could not say. She turned and gave him a quick, stiff smile. "Good morning, Harve. I hope things look a little brighter by the light of day. Your aunt's awake and making salmon on toast. She says to come on up—or you're welcome to stay here and have breakfast with us, if you want."

Josh shot her a killing look. She tried to ignore him.

Harve sat down heavily at the counter. "I hate salmon."

Briana worked to keep her smile in place. "We're having pancakes and sausage. Want to join us? Would you like a cup of coffee?"

"Coffee might help," Harve said without looking up. "I don't eat big breakfasts. They make me burp."

Josh gave a small cough and covered his mouth.

Briana tried again. "Is there something special I could make you?" she asked. "I'm probably not the cook your aunt is, but I'll try—"

"Cornflakes," Harve said in a tone of dejection. "I just

wish I had my cornflakes. In my own bowl. With my regular spoon. At my own table.''

Josh coughed again. Briana's mind spun with the irony of her situation. "I can't do anything about your bowl or spoon or table, Harve, but cornflakes I can give you."

He nodded morosely. Briana poured the cornflakes, filled the bowl with milk, put out the sugar bowl, gave Harve a napkin and spoon, flipped a pancake, then poked the sausages with a fork.

Nobody said anything. Briana listened to the sausages sizzle, the clothes dryer whir, and to Harve crunching relentlessly on his cornflakes. He nodded when she asked if she could fill his bowl a second time.

She juggled all her tasks while Josh watched and Harve went crunch, crunch, crunch.

"I'd offer to help," Josh said, "but I remember this kitchen. Two people can't work in it without bumping into each other. We'd be jammed so close it'd practically be indecent."

If Harve noticed the remark, he didn't show it. He stared sadly at nothing in particular and kept up his melancholy crunching.

The dryer stopped, and Briana's heart soared in relief. She told Josh, "If you want to help, get your clothes and get dressed."

He shrugged, went to the dryer, gathered an armful of clothes and disappeared into the bathroom.

Harve, still the picture of gloom, said nothing. He kept shoveling cornflakes into his mouth like an automaton. She filled the bowl again.

She said, "I suppose you'll want to go to your place and see how things are. And you'll want Inga to be with you. I'm sure Josh would sit with Poppa for a few hours."

"I don't want Inga with me," Harve said, not looking at Briana. "I don't want anybody with me. Unless you'd go, I'd rather be alone."

Briana felt helpless. She picked up the coffeepot. "I'm

sorry, Harve. I can't. I have to go to St. Louis. I just *have* to. It's another doctor's appointment.''

He paused, staring at the unfamiliar spoon. "You couldn't change it?"

"No," she said softly. "I really, really can't.''

She felt truly sorry for him, but she knew what he had lost was material. She thought of Nealie and Nealie's illness and knew she would sacrifice every possession she owned to make the child well.

Just to say something, she said, "Is the coffee okay? Want more?''

Harve shook his head, still in his private mourning. "It's weak," he said. "No more.''

The downstairs bathroom opened. Josh sauntered out in jeans and the faded lone wolf sweatshirt. At the same moment, Nealie burst out of her door, wearing her school clothes.

She ran down the stairs, and Josh caught her up and carried her, giggling, to the kitchen counter. He set her in the chair next to Harve, and Briana set a filled plate before her.

Nealie looked at her plate, her parents, then Harve. "Isn't this fun, Harve?" she asked. "Everybody's here. It's like you came to a sleepover at my house. Are you staying again tonight?''

Harve didn't answer. He stared at nothing in particular.

"For fun, we could all change places," Nealie said, digging into her pancakes. "Mommy could sleep with me. Or you could sleep with Daddy, and Mommy could have my bed, and Zorro and I could sleep on the couch. Or you could have my bed, and Mommy and Daddy could sleep together.''

She paused and smiled brightly. "That way they could make me a baby sister.''

Harve turned slowly and stared at her, as if she were a small, loquacious Martian who had suddenly materialized next to him. Josh stared at her, too, and so did Briana, embarrassed beyond words.

Nealie gripped her fork and looked at them all in righteous bewilderment. "Why's everybody looking at me?" she demanded. "What did *I* say?"

JOSH WALKED BRIANA to her truck. At its door, he took her by the arm and looked down at her. "Look," he said. "You've got to get Harve out of here. There are too many people around us. You and I need time alone together—it can't go on like this."

She looked at him, her dark eyes full of regret and confusion. "What can I do? Travel back in time and keep the fire from starting? Cast a magic spell and make a guest house appear? What do you want?"

"I want to be with you, talk to you, work things out."

"Let me go," she said. "I'll be late for my appointment, and Nealie'll be late for school. And here comes Penny's car."

"Penny," he said in frustration. "Good grief, it's like living in Grand Central Station."

Penny's car pulled up beside them, and Penny rolled down her window. "Hey," she said in concern. "I heard about the fire last night. Are Harve and his aunt okay?"

"They're here," Briana said, disengaging her arm from Josh's grasp. "Inga's up at the house with Poppa. Harve's inside. I think everything's going to be all right."

"Gee, I hope so," Penny said. "Is it okay if I go in?"

"Yes, fine," Briana said. "I'll see you later, Penny. You, too, Josh."

Josh had no choice but to watch Briana go. The truck disappeared down the lane, just as it had yesterday and would again tomorrow. The clinic was monitoring her with extraordinary vigilance because of the rarity of Yates's anemia.

He muttered, repeating his own words, "You and I need time alone together—it can't go on like this."

But the wind rose, sweeping his words away, out over the frozen land. It was as if the elements mocked him, saying, "Yes, it will go on like this, and you will never have her. She belongs to this place and these people and not you. Never you."

CHAPTER THIRTEEN

HARVE STOOD ALONE in the freezing wind, looking at his house.

It had taken him a long time to work up the courage to come. Inga had called, saying she would get someone to stay with Leo, that she would go to the house with him.

But Inga always tried to put a bright face on things, and he did not want that, not now. The only person he would have wanted with him was Briana, but she had said no. He and his home were not as important to her as a trip to St. Louis. Penny had tried to offer her sympathies, but he hadn't wanted them. After Briana's refusal, he wanted to be alone with his grief.

When he drove up to the house, he could not get out of his truck. He sat and stared at the damage, his mind dulled with shock and dread.

Where the shed had stood was only a blackened concrete foundation, covered with rubble and ash. It glistened under a thick glaze of ice, as if all the burning was encased in crystal.

The house, when he managed to look at it, seemed at once both ruined and impossibly beautiful. The roof had caved in, and most of the second story was gone. The outside of the first story was blackened, its windows empty sockets. But it, too, was almost completely covered with cascades of ice, a house out of a frozen fairy tale.

At last he found the courage to get out, walk around the house again and again. Then he went to the front door and found it blackened and knocked from its hinges. Gingerly he stepped inside.

Smoke still hung in the air. Everything stank of it. The living room was chaos. Most of the ceiling had caved in. Furniture had been knocked topsy-turvy and covered by rubble.

It was as bad as he expected. Yet here and there he saw the glint of something salvageable—a cast-iron lamp base, a plant stand of wrought iron, a brass picture frame.

He feared what the other rooms held. He wandered down the hall like a ghost. He was so lost in his thoughts and memories, he didn't hear the car drive up or footsteps on the sagging porch.

He stood in the kitchen, which was the greatest mess, for the firemen had burst in that way with their axes and hoses and extinguishers. He stood in the midst of the rubble, staring at the charred table lying sideways on the floor. Dishes had been rattled out of the cupboards and lay broken and mixed with bits of the partly fallen ceiling.

A woman's voice, said, "Hello, Harve. Are you okay?"

Briana! Harve thought, spinning to face her. *She had come after all!* But instead, there stood Penny in her green jacket and cap. Her hands were jammed into her pockets, her emerald eyes serious.

"What are you doing here?" he asked, disappointed and puzzled.

"It's my lunch hour," she said. "I wanted to see how you were."

He shook his head and looked around him. He made a helpless gesture. "I'm grateful anything's still standing," he said, his throat tight. "But it can't be saved. I'll have to salvage what I can, pull it down and rebuild. But—but I don't even know where to start."

Penny looked him square in the eye. "It doesn't matter *where*. Just start." She picked up a large metal trash can that had been knocked over and set it up right. She knelt and began gathering broken crockery and throwing it into the container. For a moment, Harve watched her without comprehension.

Then she examined something and said, "Look. This isn't broken. Here." She handed it to him. It was his cereal bowl. He could have kissed her.

AT FIVE MINUTES to one, Briana's downstairs phone rang. Josh leaped for it, hoping it was Briana saying she was on her way home. It wasn't. It was Penny.

Her usually brisk voice was hesitant. "Hi," she said. "I'm calling from Harve's place."

"His phone's working?" Josh asked. He felt a sense of loss that the caller wasn't Briana.

"No, I'm on my cell phone," Penny said. "Listen, I know this is irregular, because there's a lot of work in the office today. But do you think that Briana would care if I stayed over here awhile and helped?"

He knew Briana would be there herself if she could. "Stay as long as you want," Josh said. "Is it bad?"

"Yeah," said Penny. "Almost a total loss. But we've just got to roll up our sleeves and get to work."

He had to admire the spirit in her voice. She sounded determined and undaunted.

When he hung up, he looked around Briana's cheerful living room. It seemed so empty without her and Nealie that he couldn't stand it. An unbearable restlessness filled him.

He made a single phone call, and then he left.

Fifteen minutes later, he pulled up to the fire-stricken house and sucked in his breath at the damage. He'd seen worse, far worse in his time. He'd seen whole city blocks that had been destroyed, by malice, not accident.

But this was more personal. He threw his parka in the back seat, grabbed a pair of work gloves he'd found on Briana's back porch and strode up the front stairs of the Oldman homestead.

He found Harve and Penny in what was left of the

kitchen, hard at work. Josh rapped at the fire-scarred frame of the door.

Penny's eyes widened. Harve looked at him in disbelief. "You! What do you want?"

Josh pulled on the work gloves. "I came to help," he said.

BRIANA PULLED INTO her drive just as Josh did in his rental car, back from picking up Nealie at school. She grinned to see Nealie come out of the car in a tumble of skinny arms and legs and run toward her. Briana hopped from the truck, picked up her daughter and hugged her. "Hello, sugarplum. How was school today?"

"I got an A on my spelling test," Nealie said, her arms around Briana's neck. "And the teacher's reading us a book on George Washington 'cause it's almost his birthday."

"Happy birthday, dear George." Briana laughed, then she sniffed at Nealie's hair. "I swear," Briana said, drawing back to look at the child. "You smell a little smoky."

"Oh, that's Daddy," Nealie said, clambering from her mother's arms. "He's just *stinky*."

Josh climbed out of his car. His face and neck were filthy with soot, his jeans and sweatshirt permeated with ashes and dirt. A blackened pair of work gloves stuck out of his rear pocket.

Briana blinked in amazement. "What happened to *you?*"

"I've been over at Harve's," he said without emotion.

"You?" Briana asked, astonished. *"Helping?"*

"Trying to," he said in the same tone. "I'm not much of a handyman."

Nealie danced up the steps. "Daddy says he's not a handyman, but he's got a strong back. He's strong all over. I bet he has Harve's house all fixed by tomorrow."

Josh fell into step beside Briana. She looked at him. Even his ears were sooty, and he had a black streak across one cheekbone. "Can things be fixed soon?" she asked. "Really?'' She hoped so not only for Harve's sake, but for hers and Josh's, as well.

But Josh shook his head. ''No. It's going to have to be torn down. He'll have to rebuild. It's going to take at least a week to clean up the mess.''

''Oh.'' It was all Briana could say. She unlocked the front door and Nealie flew inside, calling for Zorro the cat. Briana and Josh followed, but he stopped at the rug in the entryway, kicking off his wet boots. ''I'm dirty. Let me clean up. Then can we talk?''

Nealie was going upstairs, cradling Zorro in her arms, crooning him a nonsensical song. Briana stared after her, not wanting to meet Josh's eyes.

Josh said, ''I asked if we could talk.''

''I should go see Poppa.''

''You should also lay down the law and tell him that you're staying in your own house tonight. Harve can go up there and stay. Enough is enough. You and I have to talk.''

''I know,'' she said. ''I'll try to wrangle some time for us. But I need to stay at Poppa's just another night or two—''

''Briana,'' Josh said, warning in his voice, ''this is ridiculous. There's no damn reason for Harve to sleep down here.''

''Poppa's still nervous about being alone at night,'' Briana said. ''He feels safer with me there. Now, with all this other commotion...''

Josh frowned in disgust. ''You don't want to *chance* being alone with me too much, do you? Why? Afraid you might decide you really do care for me still? More than you want to admit?''

An involuntary shudder quaked through her. Perhaps what he said was true. She let Leo manipulate her because it was safer than trusting herself alone with Josh.

She put her hand to her forehead. ''Look, my whole life seems crazy right now. I'm being shot full of these hormone cocktails until I can't think straight—maybe I do feel safer at Poppa's. I don't even know anymore.''

He took a step toward her, reached to touch her shoulder. She flinched at the anticipation of his touch, which she both desired and feared.

He saw her reaction and let his hand drop to his side. ''Okay, Briana. I understand. You're like Alice in Wonderland right now. If you think you need to stay with your father a while longer—do what makes you feel best. But I do want some time with you tonight.''

She smiled with relief. ''You understand?''

His expression was far from happy. ''I think I do. You'd better go now if you have to see Poppa.''

He said *Poppa* with sarcasm, but she ignored it. ''I'll run up there while you shower and Nealie changes,'' she said. She hesitated, then added, ''I'm proud of you for helping Harve. I really am.''

He shrugged, his brow furrowed. ''Penny started it. She went over during her lunch hour. She called to see if she could stay and help. I figured you'd let her.''

''Of course,'' Briana said. She had a sudden impulse to touch his rugged face, to wipe the dirt from his upper lip with her fingertips.

He gave her an ironic smile. ''Your brother showed up a little later, even though he's got that god-awful cold. Then some other people. Most of them are still working.''

''You and Larry and Harve working together?'' she said, still yearning to touch him. ''You must have made a strange team.''

''Yeah,'' he said. ''We did.''

LEO LEANED BACK in his recliner, holding the television remote control as if it were his scepter. ''When's Nealie going to come see me?'' he demanded. ''I miss my little Funnyface.''

''I'll bring her later tonight,'' Briana said. She sat on the sofa, clutching a fringed pillow. ''She can stay for a while and watch a video with you. Josh and I have things to discuss—about her future.''

Leo's white eyebrows rose suspiciously, like a pair of arching caterpillars. ''Her future? What things? College? That's a long way off.''

''Just things, Poppa,'' Briana said. ''But now let's talk about you. How do you feel today?''

''Worried,'' Leo retorted.

Briana hugged the pillow against her stomach more tightly. She realized it was as if she was trying to protect the child she prayed would soon be inside her. ''Worried about what?''

''You and these shots. Your brother and his cold. Harve and Inga,'' Leo said. ''Harve's sick about that house. He doesn't know which way to turn. I wish I was in shape. I could take charge. Your uncle Collin and I built that house of yours from the ground up.''

Briana nodded dutifully, although she knew that Uncle Collin had done most of the work.

''I worry about Inga, too,'' Leo said, lowering his voice to a dramatic whisper. ''I caught her drying her eyes once. Oh, she pretends she's cheerful, but she's got a tender heart, she has.''

Briana nodded again, clutching her pillow.

Leo said, ''Grief just seems to make her work harder. Notice this room? She really brightened it up. She's got a gift for that kind of thing.''

Briana had to agree—Leo's house was starting to look homey again. She was about to say so, but at that moment Inga entered, bringing two china cups and saucers on a tray.

''Hello,'' Inga said with a sort of stoic breeziness. ''How are you, Briana? Feeling better? I hope these trips to the doctor are helping. I've brought you both some nice herbal tea.'' She set down the tray and handed each of them a cup.

Briana murmured thank you, but Leo looked askance at the tea. ''This herbal stuff again? I'd rather have coffee.''

''Too much caffeine isn't good for your heart, you know

that,'' Inga said with a smile. "You need to mind the doctor and change your habits. Your loved ones want you to be around for a long time. Isn't that right, Briana?''

"Yes," Briana said. "I want you to take care of yourself, Poppa.''

"Oh, I don't want to leave this old earth yet," Leo said. "I have a farm and a family to take care of—and my neighbors.'' He beamed at Inga. "I have other plans, too. Another greenhouse. My newsletter. Inga, I must show you my newsletter.''

"I'm sure it's fascinating," said Inga. "Harve's told me how incisive your thoughts are on genetic engineering. He's pretty much decided not to just dabble in organic farming, but to go over to it full-time.''

"He's spoken of it." Leo nodded with pleasure and satisfaction.

Inga steepled her fingers and looked thoughtful. "Maybe good can come of this tragedy. Maybe he'll not only change the house, but the whole farm. To be more like yours. You're kind of an idol to him, you know.''

Leo shrugged modestly. "Hmph. Well, I guess I've taught him a thing or two along the way.''

Briana put aside her tea, barely tasted. "I have to be going. I'm getting behind, with all these trips to the city.''

Inga looked stricken. "Oh, don't go yet. Harve should be back soon—it's starting to get dark. Stay and talk to him, Briana. I'm sure you'd be a comfort to him.''

"I'm sure you'll be better," Briana said. "You're family. I'm not. I don't mean to be unneighborly, but I have things I have to do. I'll bring Nealie in a little while.''

She rose and put on her jacket, which she had flung over the arm of the sofa. Leo looked unhappy at her departure. "You just got here. I've been waiting all day to see you. You'll be back again to stay tonight?''

Briana hesitated, then nodded, feeling strangely guilty. "Yes. After I take Nealie home, I'll come back to spend the night. But I can't keep doing it, Poppa. When Harve feels more settled, he can take the spare room. I'll tidy it up for him.''

"Oh, my dear," Inga said brightly, "I've already cleaned it and rearranged it—for you. Your poppa wants you to be as comfortable as possible."

My Poppa wants to control me as much as possible, Briana thought, irritation rising. "Only a few nights more," she said. "I mean it."

Inga, standing behind Leo, must have seen the sparks stirring in Briana's eyes. She looked at Briana with kindly sternness and shook her head. Her expression clearly said, *Don't say anything to upset your father. It's not good for him.*

Briana knew that look well. She had seen it on her mother's face a thousand times. She had grown up with it. It was household law to defer to Poppa, to cosset and never upset him.

She had only violated that law once, with Josh. She was about to do it again. Her emotions spun like a whirligig, and she didn't know if it was the situation, the hormones or both.

"We'll talk about it later," she said with a calmness she didn't feel.

NEALIE DIDN'T WANT to go to Leo's.

Tears rose in her hazel eyes. The sight of them made Josh's heart tighten painfully, as if pinched in a vise.

"Mommy, I don't *want* to go to Grandpa's. I want to stay here with you and Daddy. It's hardly ever just the three of us."

"Your grandfather wants to see you," Briana explained, smoothing the girl's hair. "And I have to go to the greenhouses and work. I'm way behind on the plants."

So after supper, they drove Nealie to Leo's. She went reluctantly, carrying her video of *Beauty and the Beast.* Josh, his heart constricted, watched Briana walk their daughter to Leo's door.

When she got back into the truck, she said nothing, and neither did he. They drove in silence to the oldest greenhouse. "I have seedlings to repot," she said. "We can talk while I work. You can help if you want."

The greenhouse was warm and humid, fragrant with the scent of fertile potting soil. The shelves were full of trays of young plants, delicate and green, just starting to flourish. In the silence, they seemed to be breathing almost perceptibly, and they gave the air a strange, secretive liveliness.

Josh watched her wet the fine transplanting soil, set out the stacks of new pots, swing a tray of seedlings from a shelf on to the worktable. She plunged her hand into the soil bucket and brought up a palmful that she deftly patted into a medium-size black plastic container.

She gave him a nervous smile. "It's kind of fun. Like playing in mud."

He tried to follow suit. He wondered if she wanted them both to have their hands in the moist black earth so they would not be tempted to touch each other. She had worn a white T-shirt, as if to ward off any contact.

Josh's fingers were awkward on the fragile stems, the sensitive root balls. And Briana was clearly on edge. He knew her being flooded with hormones didn't help.

For days he had wanted to be alone with her for more than a few stolen seconds. He wanted to talk, but he felt tongue-tied. He had things to ask her and tell her, difficult things, and he did not know where to start.

At last, to break the silence, he said, "Why do you keep repotting these things? They look fine the way they are."

She firmed the soil in the bottom of another container. "To build the root system." She tipped a tomato seedling from a smaller pot into the palm of her left hand. "See this? The plant's small, but its roots are already crowded. It wants more room."

He lifted an eyebrow. "But then the same thing happens. You do it again and again."

"Of course," she said, concentrating on settling the roots

in their new home. "Tomatoes *love* to be repotted. Each time they'll grow bigger roots. The stronger the root, the better the plant. By the time these are ready to go into the ground, they'll have terrific root systems—not like those dinky little plants you see for sale most places in the spring."

"Seems like a lot of work," he grumbled.

"Good, strong roots are worth it," she said.

He looked at her, the fine-featured profile, the beautiful mouth tense with concentration.

"Good, strong roots," he said. "You believe that goes for people, not just plants."

She looked at him, and her eyes were sad. "For some people."

"People like you," he said. He thought, *She's known this greenhouse, these smells, these sights, the feel of the soil from childhood. Just as Nealie already knows them.*

She said, "People like me. Yes, I suppose." She turned and took another handful of soil.

He reached for another handful himself. He wasn't afraid of dirt. But he wasn't used to treating it with reverence, either. "And then there are people like me. Who live without roots."

She packed fresh soil around the transplanted seedling to its lowest leaves. "It's hard for people like me to understand people like you."

"And vice-versa," he said, stealing another sidelong glance at her. She'd wiped her cheek and left a dark smear of dirt along the delicate line of her jaw. He wanted to wipe it away, but his hands were as dirty as hers. He thought of kissing it away.

No. He couldn't be swept that way again. Their time was running low. Too much was happening too fast, and nothing physical was possible between them. She was terrified of an accidental pregnancy.

He took a deep breath and said, "Today when I went to Harve's—"

"It was very good of you to do that," she said. "It really was."

"No. I didn't go out of a kindly, charitable impulse. I went so *I* wouldn't feel like a turd."

She gave him a small smile. "I'll give you credit for your actions, not your motives."

He shook his head, troubled. "Don't give me credit for anything. Other people came, too."

"That's what neighbors do," she said. She said it with the simple sincerity that could turn him inside out.

"I saw that," he told her. "They came and they helped because he was one of them. They're all like him. They've all got—roots."

She frowned. "I don't understand what you mean."

"I worked with them," he said. "But I wasn't one of them. I could feel it. And I knew I'd never be one of them."

"Oh." Was there disappointment in her voice, or did he only imagine it? She carefully transferred another seedling, its roots as fine as cobwebs.

He said, "It's how I used to feel when I'd try to fit in with your father and brother. I don't belong. It's like I'm a different breed."

Softly she tamped down the soil to secure the plant, to keep it steady and nurtured. "You are a different breed. We—my family and I—we're tame. We're the hot house-plants. You flourish in the wild."

"But I love you."

The words leaped from his mouth as if they had a life and will of their own. His heart slammed in his chest, crazed by his foolishness.

Her pretty face was sad. "I—I care for you, too. Deeply. But what good does that do?"

He started to reach out to her, then saw his hand, mud-died to the wrist, and drew it back. He gripped the table instead.

He said, "I look at you—" He stopped, swallowed. "I

look at you and I want you. I want to have another baby with you. And maybe even another.''

''Babies need fathers,'' she said. ''Fathers who are there to help them grow up.''

''I'm Nealie's father,'' he said with passion. ''I love her, and she loves me, and I try to be a good parent.''

''I know,'' she said. She took another young seedling and tipped it out, taking care of its frail roots, its slender stem.

''If you'll marry me again,'' he said, ''I'll try to be a good husband. I'll love our baby, and I'll be the best father I know how to be.''

''But you'll be gone, mostly,'' she said. ''And you'll go to dangerous places.''

''It's my *job*,'' he countered. ''Lots of women marry men who have to be away—they have since the beginning of time. They've married sailors and soldiers and explorers. Men went off to wars—''

''Most of those men *had* to go,'' she said. ''You choose to. There's a difference.''

He gripped the table more tightly and leaned toward her. She drew back slightly, as if in self-defense. ''I would always come back to you. Always. And to our children.''

Tears suddenly sprang to her eyes. ''Could you come back from the dead? Because the first time, it wasn't so much that you went away. It was where you went—and why. You could have died. There was shooting. There were bombings. But you had to go there. For what? For *pictures*.''

His muscles stiffened in resentment. ''They were good pictures.''

The tears welled more brightly. ''Good for what?''

He swore to himself. She didn't understand him at all. Maybe it truly was hopeless between them. But he swept his soil-stained hand in a gesture that took in the greenhouse, the whole farm.

''What good is this?'' he retorted. ''All this work, all this clannishness, for what? So a few hundred people can chow down on a homegrown tomato? Wow. Talk about a mission in life.''

''These plants are endangered,'' she said, flaring into argument. ''They're part of our heritage, but if people don't work to save them, they'll die out.''

''Okay, so your job is to preserve things, right?''

''Right,'' she said. Her nod was pugnacious.

''So is mine,'' he reasoned. ''I preserve moments. I preserve split seconds in time. Sometimes they're pretty. Sometimes they're not. But I'm trying to capture a piece of the truth. Including what's disappearing forever from this world.''

''Do you have to put your own life in danger to do it?''

''Sometimes.''

''You do it more than sometimes.''

''I go with the story. That's all. That's all I've ever done.''

''And it's all you'll ever do,'' she accused, going to the racks and pulling down another tray of seedlings.

''Is this,'' he asked with a bitter smile, ''the root of the problem, pardon the expression? That you're scared?''

She slammed the tray down so hard the young leaves trembled and crumbs of soil jumped. ''You're damn right I'm scared. I'm terrified.''

He looked at her in wonder. ''I never took you for a coward. Not you, of all people.''

She started filling a new container. She moved with the briskness of fury. ''I don't want to be a bride one month and a widow the next. I don't want Nealie to think she's got a full-time father and then, instead, be an orphan. I don't want our baby to grow up knowing you loved some story more than him—or her.''

A tear spilled down her cheek, and she brushed it away angrily, leaving another streak of dirt.

He looked at her, his throat aching with emotion. It destroyed him when she cried. ''Life's uncertain for everyone,

Briana. Look at Harve. If that fire had started a few hours later, he might have died in his sleep.''

"Not everybody's life is as uncertain as yours," she answered. "Good grief, can't you understand? I don't ever want to believe that you're mine again. Because I can't bear the idea of losing you a second time. The first time nearly killed me. If that's cowardice, make the most of it."

The tear coursed down her face, fell from her chin and landed on the breast of her white T-shirt.

Damn the mud, he thought, and put his arms around her, pulling her close. She stifled a sob and wrapped her arms around his neck. He knew he dare not kiss her, or he wouldn't be able to stop. So he simply held her as tightly as he could.

CHAPTER FOURTEEN

THE NEXT MORNING after Briana's ultrasound, the doctor surprised her. He told her that the eggs seemed mature, and he prepared to give her a shot.

"This substance tells your system to release the eggs," he said. "We'll make an appointment for you and your husband to come in tomorrow. We'll recover your eggs and get his sperm donation."

Briana head swam, and she felt as if she were trapped in a surreal high-tech science experiment. "He's not my husband," she said. "He's my ex-husband."

"Sorry. Forgot," said the doctor, showing no emotion.

He stuck in the needle. Briana winced. She wondered what *this* dose of hormones would do to her already tumultuous emotions. But she thought of Nealie, took a deep breath and tried to be strong.

When she got home, Josh was gone, working at Harve's. Nealie was at school. Penny was at the greenhouse, planting herb seeds. Briana was glad for a respite of solitude and doing nothing. She sat for a long time on the sofa, with Zorro purring almost noiselessly on her lap.

She stroked him with one hand and lay the other on her abdomen. *What's happening inside me,* she wondered, half in awe, half in fear.

When Josh came back, he had Nealie with him. Briana wanted to stay as long as possible with Nealie and Josh. She phoned her father to tell him she wouldn't be up to his house until nine or ten.

Inga answered Leo's phone. "Please don't be too late.

He worries, you know. And stress isn't good for him. He should avoid it.''

Inga said it politely, she said it with concern and even sweetness, but Briana could only think, *I'd like to avoid stress myself.* Perhaps the safest thing to do on a night this full of ricocheting emotions was to take care of Poppa as usual—as if everything was ordinary.

At Nealie's bedtime, she and Josh took the girl upstairs, tucked her in and took turns reading her a story. Once Nealie was asleep, they talked, but with reticence. She could think of little to say. He was strangely quiet.

At last he said, ''I know what you're feeling. I'm not crazy for Harve to sleep here again, but maybe it's easiest on all of us this way. Go to your father's. Get a good rest.''

When he kissed her good-night, she felt a rush of poignance. He was holding back, she knew, for her sake. Last night he had said he loved her. He did not say it again tonight.

She was glad. To hear him speak those words might, at that moment, rend her apart completely.

THE APPOINTMENT in St. Louis was at ten o'clock. Briana could not say how long she and Josh spent at the clinic. Things seemed to happen swiftly yet in strange slow motion.

Afterward she eased herself into the passenger side of Josh's car. He helped her, treating her as if she were as fragile as spun glass. ''Are you sure you're okay?'' he asked, his brow furrowed.

She nodded. She was in slight pain, but what she felt most was a sense of unreality.

No surgery had been necessary to retrieve the eggs. She'd been given a mild intravenous sedative. Then the doctor inserted a thin needle through the vaginal wall, which he guided by ultrasound, and harvested five eggs.

She could go home, and it would seem as if nothing had

happened at all. No one should be able to detect the slightest change in her.

But she felt profoundly different in ways she did not yet understand. It was as if she viewed the world through a fine haze and had cotton in her ears, not enough to deafen her, but enough to make all sound seem muted and distant.

Josh got in on the driver's side and fastened his seat belt. He shot her another look of concern. "You told me they wouldn't hurt you," he said. "But they must have. You're pale. And shaky."

"It didn't hurt much," she said.

He frowned, then raised one eyebrow. "I think I got the better deal this time. I just had to go into the bathroom with the girly magazine again."

She tried to smile, but her lips wouldn't obey. Josh had thrust the key into the ignition, but he pulled back his hand, leaving the key unturned. He unsnapped his seat belt and leaned close to her, putting his arm around her shoulder. "Come on, babe," he said gruffly. "What's wrong? Tell me."

He wore a Scandinavian sweater, and she lay her cheek against his chest, needing to feel the strength and hardness of his body. "I feel like somebody in a science-fiction movie," she said. "There are parts of us back in that lab. A doctor is probably examining the eggs right now. And somebody's putting your sperm in a bath."

"Where do they get the teeny-tiny bathtub?" he teased.

This time she did smile, but it faded quickly. She said, "This afternoon, they'll fertilize the eggs. We won't even know when it happens. You and I might not even be together."

He sighed and held her closer. "Right. It's not very sexy."

She shut her eyes and rubbed her forehead again his sweater, just under his collarbone. He said, "It seems like I at least ought to kiss you."

She said, "I wish you would."

He bent to her, and she lifted her face. His mouth was gentle, not demanding. She could feel that once again he was holding back, repressing desire. His restraint tugged at her heart more than any passion could.

He drew away and framed her face between his hands. "So Mr. Sperm meets Ms. Egg this afternoon?"

"Yes." She studied his rugged features. His eyes so often had a guarded expression. They were not guarded now. She thought, *He really does love me. He does.*

His half-smile was tender yet sardonic. "If I'm not there and you're not there, who exactly gets our, uh, components together? A stork in a lab coat?"

He had a small scar under his left cheekbone. She resisted the urge to stroke it. "No stork. An embryologist. I think it's Dr. Chan."

"The Chinese doctor?"

"Yes. He's from Hong Kong."

Josh smiled and rubbed his nose against hers. "So you and I aren't creating our baby? The nice man from Hong Kong does it for us."

She put her hands on his shoulders. "And you came all the way from Moscow to do your part. It'll be a very international baby," she said.

His face sobered. "If there is a baby," he said. "Don't get your hopes too high. It might not work this time."

This was the specter that always haunted her. "I know. It might take more than one try. But I hope not. This is hard, Josh. It's so hard. I don't know how infertile couples go through it time after time."

He put his hand behind her head, lacing his fingers through her hair. He drew her to his chest again, and she rested there gladly. The coming days would be interminable. By tomorrow, the doctors would know if the eggs were fertilized. But not until the third day could they tell if the fertilized eggs seemed healthy. And not until the fifth day could they learn if the broken chromosome was in any or all of the eggs.

So many ifs. So much uncertainty. So many questions, some far too difficult for her to answer. Her head ached.

She told herself all that mattered was to try to save Nealie and to give the baby as good a life as possible. Boy or girl, she was certain this child would be special, as much a child of love as Nealie was.

She took a deep breath and pulled away from Josh. "I'm better, thanks. We should go home. I need to get back to work. Penny's been doing everything, and I know she'd like to go over and help Harve again."

He frowned in disbelief. "Work? This afternoon? Why don't you just go home, lie down and take it easy?"

"I'd rather keep occupied," she said.

"I guess I should go help Harve, too," Josh muttered, snapping shut the buckle on his seat belt. "But I'd rather stay with you. You still look pale."

"I'll be fine. It's just, for the first time, I think the reality's sinking in."

He sighed through clenched teeth. "Yeah. Me, too." He turned the ignition key.

She said, "You know, don't you, that I'll never be able to thank you enough for this."

"I can think of a way you could thank me."

She knew he meant marriage. For a crazy moment she wanted to say yes. But instead, she said, "This isn't the time to talk about it. You know it, and so do I."

"Will there ever be a time?" he asked.

Suddenly a picture flashed into her imagination—how he would look holding a new baby. She remembered the expression on his face the first time he'd stared at Nealie in his arms.

"Maybe," she said, so softly it was hardly audible.

But he heard. He nodded. "For now, maybe will do."

THAT AFTERNOON at Harve's, Josh stood knee-deep in snow, helping load burned debris into a pickup truck. Larry worked with Josh, but he moved slowly, and in spite of the cold, sweat stood on his forehead and upper lip.

In the ruins of a first-floor bedroom, Harve swung a sledgehammer, knocking down what remained of an outer wall. "Harve," Larry called in a harsh voice, "you ought to do that from the outside. You could fall right through the damn floor into the cellar and kill your—"

He broke down in a fit of coughing. He couldn't stop. Josh pounded his back. It didn't help. Larry coughed until he nearly choked.

Penny came running with a thermos of water. Josh filled the cup as Penny put her hand to Larry's forehead. "Good grief," she said. "You're burning with fever. You should go home right now."

Larry managed to drink a few swallows, coughed again, took another drink. "I feel like hell," he admitted.

"You were coughing yesterday, too," Penny scolded. "You should take better care of yourself."

Larry protested, but Josh could tell his heart wasn't in it. When Larry could finally stand, he seemed weak-kneed. "I'll be back tomorrow," he vowed. But when he walked toward his van, his gait was unsteady.

"Gee," Penny said to Josh in a low voice. "Do you think he should drive by himself?"

"He wouldn't let me take him," Josh said. "Or you, either."

Penny gave a sigh of disgust. "He always has to be so macho."

Josh said nothing. He watched Larry drive off. If Larry got seriously sick, it would be one more problem to weigh on Briana. Heritage Farm was already running behind schedule, and Larry was the only able-bodied man working it full-time. By working at Harve's, Larry had already sacrificed two days at his own place.

Penny screwed the lid onto the thermos. "He should be okay," she said. "He's got the constitution of an ox."

"I hope so," Josh said moodily.

Penny shrugged and headed back to work. Josh once again started flinging charred rubble into the bed of the truck. But he wasn't thinking of the ruined house or of Larry or of Heritage Farm. Instead he wondered if, in St. Louis, Dr. Chan was about to go into the lab and make Josh the father of Briana's second child.

BRIANA COULD NOT face spending another night at Leo's. She phoned and told him so. "Harve can stay there," she said. Leo fussed, but Briana was too dazed to care.

When Josh got back from Harve's, she still felt strange. She supposed it was more emotional than physical strain, and Josh seemed to understand.

They said little. They spoke of Harve's house, Larry's cough. But they were both thinking of what might be happening in St. Louis.

After supper he helped her with the dishes, kept Nealie occupied by drawing pictures with her, then joined Briana in putting the child to bed. He said he'd read the bedtime story and told Briana to rest.

When he came down at last, she was sitting on the couch, the lights dimmed. Soft music played, something haunting and Celtic. She held a mug of hot cider and had set a glass of wine on the coffee table for him.

He settled beside her. He nodded in the direction of Nealie's room. "She's asleep," he said. "She tried to hold out for you to come up and kiss her one more time, but she couldn't make it. Hope you don't mind."

Briana shook her head and gazed at the fire. "She needs her sleep."

He sighed gruffly and picked up his glass. "So do you. You look beat."

She raised her chin. "No. Not really."

"I forgot," he said, watching her over the rim of his glass. "You're never beaten. Not you."

There was no sarcasm in his voice. She knew he meant

it as a compliment. But she didn't think she deserved praise for courage. At this moment, she felt little bravery.

"I keep thinking about *it*," she said.

She knew there was no need to define *it* for him. By now, Dr. Chan had done his job. What would be the result? She had no idea, only a hoard of conflicting hopes and fears.

Josh touched his glass against her mug. "To Dr. Chan. And his success."

They each took a small drink. To Briana the cider was tasteless. She toyed with the mug nervously and stared into the flames of the fireplace.

Josh said, "They'll call tomorrow, right? To let us know if fertilization's taken place."

"Right," she said.

She nibbled at her lip. The doctors had been able to take only five eggs. The low number disturbed her, for the odds were that only sixty percent of them could be fertilized.

That meant that only three of the eggs might grow. Of those, all might be healthy—or none. All might carry Nealie's anemia. Briana would have to wait months to start the cycle of drugs again, crucial time would be lost, and help for Nealie would be even more distant.

Briana squared her shoulders. She wouldn't dwell on the negative. She said, "If we get a healthy embryo, the doctors will want you there when they implant it. Did they tell you that?"

He winced slightly. "No. Is it an operation?"

She almost smiled. "You—squeamish? You've seen everything."

"I don't want to see you being hurt, that's all."

She patted his arm. "It won't hurt. The procedure's not surgical. They'll put me in a thing that looks like a dentist chair with stirrups. I'll probably be covered up so much that only the doctor will see me."

He lifted his eyebrow wryly. "No glimpse of your irresistible nether parts? I don't get a single break in this procedure, do I?"

She knew he was trying to raise her spirits. "Nope," she said. "You don't." She added, "You don't have to be there if you don't want to. If it would make you uncomfortable."

"Briana. I *want* to be there."

Her throat tightened. "That's kind of you."

"No. I mean it. I want to. The father ought to at least be in the same room when the mother gets pregnant. Don't you think?"

She smiled. "Purist," she said.

The two of them were silent a moment. The fire crackled. Outside, the wind made a branch rub against a window, a low, whispery sound.

Zorro came padding across the floor from his food dish in the kitchen. He looked at Josh and Briana with his pale green eyes, then leaped onto Josh's lap and settled there, tucking his paws beneath him. He gave his peculiar purr.

Briana was touched and surprised. Zorro was shy. He'd never favored anyone with such intimacy except Nealie and Briana.

Josh said, "The phantom cat's materialized. What's this mean? He usually avoids me."

"I guess he'd decided you're one of us," she said, then wanted to bite her tongue.

Josh stroked the cat, but he said nothing. She stared at the profile of the man who had been her husband, the man who today might have fathered her second child.

You are one of us, Briana thought. *And you're not one of us. You belong with Nealie and me—but you don't. You're a paradox.*

She said, "I really wish you'd told me what happened to you when you were a boy. I might have understood you better."

In the shadowy light, his half-smile seemed cynical. "I doubt it."

"But if we talked—"

He cut her off. "No," he repeated. "Not now." He gave her shoulder a brief squeeze. "Try to rest. Tomorrow isn't going to be easy, no matter what happens." He finished his wine and stood. "I'll be over early tomorrow," he told her. "I want to be with you when you get the news."

She should have been relieved he was going. Instead disappointment welled in her. Reluctantly she walked him to the door, watched him don his parka. He leaned over and kissed her on the cheek. The caress was meant to be almost brotherly, but it filled her with churning emotion.

When he left, the house felt as empty as if someone had died. Zorro came and rubbed against Briana's ankles.

"I know what I want for Nealie," she whispered, picking him up and holding him close. "But I don't know what I want for myself anymore."

AT LEO'S HOUSE, Inga came out of the kitchen. Harve, standing by the living room, hardly noticed her.

"I was on the phone," she announced. "With Glenda. Larry isn't any better. She's afraid he's got bronchitis. He's prone to it."

Harve should have felt sympathy, but he didn't. He wished his problems were as small as a case of bronchitis.

Inga shook her head in concern. "She says he's also been getting sinus infections the past few years. That they hang on forever. The bronchitis might bring on another one."

Harve gave no answer. He kept staring out the window. He watched as Josh's rented car pulled away. "He's leaving early tonight," he said.

"Well," Inga said briskly, "that's good, isn't it?"

She and Harve were alone. Leo had gone to bed.

Harve kept staring at Briana's house. "She spends a lot of time with him. Why'd he have to go with her to St. Louis today?"

Inga sat in the rocking chair and took up her crocheting. She had found Briana's mother's yarn and crochet hooks and was making Harve a muffler. "Maybe he was worried about her. The roads were icy this morning."

Harve ran his hand through his hair, turned and saw the

dining room table strewn with his papers. He'd been filling out insurance forms all evening, and the task weighed on his spirit.

He was depressed that Briana seemed so caught up in herself she paid hardly any mind to him or his misfortune. He said, "I don't know why she's running off to St. Louis all the time. She doesn't seem sick to me. She doesn't *look* sick."

Inga snipped her yarn. "Actually, she looks as if she's under a strain. I noticed it that day I met her at church. I thought, there's a woman with something on her mind. And she's moody, touchy."

"She may have something on her mind, but at least her house didn't burn down," Harve grumbled.

"You still have your land," Inga told him. "You can build a new house. In every end is a new beginning."

Harve shoved his hands into the pockets of his overalls. "Who knows how long before I have a home of my own again? Months."

"Leo's invited us to stay as long as we like," Inga said. "I should think that you'd be happy to be near Briana."

"She acts like I don't exist," Harve said. "And besides, now I feel like I'm living on Leo's charity. It was better when he owed me favors."

Inga looked up sharply. "Dear, you must learn, when life gives you lemons to make lemonade."

Harve frowned. "I hate that saying."

"You shouldn't. You have a golden chance. Don't think of it as taking charity from Leo. Instead show him how well you can earn your keep. Make him think you're indispensable."

Harve's frown turned to a look of puzzlement. "Me? Indispensable?"

"Indispensable," Inga repeated with conviction. "You've seen all the things around here that need fixing. Larry's overworked. Now he's sick on top of it. Who can keep this place running? Josh Morris? Of course not. But

you could, sweet boy. You could be the salvation of this
farm.''

Harve thought. Once the ruins of his house were cleared,
it would still be months before he could plant his main crop,
corn. It would also be months before construction could
start on his new house. He could spend time helping Leo.

Inga said, ''Who knows? If you married Briana, it might
even lead to joining the two farms. Wouldn't that be something?''

He turned and faced the window again. In spite of Inga's
encouragement, he was starting to feel his chances with
Briana were hopeless. ''I—I've got this bad feeling about
her and him.''

''Oh?'' Inga snipped another piece of yarn. ''You think
they're involved again?''

He didn't answer.

Inga said, ''Would it make a difference in your feeling
for her? If she and he were having an affair?''

He spun around, his mouth falling open. ''Aunt Inga!''

She examined her handiwork, then set it aside. ''Don't
be shocked, Harve. I asked a simple question. If she had
another fling with this man, could you forgive her?''

Harve put his hand to his forehead in misery. Since Josh
had returned, he had been torturing himself with this question. Inga could read him like a book, a very simple, very
open book.

''I guess I'd forgive her for anything,'' he said.

''Anything?'' asked Inga, examining the points of her
scissors.

''Anything,'' said Harve.

SATURDAY MORNING, Briana was taking the breakfast biscuits out of the oven when the telephone rang.

Josh saw her jump at the sound. She caught her breath,
and every muscle in her body seemed to stiffen. She looked
at Josh, and he looked at her.

At the same moment, they realized the phone call was

CHAPTER FIFTEEN

OSH DECIDED what hell was. It was moving around great quantities of dirt and fertilizer. More specifically, hell was moving around great quantities of dirt and fertilizer while Harve gave the orders.

Leo's largest warehouse held his bulkiest products—special mixes of soil and what he liked to call "enrichment products." He ordered them from a company in Oregon.

Soil bags were big, heavy, unwieldy and oozed grime. The contents of enrichment products seemed picked for ow badly they stank.

Josh hauled, heaved and stacked. Sometimes a bag or ottle had broken in shipment. Soils, both the fine and the oarse, spilled out and haunted the air in a dirty, low-lying g.

Leaking fertilizer was worse. It settled over Josh in a ickly smut. Fish emulsion, which was liquid, slimed him. ulness clung around him in an odiferous cloud.

The large containers were for Leo's use on the farm and r his local customers. The smaller quantities were sold ough the catalogs.

Today's job started with storing the latest shipment from egon in the proper niches. Josh lugged the bulky bags boxes of gallon bottles. Harve told him what to lug and re to lug it.

t was not that Harve did nothing. It was that Harve knew t he was doing. Josh did not and could only follow rs.

When we finish this," Harve said, "we start filling the

too early to be from the center. It was not yet eight. Briana exhaled in relief and said, "It must be Poppa. Will you get it, Nealie?"

But Nealie had splashed orange juice all over her hands, so Josh answered the phone.

The caller was Glenda, sounding harried. "Josh? Larry's got bronchitis, I'm sure of it. And probably the start of a sinus infection. It's laid him low. I think he'd better stay in bed."

"I'm sorry," Josh said. "Is there anything we can do to help?"

Glenda sighed in exasperation. "No. I know the routine by heart. Aspirin, cough medicine, make him rest, turn on the vaporizer." She paused. "I just talked to Poppa. This is kind of awkward, but—"

"But what?" Josh prodded.

He could smell the aroma of biscuits and melting butter, bacon and coffee. He wanted to sit down to breakfast and pretend he was a normal man having a normal breakfast with his nice, normal family.

Again Glenda hesitated. "Harve is coming over to see Briana. With Larry sick, Poppa's kind of let him take charge. He wants to get copies of Briana's shipping orders. He says he'll handle the heavy items. Some of those boxes weigh a lot."

Josh thought, *I smell more than bacon. I smell trouble.*

Glenda said, "Poppa said since Harve's going out of his way to help us, it would be nice if he had some able-bodied man to help him."

Mentally Josh swore. He said, "That means me, right?"

"I'm afraid so. Poppa says he's going to phone you himself. I thought I should warn you."

"Thanks, Glenda," Josh said. He told her goodbye and hung up.

"What was that about?" Briana asked. "Sit down and tell us. Breakfast is ready."

"Come eat, Daddy," Nealie said.

The phone rang again. Josh picked up the receiver, knowing he was going to hear Leo. "Hello," he said, hearing the fatalism in his own voice.

"Josh," said Leo, almost jovially. "Harve's on his way down there to get some shipping orders from Briana. Larry's under the weather, and Harve volunteered to fill in for him."

"So I heard," Josh said from between his teeth. "Generous guy, Harve."

"Yes, indeed," said Leo. "Not one to sit around on his duff when there's work to be done. Not a lazy bone in his body. No, sir."

Perhaps we can ask that he be canonized, Josh thought.

Admiration vibrated in Leo's tone. "That he would pitch in and help like this, after all he's been through. I was wondering—could you give him a hand? I mean he's helping out Briana and Nealie, too, you know."

A cloud of gloom descended over Josh. He had just been blackmailed, and neatly, too. He said, "As soon as I've finished breakfast, Leo."

"You won't go unrewarded," Leo said. "I want you and Briana and Nealie to come up for supper with us tonight. I won't take no for an answer. I've hardly seen you since you got here. And Inga really wants to get to know you better. You've just met in passing so far."

"Daddy, come *eat,*" Nealie beseeched.

"Leo, Briana and I'll talk about it. Now I'd better—"

"You do that," Leo said cheerfully. "Why, Harve's at your place now. I can see him from here. Got a bird's-eye view from up here, you know."

I know. Oh, yes, I know.

A knock sounded at the door.

Josh looked at Briana, standing at the counter waiting for him. Their eyes met. "What's this about?" she said apprehensively.

"I'm going to have to help Harve do something," he muttered.

"But for how long?" she asked.

"I don't know," he said.

Her eyes told him, *I don't want to be alone. to be here when the center calls.* But she manage and say, "I'll be fine."

Again they heard the knock on the door. Josh w in the man who loved Briana almost as much as h

early orders. People buy a lot of this stuff. Sometimes Larry boxes and sends out half a ton of this stuff at a time.''

Josh was stacking cumbersome sacks of fertilizer mix. ''How do you know so much about this?'' he challenged.

''I used to work for Leo during school vacations,'' Harve said, loading a dolly with bags of green sand. ''My daddy wanted me to have the experience.''

This made no sense to Josh. A farm was a farm. ''Why weren't you working on your own place?''

''Because I knew all that. This was part of my education. My daddy wanted me to learn other things.''

Like how bad fish emulsion stinks, Josh thought grumpily.

''My daddy was just a regular farmer. But he saw Leo was a pioneer. And an entrepreneur. It was him that said maybe we should follow in Leo's footsteps. I'm fixing to do that one of these days.''

Josh muttered something unintelligible as he hoisted another sack.

Harve said, ''I don't suppose you ever did anything like this before.''

''Not exactly,'' said Josh, although once he had fallen into a wallow with a dead hippopotamus in it. The smell was similar.

''You just go all kinds of places and take pictures, huh?'' said Harve.

''That's about the size of it,'' Josh said from between his teeth.

''But sometimes,'' Harve said, with a hint of charity, ''you have to camp out. I used to be in Boy Scouts. I liked to camp out.''

Try camping out on Mount Everest, thought Josh. *Or in the Gobi Desert.*

''I'll give you credit, though,'' Harve said, loading another dolly. ''When you work, you pull your own weight.''

Josh paused to wipe the grime from his mouth and stare at Harve. The man was paying him a compliment?

Harve didn't meet his gaze. Instead he grunted and

pushed the dolly to the dry fertilizer storage section. He said, "I appreciate your helping at my place. I don't think I ever thanked you proper."

Josh was surprised, almost touched. "It's okay."

"I'm still kind of in shock," Harve said. He parked the dolly and began to unload the sandbags. "It helps to keep busy."

Josh picked up another bag of fertilizer. Its seam ruptured, billowing dust. Josh coughed and hacked. "No wonder Larry gets bronchitis," he said, wiping his face. "This stuff must be murder on your respiratory system."

"Yeah, it gets to him, all right," Harve said without emotion. "He needs more help in winter. Vacations, he can get schoolkids. But full time, a good man is hard to find. I mean a man who knows what he's doing. This work is specialized."

Josh thought his present task could be done by a large and not very bright dung beetle. But then he heard the sound of a truck outside. He recognized the rhythm of its motor—Briana was here.

"What the—?" Harve said. "Sounds like Briana. Is she bringing lunch? I thought Inga was." He pushed up his sleeve and looked at his watch. "It's too early. It's not even eleven."

Josh sprinted toward the warehouse door. He knew why Briana was there. She'd heard from the center. As he ran, he stripped off his dirty gloves, throwing them to the floor.

"Hey!" Harve called. "What's going on?"

Josh barely heard him. He plunged through the deep snow and reached the truck as Briana was stepping out. He stared at her, his heart thudding.

She looked at him, smiling tremulously. "Four of the eggs are fertilized," she said. "It's—it's a good start. In two more days we'll know if they're developing the way they should."

He felt a lump rising in his throat. "Babe, we're getting there. Just hang on. We're getting there."

He put his arms around her. He didn't care if he was filthy, and she didn't seem to mind a bit. She wound her arms around his neck.

"Oh, Josh," she said, shaking her head. "I was so scared nothing would happen."

"Now Nealie's got a chance," he said, pulling her closer. "And maybe we'll have a miracle."

"Congratulations." She grinned at him. "You're the proud father of four zygotes."

"I should have done it today instead of yesterday," he said, "I'm much more equipped to fertilize things."

She sniffed at his grimy neck. "Mmm. I smell fish emulsion."

"Sorry," he said. "I'll back off."

But she kept her arms around him. "To me, right now, you're fragrant as a rose."

He bent and kissed her, a long, celebratory kiss, full of affection and wild hope.

From the door of the warehouse, Harve watched in silence, his face stricken.

AT THE KITCHEN WINDOW, Leo was watching the warehouse through the binoculars he pretended he kept for bird-watching. In truth he kept them to keep tabs on his family.

"They're kissing," Leo said in horror. "I saw her drive down there and thought, what the hay? And now they're *kissing*. Right in front of Harve."

Inga's hand flew to her breast. "In front of Harve? Oh, the poor boy! Let me see."

Leo, grim-faced, thrust the binoculars at her. She seized them, put them to her eyes and stared. "My goodness! They certainly are. Poor Harve. He's gone inside. He looked so depressed. He was all slumped."

"He's always slumped," Leo grumbled.

"They've stopped," Inga said, adjusting the binoculars. "But they're still holding hands. Now she's getting back in the truck. They're waving goodbye to each other. They seem awfully excited about something.''

Leo's mouth was grim as he watched Briana drive toward her house. Inga lowered the binoculars. "Leo, you're right. Something's going on between those two."

Leo gave her a reproving look. "You doubted me?"

Inga turned to him, eyes wide. "Oh, not for a minute. I just didn't think they'd be so—so open."

Leo said, "He's got no shame, that man. And it's like he puts a spell on her." He stamped through the kitchen, banged open its door and marched into the living room. He threw himself into his recliner.

"When Nealie was here the other night, that's all she could talk about—Daddy, Daddy, Daddy. Briana used to talk about *me* like that. She never gave me a lick of trouble until he showed up."

Inga followed him. "You're upset. Let me make you a cup of tea."

"I don't want a cup of tea. I want my daughter to come to her senses." He put his elbow on the arm of the chair and settled his chin on his hand. "Nealie wants them to get back together. Phooey! It'd be a disaster."

Inga sat in the rocker next to him and touched his arm. "Children of divorced parents often feel that way, Leo. It's normal."

"Why can't Briana get back together with Harve?" Leo demanded. "What's she want with a man who runs all over the world taking pictures of penguins and yaks? I've talked to him. He doesn't know a summer squash from a snap bean. He doesn't even want to know."

"There are none so blind as those who will not see," quoted Inga. She rose, took a small pillow and put it behind Leo's head. "There. That should be a little more comfortable."

Leo settled against the pillow. It was more comfortable. He repeated her words. "None so blind as those who will not see. That's Briana, too. How to make her see Harve's the man for her?''

Inga sat in the rocking chair and took up the sewing basket. "In my very, very humble opinion,'' she began.

Leo leaned closer to her, his eyes narrowing. "In your opinion, what?''

"Josh Morris can't be here much longer,'' Inga said. "Let Harve do what Harve does best. And in the meantime…''

Once again she did not finish the thought, and Leo leaned nearer still. "And in the meantime what?''

"In the meantime,'' Inga said sweetly, "we just keep trying to make sure that Josh and Briana have as little time alone together as possible.''

She drew out the scissors and held them up to the light. "After all,'' she said, "it's for Briana's own good.''

She tested the scissors on the empty air. They went snip, snip, as if cutting time itself.

AND TIME WAS CUT. That night Leo insisted that Briana, Josh and Nealie join him, Inga and Harve for supper. Leo said Inga had been planning for the event all day and was making her special lemon-minted lamb and vegetable pilaf.

"Besides,'' Leo told Briana on the phone, "I've been wanting us all to have a big family dinner since Josh got here. I know we have our differences, but it's important that we try to get along. For Nealie's sake.''

Briana sighed and finally agreed. All evening, Harve and Leo talked about nothing except compost and vegetables. Larry was still sick and stayed home, so Glenda came with the boys. She seemed delighted to have an evening out.

Inga was an excellent cook and charming company. Her most amazing feat was making Glenda's rowdy sons behave almost like little gentlemen.

"I don't know how you do it,'' Glenda marveled when Inga smoothly intervened and kept Rupert from spitting water at Neville.

"There are ways," Inga assured her. "I taught so many years that there aren't many things kids can put over on me."

"I thought you taught high school," Briana said, puzzled.

"I did," Inga answered, talking Neville's hand out of the salad bowl. "But I taught elementary school for seven years. After I got my master's, I switched to high school. I love children. But I don't put up with nonsense from them."

"I wish I had the knack," Glenda said sadly. "Maybe you could teach me a thing or two."

"Any time, my dear," Inga said. "I'm flattered you'd ask." She turned her attention to Josh, who was helping Nealie cut her meat.

"And you, Josh," Inga said. "It's so good to have a talk with you at last. I've always wanted to know a world traveler. The rest of us must seem like provincials to you. Just stay-at-homes."

Inga's tone was friendly and bright. But Briana saw irritation spark deep in Josh's eyes. "I don't consider my wife or my daughter provincials, Mrs. Swenson," he said. "Nor anyone else here."

Inga looked contrite. "Oh, excuse me," she begged. "I didn't mean that the way it sounded. It's just that you've traveled so many places, and the rest of us have hardly traveled at all."

"I'm through eating," said Rupert. "I want to watch television."

"Then say, 'May I please be excused,'" Inga said.

"May I please be excused?" Rupert echoed in disbelief.

"Me, too," cried Neville, and Marsh banged his spoon, indicating he wanted to go with his brothers.

"Yes, you may," said Inga. "But keep the volume down."

Rupert slid from his chair and vanished into the living room. Neville sped after him, and Marsh toddled behind.

Inga sipped her coffee and turned to Josh again. "I'd love to hear some of your travel stories. Leo says you've been to some dangerous places."

"They're not dangerous if you're careful," Josh said.

"Daddy got bit by a tarantula in Costa Rica," Nealie volunteered. "And he nearly got hit by a Molotov cocktail in Indonesia."

"My goodness," Inga said, "I bet you wish he had a safer job."

"No," Nealie said, taking a tiny nibble of lamb. "I'm proud of him."

"And you should be," Inga said. She looked at Briana, and her eyes said, *This poor child really doesn't understand, does she? And you, my dear—how did you ever live with such insecurity?*

Briana's heart rapped angrily in her chest. Inga turned her attention to Josh. "How long until your next assignment?"

Again Briana saw a glitter of displeasure in Josh's gaze. He said, "I'm not sure. It could come within a couple of weeks. Maybe sooner. It's a question of permits."

"How lovely you're here now," Inga said. "It's like fate sent you when you were needed most. What with Leo convalescing and Larry sick and Harve trying to run two places at once, we so need an extra hand now. Harve says you were such a help today."

Oh, no, Briana thought with a sick feeling. *I should have seen this coming. She's backing him into a corner so he'll have to keep playing the part of the hired man.*

Inga said, "Harve says it's a blessing to have you around. I hope we can keep counting on you."

"It really was good of you to help do Larry's work," Glenda said shyly. "I can't thank you enough."

Briana knew that Glenda meant this. There was little guile in her sister-in-law, and her thanks seemed heartfelt.

Inga said to Josh, "Leo says you may be sent to Burma

or Pitcairn Island. They're both quite remote, aren't they? Why do you have to go so far away?''

"I don't know that I will. It takes a lot of red tape to get either place. Both assignments may fall through. It could be someplace else.''

"Let's hope it's someplace safe," said Inga. She smiled at Nealie. "I suppose we should clean off the table. Do you want to help the women, Nealie, like a big girl?''

"No, thank you," said Nealie. "I don't like women's work. I'll stay here with the men.''

Inga tried to laugh off Nealie's answer. She nodded toward Leo and Harve, who were having an intense discussion about muskmelons. "Oh, you don't want to listen to these men. They're just talking gardens, as usual.''

"Daddy's not," Nealie said. "Somebody's got to talk to him. So I will." She put her elbow on the table and her chin in her hand and gazed adoringly at Josh. "Tell me again about how the whales sing.''

THE NEXT DAY passed in a blur for Briana. When she and Penny weren't working in the office, she and Glenda worked in the greenhouses, thinning seedlings, repotting the tomatoes and planting herbs.

Josh had been pressed into working on more projects with Harve. Most of them were hard labor and kept him far from her all day.

That evening after supper, Inga and Leo dropped in at Briana's uninvited. Inga was taking Leo for his constitutional, she said. They stayed until Nealie's bedtime.

When they left, Josh swore under his breath.

Nealie blinked in surprise. "What did you say, Daddy?''

"Nothing," Briana said hastily. "Come on, Nealie, bath time.''

"Will Daddy read me a story?''

Josh said, "Daddy will. Now scoot.''

By the time he came downstairs, Briana had poured him a glass of brandy and settled by the fire. He went to her, picked his brandy from the coffee table and settled beside her.

"Alone at last," he said. "Unless Harve is hiding under the couch."

Briana put her elbows on her knees and her face in her hands. "I'm *so* sorry," she said miserably. "Really, I am."

"I'd take you in my arms to comfort you," he said. "But your father might be out in the bushes with a periscope."

"No," Briana said, "he uses binoculars—from the kitchen window."

"I feel his eyes on us at this very moment," Josh said. He took a hearty slug of the brandy.

Briana raised her head and stared glumly into the fire. "They'll know what time you leave, all right."

He turned to her. "Maybe I shouldn't leave."

She gazed at him. Most people's faces seemed softened by firelight. His looked more rugged, more elemental. She remembered gazing into that face, shadowed by dim lamplight, while they made love for the first time. Her heart gave a small, involuntary flip.

"I wish you didn't have to go," she said. "But this is no time to make a stand against them. Larry's sick, Poppa's sick, his house is full of strangers. My hormones are hopping around like jumping beans and—all I can think of..." She trailed off, unable to finish the sentence.

He did it for her. "And all you can think of is what's happening in that lab. To the fertilized eggs."

"Yes," she said softly. "That's exactly right. It's so strange."

He tilted his head sardonically. "It's also funny."

She stiffened, giving him a hurt look. "Funny?"

He held his glass so he could stare through it at the firelight. "What your family fears so much has already happened. Mr. Sperm has met Ms. Egg. We may already have a baby in the making."

She swallowed hard. "I hope so. I pray so."

He touched her hair gently. "Tomorrow the center phones after they examine the eggs?"

"Yes," she said. She thought of the four microscopic dots in the antiseptic lab. In nine months, one of those dots might become their child. Or perhaps this whole grueling procedure would have to be repeated again and yet again.

He finished his brandy. "You didn't have a glass of wine. You used to like one after a hard day."

"No wine for a while," she said. "I hope a long while."

He stroked her hair. "You mean if there's a healthy embryo."

She bit her lip and nodded.

They were silent for a long moment. He said, "It's strange sitting in this house again, in front of this fire. It's like I belong here and I don't."

She felt his hand move slowly and silkily over her hair. "I know."

"Your father doesn't want us back together. That's more than obvious. I feel like Romeo, sneaking into enemy territory."

"Poppa's jealous of you," she said, setting her jaw. "I didn't want to believe it when we were married. Now I know it's true. Either he's more open or I see more clearly."

"I never tried much to make him like me," Josh said, clasping the nape of her neck. "I was too young and arrogant. And now it's too late."

"It's more than jealousy," she said with a sigh. "He's afraid. He's afraid for the farm, for Larry and Larry's family. He's afraid for himself, too. He *has* been sick. He's never faked that."

Josh's hand moved to her face. He took her chin between his thumb and forefinger. "That's the long version. The short version is he's afraid of losing you. It's all summed up in you."

"And Nealie," she said. "He loves Nealie."

"Yes. He does. And so do I."

She said, "You and Poppa are so different. You're not afraid of anything."

"I'm afraid of losing Nealie. And I'm afraid I've already lost you. That when it comes to choosing between your family and me, you'll always choose your family."

She felt tears sting her eyes and blinked them back. "That's another difference, Josh. They need me. You don't need anybody."

He leaned closer, his hand on her face. "I want you. Why can't that be enough?"

"Because I have responsibilities. I have promises to keep. I have a family depending on me."

"They depend on you too much. And it's always crisis after crisis, one damn thing after another."

She drew away from him and gave him the most level look she could. "That's what family is a lot of times. One damn thing after another. You've never understood that."

He made a sound of exasperation. "No. And maybe I can't. I didn't grow up the way you did."

She rose and paced to the fireplace. "I'm sorry," she said. "I didn't mean it to sound cruel. I'm sorry about your childhood. I'm sorry you never had a real family."

He, too, stood. "I did have, Briana. My family was you and Nealie. You were enough for me. But I wasn't enough for you."

No! she thought with a roiling surge of emotion. *It wasn't that at all. I loved you, and I loved them, too—why did you have to make me choose between you?*

He came toward her, put his hand to her face once more. "I'm sorry. I'm upsetting you. We're both on edge. This isn't the time or place to discuss this."

He kissed her lightly, his lips making no demands from her. "Until tomorrow," he said.

"Until tomorrow," she said tightly. She did not know if tomorrow would bring them joy for Nealie—or a crashing desolation. She only knew that if she was ever to have an-other child, she wanted it to be his.

That was her fate, and she wondered if it was also her curse.

CHAPTER SIXTEEN

JOSH SPENT a restless night. Three times he had nightmares about Nealie's sickness that woke him up, his heart pounding, the sheets sweaty and twisted around his body.

The dreams haunted him at breakfast time, and Nealie seemed subdued, almost listless, as if she did not feel well. Briana smiled and tried to act naturally, but Josh sensed her anxiety.

He was haunted when he went off with Harve to mend a broken ventilation fan in one of the greenhouses. He knew nothing of ventilation fans, and he supposed he seemed stupid to Harve. He did not give a damn.

He did as he was told as mechanically as a robot, but his mind was on Nealie and Briana. And he thought very hard about the child who might soon be growing in Briana's womb.

"No, no," Harve grumbled, "I said the colchis bolt. The colchis bolt." He tapped it with his wrench, but Josh paid no attention. He heard Briana's truck outside and swiftly climbed down his ladder.

"Hey!" yelled Harve at him. "I need help here."

Josh ignored him. He met Briana in the doorway of the greenhouse. She hadn't buttoned her jacket, and her cheeks were bright pink, but not with cold. He could tell by the light in her eyes that her news was good.

He put his hands on her upper arms and stared at her questioningly.

"Three," she whispered, her lips twitching into an emotional smile.

"Three?" he repeated, squeezing her arms as if to assure himself she was really there, really speaking those words.

She nodded. "Three of the eggs seem to be developing normally. In two more days we'll know if the chromosomes are healthy."

"Then we've got three chances," he said. He tried to grin, but his mouth felt shaky. "Maybe we'll end up with triplets."

"Nope," she said. "One at a time."

He put his arm around her, drew her close. They had talked of implanting multiple embryos but decided against it. If there were several with healthy chromosomes, the extras would be frozen in case something went wrong with the first implantation.

He rested his chin atop her head. The door was ajar, and a cold breeze stirred her hair, tickling him. He held her a long time, stroking her back, pressing his mouth against her ear, whispering secret things to her.

Neither of them remembered Harve until he dropped a wrench. It hit the greenhouse's cement floor with a clang. Startled, Briana sprang out of Josh's embrace. Embarrassed, she looked at Harve. "I'm sorry, Harve. I had something personal to tell Josh. It was news that couldn't wait."

"Mmph," said Harve, descending the ladder to retrieve the wrench.

Briana reached into the pocket of her jacket. "And Penny asked me to give you this." She held out an envelope to him.

"Give it to Josh," Harve said shortly. "I dropped the durn bolt, too. Gotta find it." He turned his back to them and studied the floor.

Briana raised her gaze to Josh's. She handed him the envelope. "I should go. I have work to do. But I wanted you to know."

"Thanks, babe. You couldn't have made me happier."

He watched her climb into the truck. She waved and

headed up the road toward the house. Josh went back inside the greenhouse, closing the door behind him.

"Sorry, Harve," he said. "I didn't mean to leave you deserted up there."

"Mmph," said Harve again. He squatted, reached under a potting table and retrieved the lost bolt.

"Here's the thing from Penny."

Harve looked over his shoulder. Slowly he stood. He took the envelope from Josh and stuck it, unopened, in the pocket of his overalls. He started to climb to the ventilator's exhaust.

He stopped midway and looked at Josh. "It's a lot of work, keeping up a farm. You got to put your whole self into it."

Josh thought, *Yeah. It's like loving a woman.*

"YOU'RE *WHAT*?" said Inga, her blue eyes full of disbelief.

"I'm going to St. Louis," Harve said. "I'm leaving tonight."

They stood in Leo's kitchen, where Inga was making a tuna casserole. Leo was in the living room, watching television. Inga had been about to sprinkle the grated cheese, but her hand froze in midair.

"St. Louis. But you can't—"

"I'm going tonight," he said stubbornly. "I'm going to shop for a trailer house. See how soon I can get it set up on my property."

"A trailer house?" echoed Inga, setting down the cheese jar so hard that it rapped against the counter. "You mean a mobile home? What on earth—"

"I don't mind helping Leo," Harve said, setting his jaw. "But I'm tired of living on his charity."

"It's *not* charity," Inga insisted. "I explained that. You're more than earning your keep."

"I can't help it, it's how I feel," Harve said. "And that's that."

"But here you are, where you can see Briana every day—"

"Briana doesn't want to see me. I can't keep forcing myself on her. It doesn't feel right. And it's not my style."

"There's nothing wrong in going after what you want," Inga said. "As for style, you have to use some if you're going to woo a woman."

"It's no good wooing a woman that doesn't want your wooing," Harve said. "It's like trying to make a rock sit up and take notice of you."

Inga put her fist on her hip and frowned at him. "I saw her drive down to the greenhouse. Did something happen between her and you?"

"No," Harve said emphatically. "But something sure happened between her and him."

Her eyes slitted in suspicion. "Exactly what happened?"

"I don't know, but I could feel it. And she's never going to see me for sour apples. I'd never make her happy."

"He's the one who'll never make her happy," Inga countered. "You've told me so yourself. Now you're just going to quit? You won't even try?"

"Hell," Harve said with atypical fervor, "I've been trying for years. A man should know when he's beat."

"I can't believe this," Inga said in displeasure. "And what's this nonsense about a mobile home?"

"It's not nonsense," Harve said. "I'm going to have to build a new house—and wait clear till spring to even start. I'm not going to sit around here like an old begging dog. I'm going back where I belong."

Inga crossed her arms. "Well, I'm staying here as long as Leo needs me. I said I would, and *I* happen to keep my promises."

"I told him I'd help while Larry was down, and I keep my promises, too. But I'll sleep at my own place."

"In the meantime, you'll go off to St. Louis and leave us high and dry."

"No, I won't. I'll be back when I can. But I want my

own place. Because when it comes to Briana, I don't have a snowball's chance in hell. I'm done making a fool of myself.''

''Fiddle-dee-dee,'' Inga said. ''You'll change your mind. I told you, all things come to him who waits.''

''And I told you. I'm going to St. Louis. I'll be back when I can.''

''Oh, really.'' Inga huffed.

Harve went to his truck. He had little to load for his journey, but he had enough. Neighbors had donated things—clothes, toiletries, even a second-hand suitcase.

He was throwing the suitcase into the passenger seat when Penny's car came up the hill and stopped in the drive beside him. Harve winced. He didn't want to talk her.

She rolled down the window. ''Hi,'' she said. Strands of fire-colored hair danced in the breeze. ''Did you get my note?''

He'd gotten it. He nodded curtly.

''I mean it,'' she said. ''We never knew what to do with Daddy's clothes when he passed away. He wasn't as tall as you, but he was thin, and there might be a few things that would fit. You're welcome to take your pick.''

He tried so hard to keep his face impassive it felt stiff. He shook his head. ''That's mighty kind. But I got enough clothes to get me by. Franklin Hinks gave me half a closet full.''

Penny gave him a hesitant smile. ''That's great. But you're still invited for supper. I'd like you to meet my sister.''

Harve didn't want to act rude, but her invitation, meant to be kind, had hurt his feelings, make him feel even worse. ''Does your sister know you're asking me?''

She grinned impishly. ''No. She's too shy. She'd never cooperate. But I'd like the two of you to get acquainted. I think you'd like each other.''

Harve looked away. He'd seen Tammy Pfeiffer, and she

was pretty enough, but she didn't talk much, and she seemed timid as a mouse. Maybe Penny thought that if like attracted like, then dull would attract dull.

"Thanks," he said. "But I don't want to get fixed up just now."

"It wouldn't be getting fixed up," Penny reasoned, tossing her curls. "You'd just get to know each other better."

"No, thanks," said Harve. The very thought of having Tammy Pfeiffer thrust at him depressed him.

"Another time, maybe," Penny said. "Look, I just had an idea. We have other things of my dad's. I know people have been giving you stuff, but maybe this is something you haven't got. You like fishing, don't you?"

Harve looked at her in wary surprise. "How'd you know that?"

"Your picture was in the paper when you caught that big bass last summer," she said. "The story said you were an avid fisherman."

He was astonished that she would remember such a thing. He could only stare at her.

She shrugged. "We never knew what to do with Dad's fishing stuff. He'd want it to go to someone who'd appreciate it. He had some good rods and reels, a lot of lures. I'd be glad if you'd take it."

In spite of himself Harve was moved. "I might take you up on that."

"Great," she said. "You take care, hear?" She shot him another grin and drove off in her rattletrap car.

I'm going to have to fix that rear wheel, Harve thought, looking after her. *Doesn't she know it could be dangerous, driving around like that?*

He climbed in his truck and headed for St. Louis. He was about to become a free man again.

"I'LL GET IT," Briana said when the phone rang.

She set down the platter of chicken she was about to grill.

Josh was at the sink making a salad, and Nealie was on the couch with Zorro, watching *The Secrets of Nihm*.

Briana picked up the receiver.

"We've got an emergency," said Leo, his voice tense with concern.

"Oh, no, Poppa. What now?"

"Harve's going to St. Louis to buy a mobile home. He wants to move back to his own place."

"What?" Briana demanded. "Why is that an emergency?"

"Well," Leo said, "you've been talking about sleeping at your own house again, but now you can't. Harve won't stay here, and Inga and I can't be here all night without a chaperone."

"Poppa, I can't move in permanently. All these trips to the doctor are wearing me out. I want to start sleeping in my own bed again."

"It can't be done," Leo said righteously. "I won't compromise the reputation of a fine woman. She has nowhere else to go except a motel, and I can't be all by myself. I don't feel fully recovered."

"But the doctor said your attack was minor—"

"Maybe you and Nealie should just move in here for a while," Leo suggested. "If you ask me, she's spending way too much time with Josh. Then he'll up and leave, and she'll be devastated. She'd be better off up here with you. And me. And Inga. Inga's a very steadying influence."

"Poppa, this is our home. Now tell me why Harve's gone to St. Louis."

"You should know that better than anybody," Leo said, accusation in his tone. "When are you coming up tonight?"

By the time Leo said goodbye, Briana was so frustrated, she had to resist slamming the receiver into the cradle.

Josh crossed his arms and leaned against the counter. The slant of his mouth was cynical. "What have they come up with this time?"

Briana explained, feeling more angry and trapped by the

minute. No wonder Josh disliked her family. Her father was being impossible. Had he always been this manipulative? Had her marriage ever had a chance?

She said, "And to top it all off, he says it's *my* fault that Harve's gone. Somehow I hurt his feelings. I suppose it's because I came to the greenhouse. Ooh! It's like I'm in a three-ring circus."

Josh came to her, put his hands on her waist and gazed at her, his eyes serious. "Settle down. You may be about to get pregnant. You don't need to let him upset you. Are you going up there tonight?"

"I suppose I have to. The last thing we need at this point is a big confrontation. Oh, Josh, I'm sorry. This is humiliating. But what else can I do?"

He laid his forefinger against her lips. "Calm down, babe. At least Harve is out of the picture for a while." He kissed her on the tip of the nose. His nearness made her tingle. She wanted him to kiss her again, in earnest. He bent nearer, as if he meant to.

But then Nealie was there. "Is supper ready?"

Briana broke away from Josh guiltily. "In just a few minutes, honey. Do you want to help Daddy make the salad?"

"Yes." But Nealie looked wistful. "Mommy, do you have to go to Grandpa's again tonight?"

"I'm sorry," Briana said. "I do. But Daddy will stay here with you."

Nealie seemed no happier. "I'd like it better if you were here, too. Why can't the three of us be together anymore?"

Something made Briana want to burst into tears. She hoped it was the hormones.

"IT'S A fiendish plot," Leo fumed. He sat in his recliner and smacked his hand against the arm of the chair for emphasis. "That man is after my daughter. He wants to get into her pants again. I know it."

Inga winced. "Maybe you could put it a little more delicately—"

"Delicate, shmelicate," Leo retorted. "I'm a plainspoken man. He's probably got a girl in every port. I wouldn't put it past him."

Inga didn't think so. She had seen the way Josh looked at Briana. And she was starting to think that maybe Josh and Briana were already making love to each other. Harve said he would forgive her anything. Had he decided he could not forgive her that?

Still, Inga was a woman of boundless optimism. "Maybe she just has to get him out of her system. Sometimes it happens that way."

Leo sniffed in disdain. "Now she's gone and lost Harve for good. What have I done to deserve this?"

Inga picked up the teapot. "I don't think she's lost him for good." She wasn't sure of this, but she believed in looking on the bright side.

She filled a cup and said, "It might do her good to have him gone. Absence makes the heart grow fonder. When he comes back, she'll look at him with new eyes."

"And what if he doesn't want her anymore?" Leo demanded. "What then?"

Inga brought him the tea, then sat by his side. "Harve is temporarily discouraged, that's all. If he loves her, he'll be back. Love conquers all."

"Love conquers squat," Leo said grimly. "I love my daughter, and look what it's got me. She's over there with that philandering wastrel. I wanted a decent man for her. One who'd give her healthy children."

Inga, usually unflappable, was shocked. "Why, Leo. You adore Nealie. How can you say such a thing?"

"I *do* adore her. But all the good in her comes from *my* side of the family. Not his. He hardly even knows who his family is. He's the one who gave Nealie that sickly constitution. I understand genes. I'd bet the farm on it."

"Genes? You mean her allergies?"

"Her allergies, her nosebleeds, her being tired all the time and getting every infection that comes along."

"But Larry's prone to infections," Inga said. "And Briana's being treated, too."

"Briana? It's all in her mind," Leo argued. "Look at her. She's healthy as a horse."

Yes, Inga thought. *She certainly seems to be.* And it was not odd for Larry to have sinus infections. He constantly worked with things that gave off dust and molds.

But the child was another matter. Inga could see Nealie was fragile, and something in Leo's words haunted her. She thought of her students through the years, and one came to her mind with sudden, frightening clarity. A boy named Jason Castleman.

A boy who had constant nosebleeds, who was tired all the time, who got every infection that came along. A boy who proved to have a sickness that could not be cured. He'd been buried in December, when the cemetery was bleak and cold.

The memory struck her like a blow, but she tried to keep her voice neutral, casual. "Leo, tell me more about those nosebleeds, will you?"

BRIANA WENT through the next two days in a kind of surreal fog. Somewhere in the fog her father kept making demands, and Glenda was overwhelmed and needed help.

On the fringes of this fog, the Haven Manufactured Home Company caused a used mobile home to materialize on Harve's property. It was put in place as swiftly as if it happened in a dream.

Briana vaguely understood that Harve was almost camping out in the trailer. Neighbors had given him used furniture and appliances, but he still didn't have the utilities hooked up, and Inga couldn't move in with him until he did.

At the edge of Briana's consciousness Inga fluttered, trying to be helpful, but to Briana she was no more substantial than a moth. Even the solid and dependable Penny seemed as spectral as a ghost.

All she could think about was that Wednesday morning she would get a call from the clinic, a call that involved life and death. If there was a healthy embryo, it would be implanted. If it grew into a child, it would be a miracle of creation in its own right, and it might save Nealie's life, as well, a second miracle.

If there was not a healthy embryo, she would try again. And again. And again. As many times as she had to.

As she waited, something was happening to her emotionally. She deeply wanted this second child. *Body and soul, I want you,* she kept thinking. She yearned to hold this baby, to gaze in wonder at the newborn face, to feel the tiny hand curl around her finger.

It was as if Briana were on a small island in this great sea of fog, and among the few realities were her own thoughts, hopes and fears. Her beloved Nealie was real. And Josh. Always Josh.

WEDNESDAY MORNING, Briana asked Penny to work in the greenhouse repotting. Penny had done such duty before and didn't seem surprised. "Sure," she said.

Josh had driven Nealie to school. He would come straight back to spend the morning with Briana, waiting for the call from the center.

As Briana saw him pulling into the drive, the phone rang. The sound stabbed through her heart like a spear of ice, striking her numb. The ring pierced her a second time. *It's come. We'll know,* she thought, her emotions spinning almost out of control.

She made her way to the phone. "Hello?" she said. Her voice shook even over that single word.

"Mrs. Briana Morris, please," said a woman's voice. Briana knew that voice. It belonged to one of the clinic's chief nurses.

"Th-this is Briana Morris," Briana stammered, and it

seemed to her as if her whole life stood poised, uncertain, waiting to be changed forever.

"This is Anna at the IRH Center," said the nurse. "Mrs. Morris, we have good news for you. There's a healthy embryo waiting. It shows no chromosome damage whatever. Can you be in the office by nine o'clock tomorrow morning? Dr. Langdon can do the implantation then."

"Yes," Briana said, dazed and not yet fully comprehending. "Yes. We can be there."

"Fine. Nine o'clock it is. And congratulations, Mrs. Morris."

Briana's whirling mind seized on one question. "Anna?"

"Yes?"

"The other embryos?"

There was a slight pause. "They didn't survive, Mrs. Morris. Dr. Chan thinks it was the result of the genetic flaw. We've seen this sort of occurrence before. It's fairly common. The important thing is that you have one that is fine and seemingly healthy."

"Yes," Briana managed to murmur. "Yes. Thank you." She hung up the phone.

The front door swung open and Josh walked in, a burst of cold air behind him. Briana ran and flung herself into his arms, laughing and crying at once.

"We're going to St. Louis. Tomorrow at nine o'clock."

It was all she needed to say.

He held her tight.

THAT NIGHT Nealie went to bed before eight o'clock. Josh didn't want Briana to go to Leo's. She did not seem to want to go, either.

They sat together on the sofa, the lamplight low, and linked their hands. He'd put on her favorite Celtic music and built a fire in the fireplace, hoping to cast a spell that would make her linger with him.

She stared at the flames pensively. "Nealie seemed worn down tonight—and too quiet."

"Yes," he said, stroking his thumb over Briana's knuckles. The child's fatigue had worried him, too. Sometimes it seemed that Nealie kept going on pure willpower and adrenaline, but tonight her little body had run out of both.

He put his arm around Briana's shoulder. "Tomorrow, babe. We go to St. Louis, and when we come home, you're going to have her little brother or sister in the nest."

He patted her flat stomach, and she leaned her head against his shoulder. "Heaven willing," she said. She said it softly, but he heard the tension in her voice.

He kissed her hair. "Do you want a boy or a girl?" he asked.

"I'll gladly welcome either," she said, putting her hand over his and pressing it to her stomach. "But Nealie would want a girl. What would you want?"

He kissed her hair again. "Either one. Have you thought of names?"

He felt her hand tighten over his. "No. It seems too soon. I guess I'm afraid to."

"Don't be afraid," he said and drew her closer.

She was quiet for a moment then drew back and looked at him. "Josh?"

She was so beautiful in the dim and dancing light, her eyes so dark, hair darker still, mouth so full and inviting.

He said, "What, love?" Perhaps he shouldn't call her that, but that's what she was, his love, the love of his life.

She glanced away as if suddenly taken by shyness. "Dr. Langdon told me—he said—"

He leaned nearer. "He said what, love?"

"He said it might be a good idea for us to make love tonight. It could improve the chance of a successful implantation. If—you're willing?"

He could not believe he'd heard her correctly. "He said *that?* Nobody told me anything—"

She shook her head. "He said since we weren't married any longer, he'd let me make the decision. But—I want to, Josh. If you do."

He gripped her upper arms. "If I *want* to? Good Lord, Briana, I've wanted to since the second I saw you again."

She lifted her face to him, her lips parted.

He kissed her with all the pent up longing of the past weeks. He didn't understand the science of it and he didn't care. Perhaps Briana felt no real desire for him. Perhaps to her he was merely a medical prescription that might prove useful. He didn't give a damn, he wanted her too much.

She wound her arms around his neck, and he stopped thinking of anything except pleasing and possessing her. He lowered her to a lying position and pulled up her white sweater.

He kissed her stomach, savoring the silkiness of her skin, the delicately salty taste of her. She sighed and laced her fingers through his hair. His kisses moved higher and became more intense. At last his tongue explored the valley between her breasts, and his hands closed over their warm swell.

She arched her back. He groaned. "Let's get behind a closed door and get these damn clothes off you," he said.

"Let's. And yours, too," she said.

It was a difficult course to navigate, the way to the bedroom. They kept stopping, swept up in storms of kissing and embracing, and twice they found themselves lying on the stairs, almost too inflamed with sexual hunger to move any farther.

But Nealie was upstairs, and she might waken. Somehow they got into the bedroom, and soon their clothes were scattered across the floor, and he had her naked and in bed just as it used to be.

He felt the wonderful curving of her hips, her waist, her breasts. He tasted her mouth, her nipples, her navel, the moist bud of pleasure between her thighs. He loved her with his lips, his hands, his arms. His legs twined with hers.

Her hair smelled like summer flowers. So did her flesh. Her breathing grew faster and harder, and so did his. When he touched her or kissed her a certain way, she cried out softly, in the way he remembered, the way that drove him crazy.

At last he could stand it no more. "I can't hold out any longer, babe," he said, breath ragged.

She settled more deeply into the bed, her hair fanning out on the pillow. He propped himself above her as she opened her legs, and he entered her as if she were paradise.

She wrapped her slender legs around him, her calves and feet pressing against his hips, helping him even more deeply into her. He thrust, and she twisted beneath him, timing her movements with his, building to a crescendo he was sure would kill him.

When it happened, everything went black for a moment, then bursts of light shot off in flashes behind his eyes. He felt her contractions like sensual ripples inviting him to drown in her, and he did.

He withdrew at last, breathless and spent yet wanting more. "Again?" he asked, lying beside her and pulling her close.

She laughed in the intimate way he remembered. "This was just what the doctor ordered. But he didn't say twice."

"Then stay with me. Let me sleep holding you," he said, caressing her breast again.

She sighed, turning to him. She put her hand on his bare chest. "I can't. I have to go to Poppa's. He's probably already fuming."

"Let somebody else go," he said. "Stay here with me."

"There isn't anybody else." Her hand trailed down his chest, drew a circle round his navel.

"I'll call Glenda. She'll do it."

"She can't. Larry's sick."

"He isn't dead. The kids'll be asleep. I'll talk her into it."

"You can't."

"I can."

He did.

He slept the night with her nestled against him, his arm

around her and his cheek against her shoulder. He thought *I've come home.*

In the dark hours of early morning, he forced himself to leave against his will. He kissed her goodbye but didn't wake her. She needed her rest. They had to go to St. Louis, and science would try to give her his child.

CHAPTER SEVENTEEN

DRAWING A CHERRY TREE was hard work.

Nealie sat at her desk at school with her crayons. The tree's trunk was straight and brown. The leaves were a ball of green atop the trunk, like a big green lollipop on a brown stick.

She had left white spots in the green ball where she was carefully drawing the red dots that were the cherries. This was a picture of the cherry tree that George Washington had chopped down when he was a little boy.

The teacher was telling them about George Washington because he had a birthday coming up. George Washington was the first president of America and the father of his country.

This made Nealie think about her own father. He was the best of all possible daddies, but she was unhappy with him because he hadn't taken her to school this morning. She'd had to ride with Penny because Mommy and Daddy had to go to St. Louis.

She missed riding with him and was sad because she knew he soon might have to go far away again. The call might come at any time. He had to leave because it was his job to go places. Her mommy had to stay here because it was her job to help Grandpa.

Nealie loved her grandfather, but she thought he'd been acting funny lately. In fact, lately all the grown-ups had been acting funny. She pushed her glasses up on her nose and tried to sort her thoughts and feelings. She loved it

when her daddy came home, but he seemed to make everybody else act different.

Nealie didn't understand this, and it bothered her.
Grandpa and Uncle Larry didn't like Daddy, and Daddy
didn't like them. Why? Grown-ups always told her not to
fight and to get along, but they didn't do it themselves. It
puzzled her until her head spun, so she decided to stop
thinking about it.

Nealie put down her red crayon and studied her picture.
The cherry tree looked all right, but the picture seemed to
need something more. She took her yellow crayon and
started to draw a sun in the sky. She would put yellow rays
coming out of it and then color the sky blue, and that would
be really good.

She would give this picture to Daddy so he could take it
with him when he went away. There was one thought she
couldn't stop thinking no matter how hard she tried. She
wished Daddy would stay and that he'd marry Mommy
again. If they got married, they could have a baby sister for
her. She had always wanted a little sister, and for her to be
named Julia. This was Nealie's favorite name. Julia Ann.

Yes, she decided, that's truly what she wished for most.
That Mommy and Daddy would stay together and give her
a baby sister.

"Julia," she said softly to herself, drawing rays on the
sun. "Julia Ann."

IT'S DONE, Josh thought.

The implantation had been performed much as Briana
had said it would. It had taken a surprisingly short time.

During the process, he'd had the eerie feeling that he and
Briana had been kidnapped by space aliens. She'd lain on
a strange bedlike device that looked to Josh as if it came
from some future civilization. She was covered to the waist
by a white sheet. A doctor in surgical garb and gloves had
hovered over her, chatting softly, being reassuring, saying
all the right things. At least Josh supposed they were the

right things. He could not remember a word the man had said.

Too many thoughts and emotions had cascaded through him. He wondered if this was like drowning. Lifetimes flashed before his eyes.

Briana had to rest, and he stayed with her, holding her hand. "Are you all right?" he kept asking. "How do you feel?"

She said it hadn't hurt. She said the worst part was the suspense. It would be two weeks until a blood test would show if she was pregnant.

He held her hand as they walked to the parking lot. The day was crisp and sunny, with no ice on the sidewalks, but he had the absurd desire to take her by the arm and lead her as carefully as if she were great with child.

He opened the door of the car for her. She gave him a wan smile and got in. He slid into the driver's seat, but he could not bring himself to start the car. He turned to her and put his hand on her cheek. "I never felt really alone with you in there."

Her dark gaze held his. "I know."

He said, "It was so—futuristic. I had this feeling that Big Brother was watching on spy cameras."

She nodded, gave him another slightly sad smile.

"Oh, God, Briana," he said with a catch in his voice. He kissed her, long and searchingly, and she kissed him back. It was as if words were too weak to say what they felt. Their feelings could only be conveyed by touch.

Gently, she broke away. She said, "What can I tell you? I love you for having done this."

"I love you, too," he said. "Come here. Just let me hold you."

He put his arm around her, and she collapsed against his shoulder, putting her hand on his chest.

"I feel like we're doing this backward," he said against her hair. "First I get you pregnant. Now I get to touch you."

"*Maybe* you got me pregnant," she murmured. "We don't know."

He touched her cheek, which was cool and smooth. "I would pay any price right now to know if there are three of us in this car."

"So would I." She rubbed her forehead affectionately against his shoulder.

He stroked her silky hair. "Lord. The things that went through my head in there."

"Me, too," she said. "I felt like Dorothy stepping into Oz. We are definitely not in ordinary reality here."

He rested his cheek against the top of her head. "I'd look at the doctor, fiddling around under that damn sheet, and I'd think smart-ass things, like that catheter's doing the job I ought to be doing, and then—"

"And then?" Her hand slipped inside his open parka, toyed with his shirt button.

"And then I'd think—I'm watching a miracle here."

She nodded. "Me, too. One second I'd feel like a lab experiment. The next I'd feel this incredible sense of wonder. Then I'd feel naked and helpless. And then a surge of—of something like joy. It kept changing. Like a kaleidoscope."

"It's hard to think that people do this every day," he mused. "I feel like we're the first."

"I know."

"In our lifetime, the impossible has become possible. Ten years ago, this couldn't have been done." A dark thought crossed his mind. *And a child like Nealie would be doomed.*

Meditatively she said, "And ten years from now, they may have a different way to help people like us. So innocent children won't suffer."

They were silent for a moment. He felt as close to her as if they had just made love again. In a way, he supposed they had.

He said, "Now we have to go back and pretend nothing's happened."

"That will be fun," she said wryly.

They fell silent again. At last he said, "Briana, if you're pregnant—what are you going to tell your father? And when?"

She drew back, her eyes holding his. "What I want to tell him is that we got married again. Because I *will* marry you—if you still want me."

He was stunned. He put his hands on her upper arms, gripping tightly. He said, "I've never wanted you more. Briana, are you sure?"

"Yes," she said. "I knew it when I was resting in that room, just holding your hand. It's the right thing to do. If I'm not pregnant this time, we'll keep trying until I am. But we'll be a family."

"What about my job?" he asked. "You hate what I do."

"I've got to learn to cope with it," she said. "I'm older now, and I try with all my might. Do you think you could deal with my family?"

"I'll learn, too," he said. "Whatever it takes, I'll do."

"But," she said, "I'd still like to keep it secret a while. I'm going to have to break this slowly to Poppa. He's not completely well yet."

"I might have to go soon," he said. "They might call any day now."

He saw the glitter of her tears.

She said, "You may not be here when they test to see if I'm pregnant."

"Briana," he said, "in my heart I'm always here with you. I always have been. I always will be."

THE NEXT DAY, Leo was in the greenhouse, helping Briana repot. Inga had convinced him that a little activity each day would be good for his heart. As soon as Inga cleaned up the luncheon dishes, she would join them. She said she had always wanted to learn to work with plants.

Leo had not done such work since his first heart attack long ago, when Briana was pregnant with Nealie. He realized how he'd missed it. He liked the feel of the damp soil, the complicated scents and heavy warmth of the greenhouse.

It made him feel almost young again and in charge. He had lost four pounds under Inga's care and was eating better than he had in years. His house was becoming orderly and cheerful.

But his children worried him. Larry was still sick. Glenda said he laid about all day crabbing that the boys didn't behave.

And Leo was fearful about Josh and Briana. Why had Briana stayed home night before last? Josh hadn't left until long past midnight. Leo knew because he couldn't sleep and kept rising to see if Josh's car was gone. It was unsettling. At first Leo was too upset to mention it to Briana. She'd been acting so strange lately.

He decided it was time to speak his mind. "Something's going on," he said. "That man stayed until all hours the other night. And the two of you have been making eyes at each other since you went to St. Louis."

Briana gave him a calm look. "Poppa," she said, "I love you. I don't want to upset you. But yes. We still care for each other."

"C-care for him?" Leo sputtered. "I think you would have learned your lesson the first time!"

She said, "We're older now. When we got married, it was too headlong, too fast. But I still love him, Poppa. So the best thing you could do is accept it—and him."

Leo's hand was black with dirt, but he clasped it to his chest. "I'm an old man who's recuperating, and you spring this on me?"

"You knew it was happening," she said with the same repose. "You just said so."

"I hoped I was wrong," Leo retorted. He took his hand away from his chest. He'd left a black print on his apron front, and his fingers trembled. His heartbeat was fast, but it was steady and strong.

Nevertheless, he decided to let her know how disturbing he found her words. "I think I need a nitroglycerin tablet," he said.

"Do you want help?" she asked.

"No," he snapped, going to the sink. "You're right—I saw this coming. My sincere hope is that it blows over." He washed his hands, then fumbled for the vial of pills in his shirt pocket.

"Poppa," she said, "I know you don't like the idea. But please remember—he's Nealie's father."

"And I'm yours," Leo retorted.

"Yes. And I adore you. Just as Nealie adores Josh. But I have the right to live my own life."

Leo opened his medicine vial and popped a pill under his tongue. "Hmph," he said. But he took the cup of water Briana offered.

"I don't choose to discuss this anymore," he said loftily. "I'm supposed to avoid stress. Talk about something else. I'm going to repot the rest of those yellow brandywines. I forgot how soothing it is to repot."

He moved to the worktable. "Tomatoes are so much more comforting than children. They never talk back. They never defy you. They don't run around with some other tomato that's no good for them."

Briana said nothing. She gave him her dratted Mona Lisa smile.

The door opened, and Inga breezed in, her cheeks red with cold. "Hello," she chirped, as she hung up her coat. "My, don't you two look busy? I would have been here sooner, but I stopped at Larry's to see if he and Glenda needed anything."

Briana said, "How are they?"

Inga took one of the work aprons from a peg and put it on. "Larry's better, but the boys were making him cross as a bear with a sore head."

"They'd make anybody cross as a bear," grumbled Leo, but he was glad when Inga came to his side. She exuded competence, as usual, and he found comfort in her presence.

Inga said, "Poor Glenda was near tears, and she said she just didn't know what to do anymore. I said to her, Glenda, your boys are just normal boys. But children always test limits, so those limits must be firmly set."

Inga watched Leo repot for a moment, then said, "I think I see how you do it. I read about it this morning in that book you left out for me. You picked a very good one. The directions were so clear."

Leo tried to keep a smile of pride from his lips, for Briana had put him in a bad mood. How pleasant that at least Inga, a woman of uncommon intelligence, maturity and perception, appreciated him.

Inga took a scoop of soil and put it in a container, patting it around the bottom and side. *She's got a good touch,* Leo thought approvingly.

"So anyway," Inga went on, reaching for a young plant, "Glenda said that she thought Larry wasn't consistent when he disciplined the children, but he blames *her* because they don't behave. She said she was ready to go to a counselor, but he refused. He thought it wasn't manly."

Leo snorted. "That's because it's not manly. Sitting around telling some headshrinker your feelings. Phooey."

"Oh, Leo," Inga said, "that's not the way it works. There's no stigma to getting expert help when it's needed. The world is so much more complicated than when we were young."

"You can say that again," Leo said with feeling.

"My goodness," Inga said, "Larry and Glenda married so young. Three children, now a fourth on the way. They both work hard—it's no wonder they feel the stress."

"I certainly understand stress," Leo said gloomily. He shot Briana an accusing look, but she only gave him another of those cryptic smiles.

"You certainly can, poor man," Inga said. "At any rate,

I told Glenda I'd talk to Larry. She said she'd be happy if I did. Would you mind?''

"I don't know about this counselor business," Leo muttered.

"Oh, Leo," Inga said, eyes widening, "it's the enlightened thing to do these days. Even I've done it."

"You?" he said in disbelief.

"I'm not ashamed. When my husband died, I was grieving so hard, I knew I needed someone to help me through that terrible time. I mean, my whole life had been taking care of that man. Counseling was a godsend."

"Hmm," mused Leo. If someone as sensible as Inga would use counseling, it must have some merit.

"Excuse me," Briana said, glancing at her watch. "I've got to clean up and go pick up Nealie at school."

As soon as she was gone, Leo said to Inga, "I was right. She and Josh are warming up to each other again. She admitted it."

A strange expression crossed Inga's face. "Yes. I suppose it's been—inevitable. We just didn't want to see it."

"Well?" Leo demanded. "What do we do?"

Inga had been oddly quiet on the subject of Briana for the last day or so. She surprised him by saying, "We shouldn't do anything. It was probably wrong to interfere. It was certainly wrong for me to interfere. Josh is the father of your grandchild. To shut him out, to work against him—it can only make for bad relations between you."

"There've always been rotten relations between us," Leo countered. "I've tried to keep them apart, but he foils me. Lately he's been hovering over her like a vulture. At least he's gone today."

Inga looked thoughtful. "Yes. I saw him leave right before lunch. Where'd he go?"

"I don't know. I wish it was Timbuktu."

But Josh was not in Timbuktu. He was at the courthouse of the bustling tourist town of Branson, Missouri, buying a marriage license.

MISSOURI HAD a three-day waiting period for marriages. Exactly three days later, Josh and Briana married for the second time. They took the license to the nearest city of any size near Illyria, Springfield.

They were married in the chambers of an elderly judge named Arthur O. Stanhope. His secretary and the court reporter were the witnesses.

Briana's knees shook throughout the ceremony, and Josh held her hand tightly. At last Arthur O. Stanhope said, ''I now pronounce you husband and wife. You may kiss the bride.''

Josh said, ''Come here, bride.'' He bent and kissed her so long and so yearningly that the secretary giggled.

Briana felt joyous, but it was a different sort than the first time she had married him. This wasn't the swooping giddiness of a young woman eloping with a man who had bewitched her at first sight. This joy seemed stronger and deeper.

There were other differences. The first time they'd wed, she had been fearless. Now she was full of anxieties, about Nealie, about whether she was pregnant, about Josh going away again.

He kept hold of her hand as they left the courthouse. In her other hand she clasped a small bouquet of crocuses and hyacinths he had bought her at the florist's. It was the only weddinglike thing they had done—except for the wedding itself.

They had not dressed formally. They had wanted to awaken no suspicion when they left. Briana wore a dark blue jumper and a white turtleneck. Josh had on cargo pants and his Scandinavian sweater. They had not exchanged rings. They would wait.

But if the act had not been festive, the day itself was, sunny and balmy, with the sky a deep and perfect blue. There was an exciting tingle in the air that whispered that winter was old and dying, that spring was pushing to be born.

They took a walk in a small city park that, in spite of the weather, was almost deserted. Most adults were still at work, the children in school.

The snow was melting rapidly, and Briana could see patches of grass showing the first hints of green, and there were buds on the forsythia bushes. A pair of cardinals flew across their path, a darting, zigzag flight so spirited Briana wondered if they were practicing mating.

Josh gazed after them, then looked at her, one corner of his mouth quirked in an ironic smile. "This is pretty strange, you know. I've just turned the former Mrs. Morris into the present and future Mrs. Morris. I hope Mrs. Morris has no regrets."

They stopped by a pond that was still frozen. Mirrorlike pools of water had formed on its surface, blazing in the sunlight.

She reached up and adjusted his shirt collar, which peeked above his sweater. "I have one regret, Mr. Morris."

He toyed with a lock of her hair. "What's that?"

She smiled sadly. "There won't be a wedding night."

His smile turned into an expression of stoic resignation. "I wonder if you can possibly regret it as much as I do. This is killing me, Briana."

"I know," she said. "Me, too."

After the implantation of the embryo, they had been told to abstain from sex for two to three weeks. The contractions of orgasm might interfere with the delicate placement of the fertilized egg.

He took her face between his hands and tilted it toward his. "This is going to have to do for now."

Her lips parted beneath his, and their tongues played a complex and intimate game that made her want to sink against him and slide her hands underneath his sweater, feel the warm, hard flesh of him.

"I wish you didn't have on that damn coat," he murmured against her mouth. "I wish you didn't have on anything at all. Or me, either."

"This is a municipal park," she said. "We'd be arrested."

"If I'm called away before we can have sex again, when I come back, I'm going to lock the door and ravish you repeatedly."

She shook her head. "I don't think that would be good for Junior, either. You can only ravish me once or twice at a time."

"Damn!" he said, clenching his hand into a fist like a foiled melodrama villain. "Another fantasy shot to hell."

She put her fingertip on his lips. "Watch your language. There may be a child present."

His face went serious. He took her hand and held it to his chest. "I've asked you this four hundred times in the last four days. Do you feel pregnant?"

"I can't say." She could feel his heart beating beneath her fingertips. "The doctors have me on another hormone now, so if I have any sort of twinge, I don't know if it's a good sign, a bad one or just a side effect."

"Poor woman," he said, looping his arms around her shoulders. "You're as full of drugs as a pharmacy."

She laid her head against his shoulder and looked at the dazzling surface of the icy pond. "Not even an ordinary pharmacy. A very jumpy, emotional pharmacy. I'm sorry my feelings have been so—turbulent."

He moved behind her, wound his arms around her so his hands rested on her flat belly. In her ear, he said, "You've been a rock. Most courageous girl in the world."

She leaned against him, her hands atop his. She wondered if their unborn child rested beneath their joined touch. "I've had my ups and downs. And they've been doozies."

He drew her closer. "Just so you don't feel that today is one of the downs. I hope you'll never regret this, Briana. I love you."

"I love you, too." But even as she said it she felt a wave of fear wash over her. She feared for the embryo within

her. As always, she feared for Nealie. And she dreaded the
call that would take Josh away from them again.

She sighed and closed her eyes against the glare of sunlight on the lake. As if he sensed her thoughts, Josh kissed
first her ear, then the spot behind it. "This time I want to
stay married to you forever. I know I'll be gone a lot, but
I'll be as good a husband as I can. And as good a father to
Nealie and the baby."

She turned her face to him, looked at him earnestly. "I
wish you didn't have to leave again."

"So do I, babe." He kissed the tip of her nose. "But it
won't be for long. And after this one, I'll try to schedule
my assignments so we have as much time together as possible. I promise."

She put her arms around his neck and clung to him
tightly. "I told my father that we still cared for each other."

"That's putting it mildly," Josh said and nuzzled her
hair.

"He must know that this is bound to happen. I've hinted
as much. This time I won't let my family monopolize me.
You and Nealie and the baby come first."

"Likewise," he said against her throat. "I want to have
you and hold you from this day forward."

"In two weeks," she said, "we'll find out if our family
of three becomes a family of four."

"In two weeks," he said, "I'll be able to make love to
you again."

They held each other and smiled at the irony of such a
wedding day.

He kissed her again, a lingering, hungry kiss.

"It's going to be a long two weeks," he said.

AT LEO'S, Harve was almost finished reinforcing a weak
strut in the wall of the newest greenhouse. His hands were
sure, and he worked efficiently, but his mind was on other
matters.

He knew Josh and Briana had gone off together again.

Inga said they were going to do some shopping for Nealie. Harve didn't care. The more he saw Briana with Josh, the more he realized his infatuation with her was futile.

And infatuation was all it was, he knew. He'd been entranced by her looks and her spirit, true—but most of all by her unattainability. She was like the princess atop the glass hill, and only one man could ride to the top of that hill and claim her. Every time Harve had tried to ascend, he slipped back to ordinary earth, where he belonged.

And if Harve was completely honest, he had to admit that part of his attraction to Briana was that she was Leo's daughter. He admired Leo. He came close to idolizing him, and he saw Briana as a way of becoming permanently allied with Leo.

But he had been sitting alone most nights in his second-hand mobile home, thinking and thinking. Why couldn't he ask Leo about a partnership that didn't involve marriage? This wasn't the Middle Ages. A man didn't have to marry into a business arrangement.

Harve hadn't mentioned his idea to Inga because Inga was acting strangely. She had suddenly stopped encouraging Harve to court Briana. Perhaps she, too, had finally realized it was a fool's quest.

Instead, she was focusing her powers of persuasion on Larry and Glenda. Glenda had apparently confided some problem to Inga, and there was nothing Inga loved more than helping people solve their problems. Harve loved her, but he was grateful her attentions were aimed at somebody else for a change.

He tested the reinforced strut and found it secure. He put away his tools, slipped into his jacket, went out and put the toolbox in the back of his truck.

He headed for Briana's house on foot because it gave him time to think. There were things he wanted to put into words, and he needed to get them right.

When he reached the back porch, he mounted the steps

and kicked off his overshoes, setting them on the mat beside Penny's. He knocked on the back door and waited.

He took a deep breath. Penny was probably upstairs in the office. It would take her a minute to get to the door. He could feel his heart beating as hard as if he had drunk fourteen cups of coffee.

The door swung open, and he saw Penny's face, her cap of fiery curls. Surprise flickered in her eyes. "Hi. Did you come for the mail order forms? They're all small—no heavy stuff. I can fill them myself."

"I didn't come for the forms," he said. He resisted the desire to shuffle his feet.

She shrugged. "As long as you're here, want to come in for a cup of coffee? I was just about to pour myself a cup."

Harve shook his head. Coffee was the last thing he needed. This woman seemed to drink quarts of the stuff, more than anybody he knew—except for himself. "Could I just talk to you a minute?" he asked.

"Sure," she said. She made a gesture for him to enter. He stepped inside and stood in the middle of the familiar kitchen. "Take off your jacket," she invited. "Sit."

He didn't sit and he didn't take off his jacket. He stuck his hands into his pockets because he didn't know what else to do with them. He said, "I've got two things to say to you."

"Yes?" She cocked her head, waiting.

"You made me a mighty kind offer about your father's fishing equipment. I'd be honored to take it, and I thank you."

She smiled. "That's great. I know he'd want it to go to somebody who'd appreciate it. Consider it yours."

"That's the first thing I've got to say," he muttered.

She looked at him questioningly.

"The second thing—" He stopped, gathered his courage, then plunged on. "The second thing is you invited me to supper at your house to meet your sister."

Her cheeks turned pink. "Actually, I mentioned that

without asking her, and it turns out she's, uh, well, she's interested in the new civics teacher, Mr. Rudner, and he's asked her out, so—'' She stopped, clearly flustered.

"I never wanted to meet your sister anyhow," Harve said. "But I'd like to have supper. With you. Only I'd take you out. Over to Springfield. To the new steak house."

Her cheeks got pinker, but her face softened. She smiled. She had a kind of crooked smile, unique and fetching. "Why, Harve, you're asking me out? On a date?"

"That's it," he said, taking his hands from his pockets and crossing his arms. "I'm asking you out. On a date."

Her smile faded. "Is this because you're on the rebound from Briana? Because if it is, I'd rather not get into something like this."

"It's because of you, not Briana," he said, his determination growing. "I've dreamed about you three nights in a row. I took it as a sign."

She blinked and put one hand on her hip. "You dreamed about me? What did you dream?"

He uncrossed his arms and put his hands on her shoulders. He took a step closer to her. It was as if he was controlled by a force far more powerful than he was. "I dreamed this," he said. Then to his astonishment, he bent and kissed her on the mouth.

CHAPTER EIGHTEEN

JOSH AND BRIANA got to Illyria just in time to pick Nealie up from school. They would not tell her about the wedding—not yet. She was too young to keep a secret. They would decide when the time was right for everyone to know.

As her husband and daughter bantered about school, Briana put her hand gently on her abdomen. What she'd told Josh was true. She didn't feel pregnant—but it was too soon for such feelings. And she was married. It did not seem possible. It was like some strange dream.

She was jerked back to reality when Josh asked Nealie, "What's that spot on your sweater?"

Nealie said, "Oh, I had a nosebleed. I got bumped in the hall."

A chill swept through Briana, and her hand tightened protectively over her midsection.

"Did you go to the nurse's office?" Josh asked, voice taut. "Did they put ice on it?"

"Yes," Nealie said, as if the subject was boring. "It was just a little nosebleed. It stopped fast. I got a drop on my sweater, that's all."

"You're sure?" Josh asked.

"I'm just glad I didn't get it on my picture. I drew another picture for you. I'll give it to you when we get home. It's in my backpack."

Just a little nosebleed, Briana thought. *Just a little one. Nothing to panic over.* But for the rest of the trip, nothing felt dreamlike.

At home, Nealie ran upstairs to change clothes. Her limp seemed more pronounced. Josh watched as she closed her bedroom door. "I want that kid well," he said, his face hard with emotion.

"We both do," Briana said softly. She touched his shoulder. He turned, put his arms around her, bent and kissed her lips.

The office door opened upstairs, and Penny's voice called, "Briana? I needed to ask you about this customer who wants—" She stopped when she saw Briana in Josh's embrace.

Briana looked at Penny but kept her hands locked around Josh's neck and didn't move away from him. She was tired of hiding her feelings about Josh. It was time to let people know.

"Yes?" Briana said.

"Oops." Penny eased toward the office. "Sorry about that."

"It's okay," Josh said. He stepped away from Briana reluctantly.

It was just as well he did. Nealie came bursting out of her door in blue jeans and a yellow sweatshirt. As she dashed down the steps, Penny slipped inside the office.

"Here's my picture," cried Nealie, waving a piece of paper. "It's for you, Daddy. So when you go away, you can look at it and think of me."

She ran to him and thrust it at him. "See? It's a shamrock. We're studying Ireland, because St. Patrick's Day is coming. Ireland is forty different shades of green. I used all the green crayons in my box."

"That's nice work, Nealie," Josh said, studying it. "Good composition. Nice color. Let's put it on the refrigerator so we can look at it."

Nealie looked hesitant. "But it's for you to take when you go."

"I'll carry it everywhere," Josh promised her. "I'll never be without it, and I'll bring it back home to you."

"Promise?" Nealie asked.

"I swear it," Josh said, raising his hand solemnly.

Nealie threw herself at him. He set the picture aside and swept her into his arms. Warmth stole through Briana's veins. Josh loved the child so much, and the love was deep and mutual.

"It's a beautiful picture, Nealie," she said. "A very nice present. For now I'll put it by the picture of George Washington's cherry tree."

Nealie looked up at Briana. "George Washington couldn't always be home, either. He had to go during the war and be a hero. Daddy's a hero, isn't he? *I* think so."

Josh looked dubious, but Briana said, "Yes. I think so, too."

Nealie's expression went moody. "The trouble with heroes is that they have to keep going away. Can't a person stay home and be heroic?"

Josh and Briana glanced at each other and then away. He set Nealie on her feet and knelt before her, his hands on her shoulders. "There are all kinds of ways to be heroic," Josh told Nealie. "Your mother is. And she stays home."

Nealie pushed her glasses up her nose. She looked soberly at Josh. "I love Mommy. But heroic? She just stays here and works."

Josh gazed into Nealie's eyes. "You're mother is the most heroic person I know. Some day you'll understand that."

THE CALL CAME two days later.

Josh and Briana and Nealie were working in the greenhouse when Penny came with the message that there had been an urgent call from Carson Michelman. He wanted Josh to phone immediately.

Josh saw Briana's face go pale and felt his muscles tense.

Penny said, "I drove. You can ride back with me. If you want."

"Yeah," Josh said tonelessly. He turned to Briana. "I'd better go."

Briana's chin quivered, but she squared her jaw to make it stop. "Should we go with you?"

"No," he said, washing his hands. "It might be nothing. I'll come right back." He didn't bother with his parka. He left the greenhouse and got into Penny's car.

"I hope it isn't bad news or something," Penny said.

He shook his head. If it was Carson, it was bad news, all right, because it probably meant that *Adventure* finally wanted its pound of flesh. It was going to be Burma, he knew it. Well, Burma was dangerous as hell, but he couldn't stay over four weeks. That was all a visa was good for.

At the house, Penny went to the office, and Josh used the downstairs telephone. He dialed Carson Michelman's number. He thought of Nealie. He thought of Briana. He thought of the child who might or might not being growing within her, and suddenly four weeks seemed an eternity.

Carson answered on the second ring. "Michelman and Associates."

"Carson, this is Josh. I got word you called."

"Right. How's your kid?"

Josh knew this question, coming from Carson, was a mere formality. "She's holding steady."

"It's not necessary for you to be there any longer?" Carson's voice was brusque. He sounded in the mood to waste neither words nor sentiment.

"Maybe not absolutely necessary," Josh said. "But I'd like to stay longer. There are still serious family concerns."

"There are also serious contract concerns," Carson returned. "And you've had three weeks off. Vacation's over. *Adventure* calls."

"Yeah, yeah," Josh said, resigned to it, hoping Briana was. "So give me the bad news. Burma, right?"

"Nope," Carson said. "They finally made the breakthrough. *Adventure* pulled it off, by God. Pitcairn Island approved you. You've got a visitor's permit."

He felt numbed, in shock. *"What?"*

"It came through last week. We've been looking for a way to get you there."

Josh swore. "Pitcairn? Are you crazy? Is *Adventure* crazy? They really want to go through with this? Pitcairn's a rock in the middle of nowhere. There's no real story, and they don't like talking to journalists."

"The story is that it's the most remote community on earth. It's in trouble, it's dying," Carson said.

"That's been happening for years," Josh said. "It's old news."

Carson said, "The Pitcairners are considering tourism, but not too much. They're going to let *Adventure* do an article—"

Josh was full of foreboding. Pitcairn was an inaccessible and dangerous place, and nobody would pay it an iota of mind if, over two hundred years ago, Fletcher Christian hadn't led the mutiny on the *Bounty*.

After Christian seized control of the ship, he went to Tahiti, picked up the women he and his followers had left behind and set out to find the farthest-flung hiding place he could.

And that place was Pitcairn Island.

The island was close to no other civilization. It was an isolated dot in the middle of the world's biggest ocean, three thousand miles from New Zealand, four thousand from Chile.

The few people living there were mostly descendants of the mutineers. The place had a romantic reputation. But it was primitive, and there were rumors of a darker side, as well.

Josh said, "It gives me bad vibes, Carson. It's too hard to get there and back. A man could get stuck there for months."

"Right, right," Carson said. "But your visitor's permit is only for six months. By then a ship will come along."

Six months, thought Josh. *Six bloody months?* When he

was younger he would have thought half a year on Pitcairn would be heaven. Even six months ago he might have thought it. Now, with Nealie sick and Briana trying to get pregnant, it sounded like an interminable season in hell.

He said, "I don't want to stay six months. I need to be back here."

Carson swore at him. "Listen, you SOB, the islanders had to vote unanimously to grant you that permit. Right now you're the only photographer in the world who has one. Watson's the only writer."

"Watson's in the middle of an assignment in Mexico," Josh argued. "I know that."

"Not any longer," Carson snapped back. "The senior editor's hauling him out because—get this—*Adventure* found a ship willing to take you. But you've got to be in Houston in forty-eight hours."

"That's impossible," Josh protested. "You couldn't find a way there this soon."

"*Adventure* got word three weeks ago this might happen. They've been monitoring ships all over the world. And they got very, very, very lucky. You and Watson have to work your way over on a Swedish chemical tanker."

Josh groaned. "Oh, that sounds great. Watson and I become swabbies on a chemical tanker and go to the big rock. Do you have any damn idea how we get *back*?"

"I told you," Carson said irritably. "Something'll turn up. A mail boat comes three times a year. If you're lucky, you can get passage. We'll do what we can from this end. Just don't get sick or something stupid like that."

"Right," Josh said sarcastically. "You get appendicitis on Pitcairn, you're a dead man. The closest hospital's thirteen hundred miles away—and there's no way to get there."

"You sound like an old lady," scoffed Carson. "Before, it was, 'If the Pitcairn assignment comes up, I'm first in line.' You're going soft, Morris."

I have a wife, a kid, maybe another kid on the way, thought Josh. *Maybe it's time to go soft.*

But there was also honor at stake. Repeatedly he had said he wanted the Pitcairn assignment. But he no longer was hungry for it. Instead, it gave him a poisoned feeling in the pit of his stomach. "It's too long," he said. "I don't want to be gone that long."

"You want me to get tough? Call in lawyers?" Carson asked, starting to play hardball. "You've got contractual obligations to *Adventure.* You break them, you get black-balled by every Tessman publication in America. And, Josh, that's one hell of a lot of publications."

Josh cursed silently.

"Look," Carson said. "I said okay to your dropping everything else. You wanted to go back to Hysteria, Missouri—"

"Illyria, dammit."

"Whatever. You wanted to go back, and you knew you had this commitment to *Adventure,* and you were going to have to take a tough assignment from them sooner or later, probably sooner. I cut you slack to keep you in the States as long as I could."

You're all heart, Josh thought.

"Well, the assignment's now. The place is Pitcairn, and it doesn't matter if it's hell on earth, it's where you're going. The money, I might add, is excellent."

Doctor bills, thought Josh. *Big ones. Lots of them.*

"*Adventure* wouldn't ask just anybody to go," Carson said, softening. "But they figured you were good enough that the Pitcairners would approve you. You're smart and you're careful. And you've got the one extra thing that makes you the man for the job."

"What's that?" Josh asked, not buying it.

"Luck," Carson said with satisfaction. "You're the luckiest SOB I know in a tight spot. Remember that mess in Haiti? What were the odds of your hardly being touched? Face it, Morris. You've got it and you've always had it— luck."

Josh thought, *Luck can run out.*

But in the end he said yes. He had no choice.

"PITCAIRN ISLAND?" Briana said, dark eyes widening in fear. "It's so far away. It's dangerous, Josh."

"Babe, I'll watch my step," he promised, "you know I will. I've got every reason to be careful."

"But," she said, "but—" She knew about places like Pitcairn. She knew because of him. It was one of he places he used to talk about and she'd prayed he'd never be sent.

It was not for the usual reasons. There were no violent political clashes, terrorists, bombings, land mines, drug wars, firefights or tortures.

No, it was frightening in a different way. Going to Pitcairn was like going to the moon. It was barely accessible. No plane could land there. No helicopter could make it that far. There was no real harbor, and no big ship could negotiate its crashing waves.

Even to set foot there, you had to risk your life. You had to cross the deadly stretch of sea in a small boat, then climb a three-hundred-foot cliff. Once you got on the island, there was no guarantee when you would get off. It might be weeks—or even months.

She wanted to cry. It was starting all over again. She might be pregnant, and once more he was going away from her to a distant and frightening place.

He said, "I will always come back to you. To you and Nealie—" he patted her abdomen "—and whoever may be in here. I will always come back. Always."

She blinked back the tears. "When do you have to go?"

"They want me in Houston day after tomorrow. There's a tanker that's agreed to carry us if we work our way."

"A tanker?" she said, relieved. "Then you'll be near shipping lanes?"

"No," he said. "But they agreed to take us as close to the island as they can get. The islanders come get us in long boats. I—don't know yet how we'll get back. Or when."

She understood that too well. "But the baby?" She

choked the words out. "What if there's not a baby this time?"

He rubbed her nose with his. "There'll be a baby. They've got me in Popsicle form in the lab."

"I don't want you in Popsicle form," she said, collapsing against his neck. "I want you in the warm, old-fashioned form."

"Then you'll have me that way," he said. "Again and again and again.

NEALIE CRIED HARD when he left. He didn't know which was worse—Nealie's tears or Briana's stoic cheerfulness.

With luck he might be back in three months, even less. But he was haunted by ominous feelings about this trip he had once so desired. For the first time in his life, he didn't want to go. He wanted to stay put.

He sensed disapproval from Leo and Larry. *See?* the men seemed to say with silent looks. *He's deserting her again. Can't depend on him. Not that one.*

Glenda seemed concerned for his welfare, and oddly, so did Inga, who had suddenly started acted almost like an ally. Did she suspect something? Josh was starting to think she did.

Harve clasped his hand and wished him a safe journey, a speedy return. With an ironic shock, Josh realized he was beginning to like Harve. But it tore his heart out to leave Nealie and Briana. He kept telling himself it would be all right. Briana would be pregnant, and Nealie would be safe, and he would come home to his family.

By then it would be late spring or early summer. He imagined evenings sitting in Briana's porch swing, Nealie on his lap. Briana would lean her head on his shoulder, and together they would listen to the frogs and crickets. He would rest his hand on her swelling abdomen, where their new child grew.

THE SWEDISH SHIP had to drop anchor in the open ocean when it neared Pitcairn. The waves crashed violently against the great rock that was the island, and waves and reefs could tear the tanker to pieces. The ship had arrived at night. The sky was black, the sea was rough, and a chill rain fell.

By radio contact the Pitcairners knew the ship was there and set out in their longboats to reach it. They knew the tanker would stay a few hours at most, and they must dare the sea, no matter how dark and pitching.

They came across the nighttime sea guided by their flashlights and lanterns, a supernatural winking across the black water. Part of their journey was to bring barter—handcrafts and fresh fruit and fish. They easily clambered up the sides of the ship using a rope ladder and bearing bundles and baskets on their shoulders.

What they purchased, they swung in baskets over the side into the longboats that rose and fell on the waves. Trading done, the men and women scrambled over the rail one by one.

Each had to time exactly his or her drop from the swinging ladder. If they did not hit the longboat when it crested on a swell, they would plunge at least ten feet to crash into the boat—or miss it and fall into the sea.

Josh climbed down the side of the tossing ship on a ridiculously thin rope ladder that was slippery beneath his sweating hands. When it was his turn to free fall into the boat, he prayed, gritted his teeth and let go.

A group of islanders lowered his equipment in wildly swinging baskets. Then came the last man, the writer, Watson. He couldn't bring himself to let go of the ladder and had to be dragged into the boat by a burly man who cried, "Now, now! Let go now!"

Watson collapsed into a heap, but nobody seemed to notice except Josh, who pulled him up to sit on the thwart beside him. The others were already concentrating on making the arduous voyage back to land. They did not speak to the Americans.

Later Watson told Josh he'd never been as scared in his life as hanging on that threadlike ladder and tossing in that small boat over the night sea. "I almost peed my pants," he said.

Josh decided he probably shouldn't tell Briana about this part of the voyage for a while. Maybe never.

NOT MERELY was Pitcairn's shore dangerous to reach. Its one settlement, Adamstown, could be reached only after climbing a cliff aptly named the Hill of Difficulty.

But Josh knew that at the top of the hill was a prize of enormous value—a telephone that could reach the outside world. The telephone was a recent acquisition, bouncing its signal only a part of the day off a New Zealand satellite. He could talk to his wife and daughter.

On that phone, two days later, he learned that Briana was pregnant. When she told him, he was so stunned he could hardly speak.

"Hello?" she said through the static and fluttering hum. "Josh, did you hear me? The test was positive. There's going to be a baby."

At last he managed to say, "I'll get back as soon as I can. There should be a mail boat in a couple of months. Then I'm coming back to you. All three of you."

"And I'm telling my family," Briana said. He could hear the happiness in her voice. "I think Glenda has a hunch something's up. And Inga, too. I think she's been preparing Poppa that this might happen."

"Your father—is he strong enough to take it, do you think?"

"He's better than he's been in years. Inga makes him toe the line, but he loves the attention. It's so obvious, it makes Nealie giggle."

His throat tightened at the mention of his daughter. "My Panda Girl, how is she?"

Briana said, "Oh, Josh, Nealie's going to be over the moon when she finds out."

"I love you," he said. "Listen. The telephone signal's been bad lately. There's no Internet. I won't be able to talk to you as often as I want. But I'll think of you every minute."

"Josh, please be careful and come back to us soon."

"I'll say it again," he told her. "I love you. I'll be home as soon as I can. I'm counting the days."

He did count them. And count. And count.

NEALIE WAS so excited that she wanted to dance everywhere she went.

Sometimes she did dance and sometimes she got a nosebleed, and when that happened, she had to stop dancing, but that didn't stop her from being excited. What was an old nosebleed? Her daddy and mommy were married again!

They had gotten secretly married. They did it that way so that Grandpa wouldn't be upset. Grandpa got upset anyway, of course, but Inga was helping him smooth his feathers. She had grown expert at it. Still, Grandpa grumbled that Pitcairn Island was the most obscure place on the earth and nowhere for a sane married man to go. And Mommy, as usual, was worried when Daddy was away.

But unlike her mother and grandfather, Nealie would not believe anything could ever happen to her father. He was strong and smart and brave, and he would come back to them just like always. He especially had to come back because in November there would be a new baby.

Nealie convinced herself this child would be a girl. "Julia Ann," she kept whispering to herself. She would pretend to introduce the baby to people. "This is my little sister, Julia Ann."

But still, Mommy was distracted. Sometimes she stared at the horizon, almost as if, if she looked hard enough, she could see Daddy, as far away as he was. She would stand with her hand on her tummy, and Nealie knew she was thinking of Daddy. Three months was a long time to wait for him to come home.

In three months, winter turned into spring and spring was changing into summer. And Nealie noticed people changing, too. Uncle Larry was not as loud, and he made his boys behave better—finally! Mommy said this was because of Inga, who knew how to handle people like Larry. Aunt Glenda seemed happier than Nealie could ever remember.

Harve had changed, too. He was busy building his new house, and he had stopped mooning around after Mommy. Now he liked Penny, which was, to Nealie's mind, a much better arrangement.

So Nealie thought that life was good except for Daddy being gone. The doctor said the baby was healthy and strong and would be born right before Thanksgiving. Daddy would be home by then, and maybe he could stay a long time before he had to go away again.

But May came and went, and Daddy had to stay on Pitcairn. He couldn't book passage on the mail boat. It was already overcrowded. At last he called and said he would be home at the end of July. *Adventure* had found a yacht coming from a place called Mooréa, and the captain had agreed to pick up Daddy and the writer and get them to Tahiti, and from Tahiti, Daddy could be home in almost no time.

Mommy was starting to get a round tummy, and the further into July it got, the happier she seemed.

But that was before Mommy got the telephone call that made her cry.

IT WAS just after ten o'clock on a Tuesday morning in mid-July, and Briana waited for Josh's call. He tried to phone as often as possible, and always on Tuesdays.

He was late calling, but that did not upset her. The island's phone service was patchy and unpredictable. She was eager to hear from him, for she had much to tell him. At her exam yesterday, doctors had said both she and the baby were doing excellent.

Nealie's latest blood test showed she was still holding steady, and she had not had a nosebleed for a week and two days. Leo seemed to have grudgingly accepted the marriage and even seemed excited, almost against his volition, at the thought of another grandchild. Briana was eager to tell Josh everything.

But when the phone at last rang, the voice she heard was not Josh's. It was that of the writer, Tim Watson. Watson asked if she had anyone with her.

Briana was puzzled. There was no one else in the house—everyone was off somewhere, and she was alone.

"I'm sorry," Watson said. "I've got bad news."

Her knees felt suddenly rubbery, and her breath choked in her throat. "What is it?" she managed to say.

"Josh is hurt," he told her. "It's bad."

The edges of her vision went dark. All the light seemed to leak out of the room. She gripped the phone tightly, closed her eyes and forced herself to say, "How bad?"

"It's serious," Watson said. "He's got a fractured leg, a concussion and a broken collarbone."

"No!" she cried. "No. What happened?"

Her heart thudding, she listened to Watson stammer through a disjointed explanation. She could only half comprehend his words.

On the north side of Pitcairn was a ridge of rock jutting into the sea. It was called Down Isaac's, and the islanders waded from it to catch fish.

But Down Isaac's could be reached only by descending one of Pitcairn's cliffs, and after rains, the cliff was dangerously slippery. Josh had gone to photograph the morning's fishing. He had fallen, and nobody could clearly explain how it had happened.

"He's at the island's dispensary," Watson said. "Listen, we're doing all we can for him."

"The dispensary?" Briana said, still in shock. "There's no doctor there. There's only one nurse—"

"She's a good nurse," Watson said, trying to comfort her. "She was able to set his leg. It was a clean break. Thank God for that. She's got him in some kind of harness for his collarbone, but he's in a lot of pain. The circulation in his arm's affected. He may need surgery."

"B-but for surgery h-he needs a—he needs a doctor," Briana stuttered.

"Yes," Watson admitted. "He should be in a real hospital."

But he's on Pitcairn, Briana thought in panic. *The nearest hospital is over a thousand miles away.* "The yacht coming from Mooréa," she said desperately. "It should be there within a week. Is that soon enough?"

There was a long pause full of interference and whirring, and she squeezed her eyes tightly shut. She sensed more bad news coming.

Watson said, "I'm sorry. The yacht can't make it. Motor trouble. It had to turn back. Nobody's on the way that we know of."

"Oh, God," she said, and fought back tears of hopelessness.

"It wouldn't have helped," Watson said. "He needs a faster boat and one with a doctor aboard. We'll do what we can. We're sending out signals that we've got a medical emergency."

"Can I talk to him?" she begged. She was frantic to hear his voice.

"He's pretty drugged up now," Watson said. "And he wasn't very coherent when they brought him in. What he talked about mostly was you—you and your little girl and the baby."

Briana put her hand on her belly and felt the unborn child kick.

"Tell him we love him," she said, her voice breaking. "Tell him to hurry back to us."

When the call ended, she collapsed onto her desk and wept.

On Pitcairn a man could die of complications of even minor injuries, and Josh was badly hurt. How could she tell Nealie? What could she say to her?

This was the sort of thing she had always feared—that Josh would take one chance too many, that he would take one dangerous assignment too many, that one day something terrible would happen, and he would not come back.

She would never see him again, nor would Nealie, and his unborn child would never know him.

CHAPTER NINETEEN

BRIANA'S FAMILY rallied around her.

Her father said Josh was a survivor, a fighter, a few broken bones wouldn't get him down. Larry muttered that Josh was a tough guy. He'd worked side by side with him and he knew. "If anybody can make it, he will."

Nealie stubbornly said that her daddy would be fine and that he would come home. She had complete and utter faith in her father's strength to overcome any obstacle.

Glenda said to believe and to pray.

But oddly, it was Inga who most helped Briana to cope. "You have a baby to think of. You have a little girl who needs you. You can't afford to be weak. Hang on, darling, for your children."

So Briana hung on, but in her heart, she was terrified. For Nealie's sake, she put on a brave front. For the baby's sake, she made herself eat right, get rest, do all the things she was supposed to do.

Penny worked extra hours to take strain off her, and Inga pitched in, too. Inga understood business. She picked up the routine quickly. Briana lived in dread, but she knew she was not alone.

She talked to Tim Watson almost every day. On the fifth day, he told her Josh was fully conscious again, although he could not remember the fall or even setting out for the fishing expedition at Down Isaac's.

Watson had more good news. By telephone and radio, Pitcairn had been sending out medical distress signals trying to reach any ship in the area with a doctor aboard. This morning a Russian vessel, a thirty-six-thousand-ton bulk carrier, replied that it was within a hundred miles of Pitcairn.

By law, all Russian ships carried a medical doctor, and the captain agreed to make for the island. A crew of Pitcairn men would take the longboat to the Russian ship and ferry the doctor to land.

If the doctor thought Josh was well enough to be moved, he could be taken aboard the ship, which would make it to Auckland in little more than a week.

Auckland, New Zealand! In Auckland there were hospitals! Briana thought with a thrill of hope. But she was frightened, too. For a gravely injured man, such a journey might be dangerous, even fatal.

The decision was in the hands of a doctor she'd never met whose language she could not even speak.

"Can I talk to Josh?" She was almost pleading with Watson. "If I could just hear his voice."

"He's here," Watson said. "They fixed him up with a rattletrap wheelchair. The nurse didn't want him to try this stunt, but you know Josh. He's only supposed to talk a minute, though. He's got to save his strength."

She listened for what seemed an endless time to static and the ebbing and rising thrum of a fragile connection. At last she heard his voice.

"Briana? Briana? Babe? Are you okay?"

She could not stop her tears. "I'm fine. How are you?"

"My head still hurts. My ears ring. It's like I've got a carillon in my head. The nurse says it'll go away."

"Your leg?"

"It was a simple break. I was lucky. The collarbone's the worst. It's jammed up against an artery or something. How's Nealie? How's the baby?"

"Nealie's good. The baby's fine and kicking harder every day. Oh, Josh, do you think they'll let you get on that ship?"

"If they don't take me by longboat," he said, "I'll swim

out to the damn thing. I'll hang on its side like a barnacle.
I'll be back to you, Briana. You and the kids. Come hell or
high water. I love you.''

''I love you, too,'' she said, her throat constricting. Then
someone, the nurse from the sound of it, made him give up
the phone. She had only time to tell him goodbye.

But he was true to his word.

He arrived in Auckland on the second day of August.

One day later, Glenda had her baby, a seven-pound five-
ounce boy. They named him Leo Joshua Hanlon.

JOSH SPENT over two months in New Zealand, in and out
of hospitals.

Ironically, the source of his misery was the injury that
had first seemed most minor, his broken collarbone. The
fractured bone had lacerated nerves and abraded a major
artery, and as the bone tried to heal, a callus formed that
pressed on both nerve and artery. The pain was intense and
circulation to his right arm impaired.

The damage could be repaired—to an extent—but never
completely undone. He might have to have more operations
in the States. Josh was going to pay for Pitcairn for the rest
of his life.

He got back to the States toward the end of September,
still feeling rocky, but he wanted to be with Briana and
Nealie. He'd lost nineteen pounds; and on the last leg of
his long flight, he hurt like crazy because he refused to dull
himself with pain pills and was dazed by jet lag.

But when he landed in St. Louis and saw Briana and
Nealie waiting for him, the haze lifted from his mind, and
the aches vanished from his body.

Briana was bulging with pregnancy and had never looked
more beautiful to him. She flung herself into his arms. It
should have hurt his collarbone like the devil, but he didn't
feel a thing except joy. Nealie clung to his legs happily
crying, ''Daddy, Daddy, Daddy!''

She tried to climb him as if he were a tree, and she

knocked her big glasses askew, so finally he scooped her up in his good arm, and he and Briana leaned on each other all the way to the parking garage as if they were drunk with love.

Inga had driven Briana and Nealie to the airport. She'd thought Briana was too pregnant to make the trip alone. But she also knew Briana and Josh and Nealie needed privacy. Harve and Penny had followed her so she could ride home with them. Josh had assured Briana he could drive to Illyria even with one aching arm.

In Briana's truck, he held her and kissed her repeatedly, and Nealie climbed all over him, and he kissed her, too, although she was starting to send lightning bolts of pain though his shoulder.

"Ouch! Ouch! Take it easy," he pleaded. "Your old man's banged up. I've got pain imps sticking pitchforks in me."

"We'll make them go away," Nealie promised. "But Mommy and I are going to take such good care of you that you'll never go away again."

For the first time, a tiny cloud of darkness fell across his mind. He would be going away again. He would always be going away. But from now on, he had promised himself, it would be different.

On the road, Briana and Nealie peppered him with news and questions.

"The ride in the longboat to the Russian ship," Nealie said. "Did it hurt? Did it hurt when you were on the ship?"

"Not much," he lied. The trip in the longboat had been pure hell. He'd thought he'd die. The voyage in the Russian ship was excruciating, but nothing compared to being carried to the longboat and tossed about in it. He had passed out three times.

"So why do you have pain imps?" Nealie persisted. She was almost eating him up with her eyes.

"I should have got to the hospital faster," he said. "These things happen."

"Like when Harve's house burned down?"

"Yes. Like that. Stuff just happens."

"Harve's new house is all built," Nealie said. "It's pretty. Inga moved back in with him."

"Your mother told me," Josh said. He had his bad arm draped around Briana's shoulder. She'd said little. She looked at him with a glow on her face. The seat belt curved over the sweet roundness of her belly.

"I miss Inga," Nealie announced, suddenly serious. "I wish she'd come back and stay at Grandpa's. At first I didn't think I liked her much, but now I do."

Briana spoke, a smile on her lips. "She was like a rock for us. I don't know if I could have made it through this without her."

"Inga makes the best potato pancakes in the world," Nealie said. "And Harve is going to propose to Penny."

Briana laughed and put her finger to Nealie's lips. "Shh. That's supposed to be a secret until Thanksgiving."

"Everybody knows it," Nealie said in self-defense.

Josh looked at Briana and lifted an eyebrow. "My rival gave up?"

"Your rival found his true love," she said. She laid her head against his aching shoulder, and somehow she made it feel better.

"So much happened while you were gone," she said. "I think Poppa and Inga are in love. I think they're waiting until everything's settled down before telling people."

Everybody in this family tries to keep secrets, Josh thought. They thought they were protecting each other. Maybe they were. He never wanted Briana or Nealie to know what he had suffered getting back from Pitcairn. What good would it do them to know?

"I'll finally get to have a grandma," Nealie said proudly. "*And* a baby sister. Almost all at once."

"You might have a baby brother," Briana cautioned. "We don't know if it's a boy or a girl."

"*I* know," said Nealie.

Josh smiled. It was good to hear his daughter's chatter again. It was good beyond belief.

"I know because I talk to her all the time," said Nealie. "She talks to me, too. She's coming soon. And she wants her name to be Julia Ann."

"Julia Ann," Josh mused. "That's a nice name. I could live with that. What about you, Mom?"

"I guess," Briana said. "But if it's a boy, I want to name him after that Russian doctor."

"Rotislav Ivanovich Smirdnekov?" Josh said.

"He brought you home," she said and nuzzled his shoulder.

Involuntarily, he flinched.

"I'm sorry," she said, drawing back. "Did I hurt you?"

"It hurt good," he said. "Do it again."

He gazed at the Missouri countryside. In its way, it was as strange as Siberia or Tasmania or Pitcairn Island.

But it was also home, because Briana was there. And wherever she was, that was the place his heart lived.

INGA HAD DECREED a small celebration, and when Inga decreed something, it was done. Josh saw the rest of the family and was amazed that they seemed glad to see him. Leo hugged him in welcome. It hurt.

Larry was so accepting, he slapped Josh on the back. That hurt worse. Harve pumped his hand endlessly, and by this time, Josh's whole arm hurt like Hades. Penny seized him by both shoulders—this hurt, of course—and kissed him on the cheek.

Glenda wept with happiness and relief on his shoulder. That, too, hurt, but not as much.

Josh had to hold the new baby, Leo Joshua. The infant was a small, red-faced morsel who wet on him. For some stupid reason, Josh didn't mind. It felt good to hold new life.

But toward the end of the party, Nealie's nose started to

bleed. Josh seized her in his arms, regardless of the pain that flashed through him.

Inga and Briana helped him stop the bleeding. When it was over and Nealie's face was wiped clean, Inga softly said in his ear, "Enough is enough, dear boy. Go home with your family. We're so glad you're back. And so thankful."

She, too, kissed his cheek. It didn't hurt at all.

But the sight of Nealie, pale and exhausted by emotion, did.

BRIANA SETTLED onto the couch, snuggling against Josh. She reveled in the solid reality of him, the touch and firmness and heft of his body beside hers. She had a tumbler of apple cider and had poured him a glass of wine for homecoming.

He was solemn. "Nealie," he said, "how is she? You haven't been holding out on me, have you? Tell me the truth, for God's sake."

She touched her fingertips to his jaw. "She's holding steady, Josh. Honestly. I think she just got overexcited by you coming back. We were all so worried about you. Your collarbone—how is it? Really? I thought I saw you wince tonight more than once."

"I'll live," he said and kissed her ear. "But this is going to slow me down."

Her heartbeat speeded. "You mean you'll take it a little easier?" *Is it possible?* she thought, *Can he shake off his wanderlust even a little bit?*

He put his good hand on the curve of her stomach. "Oh, Briana, for a while on Pitcairn it was like I stood in front of two doors. One led to you and Nealie and this little person—"

He caressed the soft mound of her belly where their unborn child rested. He was silent a moment. "The other door led to someplace else. I think that place was death."

She shuddered and put her hand atop his. "Don't talk like that."

"I have to," he said. "I had a lot of time on that Russian freighter. I had even longer in Auckland. There was nothing to do but think. I thought about us. I thought about me. I thought about what I've done and why I've done it and why I was the one who let things come between us."

She was overwhelmed by his generosity. She took his face between her hands. "Oh, Josh, it wasn't just you. It was me, too. I thought if I left my family, it would fall apart, and all the bad things that happened would be my fault. I thought I was more important than I am."

"No," he said. "I didn't understand family at all. I never had one. I never understood the hold it can have on you, how it can tie knots around a person's heart."

She leaned closer to him, glorying in touching his well-loved face after all these months. She said, "And I never understood that I was looking backward. When I married you, I promised to commit to you and our future. To make a new family. Not to cling to the past and the family I grew up with."

He surprised her by laying his face against her shoulder. "What happened to me when I was a kid..." he murmured.

"You mean that man," she said, caressing his hair. "The one who did things to you. You mean that."

"I mean that," he said, voice muffled. He put his arm around her, pulled her tighter. "It made me feel less than a man. So I've spent my whole life trying to out-macho anybody else. I thought to be a man I had to be rough, I had to keep grabbing danger, smacking it around, spitting in its eye. I was a lean, mean lone wolf. I couldn't stay in one place. I couldn't settle down. It would mean I was—weak."

"Oh, Josh," she said, kissing his neck. "Oh, Josh—you, weak? Never. Never."

He raised his face and looked into her eyes, his expression pained. "Yeah. I was weak. And stupid. I thought the only way to prove myself was by taking chances other men wouldn't. But the chance of my life—was you.''

Again her hands framed his face. She said, ''I should never have stayed behind when you went away. Now I know I don't have to. I know you'll always have to be on the move. But I don't always have to be here.''

A light flared deep in his eyes. ''What do you mean?''

''I mean,'' she said, ''I thought I was indispensable. I'm not. Papa and Harve are talking about a partnership. Penny can take over most of what I do with the business. Inga can help her, and she's good with the family. She's doing better than I ever did. Together, they make me dispensable—and free. Nealie and I and the baby—we could go with you to California. We could have our *own* home.''

He grinned in disbelief. ''Just us? You wouldn't know what to do with yourself.''

''No,'' she said with utter seriousness. ''I've gone over this in my mind a thousand times. If we stay around here, people may start putting two and two together. It's almost inevitable. I want our kids to have childhoods that are as normal as possible. I don't want gossip about them, and the last thing I ever want is for the media to find out.''

His smile grew speculative. ''You mean that?''

''Every word of it. It's for Nealie's good. And the baby's. I've talked to Nealie about moving. I said it would be a lot easier for you to get home if we lived on the coast. She likes that idea. Besides, it would probably be good for her to live in a warmer climate.''

''My God,'' he said, ''you really are something, you know that? I could buy you a little farm. In Salinas Valley or Napa Valley. You could run it. Grow things. Maybe even some sunflowers. The first time I saw you was in that field of sunflowers. You could still go visit your family whenever you wanted—''

''You're my family,'' she said. ''You and Nealie and this child.''

The baby kicked, as if to emphasize she was right.

"I'll never take another dangerous assignment," he told her, stroking her hair. "I'll be gone sometimes. Sometimes for a more than a little while. But I'll never take foolish chances again. I learned that, this trip. A married man, a man with kids—he's got no business playing dice with death."

Tears welled in her eyes. "It's scary playing dice with life, too."

"I think I've grown up enough to try," he said. He kissed her, long and deep.

THE BABY WAS BORN November nineteenth in St. Louis, Missouri. She was a strong, healthy baby, weighing eight pounds. She had her father's pugnacious jaw and her mother's jet black hair.

Two months later, in St. Louis, blood from Julia's umbilical cord was implanted into Nealie. Nealie hated being in the hospital and didn't really understand what was happening. She thought she was having some strange operation to cure her allergies.

A month later, the center tested Nealie and pronounced the operation a success. Her sister's cells had taken hold. The anemia was arrested.

Nobody knew of Julia Ann's strange conception except the people at the center and Briana and Josh.

A few other people may have suspected, and one knew because she had unerringly guessed. That person was Inga.

After Nealie's operation, she said to Briana, "I think I know what this is about. I understood when I asked Leo more about her illness. I remember a student I had. His name was Jason Castleman. He died of Yates's anemia when he was fifteen." Inga paused. "Science hadn't learned how to save people like him yet. Now it can. I remembered reading news stories about cord blood and genetic testing. I started thinking about all those trips you were taking, the way you and Josh were acting, and it came together. I thank heaven that Nealie had a chance. And you were courageous enough to take it.''

Briana felt a frisson of alarm. ''I don't want people to know.''

''I understand. I'll say nothing to anyone,'' Inga promised. ''Especially your father. He doesn't need to know.''

Ah, Poppa, Briana thought, *you've got someone else to protect you now.*

''Thank you,'' she said and embraced the older woman. Inga and Leo planned to be married at Easter, and Briana was glad for both.

She and Josh and Nealie and Julia would move to an acreage in the Salinas Valley in California. There was no chance of anyone knowing their story there. They would be just another family. A woman who grew rare plants and seeds, a man who was often away on assignment photographing rare sights. A little girl who had once been fragile but was now growing strong.

There would also be, of course, a baby, pretty and happy, nothing terribly unusual about her. She was just a seemingly ordinary baby whom all of them loved.

And her name was Julia Ann.

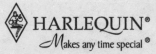

EMERGENCY!

The Family Doctor
by Bobby Hutchinson

**The next Superromance novel in this dramatic
series—set in and around St. Joseph's Hospital
in Vancouver, British Colombia.**

Chief of staff Antony O'Connor has family problems.
His mother is furious at his father for leaving her many
years ago, and now he's coming to visit—with the
woman he loves. Tony's family is taking sides. Patient
care advocate Kate Lewis is an expert at defusing
anger, so she might be able to help him out. With this
problem, at least. Sorting out her feelings for Tony—
and his feelings for her—is about to get trickier!

**Heartwarming stories with a sense of humor,
genuine charm and emotion and lots of family!**

On sale starting April 2002

Available wherever Harlequin books are sold.

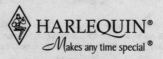

HARLEQUIN®
Makes any time special®

If you enjoyed what you just read,
then we've got an offer you can't resist!

Take 2 bestselling
love stories FREE!
Plus get a FREE surprise gift!

Clip this page and mail it to Harlequin Reader Service®

IN U.S.A.	IN CANADA
3010 Walden Ave.	P.O. Box 609
P.O. Box 1867	Fort Erie, Ontario
Buffalo, N.Y. 14240-1867	L2A 5X3

YES! Please send me 2 free Harlequin Superromance® novels and my free surprise gift. After receiving them, if I don't wish to receive anymore, I can return the shipping statement marked cancel. If I don't cancel, I will receive 6 brand-new novels every month, before they're available in stores. In the U.S.A., bill me at the bargain price of $4.05 plus 25¢ shipping and handling per book and applicable sales tax, if any*. In Canada, bill me at the bargain price of $4.46 plus 25¢ shipping and handling per book and applicable taxes**. That's the complete price, and a saving of at least 10% off the cover prices—what a great deal! I understand that accepting the 2 free books and gift places me under no obligation ever to buy any books. I can always return a shipment and cancel at any time. Even if I never buy another book from Harlequin, the 2 free books and gift are mine to keep forever.

135 HEN DFNA
336 HEN DFNC

Name	(PLEASE PRINT)	
Address	Apt.#	
City	State/Prov.	Zip/Postal Code

 * Terms and prices subject to change without notice. Sales tax applicable in N.Y.
** Canadian residents will be charged applicable provincial taxes and GST.
   All orders subject to approval. Offer limited to one per household and not valid to
   current Harlequin Superromance® subscribers.
   ® is a registered trademark of Harlequin Enterprises Limited.

SUP01   ©1998 Harlequin Enterprises Limited

These New York Times *bestselling authors*
have created stories to capture the hearts and minds
of women everywhere.
Here are three classic tales about the power of love—
and the wonder of discovering the place
where you belong....

FINDING HOME

DUNCAN'S BRIDE
by

LINDA HOWARD

CHAIN LIGHTNING
by

ELIZABETH LOWELL

POPCORN AND KISSES
by

KASEY MICHAELS

Available only from Silhouette
at your favorite retail outlet.

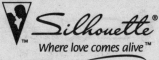

Coming in May 2002

**Three Bravo men marry for convenience—
but will they love in leisure? Find out in
Christine Rimmer's *Bravo Family Ties!***

Cash—for stealing a young woman's innocence, and to
give their baby a name, in *The Nine-Month Marriage*

Nate—for the sake of a codicil in his beloved
grandfather's will, in *Marriage by Necessity*

Zach—for the unlucky-in-love rancher's chance to
have a marriage—even of convenience—
with the woman he *really* loves!

BRAVO
FAMILY TIES

Where love comes alive™

Visit Silhouette at www.eHarlequin.com   BR3BFT

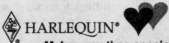